Courting
MISS AMSEL

**Center Point
Large Print**

Also by Kim Vogel Sawyer
and available from Center Point Large Print:

My Heart Remembers
A Promise for Spring
A Hopeful Heart

Courting
MISS AMSEL

Kim Vogel Sawyer

CENTER POINT PUBLISHING
THORNDIKE, MAINE

This Center Point Large Print edition
is published in the year 2011 by arrangement with
Bethany House Publishers,
a division of Baker Publishing Group.

The text of this Large Print edition is unabridged.
In other aspects, this book may vary
from the original edition.
Printed in the United States of America
on permanent paper.
Set in 16-point Times New Roman type.

ISBN: 978-1-60285-977-7

Library of Congress Cataloging-in-Publication Data

Sawyer, Kim Vogel.
Courting Miss Amsel / Kim Vogel Sawyer.
p. cm.
ISBN 978-1-60285-977-7 (library binding : alk. paper)
1. Women teachers—Fiction. 2. Parent-teacher relationships—Fiction.
3. Women—Suffrage—Fiction. 4. Frontier and pioneer life—Nebraska—Fiction.
5. Large type books. I. Title.
PS3619.A97C68 2011b
813´.6—dc22
2010042074

Dedicated to my brother
Brad,
who is an inspiration to his students
(and to me).

"In the day when I cried thou answeredst me, and strengthenedst me with strength in my soul."
PSALM 138:3, KJV

Chapter
ONE

Walnut Hill, Nebraska
September 1882

This certainly isn't the way I imagined it.

Standing on the raised planked platform with her name—*Miss Amsel*—chalked in flowing script across the center of the black-painted board behind her, Edythe searched the somber faces for any small sign of enthusiasm. Row upon row of unsmiling lips and apprehensive eyes greeted her. Her stomach trembled.

Pressing her palms to the smooth front of her taffeta overskirt, she donned a bright smile. *Someone* had to smile. "Now . . ." Her dry mouth made her voice sound growly, and a little pigtailed girl in the front row cringed. Edythe cleared her throat. "Now that you know my name, it's time I learned yours. Each of you take up your slate and slate pencil"—the shuffle of slates sliding over worn desktops indicated instant compliance—"and print your name in your neatest penmanship on the slate. Then hold it up for me to see."

Heads bent over desks. Slate pencils created a soft *skritch-skritch*. A fragrant breeze flowed through the schoolroom's open windows, and Edythe filled her lungs with a satisfied breath. Ahh, *her* pupils following *her* directions. For how many years had she anticipated this moment? At least a dozen. Pa had said it would never happen, and at times she'd believed him. Yet here she was, standing before her very own class of students.

Some dreams do find fruition, Pa.

She blinked away happy tears as a second round of scuffles signaled slates being lifted. Fresh-scrubbed fingers held slates beneath chins. Opening the student log that rested on her desk, she checked the names that corresponded with those printed on the slates. *Martha Sterbinz, Jane Heidrich, Andrew Bride, Henry Libolt, Louisa Bride . . .*

Some names were legibly written, others a bit difficult to decipher. Regardless, Edythe acknowledged each offering with a smile of approval, but not one child smiled in return. She had longed to teach in a little country school, where children from big to little mingled together like a family. Being accepted as the schoolmarm for the farming community of Walnut Hill, Nebraska, was her fondest hope come to life. But none of her imaginings had included taciturn students.

On the right-hand side of the room, two freckle-faced boys shared a desk seat and a slate.

A smile quavered on Edythe's lips as she noted their names—Johnny and Robert—penned one above the other with arrows indicating which name applied to which boy. She laid her pen on the logbook and crossed to stand beside the boys' desk. In the silent room, the gentle swish of her skirts against the wood-planked floor seemed intrusive.

"Johnny . . . and Robert." She looked fully into their faces as she spoke their names. Both stared at her with unblinking brown eyes. With thick, curling lashes, round, freckled cheeks, and matching cowlicks, they gave the appearance of a pair of bookends. "Are you twins?"

The one on the left shook his head. "No'm. Brothers. I'm eight." He jabbed his chest with his thumb and then jerked it toward his brother. "He's seven."

"I see." Edythe swallowed. Surely the other children in the room were boring holes through her, so intent were their gazes. "You've done a commendable job of writing your first names, but you've neglected to include your surname. Can you tell me what it is?"

She wouldn't have thought it possible, but their eyes grew even larger. The younger one—Robert—sucked in his lips. His chin quivered. What on earth had she done to frighten him so? She looked at Johnny and gentled her voice. "Do you know your surname?"

The pair exchanged a nervous glance, but neither spoke. The wall clock's heavy pendulum ticked off the advancing seconds as loudly as a gong. Then a slight movement from the back row caught Edythe's attention. A tall, slender girl with blond hair slicked away from her face held her hand in the air.

Edythe searched her memory for the girl's name. "Martha?"

The girl's shy nod indicated Edythe had guessed correctly.

"Did you have something to ask?"

Martha rose, licking her lips. She pressed her palms to the desktop as if in need of support. "Just wanted you to know, ma'am . . . those're the Townsend boys. They live on a farm south of town."

"Thank you, Martha."

The girl sank into her seat, her shoulders wilting.

Edythe turned back to Johnny and Robert. "So you are Johnny and Robert Townsend."

They nodded in unison.

"Do you know how to write *Townsend,* boys?"

Johnny dropped the slate with a clatter and covered his face with his hands. Robert stared at her. One tear spilled from its perch on his lower lashes and rolled down his cheek. From the front row, the little pigtailed girl began to weep, filling the room with her distress. Edythe looked around in confusion. The face of every student reflected fear or resentment.

Edythe put her hand on Johnny's shoulder. "Look at me." Very slowly he lowered his hands and peered up at her. "Why are you frightened?"

"You . . . you gonna"—his shoulders jerked as he fought back tears—"whomp me if I spell it wrong?"

Edythe frowned, confused. "Whomp you?"

"Yes'm." Johnny's lips quavered so wildly his words came out in a squeak. "I ain't wrote my second name all summer long, an' now I can't 'member how to do it. Please don't whomp me." Another tear rolled down Robert's face. The boys clutched hands.

Edythe looked around the room, meeting the gaze of each student in turn. So much trepidation—and now she understood why. Catching her skirts, she whirled to the front of the room, stopping directly in front of the bench where the little pigtailed girl continued to wail.

"Children, what means did your former teacher use as discipline in the classroom?"

A sullen-looking boy on the second row shot one hand in the air and yanked up his slate with the other. *William Sholes,* the slate read in precise block letters.

Edythe said, "Please tell me, William."

William bolted from his desk. "If we made mistakes, Mr. Shanks bent us over his knee an' whupped us good with that stick." He bobbed his head toward the tray at the front of the room.

Edythe stepped onto the teaching platform and lifted a slim, peeled hickory stick perhaps three feet in length. When she had discovered it lying in the tray the evening before as she'd readied the classroom for the first day of school, she'd assumed it was intended as a pointer. She held it aloft. "Are you referring to this stick?"

The little pigtailed girl's wails changed to frantic, hiccupping sobs. The child, so small her legs stuck straight out rather than bending toward the floor, couldn't possibly have experienced the sting of the switch—perhaps the older students had warned her of its threat. If Mr. Shanks had been in the room at that moment, Edythe would have told him what she thought of his discipline methods. Teachers should inspire more than hysteria in small children.

Edythe stomped to the front edge of the platform. Curling her fists around opposite ends of the stick, she held it chest-high. "I assure you, the only thing going over *my* knee is this."

Raising her knee slightly, she smacked the stick across her thigh. Gasps sounded across the room as the stick snapped in two. The pigtailed girl's cries ceased with a startled gulp. Edythe marched to the window and tossed the useless halves onto the playground. Then she faced the students, swishing her palms together. "From this day forward, no one in this room will be *whomped* for mistakes. Making mistakes is part of learning, and we're here to learn. All I ask is that you always do your very best. Will you promise me that?"

The little pigtailed girl stared at Edythe in wonder. All across the classroom, heads nodded. Voices rang. "Yes'm. I promise."

"Good." Edythe raised her chin and sent a serious look across the classroom. "And I promise to do my best, as well." Her heart gave a happy skip. At last, her students were smiling.

"Then she busted it—*boom!*—right acrost her knee an' threw it out the window!" Johnny gestured with his fried chicken leg, his eyes bright. "Said nobody's gonna get whomped again."

Joel Townsend paused with his fork stabbed into a chunk of boiled potato. He'd be the first to acknowledge no sorrow at seeing the former teacher go. The prune-faced man had terrorized the boys with his overzealous use of the hickory switch. But the new teacher might be making a mistake by giving the rod of discipline a toss.

He sent Johnny a thoughtful look. "Your new schoolmarm say how she plans to keep order?"

Johnny chomped off a bite of chicken and chewed, his forehead all crinkled. "No, sir."

"Just no more whompin'." Robert lined up his

peas on the edge of his plate with his stubby fingertip. "I like 'er, Uncle Joel. Like 'er a lot."

Joel tapped the top of Robert's head. "Quit playin' there and eat."

"Yes, sir." The boy grabbed his fork, poked one pea, and carried it to his mouth. He shuddered.

Joel swallowed a chuckle. "You two make sure you mind your manners. Miss Amsel might not be usin' a switch on you, but I won't spare it if I find out you've caused trouble at school."

Both boys looked at him with wide, innocent eyes. Johnny said, "I won't cause her no trouble, Uncle Joel. Honest."

"Me neither," Robert vowed. "She's just so nice." He propped his chin on one hand, a crooked grin creasing his cheek.

If Joel hadn't known better, he'd have thought the boy was smitten. But he did know better. Robert missed his ma. Johnny did, too. Having a female teacher would be good for the boys. He could father them—he'd had no trouble stepping into their pa's shoes two years ago when the boys were deposited on his doorstep—but mothering was a whole different thing.

"Oh!" Robert dropped the gnawed-clean chicken bone and shoved a hand into his dungaree pocket. "Miss Amsel sent a note home."

Mr. Shanks had sent notes when there'd been mischief in the classroom. Joel scowled at each boy in turn. "You sure you didn't cause trouble?"

"No, sir!" Robert began jabbing his fork tines into the peas with gusto.

Johnny added, "She sent 'em with all the kids—everybody got a note."

Puckering his forehead, Joel peeled open the paper and scanned the graceful, slanted script that covered the top fourth of the page.

Johnny tipped forward, his fingertips on the edge of the table, and tried to peek over the top of the paper. "What's she say?"

Joel pinched his chin. "It appears your new teacher intends to make the rounds beginning next week and visit all the families with schoolchildren." This Miss Amsel was sure different from Shanks—he hadn't even attended Sunday services with the townsfolk.

Robert bounced in his seat. "Can she come at suppertime an' eat with us? Huh, Uncle Joel, can she?"

"Settle down there, boy, and let me think." Joel looked again at the note. *Please indicate a convenient day and time, and I shall do my utmost to honor what best fits your schedule.* She sure had a fancy way of stringing words together. Old Mr. Shanks had used some highfalutin' words—and he'd also expected the kids to know them. Joel hoped this new teacher wouldn't expect too much from the kids in Walnut Hill. Mostly offspring of lowly dirt farmers, they

15

wouldn't be comfortable spouting words like *utmost*. And neither would he.

"Johnny, fetch me the pen and ink."

The boy dashed to the bowfront secretary that had belonged to Joel's mother and pulled down the drop leaf. Johnny held the pen and bottle of ink as carefully as if he were carrying a king's crown. "When you gonna tell 'er to come? Tomorrow?"

"Now, didn't she say next week? Is tomorrow next week?"

Johnny scratched his head. "Reckon not." He leaned close, bumping Joel's elbow as he dipped the pen into the uncorked bottle. "How 'bout next Monday, then? Can she come next Monday? Huh?"

"Johnny, if you're done eating, start clearing the table."

The boy huffed, but he moved to obey.

Joel hunkered over the letter, his thoughts flitting here and there like a moth around a lantern's glow. Most of the families would probably invite Miss Amsel to come for supper and stay afterward to drink coffee, eat cake, and chat a bit. Social gatherings were limited to twice-a-year church socials and a rollicking barn dance when harvest ended. Folks hankered for time to visit, and they'd be eager to host the new teacher, show her a pleasant time. And give her a good look-see.

With a critical eye, he examined the cozy room that served as parlor, kitchen, and dining room in his log house. Not as clean as it could be, since a bachelor man and two rowdy boys occupied it. He had no pretty cloth or fine dishes to put on the table, the way his ma used to do when company came. Considering the teacher's grand words, she'd probably expect to eat off something more than speckled tin plates laid out on an old oilcloth. As much as he hated to disappoint the boys, he couldn't serve up supper to the new schoolmarm. Johnny and Robert would have to be satisfied having her come for an evening visit.

He held the tip of his tongue between his teeth and carefully penned a reply. *Miss Amsel, you can visit us any school day after seven o'clock.* Compared to her neat penmanship, his lines of print looked like a squirrel had dunked its tail in the ink bottle and then flopped it around on the page. But there was nothing he could do about that—he had a hand for coaxing corn from the soil, not putting pretty words on paper.

After dipping the pen again, he continued: *Let Johnny and Robert know which night.* He nibbled the end of the pen, thinking. If he got some forewarning, he'd have time to ask Mrs. Jeffers in town to bake a cake or pie. Then at least he'd have something to serve when the teacher visited. Maybe Mrs. Jeffers would even lend him some nice dishes if he promised to be extra careful with them. He started to sign his name, but the note looked too short. Like it was missing something. Tapping his chin with his knuckles, he sought an appropriate way to end it.

At the dish basin, Johnny teasingly splashed Robert, and both boys giggled. Joel smiled, remembering their exuberance when they'd returned from school that afternoon. He set the pen nib on the paper and scrawled, *Thank you for giving the boys a good first day back to school. We look forward to hosting you.* He blew on the ink until it looked dull instead of shiny, then started to refold the note.

But he paused, taking in her neatly scripted lines and pompous wording. His gaze drifted across his closing sentence. Nervousness churned his belly. *Sure hope the good Lord'll forgive me for writin' down a little white lie.*

Chapter
TWO

Edythe dabbed two dots of paste on the underside of a paper tent, then pressed it to the desktop next to the inkwell. She held it for a few seconds, allowing the paste to take hold. Hands on her hips, she smiled at the rows of desks. Each top sported two crisp white tents with a student's name penned in black ink on both the front and back. One side faced the student, the other side the teacher, giving her an opportunity to learn the pupils' names.

She fingered the crisply folded top edge of the tent bearing the name William Sholes. According to her records, William was thirteen and entering his seventh year of school. A child of William's age and experience didn't need the handmade sign to learn to spell his name, but the younger ones would associate the written word with the person in the desk. Her gaze shifted to the signs she had hung all around the classroom, identifying the clock, the blackboard, the windows, the flag . . . Miss Amsel's students would learn to read. They would learn to read *well*.

She returned to the teaching platform and sank into her chair. Resting her arms on the time-worn desktop, she admired all she'd accomplished in the four hours since the students left for home. Apparently Mr. Shanks had been derelict in his cleaning duties. She'd discovered dust in every corner and lurking beneath the desks. A well-applied straw broom chased most of the dust out the door, but she intended to bring a mop and bucket to school over the weekend and give the floor a more thorough cleaning. Never let it be said Miss Amsel's classroom lacked in cleanliness.

Rearranging the desks to her liking had taxed

her physical abilities—my, but the scrolled iron legs were heavy!—but she was pleased with the final layout. Eighteen students, ages five to fourteen, comprised her class list, and two students could sit at each desk, so she'd formed the desks into three rows of three desks each. Two of the attached benches on the front of the first row of desks would serve as recitation benches while the third was reserved for her youngest student, little pigtailed Jenny Scheebeck. Remembering the diminutive child's copious weeping earlier that day, Edythe hoped Jenny would find no reason to cry in school tomorrow.

A gust of wind whisked through the open back door, ruffling the sign with *window* printed on it. Edythe scurried to close the door. Then she removed the little hammer from her desk drawer and tapped the tacks that held the sign to the windowsill. She looked around to make sure no other sign had been loosened in the unexpectedly strong blast of evening air.

Assured all of the identifying signs were secure on the knotty pine walls, she examined the blue-flowered paper she'd pasted to a section of the west wall to serve as a backdrop for hanging student writings and projects. She ran her fingers over the heavily blossomed paper, imagining how the expanse of morning glories would look dotted with essays, pages of arithmetic problems, and childish drawings. *A garden of projects to show how the children are blooming,* she thought with a smile. She could hardly wait to hang the first assignments.

She gave a little gasp. In the midst of all of her cleaning and organizing, she'd neglected to complete lesson plans for the next day. Lifting her skirts, she bustled to her desk. With student textbooks spread across the desk and her reading glasses perched on her nose, she opened her planning journal and set to work. The pendulum on the clock *tick-ticked* in perfect rhythm. A breeze whispered through the open windows. Pages snapped beneath the impatient flick of her finger. Edythe found herself humming as she worked, the wordless melody combining with the room's unique sounds to create a pleasant symphony.

As she recorded her plan to introduce longitude and latitude to the fourth- and fifth-grade students, the squeak of wagon wheels and the clop of horses' hooves shattered her focus. Edythe pulled her glasses free as heavy boots clumped against the cloakroom floor. She started to rise, alarmed, but then she sank back down in relief when she spotted her landlady, Mrs. Kinsley, charging up the aisle.

The older woman halted in front of Edythe's desk and set her face in a scowl fierce enough to curdle milk. "Land sakes, girl, you plan to spend the night here? I held supper long as I could, but finally had to eat. Stomach was complainin'." Her disapproving gaze whisked across the tumble of books on Edythe's desk, and she raised one eyebrow. "You readin' all these at once?"

Edythe chuckled. "I must if I'm to meet each student at his or her grade level." She scanned the room again, a smile tugging at the corners of her lips. "Every grade from one to eight is represented by these names, and each child deserves the most I can offer. I don't intend to leave any of them wanting." How she anticipated watching her charges change and grow over the course of the year!

Mrs. Kinsley craned her neck, examining the classroom by inches. Then she shook her head, releasing a low whistle. "This place looks a heap different'n it did when old man Shanks was runnin' things. He had it as cheerful as the inside of a pine buryin' box. You got pretty paper on the wall, little words everywhere for the young'uns to read, desks all spit-shined . . ." She propped her bony elbow on a stack of books on the corner of the desk. "An' I hear you done away with the teachin' switch."

Edythe's jaw dropped. "You heard that already?"

Mrs. Kinsley laughed. "You come from a big city, Miss Amsel, where folks don't much care what their neighbors are doin'. But here in the country there ain't much excitement, so news spreads faster'n whitewash on a barn wall. You set the tongues a-waggin' by breakin' that stick an' tossin' it out the window."

Edythe hadn't realized what an impression she'd made on the children. She tipped forward eagerly. "So are folks pleased with the change?"

The woman rubbed her cheek, forcing the soft skin into furrows. "Don't know so much pleased as perplexed. Wonderin' how you're gonna keep these young'uns in line without an occasional whack across the seat of the britches." That single eyebrow rose again. "I'm wonderin', too, to be honest. Never met a youngster yet that didn't require the rod of correction from time to time."

Edythe pinned her landlady with a steady look. "Rest assured, Mrs. Kinsley, it is possible to maintain discipline without the use of physical force. I'm a firm believer that when the threat of punishment is removed, children become free to explore and will learn more readily than children who expend their energy trying to evade the sting of a rod."

Another laugh rumbled from the woman's throat. "Girl, I'm a firm believer that when you give young'uns the freedom to explore, they get into things you'd rather they didn't."

Edythe scowled.

Mrs. Kinsley threw both hands in the air. "But

you're the schoolmarm, Miss Amsel, so if you want to corral these youngsters in some other way than what's been done by every teacher who come before you, then you go right ahead." She pointed one finger, her brows low. "But if after a time you change your mind, there's some good-sized cottonwoods growin' on my property. You're welcome to take a sturdy twig for . . . er . . . classroom use."

Edythe had made a promise to her students. She would honor it. "That will not be necessary."

To Edythe's chagrin, the woman laughed again. Mrs. Kinsley headed for the cloakroom, her arms swinging. "Get your things an' come on out to the wagon. Too late for you to be sittin' here all alone—folks won't approve of their schoolmarm bein' out after dark." She charged out the door.

Edythe considered ignoring Mrs. Kinsley's command. At twenty-eight years of age, she was hardly a child to be ordered about. Especially by her landlady. Hadn't she disregarded her father's order to remain in Omaha until her youngest sister left home? Only another four years, he had wheedled. Remembering his whining tone and manipulative words—*"How'll poor little Missy survive without havin' a woman to look after her?"*—Edythe shuddered. Pa didn't really care about her or Missy; he wanted Edythe at home out of selfishness. *He* had depended on her, drowning her with his despondence and neediness.

Although she chafed at being ordered to the wagon, she understood Mrs. Kinsley meant to protect her reputation with the townspeople. So Edythe swallowed her protests, gathered her planning journal and needed textbooks, and joined Mrs. Kinsley on the buckboard's high seat.

At Mrs. Kinsley's tiny clapboard house, Edythe carried her books to her little room at the top of the narrow staircase that emptied into the kitchen. Then she washed her hands and sat at the kitchen table for her late supper. The pork chop and sliced potatoes had no doubt been quite tasty when fresh from the frying pan. Cold, however, the food was less than appealing. Congealed lard whitened the edges of the meat and turned the potatoes into a sodden glob. Edythe scraped the evidence of lard away as best she could with the edge of her knife and resolved to eat every bite of the chop and potatoes.

Mrs. Kinsley bustled around the kitchen, humming while Edythe ate. She reminded Edythe of an industrious hummingbird, buzzing from flower to flower—the woman never stilled. Edythe determined to be on time for supper from now on so she could enjoy a hot meal and have the landlady's company while she ate. At home, there had always been several people seated around the table. While she had occasionally longed for solitude during the years she cared for her younger brothers and sisters, she now discovered sitting alone made for a dreary mealtime.

The moment Edythe put her fork on the empty plate, Mrs. Kinsley zipped over and snatched everything off the table. She marched to the waiting wash pan, flashing a smile over her shoulder. "Reckon you're gonna want to finish up your lessons now. Glad I thought to put that old table an' chair from the shed up in your room—it'll come in right handy as a desk, don't you think?"

When Edythe had examined her room upon arrival yesterday evening, she'd noted the table had a wobbly leg and the slatted chair's seat was cracked. Even so, using them would be better than sitting on the edge of the bed and holding her books in her lap. "Yes, ma'am. Thank you."

Edythe started to rise, but a catch in her lower back slowed her movements. Her muscles were stiff. Perhaps she should have waited and asked for help in moving the heavy desks. Mr. Libolt, who had picked her up from the stage and delivered her to Mrs. Kinsley's, had indicated the town council members were willing to assist her in whatever needed doing. But waiting for help meant a delay in making the schoolroom *hers*. She kneaded her back with her knuckles, trying to unkink the tight knots before climbing the stairs.

Mrs. Kinsley paused in clattering dishes in the pan and shot her a low-browed look. "You all right?"

"My back hurts." Edythe chuckled ruefully. "I've always been a hard worker. I cared for my father's house after my mother's death, and it never seemed to bother my back."

Mrs. Kinsley pulled a plate from the water and smacked it onto a tea towel stretched across the work counter. "It's probably the sittin'. 'Specially if you ain't used to it. My bones get right stove up if I sit for too long. That's why I keep movin'." As if to prove her words, she took up the washrag and attacked the skillet, her elbows high and her hips rotating with the energetic scrubbing.

Edythe swallowed a giggle. "Well, I suppose I—" A knock at the front door cut off her words.

Mrs. Kinsley glanced at the little windup clock on the windowsill. "Who'd be callin' at this hour of the night?" She stormed through the kitchen door, drying her hands on her apron as she went. Curious, Edythe peered around the white-painted door casing while Mrs. Kinsley swung the front door wide. A tall, blond-haired man with a narrow face stepped over the threshold. His gaze searched the room. Edythe instinctively ducked out of sight.

Mrs. Kinsley's voice carried around the corner. "Terrill Sterbinz, don'tcha know it's past eight?"

A drawling voice replied, but he spoke too softly for Edythe to make out his words. Mrs. Kinsley's throaty chuckle rumbled in response. "That so? Well, reckon I'll fetch her, then." Footsteps approached, and Edythe withdrew farther as Mrs. Kinsley charged around the corner, a knowing grin on her face. "Out there is Terrill Sterbinz, one of our local bachelors." She spoke in a gravelly whisper. "I'm guessin' he wants to be the first to get a gander at the new single gal in town."

"Sterbinz? Is he any relation to Martha?" The man's yellow hair and narrow face reminded her of the quiet girl in her class, although Martha's features were much softer. She was a pretty girl.

"Her brother." Mrs. Kinsley leaned closer. "There's six Sterbinz youngsters in all, with Terrill bein' the oldest and Martha the tail end of the family. Good folks—hardworkin'." Her expression turned wily. "A gal could do far worse than takin' up with Terrill Sterbinz."

Edythe's face became a blazing inferno. "Mrs. Kinsley, I didn't come to Walnut Hill to snag a husband. I came to teach."

Mrs. Kinsley frowned. "So what do you want me to do with him?"

Edythe suspected if she answered the question honestly, she'd shock the older woman. "Please tell him I am unavailable at the moment, but if he wishes to discuss his sister's progress, I will be happy to visit with him in the schoolhouse at the close of classes tomorrow."

Mrs. Kinsley shook her head. "All right. I'll do it." She waggled a finger under Edythe's nose. "But word o' warning . . . we got at least six unmarried men near your age in this town. They'll no doubt all want to make themselves known to you. They all start showin' up at the schoolhouse, you might be settin' yourself up for trouble. You won't have no chaperone outside o' the young'uns. Be better to talk with 'em here, where I can keep an eye on things."

Edythe raised her chin. "I prefer to keep my contact with the men of this community on a professional level. Since the schoolhouse is where I work, any meetings will be conducted there."

Mrs. Kinsley, muttering under her breath, headed for the parlor. Edythe clattered up the stairs, ignoring her aching back, and closed her bedroom door behind her. Leaning against the raised-panel door, she willed her heart to slow. If Mrs. Kinsley was correct about the single men in town seeking her out, she'd have a bigger problem than juggling eight different grades of learners. Somehow she must find a way to inform the townspeople, quite unequivocally, that Edythe Amsel was *not* interested in matrimony. Not now. Not *ever*.

Chapter
THREE

Joel Townsend drew the horses to a halt at the edge of the schoolyard. Children swarmed in the dirt yard, their feet stirring clouds of dust while their laughter gave the gray fall morning a festive feel. He couldn't remember the youngsters looking so happy to be at school. Only one week into the term and it appeared that Miss Amsel had changed all the youngsters' attitudes toward learning. Even though some folks fretted she was going to be too easy on the pupils, Joel was willing to give her a chance. He appreciated not having to fight Johnny and Robert out the door in the mornings.

He set the brake and then turned to look into the wagon bed where the boys sat cross-legged. "All right, hop on out now." Both boys bolted to their feet and clambered over the side. Joel called, "Johnny, what're you supposed to remember to do today?"

The boys paused. Johnny scratched his head, his face puckered. Then he broke into a grin. "I'm s'posed to ask Miss Amsel which day she's comin' to our house!"

"That's right. Have her write it down for you." Joel wanted to make sure he had the right day and time. Johnny was a good boy, but being only eight, his memory could be fuzzy. "And remember just 'cause I dropped you off this mornin' doesn't mean I'll be pickin' you up. You two walk on home, like always, an' don't dawdle. Chores'll be waitin'."

"Yes, sir!" The boys practically danced in place, straining toward their boisterous classmates.

"Study hard today. Behave yourselves."

"We will, Uncle Joel! Bye!" Lunch buckets swinging, the boys shot across the yard to join in the play before the school bell signaled time to come inside.

Joel sat for a moment, watching them, a fond smile lifting his cheeks. Even though he hadn't hesitated to take in his brother's orphaned sons, he'd worried about how much having the boys underfoot would change his life. He'd lived alone for a dozen years and suddenly he had two young lives to watch over, guide, and care for. But he didn't regret one minute of time with his nephews. They brought laughter and *life* to his quiet house. He hoped, someday, to marry a woman who would love the boys as much as he did. Then their family would be complete.

Joel released the brake and lifted the reins, but before he could flick them downward, the school's double doors flew open and the teacher stepped onto the porch. Arms akimbo, she scanned the play area. He knew he should move on, but Joel sat and took a good look at Miss Amsel. He'd heard about her, but he hadn't yet seen the woman who had captured his nephews' hearts and had the single men in town all abuzz. Wally at the mercantile asserted that four of Walnut Hill's unmarried fellows had bustled over to the schoolhouse at the end of the second school day, eager to introduce themselves to the new schoolmarm and ask her to join them for a meal at the restaurant in Lincoln Valley's hotel. He'd also heard she turned every one of them down flat.

In a rust-colored skirt and matching shirtwaist, with her brown hair sleek against her head and a pair of round spectacles perched on her nose, she looked very prim and proper and school-teacherish. Joel wouldn't call her beautiful. But as she watched the children, a smile formed on her lips. A fond smile. A transforming smile.

She curled her hand around the thick rope hanging along the wall and gave a firm yank. At the clang of the bell, the activity in the yard ceased. Kids scooped up their lunch buckets and discarded jackets and raced for the schoolhouse door. They jostled one another, keen to be the first one up the stairs. As they filed past the teacher into the schoolhouse, Miss Amsel greeted each student with a word or two and bestowed hugs on the smaller ones, including

Robert, who bounced through the open doors as if heading to a party.

When the last child entered the building, Miss Amsel moved to close the doors. But then she glanced outward, and her gaze collided with his. He sucked in a sharp breath. Her smile faltered. She raised one hand in a hesitant wave. Sweat broke out across Joel's forehead. A quarter mile down the road, old Miz Walters stood in the stout wind, hanging long johns on a line. Were her eyes sharp enough to witness him and the schoolmarm ogling each other across the schoolyard? And would she tell Wally at the mercantile so he could let everybody else in town know?

He needed to *git.* Clutching the reins more tightly in his gloved fists, Joel gave a quick nod of farewell. Then he brought down the reins and cried, "Get up there!" The wagon jolted out of the schoolyard.

Edythe resisted peeking through the crack between the doors at the farmer whose wagon now rolled away. After being bombarded with male visitors two days ago, she found herself suspicious of any adult man loitering near the schoolhouse. She wished she'd come out earlier to see if any students had alighted from that wagon. If he was a father delivering his young ones, she could push aside the unsettling feeling of being measured as a potential sweetheart.

Giggles carried from the classroom. Edythe quickly moved through the cloakroom, where lunch buckets sat in a neat row on a bench and jackets hung from pegs. She clapped her hands together as she headed to her desk, and the giggles stopped. Every pair of eyes in the room followed her as she opened the roll book and called names. When she finished, she sent a smile across the room.

"I'm so proud that each of you have had perfect attendance during the first week of school. If you continue coming every day for the remainder of the year, you'll receive a bright red ribbon to pin to your jacket."

William Libolt—nicknamed Little Will to distinguish him from thirteen-year-old William Sholes—raised his hand. Edythe gave him permission to speak.

"I don't much like red. Could I have a green ribbon instead?"

Children tittered, and Edythe put her hand over her mouth to hold back a snort of amusement. "I regret to inform you that perfect attendance ribbons only come in one color, so you'll have to be satisfied with red."

The boy puckered for a moment, then shrugged. "Reckon I can take a red one."

"Good." Edythe sent the little boy a smile before directing her attention to the class as a whole. "Please raise your hand if you noticed something unusual on the play yard this morning."

Most students looked at one another in confusion, but William Sholes, Lewis Scheebeck, and Patience Jeffers all thrust hands in the air.

Following the edict "ladies first," Edythe called on Patience. "What did you see?"

Patience slipped out of the bench to stand beside her desk. "I saw lots of pegs, ma'am."

Lots of pegs, indeed. Edythe had spent over an hour the evening before driving the pegs into the ground and then painting the tops either red or green. "Do you have a guess why the pegs are there?"

The little girl shook her head, making her brown braids flop. "No'm, but William bothered 'em. He put his foot on one and—"

Before Patience could finish tattling, Edythe stepped off the platform. "The pegs are there for a very special purpose. In a few minutes, we'll be going outside to put those pegs to work, but for now would my fourth- and fifth-grade students please rise and come to the recitation benches?"

With grins and nervous giggles, Ada Wolcott, Andrew Bride, and Lewis Scheebeck crowded onto the center bench. For several minutes, Edythe quizzed the children on the definitions for longitude, latitude, parallel, meridian, dissecting, degrees, and sphere. To her delight, the children described every word accurately.

"Excellent! Now, Andrew, please come forward and demonstrate the placement of the significant lines of latitude for your classmates."

Andrew's pudgy cheeks glowed red. He rose and faced the class. "If'n I was the earth—"

"You'd be even rounder!" William Sholes shouted. Titters rolled across the classroom.

Andrew ducked his head, pressing his linked hands to his roly-poly belly. His dejected pose pierced Edythe's heart. She sent William a stern look that silenced the entire room. "William, you did not have permission to speak, and what you said was exceedingly rude." Folding her arms, she kept her eyes pinned to William's face. Silence lingered for several tense seconds. "You owe Andrew an apology."

"Sorry, Andrew." His tone held no remorse.

Edythe intended to address the issue with William privately at a later time, but for now she let her gaze sweep the room. "Boys and girls, in this classroom we will follow a simple rule. Before you speak, ascertain that the comment is kind, truthful, and necessary. If it does not fit all three of those requirements, then remain silent. Is that clear?" She focused solely on William as she asked the question.

Several children mumbled embarrassed

agreement, but William slunk into his seat, a surly look on his face. Edythe eyed him for another few seconds before turning to Andrew. "Go ahead."

Andrew cleared his throat. "If'n I was the earth . . ." His eyes flitted to William and back to Edythe. He pointed to the top of his head. "Then this here would be the North Pole." He gulped a couple of times, his knobby Adam's apple bobbing. "Arctic Circle's just about here." Andrew indicated his ear, then he touched his shoulder. "Here's the Tropic of Cancer, an'—" His hand slipped to his waist—"this is the Equator. Then my toes is the South Pole."

Ada waved her hand over her head and crowed, "He forgot the Tropic of Capper-corn!" She pointed to Andrew's knees. "It's right there!"

"Hey!" Lewis bolted up, his hands balled on his hips. "What about the Ant—Ant—Ant-ar-dic Circle?"

"Ant-arc-tic Circle," Edythe corrected.

"Yep, that." Lewis darted forward and tapped his palm against Andrew's shins. "It's right about here."

Laughter rang, but Edythe held up both hands, squelching it before it got out of hand. She spent a few more minutes reviewing the purpose for latitude and longitude and how the cross-hatch patterns on the globe made it possible to find any location on the earth. Then she instructed the children to form a line with her oldest student, Martha Sterbinz, at the end to encourage stragglers to stay with the class.

She retrieved a box of cut pieces of rope that she'd left beside the back door and marched the children to the side yard. There, she put them to work running the ropes along the pegs—red to red serving as lines of longitude, and green to green representing lines of latitude. When the section of ground looked like a maze of ropes, Edythe had the children post paper signs marking the major lines of latitude and their degrees from the North Pole to the South Pole. Then they put small numbered signs representing degrees on the ropes meant to signify lines of longitude.

The children buzzed, advising one another and tripping over each other's feet, but eventually the ropes and signs took on the appearance of a huge globe. When it was complete, Edythe announced, "And now we will play 'Where Am I?'"

"Where is she?" William Sholes held both arms toward Edythe. "Teacher's right there!"

Several of the boys broke into laughter.

"William!" Edythe pointed to a spot away from the group. "Go sit down."

The boy stared at her, openmouthed.

She took three steps closer to him. "You've been disruptive, so you've forfeited your opportunity to participate in our activity. You now have two choices. You may do as I instructed and go sit on the ground and watch, or you may walk home. If you choose to go home, I will come by your house after school to tell your parents why you were dismissed from school early."

Edythe hoped William would go sit away from the group rather than leave. Sending a student home the very first week of school might be interpreted as her inability to handle the class. Each second seemed to stretch into eternity while William stood, his chin jutted stubbornly, staring at the ground. Finally he began to move on stiff legs. Edythe held her breath until he reached the spot she had indicated and plopped down. He folded his arms over his chest and glared at her, but he'd made his choice.

Relieved, she turned back to the other students to explain the rules of the game. It was really quite simple, something she'd concocted while reviewing a map. Each student would take a turn standing at the point where ropes crossed one another. He or she would call out, "Where am I?" and another student would name the spot by reciting the degrees.

They played for half an hour while the morning sun warmed their heads and a ground squirrel chattered from a nearby mound. Edythe kept one eye on the game and the other on William, who toyed with blades of dry grass and pretended he wasn't watching. But twice she caught him looking longingly toward the group. She hid a smile. Surely after having to miss such fun, he'd be more cooperative.

By the end of the game, even some of the younger children were calling out the locations. They groaned when she indicated they must go inside and begin their next lesson.

Robert Townsend put his clasped hands beneath his chin. "Aw, Miss Amsel, can't we play just a little longer?" The other children swarmed around her, taking up the cry to be allowed to continue.

Edythe waved her hands, silencing the group. "We have other things to learn today." More groans followed, but she offered a compromise. "If you all work hard the rest of the morning and through the early afternoon, we'll come back out at the end of the day and play some more before you go home." She shifted to include William, who had risen to his haunches. "Does that sound like a good idea?"

"Yes, Miss Amsel!" the children agreed.

"Inside, now, and take out your reading primers." Edythe herded the youngsters back into the classroom, giving Little Will a slight push on the back of his head to encourage him forward when he lagged behind.

The morning passed quickly and pleasantly, and at exactly noon Edythe dismissed the children for lunch. In a noisy throng, they charged into the cloakroom to retrieve their lunch buckets. Then they headed outside to choose spots around the grounds for impromptu picnics. During the winter months they'd have to eat inside, but Edythe intended to send them outdoors at lunch break for as long as the weather allowed. She sat on the steps of the schoolhouse and ate the lunch Mrs. Kinsley had sent—an apple and a sandwich of cold sliced beef and pungent cheese on hearty rye bread. Simple, yet filling.

While she ate, she kept an eye on her young charges. She smiled when she spotted Martha peeling an orange for little Jenny. At fourteen, Martha would graduate from the Walnut Hill school after this year. Edythe hoped she'd be able to attend the high school in nearby Lincoln Valley. Sweet and helpful, Martha was very bright and deserved to continue her education. In many ways, Martha reminded Edythe of Missy. She quickly shoved aside thoughts of her youngest sister—it would do her no good to reflect on her former life.

Her gaze drifted to the boys, who sat in one big circle, jabbering and bopping each other with the heels of their hands while they ate. After only a few days, she'd already become fairly well acquainted with her pupils, and she prided herself on not only knowing their names but something of their unique personalities. She looked from boy to boy, tagging each with designations such as "ornery," "studious," "determined," and "cheerful." Her smile faded when her gaze reached William Sholes. She could only define him as "obstinate."

Puckering her brow, she watched the boy snatch a hunk of cheese from nine-year-old Henry Libolt. She rose, opening her mouth to call out a reprimand, but Johnny Townsend leaned over and wrestled the cheese from William. He handed it back to Henry. William clenched his fist, and Edythe stood poised, ready to intervene. But then William shrugged and went on eating his own lunch.

Edythe sat back down, pleased the situation hadn't required her involvement. When the children solved problems on their own, they were teaching themselves. Munching on her apple, she wondered if the other children found William's rude behavior as unpleasant as she did. If so, they could possibly encourage William to behave respectfully. She would give that some additional thought. In the meantime, she'd keep a close watch over the boy. Based on his conduct thus far, she feared he might turn out to be a troublemaker.

At that moment, William spun around on his seat. He seemed to search the schoolyard, and when he looked toward the schoolhouse his gaze locked with hers. A conniving grin curled his lips before he turned away. Despite the pleasant fall day and warm sun, Edythe experienced a chill of apprehension. Yes, she most definitely must keep a close eye on William.

Chapter
FOUR

At the close of the school day, Edythe gave the oldest child in each family a handwritten note indicating the day and time she planned to meet with his or her parents. Juggling the schedules for almost a dozen families hadn't been easy, and it would take three weeks to visit all of the houses, but at least she had a plan in place.

When she had distributed all of the notes, she addressed the class. "Give your note to your parents as soon as you get home." She gave William Sholes an extra stern glance. He was the only child who hadn't brought a response to her request for a convenient meeting time. She hoped the time she'd chosen would fit his parents' schedule.

Children murmured excitedly. The ones holding notes puffed with pride while younger ones with empty hands poked out lower lips. Edythe swallowed a chuckle at Robert Townsend's crestfallen expression. Maybe Johnny would allow his brother to carry the note part of the way home.

Flashing a smile, Edythe said, "I look forward to visiting with each of you and getting to know your folks. Have a good weekend, boys and girls. Class is dismissed."

Whoops erupted. The children dashed for the doors, except for Martha Sterbinz, who approached the teacher's desk with a shy look on her face.

"Ma'am, my ma told me to ask you if you're more partial to berry or pumpkin pie. She'd like to favor you with your pick when you come to our house."

William Sholes ambled back into the room and dawdled beside the paper-covered display board. What was he doing? Edythe frowned.

"Ma'am?"

Edythe shifted her attention to Martha, offering a smile. "Thank your mother for wanting to favor me. Since I don't have a kitchen or a means of baking right now, any baked goods are a real treat. Why don't you have her prepare your favorite—then I'll know what kind of pie you like best."

The girl rewarded Edythe with a wide grin. "Thank you, ma'am."

William suddenly zipped into the cloakroom, and Edythe followed. Martha and William retrieved their jackets and lunch buckets, then clattered out the door. Edythe stood on the schoolhouse porch, watching until every child had left the schoolyard. When all of the children were safely on their way home, she went inside to straighten the room and collect her shawl. She passed the paper backdrop where essays titled "What I Did This Summer" by her sixth-, seventh-, and eighth-grade students hung in a neat row against the blue flowers. The sheet bearing Louisa Bride's essay seemed to poof out in the middle, pressing against the restraining tacks on the bottom corners. She remembered William standing there, and trepidation struck. Had he pushed something disgusting beneath the page to tease Louisa? The boy seemed to take delight in pestering the girls.

Holding her breath, she worked one corner free of the tack. A folded piece of notepaper fell to the floor. Edythe sucked in her lips, biting back a rise of fury. Even before she picked it up and unfolded it, she knew what it was.

"Oh! That boy!" Wadding the note in her hand, she marched to her desk and retrieved her shawl. She flung it around her shoulders, knotted the ends, and then clomped to the porch. She slammed the doors, pretending to box William's ears. Giving the key a vicious twist, she secured the lock and then headed for the road.

So William Sholes wanted to hide his note rather than take it home. Well, he wouldn't avoid a visit from the teacher *that* easily. She stomped toward town, dust swirling in a cloud around her feet. Mrs. Kinsley had promised her the use of her wagon and mare whenever she needed it. As soon as she reached town, she would drive to the Sholeses' place. It was time for a serious talk with William's parents.

Edythe sat stiff-backed on the edge of the parlor settee, her hands in her lap. Despite the churning in her belly, she maintained an even tone as she shared William's misdeeds from earlier in the week. His mother, a thin woman with lank brown hair straggling from a sagging knot on the back of her head, seemed more bored than indignant concerning her son's behavior. Edythe wondered if Mrs. Sholes had even heard anything she'd said.

"So I hope you agree, Mrs. Sholes," Edythe said in conclusion, "that William's behavior is not only a disruption to the class, but could very well impede his own learning. Therefore we must determine a means of building a cooperative spirit in your son."

Mrs. Sholes ran a weary hand over her disheveled hair. "I don't rightly know what you expect me to do."

Edythe drew in a breath, battling for patience. "I hoped we could work together to bring an end to William's inappropriate behavior. For instance, the notes he neglected to bring home, even though he was directed to do so. How do you intend to address those with William?"

The woman laughed weakly. "Oh, you know young'uns—their minds're on play. They're always forgettin' somethin'."

"Tucking a note beneath an assignment on the wall seems more deliberate than forgetful to me, Mrs. Sholes." Sarcasm colored Edythe's comment, but Mrs. Sholes didn't appear to notice.

"Maybe he was just embarrassed 'cause he forgot to bring us the first one, an' that was his way of pretendin' he never got it."

Although Edythe didn't agree, she chose to move to another issue. "Then let's discuss the bullying. William dunked Sophie Jeffers's pigtail in the inkwell, and I witnessed him taking cheese from Henry Libolt's hand. Additionally—"

"No reason for William to take somethin' from Henry. The boys're friends. Have been for a long time." Mrs. Sholes toyed with a loose strand of hair. "You sure Henry didn't give it to William?"

"I'm very sure Henry did not offer it. William took it."

"That just don't make much sense to me. William's got plenty of food in his lunch bucket—I pack it myself with enough to keep his belly satisfied. Can't see any reason why he'd need to be botherin' somebody else's lunch."

Frustration filled Edythe's chest. "That's just

the point, Mrs. Sholes. There is no reason for William to bother any of the other children. He simply chooses to do so."

A weak laugh left Mrs. Sholes's throat. "Young'uns . . . always playin' pranks on each other. It's harmless, don't you think?"

William's belligerent glares and sneaky behavior was not harmless to Edythe's way of thinking, but it was obvious she would get nowhere with Mrs. Sholes. The woman's eyes were blinded toward her son's misbehavior. "Might I speak with your husband?"

"He's out workin' in the barn."

"Yes, you indicated that when I arrived." Edythe used her best teacher voice. "But I believe it's necessary for me to speak with him."

Mrs. Sholes sighed. "He won't be happy about bein' disturbed. Gettin' those sickle blades sharpened is mighty important so he can be cuttin' millet next week."

"I trust his son's success in school is equally important to him." When Mrs. Sholes didn't move, Edythe rose. "Would it be better if I went to the barn rather than ask him to leave his work?" If she had to, she'd follow the man into the millet field.

William's mother jerked to her feet. "I-I'll take you, Miss Amsel."

Edythe followed Mrs. Sholes out the front door and across the dirt yard toward the barn. A

48

shadow at the corner of the house slinked away, and Edythe suspected William had been standing beneath the window, listening to every word she'd said. If he'd heard his mother's excuses, he no doubt saw himself as the victor in this particular battle. How she hoped William's father would take his son's misconduct seriously.

They entered the large log barn, and the stench of moldy hay and old manure combined with an acrid, metallic odor assaulted Edythe's nose. Swallowing, she trailed Mrs. Sholes to a small room at the rear of the barn, where the metallic scent overrode the other odors. Mr. Sholes bent forward, running a large file over a long, curved blade. With each swipe of the file, small sparks flew through the air like tiny shooting stars.

"Lloyd?" Mrs. Sholes squawked her husband's name.

The man jerked, clanking the file against the blade. He hissed through his teeth. "Betsy, whaddaya mean, creepin' up on me thataway?" He glared at his wife, who seemed to shrink inside herself. "I could've nicked this blade!"

"I'm sorry, but the new schoolmarm come out and wanted to talk to you."

The man pushed his hat to the back of his head. "What about?" He didn't flick so much as a glance in Edythe's direction. She squirmed uncomfortably.

"About William. Seems he forgot to bring

home a note tellin' us she wanted to visit, an' he's been talkin' out of turn an' such in the schoolroom." Mrs. Sholes recited William's offenses in a calm, unemotional voice. Listening, Edythe experienced a small jolt of shock that the woman remembered every misdeed. Apparently she had been listening.

Mr. Sholes worked his jaw back and forth while Mrs. Sholes talked, his brows low and his gaze aimed somewhere behind his wife's head. Edythe took hope in the man's deep scowl. When Mrs. Sholes fell silent, he plopped his fist on his hip. "That it?"

Mrs. Sholes nodded.

Finally Mr. Sholes looked directly at Edythe. "Miss Amsel—that your name?"

The furrows in his forehead deepened, and Edythe's heart doubled its tempo. She belatedly put out her hand. "Yes. I'm pleased to make your acquaintance."

The man stared at her hand for a moment. Then he wiped his palm on his dirty pant leg and gave her fingers a brief shake. "Seems to me those troubles are your troubles, not ours."

Edythe's hopes plummeted. "Surely you agree parents and teachers are in partnership when it comes to the education of children."

"Yep." Mr. Sholes tapped his leg with the file. "My part of the teachin' happens here. An' your part of the teachin' happens at school. I wouldn't want you to come to my house an' give my boy lessons on farmin' or shoein' a horse. You'd be interferin' in my job."

Edythe knew where he was leading. "I'm simply requesting your support. If William sees that you view education as important, then his attitude toward school—and his behavior— should change."

Mr. Sholes removed his hat, wiped his forehead with his wrist, and then plunked the hat back into place. "Look, you got a job to do. You want me to respect that. All right, I respect it. But I have a job to do, too, an' if I have to run to the school every time my boy gets a little ornery, I won't get my job done. So I'll say it again: I'll take care of William when he's at home, an' you take care of him when he's at school. Do your job, Teacher."

Edythe's face flamed at his insolent tone. Harsh words quivered on the tip of her tongue, but she held them back. It would be pointless to argue with this muleheaded man and his mouselike wife. "Very well." She whirled toward the wide opening at the opposite side of the barn. As she charged into the sunlight, she heard a snicker. Looking up, she spotted William in the loft window.

He grinned, the curl of his lip impudent. "See you on Monday, Miss Amsel."

Edythe snorted as she climbed into the wagon and released the brake. Taking up the reins, she gave them a little flick. "Yah!" The horse obediently lurched forward, and Edythe aimed the wagon for the road. The sooner she left the Sholeses' place, the happier she would be! And over the weekend she needed to concoct a scheme to bring William under control.

Chapter
FIVE

Joel reached over his head to the highest mercantile shelf and caught the curved handle of the lone oversized kettle. He pulled, but the kettle didn't budge.

Small hands tugged at his pant leg. "Uncle Joel, can we have some licorice now?"

Robert—always wanting candy when they came to town for their Saturday shopping.

"I . . . already told you . . ." Joel grunted with the effort of removing the kettle from the shelf. Was it caught on something? "If you and Johnny are good the whole time we're here, then you can each choose a licorice whip. But not . . . until . . . we're done."

He gave one more yank and the kettle finally slid from the shelf. The weight took him by surprise, and he lost his grip on it. Robert jumped back as the kettle clattered onto the floor. The lid rolled away, and sand spilled across Joel's feet.

At the fabric table, Miz Jenkins and her daughter, Maribelle, released surprised squawks. Joel offered a slight shrug and half smile in apology.

The mercantile owner raced around the corner. "What's—?" He came to a halt when the toes of his boots encountered the sand. "Joel, where'd that come from?"

Robert pointed to the dented kettle, which now lay on its side. "It all come out of that, Mr. Scheebeck."

Joel crouched down and began to scoop the sand back into the kettle. "Now I know why the thing was so all-fired heavy. Must've been twenty pounds of sand in there."

Wally Scheebeck scowled. His right foot tapped the wood floor. Then he cupped his hands beside his mouth and bellowed, "Lewis, you get down here!"

Robert dove behind Joel. Scuffles sounded overhead, then feet clattered on stairs. Lewis careened around the corner. He skidded to a stop in front of his father. When he looked down at the sand, he gulped, his Adam's apple bobbing in his skinny neck. "Y-yes, Pa?"

Wally pointed to the remaining sand on the floor. "You know anything about this?"

Lewis's gaze skittered from Joel to the kettle and then to his pa. "I didn't do it."

Joel stood, the kettle in his arms. Robert clung

to his uncle's leg, peering out with wide eyes.

"That doesn't answer my question." Wally caught the back of Lewis's shirt and gave him a shake. "Do you know how all that sand got in the kettle?"

Lewis fidgeted. "Y-yes, sir. William Sholes done it. He put it in there when he was over last week. Said it'd be a funny joke when someone pulled on it an' the sand poured down on 'em."

The boy looked so scared Joel almost felt sorry for him. Almost. If that kettle had come down on his or Robert's heads, somebody'd be wearing a goose egg. Or worse.

Wally aimed a swat at his son's rear end, but the boy ducked away. Red-faced, Wally pointed to the back of the store. "Get up to your room an' stay there!" The boy scuttled off, and Wally turned to Joel. "Don't know what gets into young'uns sometimes. Fool boys . . ."

Joel handed the damaged kettle to Wally. "They'll get into mischief, that's for sure."

Robert crept out from behind Joel. "William plays lots of jokes. Sometimes they're mean ones, too."

Wally harrumphed. "Well, he ain't gonna be welcome over here anymore. Land-a-mercy, somebody could've got hurt!" He shook his head. "Sure am sorry, Joel. You still needin' a cannin' kettle? This is the only one I have in stock, and it's not much use with that big dent in the rim—won't seal the steam inside. But I can order you a new one from the catalog. Be here in a couple of weeks."

"That'll be fine." Joel had never canned before, but with the boys' growing appetites, he'd decided it was something he needed to learn. "I figure I can hold off canning my beans, tomatoes, and carrots for another couple of weeks." He chuckled. "Maybe by then I'll have all the stalks turned under in my fields and have a little more time for household chores."

"You still turnin' them stalks under 'stead of burning 'em off?"

Joel smiled at Wally's skeptical tone. No one else in Walnut Hill saw the sense of putting those cornstalks back into the soil, but he figured it wouldn't do any harm and it just might feed the soil something it needed. "Yep. It's a heap more work than burnin', I'll grant you that."

Wally ambled toward the counter. "Don't see how you do it, keepin' up with the farm an' doin' all that needs doin' in the house."

Sometimes Joel wondered how he managed, too, but with the good Lord's help, he and the boys muddled through. He glanced at Miz Jenkins and her daughter, who admired a length of pink calico, unaware of his scrutiny. Most men had wives to share the burden of work. It sure would make his life easier if he had a helpmeet. Of course, if he ever married, the woman would have to love his nephews as much as he did—and not see them as an intrusion.

With a grunt, Wally plopped the kettle onto the counter and reached for a broom. While Wally swept up the leftover sand, Joel selected the other items on his list and Robert eyeballed the glass jar holding the long whips of black licorice. Joel ignored Robert's deep sighs of longing and continued shopping until he'd made a considerable pile on the counter.

Wally put the broom in the corner. "That it?"

"Yep."

Wally swished his palms together and then retrieved a pad of paper and pencil stub from beneath the high counter. He bent over the pad and began figuring the tab.

Robert licked his lips, his fingertips grazing the jar's round belly. Joel watched the boy in amusement. The boys had been good all week—behaved themselves in school, did their chores without too much fussing . . . and unlike another boy they knew, never pulled pranks like filling kettles with sand. They deserved a treat.

Joel uncorked the licorice jar and withdrew three whips. "Add this in, Wally." Robert's face lit with joy. Joel handed one whip to Robert, stuffed one in his shirt pocket for Johnny, and lifted the third to his mouth. Robert took a mighty chomp, and Joel imitated him.

"You want this on your account?" Wally

reached for the black leather-bound book where he recorded amounts owed and paid.

"That'd be fine. I'll be in the first of the month, like always, to pay it off." Joel signed his name beside the amount due and closed the book. He turned to lean against the counter, and the little bell above the door clanged. Johnny entered, holding the new schoolmarm by the hand, and headed straight for Joel.

"Uncle Joel, this here is Miss Amsel."

Miz Jenkins and her daughter aimed curious looks in their direction.

"Hey, Miss Amsel!" Robert waved his candy, his grin revealing black-coated teeth.

The teacher laughed. "It appears you've been enjoying something good."

Robert thrust the limp licorice whip at his teacher's chin. "Lick'rish. Want some?"

Another laugh rippled. "It's very kind of you to share, but no thank you." She lifted her gaze to meet Joel's. "Mr. Townsend? It's a pleasure to meet you."

He should've greeted her first. Joel swallowed the lump of candy in his mouth and swiped his lips with the back of his hand. He hoped his teeth didn't look like Robert's. "Thank you. It's nice to meet you, too."

Miss Amsel's eyes, a tawny brown with green flecks, crinkled in the corners. The town council had said she was a brand-new teacher, so Joel had expected her to be young—maybe nineteen or twenty. But looking at her up close he could see she was older. Not as old as him—probably not yet thirty—but certainly in her upper twenties. And just why was he worrying about her age anyway?

The women at the table tittered, and he turned his back to them. "I hope Johnny didn't take you away from anything important."

She glanced down at Johnny. The tender smile she aimed at the boy made Joel's heart roll over. "Oh no. He was leaving Mrs. Jeffers's house as I was walking by. When he said he was heading to the mercantile, I asked if I could accompany him."

"She's mailin' a letter." Johnny's skinny chest puffed out importantly. He pointed to the corner of the mercantile, where a windowed partition bore a sign that read POST OFFICE. "Want me to put it in the box for you?"

"Thank you, but I still need to purchase a stamp."

Johnny's face fell, and Miss Amsel touched his shoulder. "But you could check Mrs. Kinsley's mail cubby—you know how to read her name, don't you?—and retrieve her mail for me."

"Yes, ma'am!" Johnny raced for the corner where mail cubbies lined the wall. Robert pounded after him. Her gaze followed the boys, a fond smile curving her lips. Joel remembered his own mother looking at him that way.

"That was real nice of you." Joel didn't realize he'd spoken aloud until she turned her head sharply and looked at him. He added, "The boys like you a lot—talk about you at home all the time."

A blush formed on her cheeks. "I like them, too. They're fine boys."

"Yep, they are." Joel held the half-eaten licorice whip behind his back. He wished he could throw it away. "But if they ever misbehave, I hope you'll tell me. They know if they get in trouble at school, there'll be trouble at home."

Something flickered in her eyes—gratitude, and something else, too. Maybe worry. But then she smiled. "You needn't be concerned. Johnny and Robert are very well behaved and always polite."

At that moment, a scuffle broke out from the corner. Hissed whispers reached Joel's ears—the boys arguing over who would get to carry Miz Kinsley's mail to the teacher. Seems he'd bought that licorice a little too soon. He grimaced. "They're *always* polite?"

She laughed. "At school, yes."

Joel jammed the piece of licorice whip into his back pants pocket as he walked to the post office corner, aware of Miss Amsel on his heels and the amused gazes of the fabric shoppers. The boys were playing tug-of-war with a short stack of envelopes. He caught hold of each boy by his shirt collar. "You're gonna spoil Miz Kinsley's letters if you don't stop fightin' over them. Robert, let loose."

Robert puckered his lower lip but let go. Black smudges indicated where his fingers had held tight.

Joel held out his hand. "Give 'em to me, Johnny."

"But Miss Amsel said—"

"And *I* said hand 'em over."

Johnny huffed in displeasure, but he smacked the stack of envelopes into his uncle's palm. Joel shot each boy a frown before turning to the teacher. "Here you are, ma'am. Sorry they're all wrinkled. An' smudged. Hopefully the letters inside will have fared all right in spite of the rough handling."

Miss Amsel flicked through the stack, as if examining them for damage. The boys watched her, their faces remorseful. She looked up and grinned. "No harm done. And . . ." She raised the stack and sniffed. "Now they smell like licorice."

Robert beamed.

Wally bustled over. "Your supplies're in the wagon, Joel. Miss Amsel, did you need somethin'?"

"A penny stamp, please, and some sugar for Mrs. Kinsley."

He looked toward the Jenkins women. "You two all right for now? I can call down the missus if you're ready to have a length cut."

"That's all right, Mr. Scheebeck," Miz Jenkins said. The pair dropped the bolt they'd been examining and moved toward the door. "We're planning a trip into Lincoln Valley early next week. We'll probably find something there." The two left the store, their heads together and tongues wagging.

Wally turned to Miss Amsel. "I'll getcha fixed right up." He pulled off his merchant apron before slipping behind the partition. When he appeared in the window, he wore a little blue billed cap over his balding head.

Joel swallowed a grin. Wally took his position as postmaster seriously.

Now that the snoopy ladies were gone, Joel wished he could talk more to the boys' teacher. But what would he say? *You seem to like my boys plenty good. Do you reckon we could take some time an' get to know each other?* How silly. A well-bred, educated woman like Miss Amsel wouldn't be interested in a common corn farmer. Hadn't she turned down every other wifeless farmer in town? "Bye now, Miss Amsel. We'll . . . we'll see you in services tomorrow?"

She looked surprised, but then she gave a quick nod. "Oh yes. Certainly."

Well-bred, but a churchgoing woman. Before his thoughts tumbled out of his mouth, Joel urged the boys out the door.

Edythe watched Mr. Townsend herd Robert and Johnny out of the store. The tail end of a whip of licorice stuck out of his dungaree pocket. She covered her smile with her fingers. A man with a sweet tooth—endearing.

"There you are." Mr. Scheebeck slid a stamp across the counter. "That'll be one cent."

Edythe placed a penny in the man's hand and used the little bottle of glue on the counter to affix the stamp. She gave the envelope to Mr. Scheebeck, and he whisked it into a leather pouch. "When will the mail go out?" she asked.

"Monday mornin'." Mr. Scheebeck hung the cap on a nail and retrieved his apron. "Mail stage already come by today—it's always here around ten—an' of course it don't run at all on the Lord's Day."

If all went well, her sister would have the letter in hand by the end of next week. Would Missy reply or ignore it? Thinking of her littlest sister made her heart ache. How she'd hated depositing Missy with their brother Justus when she left, but she'd done the right thing. Her hands were full serving as teacher; she had nothing left to offer Missy. Missy was better off with Justus and his new wife. She only hoped by now Missy had forgiven her for leaving her behind.

"How much sugar was Miz Kinsley wantin'?" Mr. Scheebeck asked.

"A pound, please." As Edythe waited for the storekeeper to measure the sugar, a little head bearing blond pigtails peeked around from the doorway at the back of the store. Edythe smiled. "Hello, Jenny. How are you today?"

The little girl stepped into the doorway. "Lewis got in trouble."

Edythe stifled a chuckle. Why did children relish tattling?

Mr. Scheebeck formed a cone with paper. "Go on back upstairs, Jenny. Don't be pesterin' Miss Amsel."

Jenny slipped away. Edythe felt the need to defend the child. "She wasn't bothering me. I enjoy talking with her. Jenny's a delight."

The mercantile owner shrugged. "She can be a talker—like her ma, I reckon. Sayin' things that're better left unsaid."

According to Mrs. Kinsley, Mr. Scheebeck was the main news spreader in town. "I've never heard her say anything inappropriate." Although Jenny no longer cried, she sat very quietly in class, taking everything in with wide blue eyes but saying very little even in response to questions. Edythe hoped the little girl would eventually lose her shyness.

Mr. Scheebeck rolled the top of the cone and handed the container of sugar across the counter. "What she said just now—about Lewis bein' in trouble? He is, but that ain't none of your affair.

Besides, he didn't cause it all himself. He had help." The man snorted. "That Sholes boy better not come into my store again anytime soon. I'll take the broom an' chase him out again."

The fine hairs on Edythe's neck prickled. "William?"

"I'm not sayin' nothin' more," the man declared. "But this prank went too far. Fun is fun, but somebody gettin' hurt? That ain't fun."

Although she knew she shouldn't encourage gossip, Edythe couldn't resist asking, "Someone was hurt?"

Mr. Scheebeck waved his hand. "Nah, but someone sure could've been. No, sir, that boy's not welcome here anymore." The man slapped his hand to his forehead. "Oh, I nearly forgot . . ." He bustled over to the post office corner and disappeared behind the partition. When he emerged a few moments later, he wore his postmaster hat and held an envelope in his hand. "Should've thought of this when you bought the stamp. Letter come for you on the mornin' stage."

Edythe took it. "Thank you."

"I'll be gettin' you a cubby set up to hold your mail—just haven't had time yet." His shoulders lifted and fell. "Runnin' this store, bein' the telegrapher, *an'* handlin' postmaster duties is a mighty big job at times. The missus has been feelin' poorly, so she isn't able to help much these days."

Edythe fingered the envelope, eager to look at the contents. "I'm sorry your wife isn't well. Nothing serious, I hope?"

"She's in a family way," the man whispered. "Baby's due end of the year. So she's takin' it easy."

"Congratulations." Edythe inched toward the door, her envelope in one hand and Mrs. Kinsley's items in the other. "Have a pleasant day, Mr. Scheebeck."

"Bye, now."

Edythe stepped out onto the street and turned toward Mrs. Kinsley's house. Tucking the cone of sugar and Mrs. Kinsley's mail in the crook of her arm, she opened her envelope and lifted out a single sheet of paper. As she read, her feet slowed until she came to a stop in the middle of the walkway next to a picket fence. She sagged against the fence, crushing the letter to her aching chest. She might as well ask Mr. Scheebeck to discard the letter she'd sent to Missy. She was too late.

Chapter
SIX

Joel bowed his head and closed his eyes as the minister said the final prayer. Robert fidgeted on the pew beside him, and he nudged the boy with his elbow. The restless movement stopped. At Reverend Coker's "Amen," Robert bounced to his feet with a frantic look. "I need the outhouse."

"Then go."

The boy raced out, weaving his way around other parishioners who loitered in the wide aisle that separated the rows of wooden benches. Joel shook his head. He supposed he shouldn't scold, given the circumstances, but he'd need to remind Robert to say excuse me when he pushed between folks.

He shifted his attention to Johnny, who waited for permission to run out to the yard with the other kids. Before he could grant it, however, Hank Libolt sidled up beside Joel. "Hey."

"Morning, Hank." Joel gave a nod toward the doors, and Johnny grinned and headed outside. Joel turned to his neighbor. "Nice day for the end of September, isn't it? I keep thinkin' this warm weather's going to come to an end and bring the snows, but so far it's held."

"Yup." Hank frowned toward the cluster of women at the back of the church. "I see all the ladies are welcomin' our new schoolmarm."

A rush of heat attacked Joel's neck at the mention of Edythe Amsel. After their brief encounter yesterday, he'd been unable to put the woman out of his mind. Her kind attention to his boys made him envision her being more than their teacher. The idea was silly considering she was clearly a big-city gal, but he couldn't seem to set the thought aside. He needed to do a heap of praying to find out whether this interest was God's idea or his own.

"I'm not too sure what to think of her," Hank continued, his voice low. "She appears well-mannered and proper. But I've heard tell of some strange goings-on in that schoolhouse."

"What do you mean?" Neither Johnny nor Robert had mentioned anything odd, and the boys usually told him everything about their day.

"For instance, Wolcott drove by the school one afternoon, an' the kids were all outside peckin' around in the dirt like a flock of chickens. He thought maybe one of 'em had lost something important, but no—when I asked my Henry, he said they was all huntin' bugs." Hank's eyes nearly bugged from his head. "Then they pinned the bugs to a piece of wood an' spent time countin' their legs, comparin' their colors, an' just studyin' 'em. *Bugs!* Who heard tell of using schooltime for something like that?"

Johnny and Robert had come home excited about knowing which bugs were harmful to crops and which they needed to leave alone so they could eat the harmful bugs. Joel started to tell Hank his boys' feelings on the activity, but Hank went on.

"An' that's just starters. She also had 'em all out of a mornin', stepping through a spider web made out of ropes on the play yard. Still haven't figured out what that was all about. Henry told me, but it didn't make much sense to me." Hank shook his head. "I'm wonderin' if we made a mistake bringin' in a lady teacher fresh from teachin' school. Maybe we should've kept old man Shanks. He could be cranky, but I never worried about what he was teachin' my young'uns."

Joel clapped Hank's shoulder. "I reckon we got used to Mr. Shanks and his ways. But every teacher has his or her own way of teachin', just like every farmer has his own way of farmin'." Hank was one of the men who had told Joel he was addlepated for digging irrigation ditches and letting some of his soil rest each year rather than planting every acre. "I say give her a chance. The children sure seem to like her."

"Oh, I'll grant you that. All three o' mine think she's dandy. 'Specially Will—he'd been pretty scared about startin' school. But now he's all excited about goin'."

Hank had just described Robert's feelings, too. Joel looked across the small worship room to Miss Amsel, who stood with her head tipped and an attentive smile on her face while Miz Saltzmann yakked away. That woman's never-ceasing blather could try the patience of Job, but Miss Amsel didn't appear at all annoyed. Apparently her kind ways extended beyond the children, and she grew more appealing to Joel by the minute.

He jerked his attention to Hank again. "I think we oughtta just leave her be an' let her teach. I thought Shanks was rough on the kids, but we let him do his job his way. Shouldn't we give Miss Amsel the same consideration, at least for now?"

Hank ducked his head and toed the floor. "I reckon you're right, Joel. But . . ." He glanced at the teacher, his brows low. "When she comes callin' at my house this week, I plan to ask her about some of those peculiar goings-on. I'm on the town council, you know, an' it's part of my job to make sure our youngsters are gettin' the right kind of learnin'."

Edythe felt like a honeysuckle vine swarmed by bees. She smiled and answered the womenfolk's questions politely, but inwardly she hoped for rescue. And rescue eventually arrived in the form of Mrs. Kinsley, who charged into the group and took hold of Edythe's elbow.

" 'Scuse my interruptin'," the woman said, "but Miss Amsel will be makin' the rounds to your houses, where you can talk to your heart's content. We gotta be gettin' home now." Luthenia sent a no-nonsense look around the circle of disappointed faces. "Have a blessed Lord's day, ladies." She tugged Edythe away from the group.

On the wagon seat, Edythe heaved a relieved sigh. "Thank you. I wondered how I would make my escape. The ladies asked question after question, but"—she crinkled her brow—"none related to teaching. They were all very . . . personal."

Mrs. Kinsley chuckled. "They're searchin' for somethin' good they can share around the quiltin' frame or at Ladies' Mission Society."

Edythe frowned. "It's rather disheartening to think their friendliness holds ulterior motives."

"Now, don't be thinkin' ill of the whole town 'cause of what I said. They're not so much malicious as curious." Mrs. Kinsley gave the reins a gentle pull, guiding the horse around a sizable pothole in the street. "Town council needs to get those potholes filled—a body could be jarred clean off the seat if a wagon wheel clunked through one." She whisked a quick glance at Edythe. "Y'see, not much exciting happens in Walnut Hill, so a new person in town makes a mighty big stir. Just mind what you say, knowin' it'll all be repeated."

Edythe sat in silence, digesting Mrs. Kinsley's advice the rest of the way home. Mrs. Kinsley drew the wagon behind the house and called, "Whoa there, Gertie." The old mare sagged her head, as if happy to be allowed to stop. Mrs. Kinsley set the brake, then turned to Edythe. "I'm gonna put this old girl in her shed an' then I'll be in to set lunch on the table. If the roast smells burnt, get it out of the oven, would'ja? We don't want to be eatin' burnt offerings."

Edythe nodded. "I'll certainly see to the roast, and I'll set the table so it will be ready when you return." She swept her skirts to the side to avoid catching them on the wheel hub as she climbed down from the wagon. Then she hurried into the house, the enticing aroma of meat spurring her forward.

Just as she removed the roasting pan from the oven, someone tapped on the front door. She dashed to the door and threw it wide. To her surprise, she found Mr. Townsend, Johnny, and Robert on the porch. The boys beamed.

"Hi, Miss Amsel! We come for our cookies."

Edythe blinked twice, confused. "Cookies?"

Mr. Townsend looked past her shoulder, as if seeking someone. "Where's Miz Kinsley?"

"Out back with the mare. I shall retrieve her, and—"

Suddenly, Mrs. Kinsley bustled into the room, waving her hand to the little group on the porch. "Bet you're here for them cookies I promised the boys. I been carin' for Gert an' haven't got 'em wrapped yet. I gotta wash my hands." She whirled toward the washbasin. "Miss Amsel, entertain them fellas for me."

Entertain them? How? She gulped and faced the little group. Heat flooded her face. They stood in a quiet circle, examining one another in silence. When Mrs. Kinsley bustled back into the room with a brown-paper-wrapped package in hand, Edythe slunk out of the way, relieved to allow the other woman control of the situation.

"There you go, boys. Fresh-baked yesterday, so they're still nice an' moist."

The pair of towheaded, freckle-faced youngsters reached eagerly for the package. "Thank you!" Robert sniffed the air. "Mmm, smells good in here. What is that?"

Mrs. Kinsley laughed. "Roast, taters, and carrots. What're you havin' for lunch today, Robert?"

Robert wrinkled his nose. Three freckles disappeared in a crease. "Beans."

Mr. Townsend gave the boy a slight nudge on the shoulder, frowning. "There's nothin' wrong with beans." He released an embarrassed chuckle. "We probably do eat a lot of 'em. They don't need much tendin' while they simmer, so it's an easy thing for me to cook."

Mrs. Kinsley gestured to the kitchen. "Well, if you think those beans'll keep a mite longer, you're welcome to stay. I made plenty—can't seem to get over my habit of cookin' a big meal, even though Cyrus has been gone over three years now. Why don't you an' the boys sit at the table with Miss Amsel an' me? We can set out extra plates quick as the shake of a lamb's tail."

Joel's neck blotched red. "I appreciate the invitation, but the beans'll be boiled down to a mess if we don't get back soon." Robert and Johnny groaned, but their uncle's frown stilled their protests. He put a hand on each boy's shoulder and turned them toward the door. "You ladies have a good day. Boys, tell Miz Kinsley and Miss . . . Miss Amsel bye now."

The stammer surprised Edythe. Did he feel ill at ease around her?

"Bye, Miz Kinsley. Bye, Miss Amsel." The childish voices held no enthusiasm.

Mrs. Kinsley followed them to the porch and waved as they climbed into their wagon. "You enjoy them cookies now, you hear?"

When the wagon rolled away, Mrs. Kinsley hurried back in and closed the door. "Well, let's get set down to eat before—" She paused, looking fully at Edythe. "What's wrong?"

Edythe wrung her hands. "Mr. Townsend . . . he . . . he isn't married?"

"Land sakes no. What gave you that idea?"

"He was at the mercantile yesterday purchasing a canning kettle. I just assumed . . ."

Mrs. Kinsley tipped her head. "Joel Townsend's never been married. I heard speculation that—" She clamped her lips together.

Edythe's senses went on alert. "What?"

"Never you mind. The Bible advises against spoutin' gossip. I might listen in when others're talkin', but I won't be guilty of spreading falsehoods." Mrs. Kinsley sighed. "Joel's alone, raisin' his deceased brother's sons. I got great admiration for him. To my way of thinkin', anybody who'd take care of somebody else's young'uns deserves a big crown when they reach Heaven."

Edythe's nose stung fiercely. Then, much to her chagrin, she burst into tears.

Chapter
SEVEN

Edythe stumbled in the direction of the staircase, but Mrs. Kinsley caught her upper arms and held her in place.

"Miss Amsel, what in the ever-lovin' blazes is the matter?" Bewilderment puckered the woman's face. "Sit down here." Mrs. Kinsley pressed her onto the settee and sat beside her, slipping her arm around Edythe's shoulders. "What's this cryin' about?"

Edythe could never remember behaving so childishly, not even when she was young, before Mama died. Dissolving into tears as an adult of twenty-eight years brought a rush of embarrassment. Yet the comfort of Mrs. Kinsley's warm, motherly arm was strangely welcome, and she didn't want to leave the soothing touch.

"I'm so sorry." She swiped viciously at her cheeks, erasing the moisture. "I'm fine—truly I am. We'd better eat before the food grows cold." She started to rise.

Mrs. Kinsley pulled her back down. "That roast'll keep. Stay put 'til we sort this out." Cupping her hand over Edythe's knee, she gave a gentle squeeze. "I been livin' almost sixty years now, an' I've learned a thing or two about tears. Most of the time, they're for a reason. But tears in and of themselves don't solve a problem. Takes a little more—usually talkin' things out. I know we're newly acquainted an' you got no good reason to confide in me, but I'm willing to listen."

More tears gathered in Edythe's eyes at the woman's firm yet warm tone. For the past fourteen years, she'd carried every burden alone.

A part of her longed to share her concerns, but it had been so long since she'd opened herself to anyone, she wasn't sure how to begin.

Mrs. Kinsley folded her arms over her chest. "This have somethin' to do with that letter you toted here yesterday?"

Edythe stared at her landlady. "How did you know?"

The lines around Mrs. Kinsley's eyes deepened. "I seen how you kept fingerin' the envelope durin' supper last night. You hardly ate a thing. Then durin' the night you was cryin'."

Edythe drew in a sharp breath. "You heard me?"

Mrs. Kinsley shrugged. "Sound carries through the grate under your bed." She gave Edythe's knee another pat. "I think you'll feel better if you talk about it, but if you'd rather not, I'll understand."

A few seconds of silence ticked by while Edythe nibbled her lower lip, contemplating what to do. Finally, Mrs. Kinsley sighed and braced her hands on her knees. "All right, missy, I can take a hint. Let's—"

The title *missy* pierced Edythe straight through the heart. She grasped her landlady's bony wrist. "Mrs. Kinsley, what you said about Mr. Townsend earning a crown in Heaven for caring for someone else's children . . ." Tears threatened once more. She blinked several times, sending them away. "Did you mean that?"

The woman pulled back, surprise on her wrinkled face. "Sure I did."

"So . . . if you had the chance . . . you'd take in someone in need of a home?"

Mrs. Kinsley chuckled. "Seems to me I already did." She assumed a conspiratorial air. "Town's never had a lady teacher—always been a man. Nobody thinks twice if a man lives on his own, but havin' a young lady livin' all alone just didn't set right with the town council. So they asked if I'd be willin' to provide you with room an' board. Bedroom at the top of the stairs not bein' used for more'n takin' up space, so I said I'd be proud to host the new schoolmarm."

Mrs. Kinsley laughed softly. "Now, it's not that I think of you as a child—it's plain to see you're a woman grown—but you were needin' a roof over your head, an' I provided it." Her eyes flew wide. "But don't think I did it out of hopin' to earn a crown or to add a few dollars to my bank account."

Although Edythe had only known Mrs. Kinsley for a week, she already knew the woman was not selfish. Crusty, perhaps, but not selfish. Edythe hung her head. "You aren't selfish. But I am."

"You?" The word blasted out on a note of incredulity. "Why, you're a schoolmarm—givin' your time an' talent to a passel of youngsters. Why'n thunder would you say you were selfish?"

The tears Edythe had tried to squelch returned to pour down her cheeks in warm rivulets. "I did a terrible thing. I—I left home, and I left my sister behind." Once the words started, she couldn't control them any more than the tears that continued to rain down her face. "Missy is fourteen, the same age I was when my mother died. Being the oldest, I took over our entire household at fourteen. Missy was only a baby then, and I had four other siblings besides."

"Land sakes." Mrs. Kinsley's blue eyes grew round. "That's a fearsome load for a young girl."

Edythe nodded, gulping. "It was hard, being ma to my brothers and sisters. Especially when Pa . . ." She shook her head, dispelling unpleasant memories. "The children might as well have been mine alone for all the attention he paid them."

Mrs. Kinsley slipped her arm around Edythe again and gave her several pats. "Sounds to me like you've been earnin' your crown, too."

Edythe jolted away from the woman's kind touch. "I don't deserve a crown. As soon as Missy was old enough—the very age at which I was forced to grow up—I left her. All the others were out on their own. I decided not to wait until Missy grew up. I'd given my family fourteen years already . . . half of my life . . ."

Edythe paused, her mind tripping through the years of service, the years of waiting until she could grasp freedom from the responsibilities thrust upon her far too soon. "So despite my father's endless pleas for me to stay home and care for Missy and for him, I earned my teaching certificate and I left. I left them all behind."

Guilt sent her pacing the room, a feeble attempt to escape its clutches. "And now my brother Justus wrote to tell me Missy ran away. I'd asked Justus and his wife to keep her, but . . . but she missed me, so she ran away. No one knows where she is." Worry and fear struck like lightning, nearly driving Edythe to her knees. "She's only fourteen—a mere child, the same age as dear Martha Sterbinz. How could I have been so selfish? Why didn't I stay?"

Mrs. Kinsley came at Edythe with open arms, wrapping her in a tight embrace. Edythe clung to the older woman, grateful for her understanding. She sniffed hard while Mrs. Kinsley rubbed her back.

"Don't you go blamin' yourself. Seems to me you gave your family plenty—more'n most would've done." The encouraging contact of the woman's warm palm was a healing balm to Edythe's aching soul. "You need to be proud of the way you stepped in an' played mama for your brothers an' sisters. As for Missy . . ." Mrs. Kinsley took hold of Edythe's shoulders and set her aside. "We'll just be prayin' that she comes to her senses an' goes home."

Edythe began pacing again. "She'll never go home. Not to Pa. He's so . . ." Edythe came to a stop. She sought an appropriate word. "Bitter. He wears one down with his constant melancholy."

"Losin' his wife like he did could bitter a man," Mrs. Kinsley said.

Edythe shook her head. "It wasn't losing Mama that soured him. It was something much less important." But Edythe had no desire to discuss that part of her past life—it was over, it couldn't be changed, and it needed to stay buried. As a teacher, she intended to make sure none of her students ever suffered the same fate as her illiterate father. "I wrote to Missy, asking her forgiveness, but now . . ." She bit her lip as another wave of guilt threatened to overwhelm her.

"Miss Amsel, if there's one lesson I've learned more'n any other, it's worry don't add one day to our lives." The woman marched forward and gave Edythe's shoulders a squeeze. "All the stewin' in the world won't change the fact that your sister decided she wasn't going to stay put. Stewin' won't find her. Stewin' won't do nothin' more than give you dyspepsia."

Despite herself, Edythe laughed. "Mrs. Kinsley . . ."

The woman put on an innocent face. "You think I'm funnin' you? I've had my share of dyspepsia spells, an' I can tell you from experience, they don't do a body any good." She smiled. "Listen, young'uns do foolish things. Your sister's young—impetuous, yes?"

Edythe gave a hesitant nod. Missy was prone to rash behavior. Sometimes Edythe thought she behaved impulsively to garner Pa's attention—to make him think about someone other than himself.

Mrs. Kinsley continued. "Could it be that in the time it took your brother's letter to get from there to here, she already realized her foolishness an' went on home?"

A bubble of hope bounced through Edythe's chest. "I . . . I suppose it's possible."

"Then that's what we're gonna hang on to." Mrs. Kinsley slung her arm around Edythe's waist and led her toward the kitchen. " 'Til we hear otherwise, we're gonna pray, believin' that your sister is safe an' sound."

They sat at the table and Mrs. Kinsley asked a blessing for the food. The woman added, "An' thank You, Lord, for keepin' Missy safe—we trust You to take care of that girl, since we can't. Amen."

Mrs. Kinsley filled Edythe's plate to over-flowing with oven-browned vegetables and tender slices of beef. Although the food was cold from sitting so long neglected, Edythe found it surprisingly flavorful, and her stomach growled in anticipation. "I didn't realize how hungry I was."

Mrs. Kinsley harrumphed. "Considerin' you hardly ate two bites last night an' slept through breakfast this mornin', I'm not surprised." Then she grinned. "But seein' you eat good now tells me you're lettin' loose of your worry for Missy."

Should she be eating when she didn't know if Missy was at this very moment going hungry? She lowered her fork.

"You stop that right now." The woman's sharp words startled Edythe. The landlady pointed to Edythe's plate with her fork. "Don't just sit there starin' at your plate. Eat up." When Edythe didn't reach for her fork, Mrs. Kinsley snapped, "Is not eatin' gonna make any difference for Missy? 'Course not—it'll only make you sick. Gal as thin as you can't afford to be skippin' meals. So eat." She gentled her voice. "Things're gonna be fine—you mark my words."

Desire to believe Mrs. Kinsley's proclamation created a pressure in Edythe's breast. "How can you be so sure?"

"We placed your sister in God's hands. He's capable of takin' care of her better than you or me or anybody else could." Mrs. Kinsley went back to eating, unconcerned.

Edythe forced herself to lift her fork to her mouth. But while she chewed and swallowed, eating by rote rather than for pleasure, she replayed her landlady's words. *"We placed your sister in God's hands . . ."* "We" intimated Edythe had done so, too, but she had no concept of what it meant to place something in God's hands.

Chapter
EIGHT

By midweek, Edythe began to question the wisdom of visiting all her pupils' folks. She still believed becoming acquainted with each family was a good idea, but exhaustion plagued her.

After teaching all day—and dealing with William Sholes's persistent shenanigans; what would it take to make the boy settle down and behave?—she lacked energy to carry her through the evening. In hindsight, she wished she had planned the visits for every other evening rather than back to back, which would have given her some time to recuperate in between. But the schedule was set, people expected her—many of whom had insisted on cooking her supper—and she would honor the commitment. Surely she could handle the hectic pace for a mere three weeks. . . .

She gave the traces a little tug, prompting Mrs. Kinsley's mare to turn in at the lane leading to the Libolt place. A square log house surrounded on three sides by now-empty fields waited at the end of the dirt lane. With its porch lit by two lanterns and yellow light glowing behind the uncurtained windowpanes, the little house sent out a cheery welcome despite its plain appearance. Gertie seemed to think so, too, because she broke into a trot that closed the distance.

Edythe set the brake and hopped down. She wrinkled her nose as the ceaseless wind carried the acrid scent of charcoal to her nostrils. Apparently Mr. Libolt, like many of the other farmers around Walnut Hill, had been burning off the stubble in his fields.

Brushing the travel dust and wrinkles from her full skirt, she stepped onto the porch and lifted her hand to knock on the planked door. But before her knuckles connected with wood, the door swung open and nine-year-old Henry greeted her with a gap-toothed grin. He hollered over his shoulder, "Ma! Schoolmarm's here!"

At once, Mrs. Libolt bustled from the stove, where an enticing scent wafted from a large black pot. A toddler trailed beside her, clinging to his mother's skirts. Mrs. Libolt held her hands out in greeting. "Miss Amsel, come right on in. Henry, close that door tight, now—evening air's turned cool. Anna, don't dawdle—finish settin' that table. Willie, come get Claude before he trips me."

The children all bustled to obey. The littlest one wailed when Willie grabbed him around the middle and hauled him to the opposite side of the room, but Mrs. Libolt's laugh carried over the child's high-pitched protest. "Young'uns . . . always underfoot." The woman's bright smile put Edythe at ease. "We're proud you come to join us for supper. The children've been excited."

From the table, Anna chirped, "Mama made biscuits an' heart stew!"

Edythe swallowed. "H-heart stew?" Suddenly the aroma didn't seem quite as pleasant.

Mrs. Libolt nodded, her smile never dimming. "Oh yes, the heart's the most tender part of the beef. It's one of our favorites, an' when we butchered last weekend, the young'uns insisted I save the heart an' cook it up for their schoolmarm's visit."

"My . . ." What could she say? "How thoughtful of them."

Catching Edythe's arm, Mrs. Libolt drew her farther into the simple, unadorned room. "You don't need to stand there by the door. Give Henry your cloak—sure is a pretty one. Don't see many velvet cloaks around Walnut Hill." The woman stroked the expanse of red fabric draping over Edythe's shoulder. "I'm thinkin' Miz Scheebeck's got one, but bein' the mercantile owner's wife an' gettin' a discount from the catalog, she can afford one better'n the rest of us."

Edythe, uncertain how to respond, slipped her cloak free and laid it across Henry's waiting arms. Mrs. Libolt's gaze followed Henry as he moved to the sitting area of the room and placed the deep red cloak over the back of a chair. The longing in the other woman's eyes made Edythe feel guilty. She'd chosen her nicest worsted suit and fine velvet cloak out of deference for Mr. Libolt's position on the town council. Now, looking at the rustic cabin and the woman's humble calico skirt and muslin shirtwaist, she felt decidedly overdressed and out of place.

Smoothing her hands over the well-fitted waist of her garnet dress, she said, "May I help with anything?"

Mrs. Libolt's jaw dropped. "You're our guest! You just sit down over there—the young'uns'll keep you company while I finish up. Soon as Hank comes in—he's seein' to the barn critters— we'll commence to eatin'. Won't be long now. Go ahead an' sit." She shooed Edythe the way Edythe often shooed her students from one area to another.

Edythe allowed Anna to lead her past the table set with dented tin plates and mismatched cutlery to the sitting area. She and Anna sat side by side on the sawdust-stuffed settee, and the toddler brother sidled up to lean on her knees. When

Anna tried to get him to talk, he put his finger in his mouth and turned shy. But Henry, Anna, and Will made up for their little brother's lack of words. Their comments tumbled one on top of the other as they each shared whatever they deemed important.

Listening to the children's jabber while their mother worked cheerfully at the stove and occasionally sent a smile in their direction, Edythe felt better about planning these visits to the children's homes. Not only did the parents seem pleased to host the new teacher for an evening, seeing the children at home gave her a completely different perspective of them.

On Monday evening, Jane Heidrich, who rarely spoke or smiled in class, nearly bubbled while showing the schoolmarm her chickens and the pigs she'd raised. Clearly, Jane felt more confident on her family's farmstead than in the classroom, and Edythe had made a mental note to offer the girl lots of encouragement. The two little Ellsworth girls, magpies in class, were apparently overwhelmed by having their teacher in their home on Tuesday. They'd sat wide-eyed and silent through the entire meal. Now, on her third night of visiting, the Libolt children, whom Edythe had dubbed "animated," proved they were much more energetic in their home than in the schoolhouse.

By the time Hank Libolt entered the room and

Mrs. Libolt called everyone to the table, Edythe was grateful Henry, Anna, and Will exhibited restraint in the classroom; their enthusiastic chatter wore out her ears. They fell silent, however, when their father folded his hands to say grace. Mr. Libolt's formal, almost terse, way of addressing God differed from Mrs. Kinsley's ease in speaking with her Maker, but Edythe reminded herself she shouldn't try to assess prayers. She knew little, if anything, about what it meant to talk to God. She ought to pray for Missy each day, the way Mrs. Kinsley did, but thus far Edythe had allowed her landlady to offer all of the prayers.

"Here now, Teacher, you hand me your plate." Mrs. Libolt held her hand toward Edythe, a smile splitting her face. "Guests first."

Edythe did as she was bid, and Mrs. Libolt ladled a huge serving of meat and vegetables swimming in a thick brown gravy onto Edythe's plate. Edythe kept her hands in her lap and waited while Mrs. Libolt filled the other plates. Mr. Libolt and the children plucked up spoons and began to eat as soon as they had food in front of them. A year ago, Edythe would have done the same thing, unaware of societal niceties. But she'd learned more than teaching skills at the normal school—her fellow students, many of whom came from more genteel backgrounds, had unwittingly taught Edythe how to be a lady. So whether those around her exhibited proper manners or not, she chose to do so. Perhaps her students would absorb some of the social graces.

Anna, seated on Edythe's left, gave her a puzzled look. "Why ain't you eating, Miss Amsel? Don't you like stew?"

"Oh yes, I like stew a great deal." *Heart* stew, though? She wasn't sure. "I'm letting mine cool a bit so I don't burn my tongue."

Anna grinned. "Just blow on it." She blew so hard, broth spattered across the table. Mr. Libolt scowled, and Anna hunched over her bowl.

Edythe lifted her spoon and took a hesitant bite. The flavor was exactly like beef roast stew, but the thought of what she held in her mouth made it hard for her to swallow. She silently congratulated herself for achieving one bite and dipped her spoon a second time.

"So, Teacher—" Mr. Libolt met Edythe's gaze from across the table. No smile lit his face. "What were you doin' with the young'uns out on the play yard with all them ropes?"

Edythe lowered her spoon, confused until she remembered the activity from last week. "Oh, you're referring to the learning project on latitude and longitude." She flashed a smile at Henry. "Although it was a lesson for the fourth- and fifth-grade students, your Henry caught on to naming the degrees quite well. I was proud of him."

Henry beamed, but Mr. Libolt's frown deepened. "Latitude and long . . . what?"

"Longitude, Pa." Henry's skinny chest puffed. "It's like the earth is all covered with lines an' people use 'em to find a place anywhere in the world—even in China!"

Angry streaks rose from Mr. Libolt's neck to his cheeks. He gave his son a stern glare. "You just hush there." Henry ducked his head, and the man pinned Edythe with the same glower. "The young'uns around here'll be farmers one day. How is knowin' how to find some place like . . . like *China*"—he made the word sound offensive—"gonna do 'em any good?"

Mrs. Libolt released a high-pitched laugh, and her hand fluttered by her throat. "Oh, now, Hank, I'm sure Miss Amsel's got her reasons for teachin' what she does. She means well."

Edythe squirmed as the man shot his wife a silencing scowl. "Mr. Libolt, I—"

"Our youngsters don't need anything fancy. Teach 'em readin', writin', arithmetic . . . some history so they know about their country." Mr. Libolt plunked his spoon onto the table, nodding at his own words. "Maybe use the *Farmers' Almanac* for lessons on weather an' when it's best to plant—that'd serve 'em fine. But all that jumpin' around on ropes seems plumb foolish to me."

The man's comments carried Edythe backward

in time. Her father's voice rang in her memory: *"You . . . becomin' a teacher? Plumb foolishness. You're an Amsel, girl—mule stubborn an' rock dumb. You can't teach nobody nothin' worth knowin'."*

Determinedly, she met Mr. Libolt's narrowed gaze. "It seems you and I view the purpose of an education from opposite perspectives. You believe teaching should be limited to fundamentals. While I certainly see fundamentals as the base of learning, I believe a good teacher also strives to expand a child's knowledge, to open him to new and exciting ideas and worlds beyond the limited scope provided by the basic subjects."

Edythe lifted her chin and continued, her voice strong. "When the children finish their year with me, I hope they will have made strides in their reading and ciphering skills. But more importantly, I hope they will be better *thinkers*. It is my goal that the children grow as students, but also as people living in a constantly changing world."

Mrs. Libolt stared at Edythe, her jaw slack. The children, with the exception of little Claude, who went on eating, held their spoons in their motionless hands and gaped at their teacher. Edythe realized her voice had risen during her lengthy discourse. Aware that she'd made everyone around the table uncomfortable, she sank a bit lower into her chair.

Mr. Libolt's face glowed bright red, and he folded his thick arms over his chest. "Sounds to me like you're wantin' to make our young'uns unhappy with the life they got here. You're wantin' 'em to think about takin' off"—he threw one arm outward, nearly clopping Claude on the side of the head—"an' bein' more'n farmers. Aren't farmers good enough for you, Teacher?"

How had the conversation turned combative so quickly? Although many of the students in her classroom would certainly turn to farming when they finished their education, she wanted them to know other opportunities existed. But how to explain that without making the man feel inferior for choosing farming as his vocation?

Finally, settling on an answer, she swallowed and spoke in a calm, reasonable voice that belied the nervous churning in her belly. "Mr. Libolt, I assure you I do not view farming as less important than other occupations. In fact, my own father was a farmer." *Until he lost our family's homestead . . .* "I have no intention of *dissuading* students from becoming farmers. If that's what they choose, I will encourage them in the endeavor and attempt to instill in them the skills they need to be successful."

Mr. Libolt's frown did not lessen, but Edythe plunged bravely onward. "But I feel it is my duty to let the children know how many opportunities exist." She held out her hands in supplication.

"What if Henry or Little Will wishes to become a doctor, or to one day move to a big city and work in a factory? Shouldn't he be given the chance to explore other occupations that might be of interest to him?"

The man snorted. His wife chided, "Hank . . ." He snorted again.

Edythe bristled. Mr. Libolt's reaction too closely mirrored her father's behavior. Despite her intention to speak calmly, her tone turned sharp. "You would deny your son the pursuit of his own dream because it doesn't align with what you chose for his life?"

"You're bein' impertinent, missy."

The man's growling tone sent a warning Edythe knew she should heed. How would Mr. Libolt respond if she told him she would have been trapped in a life of servitude, battling bitter regret, had she followed her father's plans for her? Having discovered the courage to flee Ed Amsel's entrapment, she could not sit idly by and watch this father squelch his children's dreams.

She took a deep breath. "Mr. Libolt, I'm sincerely sorry that you don't see the value in subjects beyond the rudimentary. But I cannot modify my personal objective as a teacher to bow to your"—*narrow-minded* quivered on her tongue, but she caught herself and replaced it—"opposing view. I hope you will respect my position as much as I respect yours."

Mr. Libolt stared at her, his lips forming an upside-down U of displeasure. Before he could speak, Mrs. Libolt screeched her chair backward and rose. She flashed a too-bright smile around the table. "I baked up an apple-walnut cake for dessert. Who'd like some?"

Without waiting for a response, she bustled to the stove. She retrieved the cake from the warming hub and offered the first good-sized wedge to her husband. But he shook his head and pushed away from the table. "I got work to do in the barn. Henry, I need your help. C'mon."

Henry cast an embarrassed look at Edythe before trailing his father out the door.

Edythe accepted a piece of cake, but she only managed to choke down a few bites of the richly spiced, moist concoction. Her stomach, filled with dread at having created an enemy of a town council member, resisted accepting food. Less than half an hour after Mr. Libolt stormed out the door, she bid Mrs. Libolt, Anna, and Little Will good-bye and climbed into the wagon for the drive back to town.

As she turned from the Libolts' lane onto the main road, she sighed, her breath forming a puff of white. Tomorrow evening after supper she would ride to the Townsend farm. She intended to take her landlady with her; it wouldn't do for her to spend time alone with a single man, even though his nephews would be in attendance.

Would Mr. Townsend, like Mr. Libolt, berate her for her desire to broaden the children's views beyond the limited scope of their farming community? For some reason, she wanted to believe he would be more accepting.

She raised her tired gaze skyward and loosened her grip on Gert's traces; the reliable mare knew the way to town. "At least," she muttered to the dusky sky, "I didn't have to eat that heart stew. . . ." Then she laughed at her own expense. Such a meager reason to be thankful, but a meager reason was better than none.

Sighing again, she gave the traces a little flick. "You're lollygagging, Gertie—I need to get back." A stack of papers required grading, and she needed to plan the means of demonstrating the geographical landscapes of the United States. Would river clay be suitable for molding mountains? She could already hear Mr. Libolt's snort of displeasure when he found out his children were playing with clay in the classroom.

"I will not allow that man's shortsightedness to prevent me from being the very best teacher I can be!" Saying the words aloud heartened her. Education gave power, and as long as she was the schoolmarm of Walnut Hill, she would empower her students to think expansively.

But as she looked ahead to tomorrow's meeting with yet another farm family, her resolve wavered. What would she do if the local farmers banded together in support of Hank Libolt's feelings about appropriate subjects for the town's students?

As much as she disliked the thought, her beliefs about the fundamentals of education might create dissension—and cost her a job she couldn't afford to lose.

Chapter
NINE

"Miz Kinsley's wagon's comin', Uncle Joel! I see it!"

Johnny's shout carried through the closed front door, startling Joel. *Here we go . . .* His belly churned. He gave the tabletop one more swish with his palm in case he'd missed a crumb or two earlier and then smoothed the front of his shirt. Yep, it was still neatly tucked into his britches. After a quick glance around the cabin's main room, he pulled in a breath of fortification. Nothing fancy to offer the new teacher, but she'd see the real Joel Townsend. He hoped he measured up. Why he needed to measure up he couldn't explain—not even to himself. He just knew it was important that Miss Amsel not think ill of him or his boys.

He stepped out onto the porch. Johnny and Robert stood on their tiptoes with their arms dangling over the roughhewn top bar of the porch railing. They'd fidgeted all through supper, eager to be excused to watch for their teacher. Even though the evening air had turned cool, Joel had let them wait on the porch rather than stay penned up inside. Miss Amsel had surely wormed her way into his nephews' affections.

"See there?" Johnny pointed as the wagon rolled through the gate. "Miss Amsel—an' Miz Kinsley, too." He puckered his face. "Why'd Miz Kinsley come, you reckon?"

Robert bounced on his heels. "Maybe she brought us more cookies!"

"You haven't even finished the ones she gave you Sunday."

"Only 'cause you wouldn't let me," the boy replied, sending Joel an impish grin.

Joel laughed, but his laughter died when the wagon reached the yard and the boys rushed out to greet the schoolmarm. Her smile, although aimed at Johnny and Robert, warmed him from the distance of twenty feet. If she turned it at him at close range, he just might melt.

Knock it off, Townsend. You're actin' like a moonstruck boy.

Joel moved to the wide opening between the rails and held his hand out to Mrs. Kinsley. She took hold, and he hefted her onto the porch. It didn't take much effort—there wasn't a whole lot to Miz Kinsley in size. But what she lacked in size she made up for in spunk.

As soon as he'd let her go, she set her hands on her hips. "When're you gonna put a step out here so's a person doesn't have to get winded climbin' on up?"

Her words sounded like a challenge, but Joel heard the teasing note beneath the brusque tone. "The boys an' me just give a hop, but I reckon it's not so easy for you ladies with your skirts."

Miss Amsel and the boys approached. The boys leaped onto the porch, agile as young deer, but she looked dubiously at the distance between the hard-packed ground and the porch's planked floor.

Joel cleared his throat. "Here, Miss Amsel, catch hold."

For a moment she stared at his leathery palm, her lower lip tucked between her teeth. She flashed a quick look at Mrs. Kinsley, then gingerly lifted her deep red skirt with one hand and placed her other hand in his. His fingers closed around hers. Her hand fit perfectly in his grasp. He gave a tug, and she stepped onto the porch.

A smile wavered on her lips. He stared, mesmerized. The schoolmarm's face was graced with full, rosy, inviting lips—even more inviting than Susannah's had been, and he hadn't thought any woman could possess a more kissable mouth than Susannah Mohler. Pushing the ridiculous recollection aside, he scrambled for the proper way to greet a guest. "So . . . won'tcha come in?"

Johnny bolted forward and opened the door, and the two women stepped over the threshold. Robert darted in front of Joel to catch his teacher's hand and lead her to the table. Joel latched the door and followed. He might not know how to greet guests, but his nephews held no such compunctions. They took charge. Joel couldn't decide if he was grateful or jealous.

"Miss Amsel, sit here." Johnny pulled out a straight-backed chair from the table. "Miz Jeffers baked us a pie for your visit. Rhubarb an' strawberry. I can get you some." He threw his shoulders back, beaming at his teacher. "Uncle Joel lets me use the carvin' knife if I'm real careful. Want a big piece or a little 'un?"

Joel caught the boy by the shoulders before he could dash to the breakfront cabinet and start cutting into the pie. "Let the ladies sit for a minute or two first, Johnny. We'll break out the pie when the coffee's done perkin'." He'd put on a fresh pot—he hoped Miss Amsel would be happy with coffee. Judging by her ruffly-front blouse and skirt with a bustle that forced her to sit on the front edge of the chair, she probably preferred tea. But he never kept tea in the house. Maybe he should add it to his shopping list for the next time he visited the mercantile.

"Since Mrs. Kinsley and I just finished our supper, pie and coffee a bit later will be perfect."

Miss Amsel glanced at the circle of empty seats around the table, and Joel sensed her desire for someone to join her. Jolting forward, he yanked out a chair. "Miz Kinsley?" He waited until the older woman slid into the seat, then he plunked himself in the chair across from Miss Amsel. The two boys shared the single remaining chair.

Joel cleared his throat. "Well . . . Miss Amsel . . ." He wished he could call her Edythe, but that wouldn't be proper. "You been enjoyin' gettin' to know the folks around here?"

Although her smile remained intact, he thought he detected a slight recoil. Then she laughed lightly. "It has been very . . . enlightening."

Did she stumble over the word or did he only imagine it? And what exactly did she mean by "enlightening"?

"Of course, I've only begun my visits. Yours is the fourth family thus far." She bobbed her chin to indicate her companion. "Although this is Mrs. Kinsley's first."

When Joel had seen both women on the wagon seat, he'd assumed Mrs. Kinsley had been Miss Amsel's guide to all of the local farmsteads. "You didn't go on the others?"

"No need." Miz Kinsley's eyes shone with approval. "Miss Amsel thought—rightly so—it'd be better to have me along for this one, seein' as how you're a single man an' she's a single gal. She don't want any ill conjectures for her, or for you."

If the folks from town had any inkling where his mind had run earlier when he'd focused on the schoolmarm's lips, they'd certainly harbor some ill conjecture toward him. He needed to watch himself.

Miz Kinsley released a throaty chuckle. "She don't know it yet, but I'm fixin' to go with her to the Sterbinzes, too. Wouldn't be a problem if it were only Martha an' her ma, but with no pa in the house *and* Terrill still livin' there . . ." She pulled her eyebrows together in an uncertain scowl. "I'm thinkin' it's best not to encourage Terrill to get a wild notion."

Even though the town gossips had it Miss Amsel was refusing the attention of any single man in town, Terrill Sterbinz possessed a stubborn streak as long as the Platte River. He just might turn a visit concerning Martha into an opportunity to pursue courting. Jealousy struck at the idea of Terrill and Miss Amsel keeping company, and Joel gave himself a mental kick.

"That's sound thinking," he finally responded, relieved when Miss Amsel's posture relaxed. He searched for something else to say and wished the boys would pipe up, but they just sat there smiling at Miss Amsel. "The boys here"—

Johnny and Robert's heads turned in unison to face Joel—"come home full of good reports about what they're doin' in school. They especially liked the lesson on bugs."

"They did?" Miss Amsel seemed surprised. The boys' heads swiveled toward her again. "And you . . . you thought it was a worthwhile activity?"

"Sure did." Joel hid a smirk as Johnny and Robert promptly swung their faces toward him again. They'd get dizzy with this back-and-forth looking if they weren't careful. "We rely on the crops to make our living. The boys here were always catchin' ladybugs, puttin' them in jars. But after you talked about how ladybugs eat plant lice, they've promised to let them be. I'm thinkin' my cornstalks'll be grateful."

Delight bloomed on Miss Amsel's face, causing Joel's heart to thump hard in his chest. Did she have any idea how beautiful she looked when she let herself relax and smile that way?

"Mr. Townsend, I must be honest, I had a rather unpleasant exchange with . . . another parent . . . concerning some of the activities in which the children have engaged at school."

Most women would just blurt out everything, including the name of the other person. But apparently she refrained from gossip. *Attractive, kind to the boys, churchgoing, a controlled tongue . . .*

"I'm relieved that you see value in the study of entomology."

Joel laughed self-consciously and scratched his head. "What's that you said?"

Johnny poked his uncle's arm. "She's talkin' about studyin' bugs . . . I mean, insects. Miss Amsel says it's an important part of zoology. That means animal science." The boy grinned at his teacher. "Right, Miss Amsel?"

Miss Amsel nodded. "That's exactly right, Johnny, and your explanation proves you do a wonderful job of paying attention in class." Her expression turned pensive. "I wish all fathers were as supportive as you are, Mr. Townsend."

"He ain't our father," Robert inserted. "He's our uncle. Our pa an' ma went to Heaven." The boy tipped his head. "Where's your pa an' ma, Miss Amsel?"

Of course the boy couldn't know he was asking a personal question, but from the pained look on Miss Amsel's face, she'd been caught by surprise. Joel tousled Robert's hair. "Don't be nosy, Robert."

"But I just asked—"

Joel frowned.

Robert ducked his head, peering at his teacher through a heavy fringe of bangs—Joel needed to get out the shears again. "Didn't mean to be nosy. Sorry, Miss Amsel."

Joel's heart turned over at the tender look the

schoolmarm gave his talkative nephew. "That's all right, Robert. And it seems we have something in common. My ma is gone, too."

Robert's head shot up, his eyes wide. "To Heaven?"

"That's right."

There was no mistaking the pain in Miss Amsel's voice. As if acting independently of Joel's good sense, his hand shot across the table and loosely cupped hers. "I'm sorry for your loss."

Her gaze met his, her expression both shocked and appreciative. "Why . . . thank you, Mr. Townsend." She sounded as if she'd been running a footrace. Very slowly, she pulled her hand from beneath his. "She's been gone for many years, but I find I still miss her. Just as Johnny and Robert must miss their parents."

A glance at the boys confirmed her statement—the pair wore matching frowns. But then Johnny sat up. "Least you still got your pa. An' me an' Robert got Uncle Joel. So we're lucky, huh?"

"You're very right, Johnny." Even though Miss Amsel's words agreed, her eyes sent a different message. Something bothered her. Badly. Joel wished he could ask why she looked so uncertain, but after accusing Robert of being nosy he couldn't question her.

Miz Kinsley suddenly cleared her throat, startling Joel. He'd been so focused on Miss

Amsel, he'd forgotten the other woman was in the room. "You 'bout ready to serve up that pie an' coffee? Been sittin' here smellin' it so long my belly's convinced I didn't feed it supper."

Joel laughed and pushed to his feet. "Sure, Miz Kinsley. Johnny, you get the pie. I'll fetch some plates an' the coffee." Robert's lower lip poked out. "An', Robert, why don't you put out some of those molasses cookies. Might be Miz Kinsley or your teacher'll want a little somethin' more than pie."

Robert dashed for the cookie crock.

As they sipped coffee from rose-painted teacups borrowed from Miz Jeffers and ate their pie, the talk returned to school and the boys' progress. Miss Amsel's praise made Joel's chest swell with pride in his nephews. But even while he laughed at the boys' antics and held up his end of the conversation, a niggling question rolled in the back of Joel's mind: Why did Miss Amsel look so sad when talking about her father?

Chapter
TEN

Edythe stomped onto Mrs. Kinsley's porch, threw open the door, and then slammed it closed behind her with enough force to make the windows rattle. A startled gasp sounded from the doorway to the kitchen, and Edythe whirled to find Mrs. Kinsley staring at her with wide eyes, a damp cloth pressed to her chest.

"Land sakes, girl, you tryin' to scare me outta my wits?"

Ignoring the rebuke, Edythe tromped to the kitchen table, dumped her armload of books, and then held up her fists. A growl escaped her throat. Her irritation increased when Mrs. Kinsley released a humorous chortle. She spun and charged for the stairway, but Mrs. Kinsley darted forward and caught her by the elbow. She planted her feet and glared at the older woman. Mrs. Kinsley laughed even harder.

"Mrs. Kinsley, I—"

"Oh, forgive me, girl, but if you could've seen your face . . ." Mrs. Kinsley bent forward slightly, bracing one arm on her stomach. "Why, you were stormier than the thunderclouds rollin' in the east. I wouldn't think a pretty gal like you could look so fearsome."

Edythe grunted in irritation. "I suppose I should be relieved *someone* is able to laugh. I certainly hope my meeting with Mr. and Mrs. Jeffers this evening is a pleasant one, or I may pack my bags and return to Omaha."

All jollity fled at her comment. Mrs. Kinsley guided her to the kitchen table and pulled out a chair. "I'm not usually one to eat dessert before eatin' dinner, but I'm thinkin' you could use a little something sweet. I just took a peach cobbler from the oven. Let me dish us out some an' you can tell me what has you so all-fired up."

Edythe sat tight-lipped until Luthenia plunked a bowl of cobbler and a spoon in front of her. But the moment she jabbed the spoon through the crust into the moist peaches, her tongue loosed. "That boy will be the death of me yet!"

Mrs. Kinsley sank into her chair. "William Sholes again?"

"None other." Edythe chewed vigorously, cinnamon exploding on her tongue. "I cannot understand why he takes such joy in creating conflict!" She waved her spoon in the air. "On Monday, he put a tack on Jane Heidrich's chair and a dead gopher in Robert Townsend's lunch pail. On Tuesday, he tied a rope around the outhouse while Patience Jeffers was inside. I had to saw through the rope with a pocketknife—it took me nearly half an hour—because poor little Patience completely panicked and pushed on the door so many times she tightened the knot beyond loosening.

"Wednesday, he not only dipped Mable Saltzmann's braid in the inkwell *again,* he took all the identification cards I'd created for the skeleton diagram, wrote his own words on the backs, and reapplied them to the skeleton." Heat flooded her face. "I found some of his choices quite repulsive."

She paused long enough to take another bite of the cobbler before continuing. "And today he stuffed Lewis Scheebeck's arithmetic assignment in the woodstove's chimney. When Lewis cried, William called him a baby and tripped him when he tried to come tell me. Then he poured ink on Louisa Bride's bench. If Sophie hadn't spotted it, Louisa's dress would certainly have been ruined." Edythe shook her head, her shoulders drooping. "I've tried disciplining him—making him stay in from recess, stand in the corner, or write sentences—but as soon as his punishment is over, he's misbehaving again."

Mrs. Kinsley spoke around a bite of cobbler. "Sounds like you need to have a talk with his pa."

Edythe blew out a noisy breath. "It won't help. His father told me quite emphatically that it is *my* duty to make William behave when he's at school. Mr. Sholes won't involve himself in any discipline problems. And William knows it, so he thinks he can do as he pleases." She poked at the remaining cobbler in her bowl. Defeat sagged her spine. "I want to teach, Mrs. Kinsley. It's so important to me that the children *learn*. But William's misbehavior interferes with everyone's attentiveness. The children all watch him, waiting to see what he's going to do next."

"Miss Amsel . . ." Mrs. Kinsley sighed. "Y'know, I'm gettin' a mite tired of always bein' so formal. Can we stop the mizzin' and missin' an' just go right to our given names? Feels a lot friendlier, to my way of thinkin'."

Edythe looked at Mrs. Kinsley in surprise. "I think that's fine." A shy smile pulled at her lips. "It will be nice to feel as though we're friends rather than merely landlady and boarder."

Mrs. Kinsley gave the tabletop a light smack. "I agree. So from now on, I'm gonna call you Edythe, and you call me Luthenia."

"What a lovely name . . . so unusual."

Luthenia puffed with pride. "Ain't it? I was named for my grandmother on my pa's side. She raised my pa, him bein' orphaned when he was knee high to a cricket. Always made me feel special, carryin' her name since she was such a dear woman." She spooned another bite of cobbler. "Is Edythe a family name?"

Edythe flicked bits of crust with her fingertip. "My pa's name is Ed, so maybe that's why Ma chose it. But Pa used to say it was too highfalutin' for the daughter of a dirt-grubbing farmer. He called me Edie instead."

"I think Edie's a real sweet name."

Edythe pursed her lips. "Not to me. The shortened version of my name—the way he said it—felt like an insult. I prefer Edythe."

"Then Edythe it is." Luthenia scooped up the bowls and spoons and dumped them on the dry sink. "But gettin' back to William Sholes . . ."

Edythe groaned. "Must we?"

Luthenia propped one fist on her hip. "Yes, ma'am, we must." She waved her hand in the direction of the backyard. "I'm still thinkin' your best bet with that young'un is to march yourself out there, cut a good-sized twig from the cottonwood, an' have it handy for the next time he misbehaves. He's gonna keep a-pesterin' until he has reason to stop it. So give him a reason right across the seat of his overalls."

Sinking back into her chair, Luthenia took Edythe's hand. "Listen, Edythe, I know you're not wantin' to be like old man Shanks an' have the young'uns livin' under a cloud of fear, but there's times you gotta be firm with young'uns. Don't you see William has taken charge of your classroom? *Your* classroom! You gotta get back in control, or the lesson the kids'll be learnin' isn't one you want to teach."

Edythe hung her head. "I know you're right. But I made a promise to the entire class." She raised her head, helplessness making her eyes sting. "When I broke that switch in half and threw it out the window, I instantly became a champion to seventeen children. Only one child has chosen to take advantage of the switch's absence. But if I bring in a switch and use it on William, then I'll feel as though I'm breaking my promise to all of the children. How can I expect them to trust anything I say if I go back on my word?"

Luthenia snorted. "I think most of them young'uns would cheer if they saw William gettin' his just dues."

"They might at that, but the elation would last only as long as the realization that they could be next. I won't plant that worry in their hearts."

Luthenia sighed. "As I've said before, you're the schoolmarm, so you gotta decide what's best. But if you refuse to use a switch, you better be thinkin' of some other punishment that will work."

A clap of thunder sounded, rattling the windows. Luthenia sprang to her feet. "I knew a storm was brewin', but I didn't expect it to sweep in so quick!" She slammed the kitchen window shut, then peered outside. "Why, look how gray it's gotten . . . and still an hour 'til sunset."

Edythe looked out the window, her pulse accelerating at the sight of the wind whipping the tree branches. Dry leaves danced wildly across the ground.

"You're goin' to the Jefferses' tonight?" Luthenia said. "It's only a short walk down the street, but the way that wind's a-blowin', it might just pick you up an' plant you in the next county. I'm thinkin' you'd be wise to stay put tonight."

Edythe put her fingertips against the window, willing the wind to calm. "But Patience and Sophie will be so disappointed. Sophie told me today she'd helped her mother prepare a pumpkin cake." Lightning flashed, followed by a resounding boom. Fat raindrops splatted the windowpanes.

"Is pumpkin cake worth gettin' soaked to the bone?"

"It is if it was baked by a twelve-year-old girl who's waited three weeks for her teacher to come to her house."

Chuckling, Luthenia shook her head. "You are the most dedicated teacher I ever did see. Well, if you're of a mind to go out in this, then—"

Pounding interrupted, competing with another roll of thunder. Luthenia scowled. "Sounds like somebody else is silly enough to brave the storm." She bustled to the front door and threw it wide. Mr. Jeffers stood on the porch with his hat in his hands, dripping wet. Luthenia stepped back and gestured to him. "August! Come on in here."

The man shook his head, sending a little shower of raindrops across the porch. "No'm. I'll get your floor all wet." Cold wind gusted through the open doorway, carrying the scent of rain. "Won't stay but a minute." He looked past Luthenia to Edythe, who'd followed and stood behind Luthenia's shoulder. "Teacher, the missus sent me to tell you not to come tonight. She worried you'd catch a chill." He let out a mighty sneeze, then shrugged. "Figure she's right to worry—sure is some rain!"

Edythe nodded. "Thank you for saving me the trip, Mr. Jeffers. Please send the girls my regrets. Perhaps, if the storm clears, I can come by tomorrow afternoon—say around three?"

"We'd be pleased to have you. Tomorrow, then, assumin' the sun remembers how to shine." He plopped his soggy hat into place, yanked his jacket collar tight around his neck, and strode from the porch. In moments, the gray sheet of rain swallowed his shadowy form.

Luthenia closed the door and released a sigh. "Can't say I'm not pleased to keep you in tonight. When it's stormin' like this, best place to be is snug inside a house." She headed for the kitchen. Edythe trailed on her heels. "I'll get that chicken to stewin' now. We'll have us a nice supper. You gonna take your books up to your room an' work on next week's lessons?"

Edythe nibbled her lower lip. "Would you mind if I sat here in the kitchen and worked? I appreciate having the table in my room, but it's rather lonely up there by myself."

Luthenia beamed. "I don't mind at all! Nice to have company." She waved her hands. "Sit. I'll be real quiet, so I don't disturb you."

Edythe grinned and scooted up to the table. She opened the closest book and bent her head over the pages. Luthenia turned toward the stove, but as she began to ladle water into the waiting stew pot, something else banged on the front door—

deep thumps, not sharp raps like a fist would create. "What'n thunder . . . who else'd be callin' in this storm?" *Thump, thump, thump!* Luthenia frowned. "They're tryin' to break the door down!" She bustled through the parlor.

Edythe, curious and concerned, rose and followed Luthenia. The woman flung the door wide. August Jeffers stood on the front porch again. His arms were filled with the limp, bedraggled form of a young girl.

Edythe gasped. She pushed past Luthenia to grab August's coat sleeves and drag him over the threshold. She cupped the pale, rain-streaked face of the girl and cried out, "Missy!"

Chapter
ELEVEN

"Uncle Joel, make it stop!"

Joel set aside the *Farmers' Almanac* he'd been reading and opened his arms. Robert dashed across the floor, his nightshirt flapping, and burrowed against Joel's chest. Although fearless to the point of foolhardiness at times, the one thing Robert couldn't abide was a thunderstorm. The wind, rain, and claps of thunder sent the boy into spasms of fear. Joel suspected Robert's reaction related to the night the boys lost their ma and pa—the local sheriff had indicated the boys spent a stormy night alone after their folks' horses got spooked by lightning and overturned the wagon.

Joel understood why Robert shook in terror. But understanding the fear didn't tell him how to heal it. He rubbed his hand up and down Robert's quivering back, his heart twisting in sympathy. "Shh, boy. Remember? It's just noise—that's all. The clouds are bumpin' into each other. The boom can't hurt you."

Robert wriggled his face into the curve of Joel's neck. His fingers clung to Joel's shirt. "But I don't like it. I want it to stop."

Johnny stepped into the doorway of the boys' room, rubbing his eyes. He cringed when thunder crashed overhead. "Is Robert okay?"

Even though only thirteen months separated the boys, at times Johnny seemed years older than Robert, the way he looked after his brother. Joel said, "He'll be all right. Thunder's got him spooked."

Johnny nodded wisely. He pattered across the floor and touched Robert's back. "Wanna sleep in my bed, Robert? I'll read to you from *Aesop's Fables*, if Uncle Joel'll let me light the lamp."

Joel gave Robert a gentle shake. "You hear that, Robert? Johnny'll read to you—would'ja like that?"

Slowly, Robert lifted his face and looked at his brother. He held his lower lip between his teeth.

Tears stained his pudgy cheeks. Joel'd never seen such a look of uncertainty. *Crash! Boom!* Robert curled into a ball and huddled in Joel's lap, clinging hard.

Joel patted Robert's back again. "Johnny, go get the storybook and bring it out here. I'll read to both of you."

Johnny scampered to obey. Joel rocked his nephew while a silent prayer rose from his heart. *Lord, let this storm blow out fast. An' help me find a way to ease this boy's fear of storms. Gonna be lots of them in his life—best he learns to see 'em through instead of hidin' from them.*

"I'll go fetch Dr. Seilstad." Mr. Jeffers deposited Missy on the parlor settee. "Looks like she's gonna need him." He dashed back out into the storm.

Edythe sank to her knees beside the settee and stroked Missy's pale cheeks. Tears rained down her own face. The girl's disheveled appearance suggested she must have walked the hundred miles between Omaha and Walnut Hill. Agony born of guilt twisted Edythe's heart. How many days had Missy been on the road, all alone, trying to reach her sister? Had she eaten during her days of travel? What if Mr. Jeffers hadn't found her? A sob wracked Edythe's body and she pressed her fist to her mouth. If her sister died, it would be all her fault.

Warm hands curled around her shoulders and tugged her aside. "Let's get this girl out of those wet clothes. I got a nightgown here." Luthenia held up a voluminous flannel gown. "It'll swallow her, but it's a heap better'n that soggy dress she's wearin'. Figure the doc would want us to get her dry an' warm."

Edythe assisted her landlady in stripping Missy of her rain-soaked dress and underthings. Using a rough length of toweling, she rubbed her sister's cold limbs before holding her upright so Luthenia could tug the gown over her head. As a baby, Missy had always fought Edythe's hands when she changed her diaper or buttoned her into a tiny frock. To see her lying so still and unresponsive, unaware of their ministrations, brought a fresh rush of tears to Edythe's eyes. It seemed all the life had drained from the girl.

"I'll get these to soakin' in the washtub." Luthenia carted the wet clothes away.

Edythe tucked a quilt around Missy's frame and then sat on the edge of the settee and smoothed her sister's tangled hair away from her face. Rain continued to lash the house, driven by furious gusts of wind. Flashes of lightning lit the room, followed by rolls of thunder. Edythe shivered, imagining Missy slogging through the storm, determined to reach shelter.

Luthenia returned with a cup of something hot and steamy held between her palms.

"Chamomile tea with honey. See if you can get her to swallow some of this. It'll warm her innards."

Edythe propped Missy against a pile of pillows and poured a scant spoonful of tea between her slack lips. The first spoonful dribbled down Missy's chin, but mercifully her lips closed and her throat convulsed with the second spoonful. Heartened by the small success, Edythe tipped another spoonful into Missy's mouth. At the third swallow, her eyelids fluttered and she grimaced.

Edythe jerked backward, protecting the cup of tea, as Missy's hands flew outward. Her eyes opened and she looked around in confusion. Then her gaze settled on Edythe. "I found you." Her voice sounded croaky and raw.

Edythe passed the cup to Luthenia and gathered Missy in her arms. "You found me." She pressed her cheek to Missy's damp, tangled locks. For long seconds, she rocked her the same way she had when Missy was a colicky baby, relief making her bones feel like rubber.

Missy planted her hands against Edythe's shoulders and pushed. Although it was a weak gesture absent of any real force, Edythe instinctively released her sister. Missy collapsed against the pillows and glared at Edythe. "Why'd you leave me in Omaha?" Resentment laced Missy's tone.

Edythe gulped. "I—" Before she could finish, the sound of feet stomping onto the porch intruded.

"Must be the doc." Luthenia threw open the door and waved the young doctor into the house. She pointed to the sofa. "Your patient's right there—just now woke an' started talkin'."

Edythe scuttled aside and watched Dr. Seilstad take her place on the edge of the settee. He felt Missy's forehead, peeked down her throat, poked her chin and neck, and listened through a tube placed against her chest. Missy sat quiet and stiff throughout his inspection.

The doctor gave a brusque nod. "Lungs sound clear . . . that's good. But she's got a high fever." Snapping open the black leather satchel that rested beside his feet, he rustled around inside the bag and withdrew a brown glass bottle. He handed it to Luthenia. "One tablespoon twice a day. Keep her warm and make sure she drinks— tea is good. Could add a touch of whiskey, if you've got it in the house."

Luthenia frowned. "I do not."

Dr. Seilstad shrugged. "Then put lots of honey in the tea. Make her stay down for the next few days 'til she regains her strength." He clicked the latch on his bag and rose, his attention still aimed at Luthenia. "I'll come back Monday morning and check on her."

Edythe stepped forward. "Thank you, Doctor. I

appreciate your coming out in the storm to see to my sister's needs."

The doctor nodded. "If she gets worse over the weekend, have someone fetch me." He tugged his collar up around his jaw, lifted his bag, and headed for the door. The moment the door closed behind him, Missy tossed aside the quilt and swung her feet to the floor. She rose, but then she swayed and tilted forward. Edythe caught her and lowered her back onto the settee.

Luthenia hovered near, her face twisted into a scowl of concern. "What're you doin', young lady? Didn't you hear the doc say you were to stay down?"

"I heard." Missy's voice, although weak and raspy, carried a strong thread of defiance. She aimed an accusing glare at Edythe. "Took me a full week to get here. Come near to walkin' the soles off my shoes. I want to know—why didn't you take me with you when you left?" Her voice broke and she coughed, her face contorting.

Edythe sat beside Missy and curled her arm around her sister's waist. Through the thick folds of flannel, she could feel Missy's ribs. Remorse stabbed. When the coughing spell passed, she gave Missy a gentle hug. "I didn't want to leave you. But I didn't think I'd be able to take care of you *and* do my job as schoolmarm. I thought you'd be better off with Justus and Eulah."

Missy pushed Edythe's arm away. "So you'd

rather teach a bunch of kids you don't even know than be with me?"

Luthenia stepped forward. "Seems to me we'd be wise to follow the doc's instructions an' let Missy rest." She tipped her head, her forehead crinkling. "Sounds like the storm's finally blowin' itself out, so you oughtta be able to sleep easy." She held up the half-empty cup. "I'll fetch a fresh cup for you to sip, Missy, an' then you'd best get some sleep."

Edythe gently eased Missy against the pillows and tucked the quilt around her again. "Luthenia is right. We'll have lots of time to talk over the weekend. For now, you should rest."

To Edythe's relief, Missy didn't argue. She nestled against the pillows, and her eyes slipped closed. Luthenia caught Edythe's elbow and drew her into the kitchen. She bustled to the stove and began filling the little silver strainer with crumpled leaves to brew a fresh cup of tea.

"Well, if this ain't the surprise to beat all surprises, havin' your sister just show up. An' in the middle of a storm to boot!" The older woman shook her head.

Edythe couldn't determine by Luthenia's tone if she was upset to have an unexpected overnight guest or merely concerned. She clasped her hands together and stared at her entwined fingers. "I never considered that she might walk from Omaha to Walnut Hill. Missy possesses the impetuosity of the young, but she's never been so recklessly bold."

One eyebrow raised high, Luthenia twisted her lips into a thoughtful frown. "She went to a heap of trouble to avoid bein' with her pa. Is there a sound reason for that?"

Edythe wasn't certain how to answer. She couldn't honestly say her father was abusive. He'd never raised a hand to any of his children—he was too lazy even for that. But his perpetual melancholy, his whining insistence that the world was out to get him, wore away any semblance of happiness or hope. Pa didn't inflict bruises; he destroyed his children's spirits.

"I . . . I suppose there were reasons." Swallowing the lump of sadness that filled her throat, Edythe sank into a kitchen chair. "I should have waited until Missy was grown before I left."

Luthenia turned from the stove and gave Edythe's shoulder a pat. "No sense in findin' fault—not with yourself nor anybody else. It's done—she's here. We'll just have to make the most of it, I reckon."

Edythe jerked her face upward to meet her landlady's gaze. "You mean . . . you don't mind that she's here?"

Luthenia bounced the slotted, silver-plated ball in the steaming water a few more times and then set it aside. "When I opened my house to you I wasn't plannin' on someone else joinin' us, but how much trouble can one young'un be?" Picking up the teacup, she smiled brightly. "I raised boys, y'know. Might be fun havin' a girl livenin' things up around here."

"And you might be biting off more than you can chew." Edythe cringed. "My sister can be . . . unpredictable."

Luthenia grinned. "Might've only raised boys, but I've been around the young ladies of Walnut Hill enough to know that girls her age are giggly. Sometimes moody."

Edythe released a tired chuckle. Perhaps Luthenia did know what she was getting herself into.

"Even so, she's welcome to stay." Luthenia held the cup high. "Best get this to Missy before it cools an' she drifts full off to sleep. From the looks of her, she needs a little somethin' in her belly—the girl's vine thin." She gave Edythe's cheek a quick caress. "Don't worry, now. Go get into your nightclothes. I'll sit with your sister 'til you come back down."

Chapter
TWELVE

Just as he did every Sunday, Reverend Coker asked for prayer concerns before he closed the service. Joel glanced at Robert, who sat quietly beside him. He was tempted to raise his hand and request help in defeating the fears that took hold of his nephew every time the sky turned dark and let loose a storm. He didn't want to embarrass the boy, but he felt helpless against the unhealthy terror that gripped Robert during stormy hours.

While he was still considering making the request, the reverend's gaze settled on someone behind Joel. A bench creaked, indicating one of the worshipers had risen, and then a familiar voice reached Joel's ears.

"I'd like to ask for prayers for the schoolmarm's sister."

Joel twisted sideways and looked at Luthenia Kinsley. The older woman's face wore an anxious grimace. He'd been disappointed when Miss Amsel hadn't shown up for Sunday service. Now his disappointment changed to worry.

"The girl—her name's Missy—turned up the other night durin' the thunderstorm. August Jeffers found her lyin' in the street, mumblin' Miss Amsel's name."

A murmur went around the congregation. Apparently, like Joel, most were hearing this news for the first time. Of course, the storm was only a day ago, but even so, news usually spread quickly in town.

"She's fightin' a mighty high fever, and Miss Amsel's doin' a lot of frettin' over Missy. Prayers for the girl's recovery an' for the schoolmarm's peace would be welcome."

"Will the school need to be shut down for a day or two?" Hank Libolt called out. Judging by his gruff tone, he wasn't keen on the idea. But youngsters fidgeted, nudging each other with hopeful grins on their faces.

Miz Kinsley shook her head. "Miss Amsel's too devoted to her pupils to close school. She'll be at the schoolhouse tomorrow, same as always. I'll be carin' for Missy while school's in session." A couple of boys groaned, but they were quickly hushed by stern glances from their parents. Miz Kinsley sat down amidst another round of murmurs.

A few others voiced their requests, but Joel chose to keep his worry for his nephew to himself for the time being. He and Robert would work through the fear together. The minister closed in prayer, and people filed out. Several women surrounded Miz Kinsley, questions flying. The womenfolk no doubt hoped to extract all the details of the surprise visit from Miss

Amsel's sister. Curiosity filled Joel, too. He knew so little about the schoolmarm—hadn't even known she had a sister. But beyond his curiosity, he felt concern. Miz Kinsley had said the schoolmarm was fretting.

"You boys go on out an' play for a little while." Joel gave the boys' shoulders a gentle push. "But stay out of mud puddles. Keep your good clothes clean."

"Yes, sir!" The boys snatched up their jackets and raced out the door.

Joel dallied in the aisle until the womenfolk cleared away. Then he caught up to Miz Kinsley. "Will Miss Amsel's sister be all right?"

The older woman chuckled, shaking her head. "You mean you don't want to know how old the girl is, where she come from, or how long she's stayin'?" She aimed a wry grin at the retreating backs of the women who'd just scurried away.

Joel decided to be honest. "I reckon I do. But I'm more worried about how she's doin'. You said fever from bein' in the rain. Isn't pneumonia, is it?" Pneumonia could be deadly— he'd never forget the sound of his mother's final labored breaths.

Miz Kinsley shook her head. "Doc said her lungs were clear. It's just a fever an' all-over body achin'. An' she's all worn down from lack of eatin'. She's none too pert, I can tell you that. Poor Miss Amsel's not gettin' any rest 'cause she's sittin' up day an' night, tendin' to her sister."

Joel's heart lurched in sympathy. He hoped she wouldn't fall sick herself from worrying.

"Glad she's headin' to school tomorrow. It'll do her good to get into the classroom an' leave her sister's care to me." Miz Kinsley heaved a huge sigh. "Don't mind tellin' you, Joel, I'm a mite troubled over Edythe. She near wore herself to a frazzle with all the home visits, an' now this."

Edythe . . . The schoolmarm's given name reverberated through Joel's chest. "Anything I can do? You need stove wood chopped or errands run? Now that things're slowin' down on the farm, I can come in an' help with chores—whatever needs doin'."

Miz Kinsley's expression softened. "I appreciate that, truly I do. 'Specially comin' from you, who has more'n enough to handle what with keepin' up with those nephews of yours. For now we're doin' all right. Gonna depend on how long Missy is down to bed. Don't feel as if I can leave her alone while she's ailin', not even for a run to the mercantile." She tapped her lips with a spindly finger. "Could'ja maybe stop by the house on Tuesday? If the girl's still down, I might have need of a few provisions."

Eagerness rushed through Joel. "Be glad to, Miz Kinsley. Until then, you take care of yourself. Don't want to see you gettin' run down, too."

"Oh, bosh." She waved her hand at him. "Ol' hen like me just keeps on a-peckin'."

On Monday morning, when he sent the boys out the door with their lunch pails in hand, he admonished, "Be on your best behavior today for Miss Amsel, you hear? She's got a lot on her mind with her sister ailin'—don't give her reason to fret."

With wide innocent eyes, both boys vowed to be extra good. When they returned from school with tales of William Sholes's misconduct, Joel was tempted to ride over to the Sholes farm and haul William to the woodshed himself—Miss Amsel shouldn't have to put up with the boy's deliberate naughtiness. His protectiveness puzzled him. He'd never worried about how old man Shanks was managing in the classroom. But old man Shanks didn't have rosy lips, soft brown eyes flecked with green, and a heart as big and open as the Nebraska plains.

On Tuesday, Joel gave the boys a ride to the schoolhouse, hoping he might get a chance to say a kind word or two to Miss Amsel, but she was busy inside with something and he had to ride on to town without seeing her. He went straight to Miz Kinsley's place, his heart thumping with anticipation that she'd have a list of chores so long it'd keep him in town for several hours.

Maybe he'd get to see Miss Amsel after school was over for the day.

He clumped up onto Miz Kinsley's porch, his palms sweating in spite of the cool mid-October morning. If Miz Kinsley told him he wasn't needed, he just might dissolve from disappointment. He gave the door a few good whacks with his knuckles, then held his breath while he waited for her to answer. Only a few seconds passed before the door swung open and Miz Kinsley gestured him inside.

A cinnamony, yeasty smell greeted his nose, and his nostrils twitched in pleasure. Miz Kinsley grinned. "You had your breakfast yet, Joel? Baked up some raisin bread this mornin'—thought it might entice Missy here to eat."

Joel's gaze flitted sideways to find a young girl stretched out beneath a pile of quilts on Miz Kinsley's parlor settee. The girl reminded him of Miss Amsel with her tawny eyes and straight brown hair pulled back into a simple tail. But where Miss Amsel's face always held a soft smile, this girl looked sullen and dull.

"Missy," Miz Kinsley said, "this here is Mr. Townsend. He's got two boys in your sister's school. Fine boys—bright as new pennies an' well-mannered to boot."

Joel gave Missy a hesitant smile and nod in greeting.

Missy tugged the top quilt a little higher and stared at him with unblinking, somber eyes.

Miz Kinsley tugged on Joel's elbow. "Come on into the kitchen, Joel, an' I'll whack you off a thick slice o' that bread."

Joel eagerly accepted the hunk of still-warm bread dotted with plump raisins and striped with cinnamon. He took a huge bite. The flavor burst on his tongue, and he released a groan of enjoyment. "Miz Kinsley, this is the best bread I ever tasted."

"Well, then, I'll have to send home the extra loaf for you an' the boys. Heaven knows we won't finish it here." She sighed, and her voice dropped to a raspy whisper. "I can hardly get that sister o' Edythe's to eat more'n two bites of anything. An' with Missy not eatin', Edythe won't hardly eat, either." She sounded more disheartened than disgusted.

Joel glanced toward the parlor. He lowered his voice to match Miz Kinsley's. "She givin' you trouble?"

"It's probably just the sickness—Doc says she's still runnin' fever, an' you know nothin' tastes good when you're feelin' puny." Miz Kinsley clicked her tongue, her expression sad. "But how's she gonna get her strength back if she don't eat? She's got Edythe an' me terrible worried." Then she threw her arms outward and let out a little huff. "But you didn't come to listen to me spill my woes. You still willin' to do some errands for me?"

Joel shoved the last of the bread into his mouth and swished his hands on his trouser legs. "Sure am." He hoped the list was long—more than ever, he wanted to stick around long enough to offer a few words of encouragement to Miss Amsel when she returned from teaching. After watching his own mother pine away, day by day, he understood how her sister's illness would trouble her. He offered a quick, silent prayer for the girl's recovery and Miss Amsel's peace while Miz Kinsley wrote out a list of items she needed from the mercantile.

She handed him the yellow slip of paper. "Could do with that ol' osage orange tree the Sterbinz boys hauled in for me chopped up for my stove, as well, if you've got the time an' are of a mind to."

Joel pocketed the list and grinned. "I can spend the day if you'd like. Whatever needs doin', let's get it done."

Miz Kinsley's eyes twinkled with mischief. "You're a good man, Joel Townsend. Don't see how she'd do any better."

Joel's face flooded with enough heat to bake another loaf of bread. Her words confirmed she understood his secret motivation for wanting to stay until school let out. Before he could stammer out a defense, Miz Kinsley continued.

"Mercantile first, though—Wally'll let you sign your name in place o' mine, since he knows we got an ailin' girl over here. I'll see what'n all I can find around here to keep you occupied." The teasing grin returned to her face, making her seem years younger. "An' I'm hopin' Miss Amsel's appreciation for your willingness to help might send her thinkin' in the same direction I am."

Joel dashed out the door before he could say anything that might embarrass him. Bad enough to have Miz Kinsley speculating he was stuck on the new schoolmarm—it would plumb mortify him to prove her right.

As Miz Kinsley had indicated, Wally allowed Joel to sign off in the credit book, even though the supplies weren't for him. Wally also plied Joel with questions about Miss Amsel's sister, but Joel could only say what he knew—that the girl was stove up in bed and looked mighty puny. Wally seemed disappointed by the simple report, but Joel didn't have time to worry about that. He had work to do at Miz Kinsley's.

When he returned to Miz Kinsley's, he drew the wagon around to the back rather than open the front door and bring cold air in on Missy. The older woman dove on the crates like a bear on a honey-filled beehive. While she bustled around, putting away her stores, Joel buttoned his jacket to the neck, fetched Miz Kinsley's axe from the shed at the back edge of the property, and set to work hacking the osage orange into usable chunks.

Just as the bell in the church steeple clanged the noon hour, Joel divided the final hunk of wood into arm-sized wedges perfect for stacking in the stove's belly. He stood upright, swiped his arm across his sweaty brow, and released a sigh of satisfaction. Now that the wood was cut, he'd get it stacked nice and neat right outside Miz Kinsley's back door so the ladies wouldn't have to wander out in the snow to retrieve fuel once winter hit.

As he stooped over and lifted two chunks, the back door opened and Miz Kinsley stuck her head out. "Joel? Can I talk you into runnin' a quick errand for me?"

Joel tossed the pieces of wood aside and trotted to the dirt patch that served as a back stoop. "What's that?"

Miz Kinsley held up a tin pail. "Edythe left so quick this mornin' she forgot her lunch pail. She might not feel like eatin', considerin' her worry for her sister, but I don't want her to get the idea I approve of her skippin' meals."

Joel's heart doubled its tempo at the thought of Miss Amsel seeing him dirty and sweat-stained from his morning's labor. Or maybe it quickened at the thought of seeing Miss Amsel. "Miz Kinsley, I'd like to oblige you, but I'm in a sorry state." He sniffed his armpit and made a face. "I'd scare away a skunk right now, the way I smell."

To his consternation, the woman laughed. "Joel Townsend, there's nothin' displeasin' about a man's sweat, 'specially when it's the result of hard work. The schoolmarm ain't the kind to turn up her nose. Besides, you can take a minute or two an' clean up quick in my washbowl."

Joel cast a dubious look at the round washbowl. It'd surely take a tubful of water to get him clean again.

Miz Kinsley shrugged. "But I reckon if you're too shy, she'll just have to—"

Joel's hand reached out and grabbed the pail's handle. "I'll take it to her."

The same mischievous grin that had lighted Miz Kinsley's eyes earlier that morning returned. She scurried out of his way when he charged toward the washstand. As clean as he could get under the circumstances, Joel turned to retrieve his jacket.

As he headed out the door, Miz Kinsley called, "I put two ham 'n' cheese sandwiches an' half a dozen cookies in that pail—plenty for two, if you're of a mind to sit down an' eat with her. Who knows—havin' your company might convince the schoolmarm to eat a proper lunch."

Chapter
THIRTEEN

Edythe's stomach growled. She shifted on the porch of the schoolhouse, pressing her hand against her tummy to still the sound. In her rush to arrive early and get the stove started so the schoolroom would be warm for the students, she'd forgotten her lunch pail. For the first time since August Jeffers had deposited Missy on the parlor settee, Edythe experienced hunger pangs. And she had no way to appease them.

Although the October breeze had turned cold, the children still seemed to enjoy eating outside. The ground was soggy from last Friday's storm, but the children located the driest patches and sat in little groups under the bright sunshine, coats on and shoulder to shoulder. Their happy voices carried to Edythe's ears, and a smile tugged at her lips. How she loved listening to their giggles.

William Sholes sat off by himself today. Had he chosen to separate himself, or had the others refused to allow him to join their groups? The boy continued to create disturbances in the classroom, and none of her disciplinary tactics seemed to affect him. If she instructed him to stand in the corner, he whistled the entire time; if she assigned an additional page of arithmetic problems, he finished them in record time and smiled as he handed them in, seeming to view their completion as triumph. Nothing deterred William, and each day Edythe's frustration grew as she battled for victory with the boy.

The rattle of a wagon interrupted her thoughts, and Edythe heard Johnny Townsend call out, "Hey, Uncle Joel!"

Her heart gave a startled leap. Why would Joel Townsend visit the school in the middle of the day? She rose as he drew the wagon to a halt. He hopped down and greeted his boys before ambling across the yard to the porch and offering her a lopsided grin. "Afternoon, Miss Amsel. Miz Kinsley sent me out."

Fear exploded in Edythe's middle, sending a sharp taste to the back of her tongue. She pressed her hand to her chest. "Is . . . is everything all right? Missy?"

A look of sympathy creased the man's sunbrowned face. "Your sister was restin' easy when I was at the house." He hefted the little bucket she used to carry her lunch and swung it gently to and fro. "Miz Kinsley said you left your lunch behind. She asked me to tote it to you."

Relief turned Edythe's bones to jelly. She sank back onto the porch step.

Mr. Townsend went down on one knee in front of her, worry evident in his furrowed brow. He plunked the little pail next to her and leaned close. "You all right? Miz Kinsley said you haven't been eating much. Not eating will make a body weak. Here . . ." He tugged aside the cloth napkin that covered the pail and pulled out a square, paper-wrapped packet. "Ham 'n' cheese. Get that in your tummy, and quick as a wink, you'll feel stronger."

His kind tone coupled with the gentle teasing in his blue eyes made Edythe feel as if he viewed her as a child to be cajoled. Yet, oddly, she experienced no resentment. Without thinking, she asked a wistful query. "You promise?"

Her brief question seemed to surprise him as much as it surprised her—the comment could be construed as flirtation, and Edythe never resorted to flirtation. After a moment's pause, he released a short laugh. "Yep, I promise."

He slipped from his spot on the ground to sit on the lowest stair riser. Resting his back against the railing, he bobbed the sandwich on his broad palm. "So . . . you gonna eat or not?"

The twinkle in his blue eyes reminded her of the ornery glint Robert sometimes displayed. Her lips twitched, fighting off a smile. She'd have to be careful around Joel Townsend. The man was appealing. But as she'd emphatically told Luthenia, she was here to teach, not chase—or be chased by—a man. Especially not this encumbered man.

"I shall eat." She quickly plucked the sandwich from his hand and began peeling back the paper.

His fingers inched toward the pail, which sat midway between the two of them. "Miz Kinsley put an extra one in there—for me, she said. Mind if I eat it? I worked up a powerful hunger choppin' wood all morning. That's why I look like I've been wrestling a pile of tumbleweeds."

Edythe bit into the sandwich to keep from laughing. He did have the appearance of one who'd been rolling in dirt and branches. Little pieces of dried leaves stuck in his thick wavy hair, and his clothes were sweat-splotched and dusty. But his friendly grin and open demeanor chased away any offense. Even covered in dirt and bits of leaves, he was attractive.

Edythe flipped her hand toward the pail to give him permission to help himself. He bowed his head before lifting the sandwich to his lips, and Edythe's face went hot. Luthenia always prayed before meals. By now, the habit should have become ingrained, yet she'd neglected to give thanks for her sandwich. Would he think ill of her, since she'd forgotten to pray?

To cover her discomfiture, she stammered out a question. "Y-you chopped wood for Luthenia this morning? I thought the Sterbinz boys were going to do that for her."

Mr. Townsend shrugged, his jaw muscles contracting as he chewed. "Dunno. She asked me to do it. It's all done, too—just need to stack the pieces before I head for home."

He'd chopped the entire tree in one morning? Edythe recalled her father needing a full week to chop enough firewood to carry them for two wintry days. Consequently, their home was always cold. "Small wonder you look worn out." She couldn't hide the admiration in her voice. "That's quite a task, turning an entire tree into firewood."

He took another bite. "It wasn't real big, as trees go, an' the wood had been dead for a while, which makes for easier splitting. Get a good rhythm goin' with a sharp axe, and it's not so much work."

Edythe opened her mouth to disagree, but a movement on the playground captured her attention. William Sholes, his body bent into an apostrophe, crept up behind the group of girls. He held a stick. Just before he poked the back of Jane Heidrich's head, Edythe leaped to her feet, tipping over the lunch pail.

"William Sholes!"

The boy jolted upright.

"Take the stick to the woodpile and leave the girls alone."

"I didn't do nothin'."

His quarrelsome tone stirred Edythe's ire. She started to snap, "Only because I caught you before you could act," but Mr. Townsend sat looking at her. She'd already forgotten to bless her food before eating; she wouldn't allow him to witness impatience with a student.

Forcing her irritation aside, she formed a calm reply. "Lunch recess will be over soon. Put the stick in the pile, as I instructed, and use the remainder of the break constructively." She waited until William began sauntering toward the kindling pile at the far corner of the school-house before sitting back down. Only then did she notice broken cookies scattered across the steps.

"Oh, my . . ." She gathered the cookie pieces and dropped them in the pail. "Such a waste." Her words carried a deeper meaning than the loss of the cookies. William was a bright boy —why did he use his intelligence to stir up trouble instead of for good?

Mr. Townsend brushed the crumbs off the steps with several sweeps of his hand and offered an apologetic grimace. "Johnny an' Robert carry home plenty of tales about William's shenanigans. I reckon he makes things a mite difficult for you."

Although Edythe wished she could dispute his comment, she wouldn't lie. Drawing in a deep breath, she admitted, "He is a . . . challenge."

"Can I help?"

She shifted her head to meet his open gaze. Not even a hint of condemnation showed on his face. Asking for help was tantamount to admitting she couldn't control William, but Mr. Townsend had boys of his own—well-behaved boys. Perhaps he could offer some advice.

She sighed. "Luthenia tells me I need to give him a good switching, but I made a promise to the students that I wouldn't use the switch." She searched Mr. Townsend's face for signs of disapproval. Seeing none, she continued, "Besides, punishment seems to have no effect on William. In fact, to be perfectly frank, he seems to welcome the attention punishment brings."

The realization took her by surprise. She'd never really considered it before, but instead of discouraging William, any kind of attention—including punishment—seemed to spur him on. Aloud, she mused, "Perhaps I should ignore him. Then I would be withholding what he apparently craves."

A low chuckle rumbled from Mr. Townsend's chest. "If he sees havin' your attention—even unpleasant attention—as a reward, then ignorin' him would be the only real punishment." He tilted his head. Sun glinted on the honey strands lacing his walnut-husk-colored hair, momentarily stealing Edythe's attention. "But can you overlook his bad behavior without makin' problems for the rest of the class? Doesn't seem fair somehow, forcin' them all to put up with William's misbehaving."

"They're already forced to tolerate William's

misbehaving, I'm afraid." Regret threaded through Edythe's middle. How she wished *something* would work so the classroom would be a pleasant place of learning for all of her students. "Far too much of my day is spent dealing with William. Sometimes I worry the others are being neglected because William steals so much of my time and energy."

Mr. Townsend drew squiggles with his finger in the dirt between his feet. "Neither of my boys have ever mentioned feelin' neglected, so I wouldn't worry too much about that. But I agree you need to get William under control. He's gonna wear you out. An' we'd hate to have him run off a good teacher."

Edythe's cheeks burned at his praise. She shifted her attention to the sandwich in her hand.

"If he's likin' all the attention his tomfoolery brings, then seems to me you need to quit givin' him what he wants. Ignore him, like you said." Mr. Townsend gave her a serious look. "But the other kids need to understand what you're doin', or they'll just think you're lettin' him get by with misbehavin'. Might start a whole string of trouble."

Edythe nodded slowly. "That's very sensible, Mr. Townsend. But how would I go about explaining this new plan of ending William's pranks? He's often one of the first to arrive and the last to go home."

A sly grin crept up Mr. Townsend's cheeks. "I might be able to help you with that."

She raised one eyebrow, both eager and hesitant to hear his plan. "Oh?"

"Seems to me your woodpile could use some bolstering. How about I take William with me to gather up a few limbs—him bein' the oldest boy in school, makes sense he'd be asked to help."

His grin climbed higher, bringing out a dimple in his left cheek. Edythe found herself mesmerized by the beguiling little dent in his smooth-shaven skin. She had to force herself to listen as he continued speaking.

"While he's with me, you could gather the other youngsters an' have a talk with 'em—make sure they understand what you're doin' an' get them to help you. After all, if ignorin' is what it'll take to bring William around, it'll take everybody ignorin' him—not just the schoolmarm."

Edythe stared at him, amazed. "You'd really do that?"

He shrugged. "Why not? His pranks cause Robert an' Johnny plenty of aggravation. It's the only part of school they don't like—dealin' with William."

Shame struck. She wanted the children to feel at ease and comfortable in school. She'd failed them by allowing William such control. "I'm sorry, Mr. Townsend."

"Don't feel bad, Miss Amsel." His gentle voice soothed her battered feelings. "Used to be, the boys didn't want to go to school at all. That's changed because of you. This is just one little problem, an' you'll get it solved. Now . . ." He slapped his thighs and pushed to his feet. "I'll fetch William an' take him on that errand, an' you have a good talk with your pupils."

Edythe rose and held out her hand. Without a moment's pause, Mr. Townsend took it. Gooseflesh broke out across her back and arms at the feel of his strong fingers around hers. She swallowed. "Thank you for your advice and your lack of criticism, Mr. Townsend. Now I understand why Johnny and Robert are such kindhearted boys. They've had a very good teacher."

The man's cheeks flushed red, and he released a light chuckle. "All we can do is our best with the good Lord's help, ma'am."

He stepped backward, releasing her hand. She experienced an unexpected rush of melancholy with the loss of contact. He strode in the direction of the play yard.

Edythe stared after him, her heart pattering in an unfamiliar pattern. Clutching her hands together, she berated herself for her childish reaction. This man's kindness was igniting ridiculous ideas in her mind.

Lifting her skirts a few inches, she skipped up

the steps. She took hold of the bell's pull-rope and gave it a sharp yank. The children ran from all directions. Waving her hands, she hurried them through the door. "Inside, children. We have something important to discuss."

Chapter
FOURTEEN

"I'm glad the young'uns are so all-fired eager to help." Across the dinner table from Edythe, Luthenia sopped gravy with a folded slice of bread. "Tells me they don't care for William's shenanigans. Also tells me they think a good deal of their schoolmarm."

Remembering the children's enthusiasm, some of them sharing how much it bothered them to witness their teacher's frustration, Edythe knew she'd gained their affection. But their feelings toward her might crumble if William continued to rule the schoolhouse.

Luthenia raised one eyebrow. "But can you ignore everything? How's it gonna work when he starts dippin' some girl's pigtail in the inkwell again?"

She and the students had discussed several different situations and how to handle them. Dunking a pigtail in an inkwell was one of the first issues mentioned. "Martha is bringing a supply of hairpins to school, and she intends to pin up the girls' braids. If they aren't dangling, William won't be able to dip them in the inkwell."

"Sound thinkin'." Luthenia munched the last bite of her bread, her forehead crinkled in thought. "An' out on the schoolyard, when he gets impish an' starts trippin' or pushin'? Somebody might get hurt."

Edythe wished her landlady wouldn't point out the weak parts of her new plan. She had nothing else on which to draw—ignoring William *had* to work. "There may be times I'll need to intervene for the safety of the other children. But if they play their games as if he doesn't exist, I trust eventually he'll grow tired of being left out and will choose to behave simply to be included again."

"So you're all really gonna pretend he's not even there?"

The woman still sounded skeptical. Edythe reined in her misgivings. "That's right. When he's misbehaving, he'll be invisible. But the moment he behaves appropriately, he will be immediately acknowledged. He'll receive attention for good behavior rather than bad."

Clicking her tongue against her teeth, Luthenia stabbed a chunk of tender beef from the serving bowl in the middle of the table and plopped it on her plate. "I still think you oughtta—"

"I *know* what you think!" Edythe hadn't intended to snap. She lowered her fork and sent the older woman a penitent look. "I'm sorry. But I've made my feelings quite clear about using a switch."

Luthenia waved her hand. "Oh, botheration, I'm sorry, too. Seems like such an easy fix—light a fire in his britches an' *make* him be good. Prob'ly easier for a man teacher than a lady to swing a switch. I should let you run things your way, just like I keep tellin' the others in town." Luthenia's face flooded with pink.

A prickle of apprehension climbed Edythe's spine. "Have people in town expressed concern to you?"

Luthenia began hacking her slice of meat into bite-sized pieces. "Oh, you know how folks like to blather. They're just curious about your newfangled ways o' teachin', that's all. Don't make much sense to 'em. Readin', writin', cipherin' . . . them are the subjects most think are good enough for the young'uns."

Her words tumbled out faster, and bits of meat scooted around her plate as she continued. "I keep tellin' 'em the youngsters're lucky to have a teacher as young an' smart an' full of ideas as you. Good for 'em to expand their thinkin' beyond the ordinary. So you don't worry none about the old naysayers an' do what you been called to do—teach."

Edythe twisted her lips as she thought about what Luthenia had revealed. "I suppose I shouldn't be surprised, based on the questioning I received during some of my visits to the students' families. But I truly thought my assurances had put everyone's fears to rest. Except for Mr. Libolt's, of course." The man scowled at her in church or when their paths crossed in town. Yet she clung to the hope that *all* the town council members, including Mr. Libolt, would eventually come to accept her ways of teaching. She'd grown to love the children—well, with the exception of William Sholes—and she wished to remain in Walnut Hill for several years so she could watch the children grow into maturity.

"Hank Libolt's a noisy one, for sure." Luthenia released a snort of laughter. "Maybe we could get the town to do like your pupils're gonna do with William. Not much fun to blabber when nobody'll listen."

Edythe imagined Mr. Libolt standing in the middle of the street, shouting his opinions, while everyone scurried on with their own business, oblivious to his noisy haranguing. Despite her earlier irritation, she giggled.

A creak sounded from the stairs, and Edythe turned and glimpsed a pair of bare feet beneath the hem of a nightgown. "Missy, why didn't you call me? I would have helped you." She leaped up to meet her sister. Curling her arm around Missy's waist, she accompanied her the rest of the way into the kitchen.

When they reached the table, Edythe pulled loose and shook her finger. "Until you've regained your strength, do not go up or down the stairs on your own."

Missy scowled. "I called for help, but you were talking and didn't hear me. So I came down by myself." She tossed her head and sniffed. "Besides, I'm not a baby, you know."

"Of course you're not." Luthenia bustled forward and gently pressed Missy into a chair. "But you hardly have the strength of a newborn lamb right now." Luthenia flashed a quick grin at Edythe, then reached for a clean plate. "Now that you're awake, I expect you to eat a goodly portion of beef an' taters. Food'll help build your strength so your sister can stop frettin' over you."

"She stopped frettin' over me a long time ago."

Missy's mumbled words stung Edythe's heart, but before she could reply, Luthenia came to her defense. "Don't be mistakin' movin' on with her life as a sign of not carin' for you." Luthenia reached out to tuck a stray strand of hair behind Missy's ear. "She cares about you a heap, Missy."

Missy twisted her face away from Luthenia's touch and didn't reply. Luthenia sighed and ladled food from the serving bowls onto Missy's plate. Watching, Edythe battled between taking Missy to task for treating the dear older woman so rudely and wrapping her sister in her arms. What had happened to create such fury within Missy and send her on a lengthy journey by herself? So far, Missy had refused to answer any of Edythe's gently worded questions. When the girl was completely well again, the two sisters would have a serious talk.

She placed her hand on Missy's arm. "Are you chilly? I can get my robe for you." For a moment, it appeared Missy would refuse, but then she gave a slight nod. Edythe dashed up the stairs to retrieve the robe. It was her favorite—one she'd sewn for her mother when she lay ill after Missy's birth and complained that she never felt warm. Putting on the robe always made Edythe feel as though she was wrapped in her mother's presence. She hoped it would have the same effect for Missy.

With the robe over her arm, she hurried back downstairs and found Missy cautiously lifting small bites of gravy-soaked potatoes to her mouth. Edythe couldn't hold back a smile of relief. "It's so good to see you eating! Here, stand up for a minute . . ." She placed the robe over Missy's shoulders. "That should keep you toasty warm."

Missy slid back into the chair and went on eating in silence.

Edythe caught Luthenia looking at Missy. With

her brows low and lips pinched tight, she seemed to hold back a sharp comment. But when she met Edythe's gaze, her face relaxed into a smile. "I know you've got papers to grade. Let me clear off your side of the table while you fetch your work. Then you can sit down there an' get started while Missy finishes up her supper. She's slept most of the day away all by herself upstairs—I reckon she'll be happy to have your company while she eats."

Edythe looked at Missy, hoping for some sign of confirmation that her sister would enjoy having her company. But Missy kept her head low, seemingly oblivious to the conversation around her. Edythe inched toward the stairway. She was halfway up the stairs when someone pounded on the front door. An angry voice called, "Where's the schoolmarm?"

Even though Edythe couldn't see the person, she recognized the voice. She scurried back down. Missy shot her an apprehensive look, and she managed to offer a quick smile of assurance before entering the parlor, her head high. "Good evening, Mr. Libolt."

The man charged forward, forcing Luthenia to stumble backward or be run down. A severe frown turned his face into a series of deep furrows. "My young'uns came home today with some tale about how they're gonna make the Sholes boy behave in school."

Edythe cringed. Apparently she hadn't emphasized the need for secrecy stringently enough. Their carefully laid plans would be destroyed if William knew what they were doing.

Mr. Libolt's cheeks mottled red. "Not only are you teachin' worthless subjects, now you're expectin' the young'uns to control one of their own? Lady, I'm to the point of tellin' the town council we made a mistake by askin' you to teach here in Walnut Hill. If you don't stop this foolishness an' *do your job,* then I'm gonna see to it you won't be teachin' here no more—an' no place else, either, if I can help it."

Fire attacked Edythe's face. She wanted to defend herself, but she could hardly draw breath. She willed herself to calm, to find words that would diffuse the situation. But before anything formed on her lips, Luthenia bolted forward.

"Hank Libolt, you got a lot of nerve bargin' into my home an' flingin' threats."

Edythe tried to wiggle her way in front of the landlady, but Luthenia thrust out her elbow, holding Edythe back. The diminutive woman stood on tiptoe, bringing herself nose to nose with the man. She reminded Edythe of a bluebird attacking a hawk.

"How can you say Miss Amsel isn't doin' her job? Are the young'uns learnin'? Yes! Are they enjoyin' bein' in school? Yes!"

Mr. Libolt thundered, "She was hired to—"

"Teach!" Luthenia didn't back down an inch. "An' that's exactly what she's doin'!"

"She's teachin' nonsense!"

Had the pair forgotten Edythe was in the room? This should be her fight. She pushed her way between the two. "Luthenia, please go see to Missy." Luthenia pinched her lips into a grim line, but she marched into the kitchen without another word. Edythe faced her nemesis. "And, Mr. Libolt, kindly temper your voice. I don't expect you to approve of everything I've done, but I do expect to be treated respectfully."

Mr. Libolt opened his mouth as if ready to bellow, but then he gulped and drew in a deep breath. When he spoke again, his tone was harsh but no longer at full volume. "I've held my tongue on your strange teachin' methods"—a snort carried from the kitchen, letting Edythe know Luthenia was listening to every word—"but I won't be silent on this. It ain't the pupils' responsibility to make one o' their own behave."

"You're right—it's *my* responsibility to maintain order. Just as it's my responsibility to keep the schoolhouse clean and the woodstove blazing." Edythe assumed the kind, reasonable tone she'd perfected when quelling her father's irrational rants. "But someone else makes sure the woodpile is well stocked." A picture of Joel Townsend flashed through Edythe's mind, but she pushed the image aside. "The town council

153

provides cleaning supplies for my use. The responsibility is mine, yet others contribute."

Mr. Libolt's face was slowly returning to its normal color. Gratified, Edythe went on. "I've concocted a means of denying William what he desires—attention. But for the discipline to be effective, I will require assistance. Just as the townsfolk and town council assist in providing supplies for the school, the students will assist in William's discipline. After all, bringing an end to his troublemaking will be to their benefit, too."

For long seconds, the man remained silent, his jaw muscles twitching. Then he huffed. "Fine. I won't share my worries with the other members of the town council . . . for now." He aimed a thick finger at her nose. "But I'm gonna be watchin'. An' mark my words—if I'm still feelin' this unsettled by the end o' the year, I can guarantee you won't be asked back again."

He grunted, smacked his hat onto his head, and slammed out the door.

Edythe sucked in a mighty breath, her chest heaving with the intake of air. She released it in a whoosh and then turned toward the kitchen. Missy, her face ashen, stood in the doorway. She stumbled forward a few steps, dragging the hem of Mama's robe across the floor. "Edie, I don't like this place. It's just like Pa said—you're not doin' any good here."

Missy's words pierced Edythe to the depth of

her soul. She'd thought she'd escaped her father's gloomy discourses, but now his scornful voice filled her ears, carried by her beloved sister. She pressed her palms to her aching heart, wishing she could cover her ears instead.

"Please . . ." Tears swam in Missy's eyes. "Can't we go back to Omaha?"

Chapter
FIFTEEN

As Edythe walked to school on Friday morning, she reflected on the past two weeks. There had been times she'd nearly swallowed her tongue to keep from laughing. William Sholes's obvious confusion when his pranks went unacknowledged was the most comical thing she'd ever seen. And her other pupils had never been so intent on their studies. Ignoring William seemed to have a positive effect on their concentration.

A chilly gust lifted her scarf and tossed it over her face. She shook her head, dislodging it, then shivered. With the end of November waiting around the corner, it wouldn't be long before the first snow fell. The short walk from town to the schoolhouse, which had been pleasant in the early fall, would quickly lose its charm when she had to trudge through snow. Yet there was a magic to the first snowfall. She'd have the children go out and arrange themselves from tallest to shortest and then make a line of snow angels. Surely she could invent a lesson on measurement to correlate with the activity.

Lost in thought, Edythe almost missed seeing William hunched on the schoolhouse steps. He pushed to his feet as she approached. Judging by his rosy nose, cheeks, and ears, he'd been at the schoolhouse for quite a while already. He shifted from foot to foot, blowing on his hands as she closed the distance between them.

"William?" She paused at the base of the stairs. "Why are you here so early?" He always arrived before the other children, but he'd never beaten her to school.

"So cold this mornin', thought you might want help gettin' the stove goin'."

William Sholes wanted to be helpful? Edythe blinked in pleased surprise. "Th-that's very thoughtful of you. I would appreciate assistance. Why don't you gather an armload of wood while I unlock the doors?"

He darted off without a word, and Edythe quickly entered the building. Her body shuddered in appreciation of being out of the gusting wind, yet the room held a sharp chill. She deposited her armload of books on her desk and removed her scarf. As she hung it on a hook, William burst into the room with several short logs balanced in his arms.

She reached for the wood. "I'll get the fire blazing quickly so you can warm up."

"I'll start the stove."

Edythe paused, uncertain. Should she allow one of her students to bank the stove?

"I do it at home all the time. Won'tcha let me?"

His hopeful grin melted Edythe. "Very well. Thank you, William."

William spun toward the stove and clanked the door open. Leaving him to work, Edythe returned to her desk and organized her books for today's lessons. One by one, the children arrived, their cheeks reddened from cold. William greeted each by name and invited them to warm up by the stove. Although they cast puzzled glances in their teacher's direction, all but Jane Heidrich accepted his invitation. The middle of the room became crowded with the children huddling around the round-bellied stove, their hands outstretched to catch the warmth.

William wiggled his way to the outside of the group, a smile on his face. Edythe silently rejoiced at his pleasure in making things comfortable for his classmates. She marveled that the boy who usually pushed his way to the center now stood on the outer rim, allowing the smaller children the warmest spot in the room. Apparently his desire to be included had overcome his desire to create conflict. Ignoring him had worked! She congratulated herself on the transformation. Wouldn't Mr. Townsend be pleased?

She gave a little start. All of the parents should be pleased to have William's misbehavior under control. Why had she focused on Mr. Townsend?

Clapping her palms briskly, she addressed the class. "Take your seats. We need to start our day." Looking directly at William, she added, "Thank you, William, for getting the fire started this morning."

The boy straightened his shoulders, his head held high. "You're welcome, Miss Amsel."

Still smiling, she opened her roll book and put a check beside the names of the students in attendance. All but Johnny and Robert Townsend were present. Edythe scowled at their empty desk. Something must be amiss—they'd never been late before. Worry nibbled at the fringes of her mind, but she pushed it aside.

"Shall we start with a Scripture reading? Perhaps something from Psalms." She lifted the Bible from the corner of her desk. Left behind by the previous teacher, the Bible's worn cover felt smooth and comfortable in her hands. The town council encouraged using the Bible in the classroom, and Edythe had no objections. She had discovered it was a peaceful way to begin their day. Considering the wonderful change she'd witnessed in William, it seemed especially appropriate to read from God's holy book today.

She flipped the pages open to Psalm 139 and began to read. " 'O Lord, thou hast searched me, and known me. Thou knowest my downsitting and mine uprising, thou understandest my thought afar off.' " Her voice caught as the meaning of the beautifully woven words settled around her heart. Might it be that God Almighty knew Edythe Amsel's every thought? Could He understand how much she wanted to guide and protect and teach these children?

She flicked a glance at the pupils. All peered back at her, hands folded on desks, faces attentive. She continued. " 'Thou compassest my path and my lying down, and art acquainted with all my ways. For there—' "

A sudden *pop!* interrupted. Edythe jumped, nearly dropping the Bible.

"What was that?" Ada Wolcott exclaimed, her eyes wide. The children looked around and murmured in confusion.

Although similar in sound to a firecracker, the pop had seemed much less intense. Had it come from a distance? Edythe crossed to the window and peeked out at the brown landscape. From behind her, a *pop-pop!* exploded. This time she realized it had come from the stove.

The children bolted from their desks, their voices rising in alarm. Jenny Scheebeck began to cry. Edythe raised her hands to restore order. "Children, sit down, please. Remain calm." They continued to mutter excitedly, but they slipped back into their desks. Only William Sholes hadn't leapt to his feet. He sat with his hands folded, a satisfied smile on his face, not at all concerned.

Remembering his eagerness to light the stove this morning, a feeling of dread crept up Edythe's spine. Stepping down the center aisle, she approached William's desk. "William, what—" Before she could complete her sentence, a foul odor filled the air.

The girls shrieked and the boys coughed. Little Will Libolt bent over his desk, gagging. The children covered their noses. Although Edythe wished to remain composed, the stench made her stomach roll. She staggered backward two steps, trying to escape the odor. But it followed her. William pinched his nose, but his smile remained intact.

Her eyes watering, Edythe pinned the boy with the sternest gaze she could muster. "William, what is this . . ." She couldn't think of a word strong enough to define the odor. She waved her hands, indicating the smell that filled every corner of the room.

William smirked behind his hand, his lips slightly parted.

The intensity of the odor made her sick. Tears ran from her eyes. The children wailed and spluttered, begging her to do something to make the smell go away. Edythe grabbed William by the shirt front and gave him a shake. "What did you do?"

"Smells like rotten eggs to me."

The deep male voice carried over the sounds of the children's distress. Edythe released William and spun toward the cloakroom door. Joel Townsend strode forward, leaving Johnny and Robert huddling together in the doorway with their hands clamped over their noses. The man moved to the nearest window and screeched it open. Air whisked into the room—frigid but with a welcome fresh scent.

While Mr. Townsend opened the windows on the north side of the room, she opened those on the south. The room quickly turned cold with the cross breeze, but mercifully, the odor lost its bitter bite. The children sank back into their desks, hugging themselves and jabbering. Edythe's shoulders sagged. So much for bringing William under control. This had been his most disruptive prank to date.

Mr. Townsend ambled to William's desk and propped his hand on its corner. "Was I right? Rotten eggs?"

William scowled, but he nodded.

"Put 'em in the stove, did you?"

Again William nodded, slinking low in his seat.

Edythe gawked at the boy. Where did he get such ideas?

Mr. Townsend turned to face Edythe. "It's gonna stink like the dickens for a while, I'm afraid." He tugged his jacket collar around his clean-shaven jaw. Edythe noted he had a nice jawline—firm and square. She gave her head a little shake. Apparently the odor had leaked past her nose into her brain, jumbling her thoughts. She focused on his next words. "Leave the windows open all morning—hopefully that'll be long enough to clear the smell."

"M-miss Amsel?" Sophie Jeffers raised her hand.

"Yes?"

"I'm c-c-cold!"

Several others added their agreement.

"Well, we don't have much choice." She heard the tartness in her voice and immediately tempered her tone. "Fetch your coats, children. While the windows are open we'll stay bundled to stave off a chill." The children dashed for the cloakroom, their feet thundering on the planked floor. Edythe clamped her teeth together. If everyone came down with fevers because of William's prank, she just might break her resolve and take a switch to the boy after all.

Edythe drew Mr. Townsend to the far corner of the room. "Thank you for your assistance with the windows. I don't know why I didn't think to open them."

His grin revealed the dimple in his left cheek. "I reckon your mind was on other things."

"Yes." She shot a sour look toward William. He hadn't retrieved his coat but sat low in his seat with his shoulders hunched.

Mr. Townsend dipped his head toward the boys. "Sorry I had them here late this mornin'. I went out to milk, and my cow had escaped her enclosure. Had to round her up and then milk her before I could get the boys' breakfast. Didn't want to send 'em on an empty stomach." He chuckled. "'Course, if I'd known you were cookin' eggs in the heat stove . . ."

Despite her aggravation with William, she chuckled. How wonderful to find some humor in this trying situation. She rested her fingertips on Mr. Townsend's forearm. "Thank you for making me laugh. I sorely needed it."

A soft smile lit his eyes. Then he gave a little jerk and shuffled toward the door. "I best skedaddle an' let you get to teachin'." He waved good-bye to the boys and clomped out the door.

Edythe watched him go, an odd sadness clawing at her heart. As if in response to her inner feelings, a childish voice began to wail. Jenny Scheebeck drew up her knees and buried her face in her lap.

Edythe hurried to Jenny's bench and put her arm around the little girl's shoulders. "What's wrong, Jenny? Are you still cold?"

"No'm." Jenny snuffled, her face hidden. "I'm sad."

Me too. Yet she couldn't pinpoint the complete reason for her sadness. Edythe caught Jenny's chin and lifted her face. "Why are you sad?"

Jenny's eyes filled and spilled over. "I promised to ignore anything bad that William done, but I didn't ignore the stink. I'm sorry I didn't mind you!"

Edythe shot a quick look at the class. William's knowing smirk taunted her, and she stifled a sigh. "Everyone take out your McGuffey Readers and turn to the stories we started yesterday. Read quietly for a few minutes." She turned her attention to consoling Jenny. She wished someone could console her.

Clearly, she hadn't made any progress with William. And now, thanks to Jenny's innocent outburst, continuing to ignore him would be useless. She'd assured Mr. Libolt she could do the job she'd been hired to do. *But can I really?*

Chapter
SIXTEEN

Joel held loosely to the wagon traces and hunkered deeper into his jacket. The wind whisking across the plains could cut clear through a man's skin and freeze his bones. He hoped the youngsters and Miss Amsel wouldn't be too cold with those windows open.

He snorted, his breath momentarily hanging like a cloud under his nose. Cold had to be better than smelling rotten eggs. When he'd entered the schoolhouse, the stench had nearly knocked him backward. William Sholes must've buried those eggs weeks ago to get that much stink out of them. Joel shook his head. It was a devilish trick, but hiding them in the stove was clever—nobody'd know they were there until the heat popped their shells.

Giving the reins a little flick, he pondered William's penchant for mischief. He'd seen Lloyd Sholes twist his son's ear for fidgeting in church and scold him for disobeying an order. From all appearances, the boy received proper instruction. William knew how to behave properly, he just chose not to. Joel whispered a quick prayer of gratitude for Johnny and Robert. They could easily be resentful, troublemaking boys, given all they'd lost at such a young age, but they were loving, well-mannered boys instead. He intended to do all he could to make sure they stayed that way, too.

And Miss Amsel would do her part. He glanced down at his arm where her fingers had pressed into his sleeve. Such a prim and proper lady—she probably hadn't even been aware she'd touched him. But he'd been aware. The touch had gone clean through the thick bulk of his coat sleeve to his flesh, the same way the gusting wind was now doing. But instead of chilling him, her touch had warmed him all the way to his toes.

He was thirty-two years old and smitten for the second time in his life. Without warning, images of Susannah filled his mind. Small, fine boned, with an airy laugh—the way he imagined a fairy might laugh when amused. He'd tumbled head over heels for Susannah Mohler, and she'd liked him back. Until she met his brother John.

Joel's fists tightened on the reins. He'd loved his brother fiercely, but it had taken a heap of praying to forgive John for stealing Susannah from him. Seeing his brother so happy had helped, even if he'd had to move away to keep from giving in to jealousy. Buying the land in Walnut Hill, miles from his father's farm in Geneva, had given him the space he'd needed to let his broken heart heal.

He gave the reins a tug, guiding the horse to turn in at his lane. His little log house waited, plain in appearance but welcoming all the same. His place of refuge, of peacefulness. Eagerness to go in, to sit in front of the fireplace and warm up, made him snap the reins. The horse broke into a trot.

He drew the horse to a stop outside the barn and hopped down. Releasing the horse from the rigging, he heaved a big sigh and admitted aloud, "Susannah wasn't meant to be mine." The horse blinked at him, and Joel rubbed the animal's nose. "Nope. God surely has somethin' else in mind for me. And I'm wonderin' if it might be . . ."

He didn't allow himself to finish the thought out loud. He'd lost Susannah to John. The town might very well lose Edythe Amsel to another school if the Sholes boy kept up his tomfoolery. He shouldn't set his hopes on courting the schoolmarm. But as he led the horse into its stall and forked hay into the feeding box, he couldn't help wondering how much more inviting his little house would be if a wife—if Edythe Amsel waited on the other side of the sturdy plank door.

Edythe burst through the front door of Luthenia's home, propelled by a stout wind. The mingled aromas of beef and vegetables reached her nose, and she inhaled, allowing the scent to chase away the remembrance of the one that had clung to the classroom all day despite the wind coursing through the windows.

Luthenia stuck her head around the corner. "You're home earlier'n usual—thought you'd stay an' do some cleanin', since it's Friday."

"I'll go over tomorrow morning and do the necessary mopping and dusting."

Surely by tomorrow the rotten egg smell would be completely gone. She'd left two windows cracked, just in case. Placing her books on the table beside the door, she started to unbutton her coat.

"Before you get yourself all undone, could'ja run to the mercantile?"

Edythe didn't want to refuse Luthenia's request, but the unpleasant day had exhausted her. Besides that, she was ready to be out of the cold wind.

"I'm out of tea," Luthenia continued. "Now that the weather's turned wintry, I rely on a cup o' hot tea of a mornin'—it unstoves my old bones." She sighed. "Meant to go myself, but I started cuttin' squares out of some old clothes—thought to make a little quilt for the comin' Scheebeck baby—an' the time got away from me."

Edythe smiled. Luthenia had the busiest hands of anyone she'd ever known. How could she refuse a favor for such a giving woman? She rebuttoned her coat. "I'd be glad to."

Luthenia disappeared around the corner, and Edythe heard a kettle lid clang. Her landlady's voice carried from the kitchen. "While you're there, you could check the mailboxes."

Even though Luthenia made a daily trek to the mercantile in search of a response to the letters Edythe had sent to her siblings, asking them to keep Missy, the trips had been in vain. Could her letters have gotten lost in the mail? Such things did happen. She didn't want to think her brothers and sister were ignoring her. From long ago, she heard her mother's voice: *"Don't borrow trouble, Edythe."* Tears pricked behind Edythe's eyes. If only Mama hadn't died, Missy would have a secure home.

Edythe called, "Where's Missy? Maybe she'd like to bundle up and go with me."

Luthenia bustled back through the doorway and into the parlor, wiping her hands on her ever-present apron. "She's upstairs. I think she'd welcome the chance to get out. Been cooped up here with me for weeks." She quirked one eyebrow. "Doc deemed her well enough to be out an' about. Kinda surprised you didn't take her to school with you."

"Not knowing whether she'd be staying, I didn't think it wise to start a routine." Edythe moved past Luthenia to the base of the stairs. "Missy?"

Floorboards creaked, and then the bedroom door squeaked open. "What?"

"I'm walking to the mercantile for some tea. Put on your coat and come with me." Edythe took care to avoid using a demanding tone, hoping Missy's hackles wouldn't rise. To Edythe's relief, her sister came down the stairs with her coat draped over her arm. Edythe greeted her sister with a smile. "It's chilly, but I thought you might enjoy a short excursion."

Missy shrugged disinterestedly, but she slipped

on her coat and buttoned it to her throat. Edythe wrapped her own scarf over Missy's head. Satisfied that her sister would be warm, she gestured to the front door.

The two walked elbow to elbow down the street. The cold air stung Edythe's nose. She heard Missy sniff a time or two, as well, but to her credit, the girl never complained. They reached the mercantile, and Missy scurried inside, releasing a little shiver. She went directly to the potbellied stove in the middle of the store and aimed her backside at the grated door. Edythe moved to the counter and rang the little bell that sat on the corner of the scarred wood top. Several minutes passed before feet pounded from upstairs, and Mr. Scheebeck burst through the doorway at the back of the store.

He scowled at the front door. "Thought I'd put out the CLOSED sign . . ." He ran his hand over his thin hair, smoothing the wild wisps into place, and then spun on Edythe. "What'cha need, Miss Amsel?"

Accustomed to a businesslike but personable demeanor, his brusqueness took Edythe by surprise. "I came for tea, and to check our mail cubbies."

"Tea . . . tea . . ." He fumbled around on the shelves for a few seconds, his hands clumsier than Edythe had ever seen. Finally he located a box of tea leaves. Plunking it on the counter, he barked, "That it?"

Edythe frowned, concerned. "Mr. Scheebeck, are you all right?"

His eyes darted toward the back of the store. "What? Yes. Me? I'm fine. It's my wife. It's . . ." He gulped twice, his Adam's apple bobbing in his skinny neck. Leaning close, he whispered, "It's her time."

It took a moment for his meaning to soak in. Then Edythe jerked upright. "Oh!" But the baby wasn't due until late next month. Involuntarily, her gaze swung to the ceiling. Somewhere in the rooms above the mercantile, Mrs. Scheebeck labored to bring forth a child. Fear smote Edythe, followed by a longing to offer a prayer for a problem-free delivery and a healthy baby. She should hurry back and tell Luthenia so her landlady could pray for Mrs. Scheebeck and the new babe.

"We'll get out of your way, then. Would you like me to put out the CLOSED sign?"

"Yes, yes, that's fine. Good-bye, now." The man scurried around the corner as he spoke.

Missy dashed to Edythe's side and tugged on her coat sleeve. "Is his wife having a baby?"

Edythe nodded. "I wonder if I should take Lewis and Jenny to Luthenia's with me so they're not underfoot." *And if—Heaven forbid— a tragedy occurs, they won't be here to witness it.*

She tipped her head, listening intently. Not so much as a peep of childish noise reached her ears. Perhaps Mr. Scheebeck had already shuffled the children off somewhere.

"Edie, can we go now?" Missy sounded irritated.

Edythe sighed and pocketed the little box of tea. "Very well. Let me—oh!" She yanked the box from her pocket and stared at it. "He didn't record my purchase."

Missy snickered. "He probably won't even remember you were here."

Edythe tended to agree, but she wouldn't walk out the door without pledging to pay for the tea. Feeling like a burglar, she scrounged under the counter and found a piece of paper and a pencil stub. She wrote a note reminding Mr. Scheebeck of her visit and placed it near the cashbox under the counter.

Missy put her hand on her hip. "Done now?"

"I must check the mail." Edythe headed for the cubbies in the back corner of the mercantile.

"That eager to be rid of me, huh?"

Underneath the belligerence in her sister's voice, Edythe heard a note of melancholy. She turned slowly. "Missy, no matter what you might think, I'm not eager to be rid of you. I love you. I want what's best for you."

"Then, why can't we go back to Omaha?" Missy's lower lip poked out petulantly. "You could teach there, and I can be near my friends. Do you *have* to teach in this town?"

Edythe had chosen Walnut Hill to separate herself from Omaha. From Pa. From all the unhappy memories. "I made a commitment to the town council and to the children of the town. I can't go back on my word."

Missy folded her arms over her chest, her brows crunched downward. "So you're just going to ship me off to someone else?"

Edythe closed her eyes for a moment, gathering patience. "We have to find a place for you to live, Missy."

"But I want to be with you." The girl's expression turned pleading.

Edythe sighed, wishing she had the means to care for her sister.

"Too bad I'm not a boy," Missy continued. "I could do like Albert and Loren, an' just go off on my own. They were only fifteen when they left home, an' nobody complained." She chewed on her thumbnail, a sign of distress. "Then I wouldn't be a bother to anybody. Nobody worries over boys."

Edythe wrapped her sister in a hug. "I worry over our brothers, just as I worry over you. But boys are usually more independent, and it's easier for them to find honorable work. Girls are . . . different." Edythe shuddered to think of the jobs some young girls took in the big city

173

just to eat and keep a roof over their heads.

Missy huffed in Edythe's ear, but she didn't try to pull away.

Edythe gave her another squeeze, then stepped back. "Let me check the mail cubbies and then we need to hurry back to Luthenia's. That stew is probably scorched by now."

A slight grin creased Missy's face. "She's a good cook, isn't she? Almost as good as you."

So rarely did anyone praise her cooking, Edythe paused for a moment to savor the compliment. Then, with a smile, she dashed to the mail cubbies and peeked in the boxes. Luthenia's was empty, but a lone, thick envelope waited in Edythe's box. She pulled it out, her heart pounding. Justus's bold, messy script filled the front of the envelope.

Missy scooted to Edythe's side and peeked at the envelope. "From Justus?"

Edythe nodded.

"Well, why are you just standing there? Open it."

Edythe wasn't sure why Missy sounded so eager, but she automatically followed the command. Her hands quivering, she tore the flap loose and pulled out a bulky wad of folded pages. She unfolded them and glanced at the variety of handwritings—a missive from each of her siblings. Her heart pounding with hope, she began to read. Missy leaned against Edythe's arm, reading too as Edythe whisked through each page.

As soon as they'd read the last letter, their gazes collided. Missy appeared smug, but Edythe felt certain her expression reflected disappointment.

"They all said no," Missy confirmed.

Edythe nodded, folding the letters again.

"So you'll keep me, right? An' we'll go back to Omaha?" Missy tugged at her arm, hindering her efforts to put the letters into the envelope.

Edythe pulled loose of Missy's grasp. "Please, Missy, let me think."

Missy fell silent. Edythe pushed the thick envelope into her coat pocket with the tea and steered Missy toward the door. As she'd promised Mr. Scheebeck, she turned the little sign to CLOSED as they left the store. Arm in arm with Missy, she headed for Luthenia's again. She fingered the envelope, envisioning its contents.

Missy was her responsibility—but how would she care for her sister *and* teach?

God, I need some answers. Are You even up there at all?

Chapter
SEVENTEEN

Soft lantern glow beckoned Edythe down the stairway. She reached the bottom and peeked around the corner. Luthenia sat at the kitchen table, busily stitching, but her hands stilled when she spotted Edythe. Two joined triangles of fabric, suspended on a slim silver needle, swung from her fingers. The light glinted on the needle as Luthenia put her hands to work again.

"What'cha doin' up so late?"

Edythe stepped around the corner on bare feet, gripping the collar of her threadbare robe. "You're up late, too."

Luthenia gestured to the fabric scraps scattered across her lap. "Workin' on that quilt for the Scheebecks' new one." She chuckled. "Since the baby's comin' early, I'm havin' to hurry. Figure if I use every spare hour, I'll have it done by the first time the tyke shows up at Sunday service. Knowin' Wally an' Mary, that'll be the very first Sunday Doc gives approval."

Edythe worried her lower lip between her teeth for a moment. "Do you suppose the baby will be all right?"

"Miz Scheebeck's last 'un came early, too. Nothin' wrong with Jenny, now, is there?"

"No, but . . . things can go awry. Aren't you worried?"

The older woman released a soft snort. "Worry don't fix anything. Prayer does." She glanced at Edythe, her brows low. "You didn't tell me why you're up."

"My throat's dry. I need a drink."

Luthenia's gaze dropped to her work. Needle in, needle out. "Fresh water in the pail—fetched it right after supper."

Edythe scuffed to the water pail and took down the drinking dipper. She downed one full dipper, then a second. She headed for the stairs, but Luthenia's voice stopped her.

"Awful quiet at supper tonight . . . you 'n' Missy both. Somethin' on your mind?"

Edythe sent a cautious look toward the stairs.

"She's likely asleep, quiet as it is up there. An' even if she ain't, the heater grate won't pick up voices from the kitchen. You're safe talkin'."

How did Luthenia always know what she was thinking? With a sigh, Edythe pulled out a chair and sat. She hooked her heels on the chair rung and fingered one of the finished quilt blocks laid out on the kitchen table. "I heard from my brothers and my other sister. None of them are willing to let Missy live with them."

Luthenia chose two more cut triangles from the pile in her lap and lined them up. "That what's got you all fretful?"

"Well, of course!" Edythe tossed the little block aside. "What am I supposed to do with her?"

Luthenia poked the needle through the fabric and started stitching. "Haven't you been prayin' on that?" Edythe didn't answer, and Luthenia blew out a noisy breath. "Well, I've prayed plenty, askin' God to make it clear about where Missy's s'posed to live."

"He hasn't told me anything."

"Seems to me He has."

Edythe stared at her, silent.

"What were your choices? Send Missy back to your pa, which you didn't want to do, so it wasn't really a choice . . ." Luthenia's fingers sent the needle in and out in a steady pattern. "Or have Missy live with one o' your siblings. Or keep 'er with you. God closed the door on her livin' with your siblings, so what does that leave?"

"Keeping her with me, but—"

"But you don't think you can take care o' her an' do your teachin', I know." Luthenia looked up from her stitching long enough to give Edythe a stern look. "Problem is, you keep thinkin' of what you can get done on your own strength 'stead of relyin' on God to help you. Don't know how much Bible readin' you do, but—"

"I don't own a Bible."

"—there's a perfect Scripture for this situation." Luthenia shot her a low-browed look, daring her to interrupt again. "You'll find it in Philippians, the fourth chapter. Verse thirteen, if my memory isn't slippin'. Says, 'I can do all things through Christ which strengtheneth me.'" Luthenia jabbed a finger at Edythe. "*All* things . . . includin' carin' for a sister while teachin' school."

She put the needle to work again. "The secret is to let Him carry your burdens for you. His hands are a heap stronger'n ours. When you let go of the things that wear you down, then you have the freedom to *be*. I learned a long time ago, there ain't nothin' I can't handle as long as I'm leanin' on His strength."

She tied off the thread and laid the block aside. "My eyes're tired." She yawned and then chuckled. "Guess the rest of me is, too. I'm headin' to bed—work on this more tomorrow." She whisked the fabric pieces into a basket and rose.

Edythe stood, tangling her hands in her robe. "If you'd like, I can do the cooking and cleaning tomorrow. Then you'll be able to work on your quilt all day."

Luthenia tilted her head. "You sure? You got cleanin' to do at the schoolhouse, too."

"Missy can help. Then we'll come back here and do all the chores." Edythe's shoulders squared as she spoke. "It's the least we can do to thank you for putting up with the *two* of us."

Luthenia reached around to untie her apron. "I

enjoy havin' company. Even if Missy isn't the most agreeable girl, she's someone to talk to. And surely, once she settles in, she'll lose that sulky face and be more pleasant."

Edythe appreciated Luthenia's positive, giving attitude, but she felt guilty forcing her sister on the kind woman. "But you only agreed to board the schoolmarm. As soon as possible, I'll find us—"

Luthenia flapped her hand. "You got enough to do, what with teachin' an' now lookin' after your sister. You don't need the care of a house, to boot. Just stay here."

"Are you . . . sure you don't mind?" Staying with Luthenia would ease Edythe's burden considerably, but she didn't want to impose. She held her breath, waiting for an answer.

"I'm more'n sure. We'll make do." Luthenia smiled. "You'll be the one doin' most of the adjustin'. You gotta share your room with her."

Gratitude flooded Edythe's frame. "I know the town council pays you for my keep. You tell me what it is, and I'll pay you the same amount out of my salary to cover Missy."

Luthenia waved her hands at Edythe. "We'll argue that out another day. I'm too tired for it now. Head up to bed so I can blow out the lamp. We'll be draggin' like a pair o' tomcats after a full-moon night if we don't get to bed soon."

Edythe laughed loudly, then clamped her hand

over her mouth to stifle the sound. She whispered, "Good night, Luthenia."

Luthenia cupped her hand behind the lamp's glass globe. But before she blew, she bolted upright. "Edythe! I just recalled somethin', an' before I forget it again . . . you said you'd be willin' to cook tomorrow?"

"Certainly."

"Well, then, would you consider helpin' me cook up a big dinner next week?" Luthenia seemed to cringe as she asked. "Thanksgivin', y'know. Past few years I been invitin' folks who'd otherwise be alone to eat with me. The table's grown a mite crowded, an' it'll be even more so this year addin' you an' Missy. I could use an extra pair o' hands."

"Missy and I will both help."

Luthenia beamed. "Good! There's a few older folk—a couple o' widows an' old Mr. Crank, who lives out south o' town all by his lonesome. I already asked the Coopers—young couple, new in town—if they'd like to come. Gonna invite the Scheebecks so Mary doesn't have to cook after just havin' a new baby. That'll work nice if they come. Give Johnny an' Robert a couple of other kids to play with."

Edythe's mouth went dry. "J-Johnny and Robert?"

"Why, sure, I always invite Joel an' his boys. They've got no woman to cook for 'em."

"I . . . I see."

An amused smirk appeared on the older woman's face. Did Luthenia guess the source of Edythe's discombobulation?

Luthenia quirked an eyebrow. "That sound like too many for us to handle?"

Edythe inched toward the stairs. "No, I . . . I think it's fine. Missy and I will help, of course. Good night, now." She lifted her nightgown's hem and dashed up the stairs. Pausing on the landing, she tried to catch her breath. Come Thanksgiving, she and Joel Townsend would spend the whole day in this house . . . together.

Chapter
EIGHTEEN

"Betcha there won't be any beans." Robert's voice held elation.

Joel took two wide strides and caught hold of Robert's coat collar. The boy came to an abrupt stop in the middle of Miz Kinsley's front pathway. He peered up at his uncle. Johnny kept trotting toward the porch, but Joel called, "Johnny, you come here, too."

Johnny spun on his boot's well-worn heel and galloped to his uncle's side. "What is it?"

Joel released Robert, leaned forward, and gave both boys a serious look. "What'd we talk about before we rode over here?"

The boys exchanged a quick glance. Johnny answered, "We gotta eat everything on our plate an' tell Miz Kinsley thank you when dinner's over."

"That's right." Joel squinted down at Robert. "It's not polite for a dinner guest—an' that's what we are here—to turn up his nose at what's bein' served. So if she serves beans . . . ?"

"I'll eat 'em, but . . ." Robert hunched his skinny shoulders, burying the lower half of his face in his jacket collar. "I don't hafta like it, do I?"

Joel knew he served beans too often at home, but what else did bachelors eat but beans and hardtack? "You don't have to like it, but if she serves 'em, you're gonna eat 'em. And without complainin'. We'll be polite guests. Or . . . ?"

Robert puffed out a breath. "Or next year we'll eat at home 'stead o' comin' to Miz Kinsley's for Thanksgiving."

"That's right. Now go on in." Joel gave the boys a light push with his fingertips, aiming them for the porch.

Johnny threw his arm around his brother's shoulders. "Don't worry. Doubt she'd make beans today, it bein' Thanksgiving when we're s'posed to be thankful."

Joel stifled a laugh. Johnny had Miz Kinsley figured. She'd never yet served him and the boys beans when they came for a meal. Of course, it had been a few months since they'd eaten at her place—not since the new schoolmarm moved in.

His feet slowed, and he checked the ribbon tie at his throat. The boys had fussed some about putting on their Sunday go-to-meeting clothes to eat dinner on a Thursday. But he'd wanted to wear his good suit, and he felt funny about coming dressed like a dandy while the boys wore their everyday clothes. So they all looked like they were heading to Sunday service. Or a funeral.

"Uncle Joel, hurry." Robert danced in place outside Miz Kinsley's front door.

Joel drew a breath of fortification and trotted the final yards to reach the porch. As soon as his boot found the first riser, Robert knocked on the door. Miss Amsel's younger sister opened the door to them.

"Happy Thanksgiving. Please come in." She sounded like a child reciting a memorized verse.

"Happy Thanksgiving," Johnny and Robert chorused. Their voices rang like bells compared to the girl's subdued tone.

Joel gave the girl a bright smile, but she didn't respond in kind. She'd been distant at church on Sunday, too. For reasons he couldn't rightly explain, he wanted to set her at ease. But he had no idea what to say to a young woman. So he popped off his hat and handed it to her. The boys gave her their coats, and the girl disappeared through a side door before reemerging empty-handed.

She turned toward the kitchen. "Everybody's gathered back here. Mrs. Kinsley's almost ready for us to eat."

Wonderful aromas enticed Joel to follow her. Saliva pooled under his tongue, and he swallowed several times. Johnny and Robert licked their lips, their eyes alight with anticipation. Joel had eaten many a meal at Miz Kinsley's table, but it never ceased to amaze him how many people she managed to squeeze into the cozy kitchen. Her time-battered table stretched from the dry sink nearly to the parlor doorway, expanded by three homemade leaves. Mismatched chairs circled the table, half of them already occupied.

Miz Kinsley looked up from the stove, where she stirred a simmering pot that sent up swirls of steam. "Joel! An' boys! Glad you made it—just need to finish this gravy, get everything all dished up, an' we'll be eatin'. Hope you brought your appetites, 'cause me an' Edythe fixed enough to feed half the town of Walnut Hill."

Miss Amsel was doing something at the far side of Miz Kinsley's double-sized stove. He could only see her deep pink bustle perched over a striped skirt of pink and green. His face went hot when he realized he was staring, and he whirled to face the guests seated at the table—all familiar faces from town.

"Missy," Miz Kinsley said, reaching to the shelf above the stove for the salt bag, "see if you can get Mr. Townsend an' the boys to sit. Then you can help us put these platters on the table."

Missy pointed, unsmiling, to three chairs in a row along the back wall. Joel motioned the boys in first, then he took the seat closest to the head of the table. The boys did him proud, sitting quiet and patient while Miss Amsel, Miz Kinsley, and Missy carried steaming, overflowing platters and bowls to the table. It took nearly five minutes just to set out all the food.

The older woman stood at the edge of the table and used her finger to point at the bowls by turn, as if counting in her head. "Oops—still need butter. Edythe, Missy, set yourselves down. I'll fetch butter from the cellar, an' then we'll commence to eatin'." She dashed out the back door.

Miss Amsel removed her apron and then she and Missy sat, leaving the chair at the head of the table open for Miz Kinsley. Joel found himself looking directly across at Miss Amsel. She fussed with something in her lap, allowing him the chance to give her a furtive once-over. Her cheeks wore bright pink, matching her dress. Wisps of hair, loosened from the stern bun she always wore, clung to her moist forehead and neck in damp coils. His ma had always looked a little bedraggled after a long morning of cooking, but the wispy, curling strands gave Miss Amsel a soft, relaxed appearance.

She lifted her head and caught him looking. For a moment, alarm flashed in her eyes, but then she shifted her gaze to the boys, and she smiled. Her lips parted, but before she could speak, Miz Kinsley bustled into the room and thumped a bowl mounded with creamy butter onto the table.

"There now!" She plopped into her chair and placed her hands, palm up, on the table. The guests formed a chain by joining hands. She gave Joel's hand a squeeze. "Would you do the honors, Joel?"

Joel gulped, taken by surprise, but he nodded and bowed his head. "Dear Lord, on this day of thanksgiving, we come before You with thankful hearts. Thankful for our homes, for a good harvest, and for good friends. I thank You especially for Miz Kinsley an' her willingness to serve us all such a fine dinner this day. An' thank You, too, for . . ." His mouth went dry, and he had to swallow. "For Miss Amsel, who teaches our children an' also loves 'em. She . . . she's a blessin' to our town." Heat rose from his chest. He hurried on. "Thank You, Lord, for this food. Let it nourish our bodies. May we be faithful in following Your ways. Amen."

A chorus of "amens" rang, and Joel looked up.

Miss Amsel dabbed at her eyes. His heart fluttered in an unfamiliar manner. Her gaze met his, and her lips curved into a sweet, appreciative smile. The flutter in his chest increased to a gallop. He held his breath, his gaze locked with hers, wondering if her skin was all a-tingle like his was.

Then Robert bumped his elbow. "Uncle Joel, can I have some potatoes, please?"

Folks were passing bowls. Embarrassed, Joel snatched up the potatoes and spooned a sizable serving onto his plate before helping the boys. Platters kept coming, bearing sliced turkey, juicy ham, sugar-crusted yams, string beans, corn swimming in butter, round green peas, applesauce, moist stuffing, jellied cranberries, noodles in a rich broth, thick slices of hearty wheat bread, and more. He filled his plate until it couldn't hold another crumb.

Miz Kinsley called out, "Leave room for dessert! Got pumpkin pie an' apple pie an'—"

Groans sounded, followed by laughter, and then forks clinked on plates as everyone dug in. Folks chatted, several conversations going on at once—it was almost dizzying. But Joel enjoyed listening while he kept one eye on the boys and the other on Miss Amsel. He couldn't seem to keep himself from looking at her. Her location, straight across the table, made it too easy. And he found he didn't want to *not* look. Sitting there, enjoying the meal, he imagined himself in his log house with her across his table.

"Anybody know how the Scheebeck young'un is farin'?" old Mr. Crank called out.

Miz Kinsley raised her voice to a holler, the way everyone in town did for the hard-of-hearing man. "Doc's feelin' encouraged that the little feller's gonna make it. Smallest babe he ever delivered that lived past the first few days. Every day he gets a bit stronger."

A thankful murmur went around the room, and Joel observed Miss Amsel once more lifting the napkin to her eyes to wipe tears. Such a tender heart . . .

"Don't reckon we'll see mother an' baby out until close to Christmas," Miz Kinsley went on. "I asked 'em to come here today, but they said they'd best stay home. They want to protect the babe from chills an' so forth."

"Heard the Sholes boy is ailin'," the widow Meiner commented. "Out o' school this week . . ."

"You don't say?" Young Miz Cooper's forehead puckered with worry. "Nothin' serious, I hope?"

Miss Amsel replied, "Nothing serious. He just caught a chill." Her lips twitched into a grin, and Joel answered it with one of his own. William deserved that chill, and they both knew why.

Miz Cooper released a breath of relief. "Back in Walker last November, we had an outbreak of measles that near turned the town inside out. Hate to see that happen here."

From there, the three oldest guests launched into tales of illnesses that had swept through Walnut Hill in the past. Joel didn't think it the best dinner talk—especially at Thanksgiving—but Miz Kinsley would bring it to an end if she deemed it unseemly.

Missy, who'd kept her head low and hadn't spoken a word throughout the entire meal, looked up and blurted, "My mama died from anemia after birthin' me."

Everyone fell mute. Edythe's jaw muscles quivered. Joel bit down on the tip of his tongue, trying to find words that would end the uncomfortable silence.

"Our ma an' pa died, too." Johnny spoke, his childish voice so innocent it stung Joel's soul. "Their wagon turned over on 'em an' they died."

"Then they went to Heaven," Robert contributed.

Missy leaned forward, her expression intent. "How old were you? When they died, I mean."

"Robert was five. I was six," Johnny answered matter-of-factly.

"I was two months old when my mama died." Missy kept her gaze on the boys, and Joel got the impression she'd forgotten anybody else was in the room. "So mine's been gone lots longer than yours, but I never knew her. Must've been harder for you." Suddenly, she jolted and looked around the table. Her face flamed bright red. She screeched her chair against the floor and tossed her napkin over her plate. "Excuse me." She whirled and clattered up the stairs.

Miss Amsel started to rise, but Miz Kinsley caught her arm. "Let her go." The older woman's face wore a sad smile. "Might do that youngster good to reflect a bit, realize others besides her have had losses, too."

After a moment of hesitation, Miss Amsel settled back in her chair. Miz Kinsley gave the schoolmarm an approving nod, then looked down the length of the table. "Anybody ready for pie? Would'ja like pumpkin, apple, mince, berry, or buttermilk pie?"

"Yes!" Robert shouted, and everyone laughed.

Miss Amsel carried away the dinner plates while Miz Kinsley cut pies into good-sized wedges. To Joel's amazement, Johnny and Robert ate three slices apiece. Where they put all that food, he could only imagine. He enjoyed a slice of pumpkin and then ate most of a piece of mince. He had to leave the last few bites—the buttons on his suit coat strained against his full stomach. If he didn't quit, he'd have a bellyache for sure.

When they'd finished eating, the boys stretched out on the sofa in Miz Kinsley's parlor and napped. The grown-ups sat around the table, sipped tea, and visited for the better part of the afternoon. Joel removed his suit jacket and tie. He even unbuttoned his collar. Then, hooking his elbow over the back of the chair, he held his end of the conversation.

Shortly after three, the Coopers thanked Miz Kinsley and took their leave. Mr. Crank left with them, accepting their offer of a ride home. The two widow ladies finished their tea, hugged Miz Kinsley, and tottered out the door together. That left Joel with Miz Kinsley and Miss Amsel. He should go, too, but he didn't want to leave. He'd had half a dozen Thanksgiving dinners at Miz Kinsley's table, but he'd enjoyed this one more than any other.

"Can I help with the dishes? You've got a heap of 'em to wash."

"It's kind of you to ask, Joel, but Edythe, Missy, an' me'll get 'em done." Miz Kinsley chuckled. "After we take a little nap. I'm plumb tuckered."

Joel took that as a hint. "Well, then . . ." He tugged his jacket on and wadded the tie into his pocket. "I'll wake the boys an' go. Thank you for dinner. Everything was delicious, like always. The stuffin' was especially good this year."

Miz Kinsley flashed a smile. "I can't take credit for that—Edythe made it. Her ma's recipe."

"Dried cranberries, walnuts, and rosemary,"

the schoolmarm said. Then her face flooded with pink. "I'll wake the boys for you." She skittered out the door.

Miz Kinsley wrapped up a generous portion of turkey, half a loaf of bread, and the rest of the apple pie and gave it to Joel. Juggling the items, he entered the parlor. The boys were buttoned into their coats, their eyes bleary. They offered sleepy good-byes before they scuffed out the door. Joel hovered in the doorway, looking at Miss Amsel, who stood looking back with an unreadable expression on her face.

"Thank you for the meal, Miss Amsel." His lips quivered when he tried to smile. His palms turned sweaty, his heart pounded, and his tongue felt clumsy. Even Susannah hadn't had such a strange effect on him. "It was all real good. Enjoyed the visiting, too."

She tugged at the rounded hemline of her long shirtwaist. "I . . . I did, too. It was nice to get acquainted with more of Walnut Hill's residents. The . . . the Coopers seem very nice, and . . ."

Her voice drifted off, and she lowered her chin, showing him the neat part down the center of her head. Her hair looked sleek and shiny in the sunlight pouring through the open door. Joel decided it was a good thing he had his hands full of turkey and apple pie, because if they were free, he'd be lifting her chin and planting a kiss on her mouth.

He gulped. "I—"

"I—" She raised her face and spoke at the same time. The pink in her cheeks deepened to red. "Go ahead."

Joel couldn't remember what he'd planned to say. "That's all right. You go ahead."

Her rosy lips formed a timid smile. "I wanted to thank you for your kind prayer . . . when you said I was a blessing." To Joel's surprise, tears winked in her green-flecked eyes. "It meant a great deal to me."

"I meant it." His thick tongue managed to form the words. "You're a fine teacher, an' my boys are lucky to have you. You are a blessin', E— Miss Amsel."

Her smile blossomed, and with her face all aglow from sunshine, she might have been an angel come down from Heaven. Joel took a stumbling step toward the door. "Boys're waitin' in the wagon. I . . . I best go."

She stood near, her hands clasped sweetly at her waist. "Good-bye, Mr. Townsend. Happy Thanksgiving."

"Happy Thanksgiving." He dashed out the door before he tossed aside the turkey and pie and gathered the woman in his arms.

Chapter
NINETEEN

Throughout the month of December, Mr. Townsend's Thanksgiving prayer echoed through Edythe's heart time and time again. *A blessing,* he'd called her. The weather turned frigid, and snow blanketed the prairie. Wind shaped the glistening flakes into drifts that made trekking to school a challenge. But she bundled up and set out each day, undeterred and determined to prove his words true.

She had company for the chilly walk. Although Missy had argued that she was "too old" for book learning, Edythe enrolled her in school. She made clear her intention for Missy to graduate from the Walnut Hill school and then go on to high school . . . somewhere. If they remained in Walnut Hill, she'd send Missy to Lincoln Valley for high school; if they returned to Omaha, she'd insist her sister attend high school there. Either way, Missy would be educated. Edythe refused to compromise on that issue.

Missy spoke often of returning to Omaha at the end of the school year so they'd be close to Justus and Eulah, who were expecting their first child. As much as Edythe longed to spend time with her new niece or nephew, she also wanted to stay in Walnut Hill. To teach. To be a blessing. Nobody—except Mama, who'd been gone for more than a decade—had ever called her a blessing.

The Monday after Thanksgiving, Martha Sterbinz had shyly approached Edythe and asked if they could have a Christmas program at the school. "The teacher we had before Mr. Shanks let us do a program at Christmas, an' it was real nice to have all our folks here. May we do one again?" she'd said. Edythe initially considered refusing—at times she felt overwhelmed keeping the multiple grade levels on task and moving forward. But after considering the girl's request, she decided it might be the perfect way to bring all of the parents in Walnut Hill together. And it opened the door to a study of world cultures that excited her as much as she hoped it would the children.

Using geography textbooks and a children's storybook called *All Around the World*, they researched Christmas traditions from different countries. She divided the class into four groups, mixing younger students with older ones. Edythe allowed each group to select one of the countries from which their ancestors had originated— Germany, Sweden, or England; or the country that was now their home—America. Lively arguments ensued, but eventually each group settled on a country.

The children cut twelve-inch-tall paper dolls from brown paper and used fabric pieces from Luthenia's scrap basket to dress the dolls in ways that reflected their chosen country. Younger students drew maps, and older ones wrote reports. Edythe became accustomed to hearing them share snippets about "their" country's imports and exports, famous leaders, or unique geographical features. The display wall proved inadequate to hold all of their handiwork, so Edythe allowed them to tack their projects on every available space. Soon the classroom walls wore a patchwork of colorful drawings, brightly costumed dolls, and neatly written essays.

Watching the children work together thrilled Edythe's teacher heart. In addition to gaining information about the world, they were learning cooperation, compromise, and organization—all crucial life skills. Edythe thanked Martha repeatedly for suggesting the program. The girl's idea had opened the door to a wonderful experience.

Each day, in place of recess, they practiced for the upcoming program. The children already knew the Christmas hymn "Silent Night," but Edythe taught them the German words as well. She wished she could teach them the lyrics in Swedish, but Martha suggested having a Swedish treat in place of a Swedish song. Edythe deemed it a perfect suggestion and added,

"Martha, you would make a wonderful teacher." The girl's pleased blush had given Edythe's heart a lift.

The month of December was the cheeriest month of the school year despite the cold and snow, despite the toes-freezing walk, despite the runny noses and the musty smell of wool mittens drying on the woodstove's fenders. Edythe would have called the final weeks of 1882 perfect had it not been for two students who proved to be the proverbial flies in the ointment.

William's uncooperative attitude didn't surprise Edythe. She'd deliberately placed him in a group with the two little Ellsworth girls—who were so dependent on each other they even needed the outhouse at the same time—Henry Libolt, and Missy. She hoped his position as the group's oldest boy would encourage him to assume leadership. And certainly William led . . . but not in a positive manner.

For reasons beyond Edythe's understanding, Missy giggled at everything William did. No matter how many times Edythe lectured her sister on the importance of focusing on her studies instead of dallying with a boy, or how many times Missy promised to try harder, each day ended the same—with Edythe frustrated by William's behavior, angered by her sister's blatant flirtation, and heartsick. The other girls didn't like William, so Missy's fascination with the boy distanced her from the ones who could become her friends if only she would allow it.

The closer they came to December twenty-second—program day—the greater the children's excitement grew. Each student created an invitation for their parents or someone else in the community, and their voices rang with enthusiasm when they shared with Edythe that Uncle Milton or Grandma Betty was planning to come. Edythe hoped the little schoolhouse would be able to hold everyone. She also hoped the visitors would enjoy the program. Her students would be so disappointed otherwise. And so would she.

"Boy, are you tryin' to grow potatoes in your ears?" Joel dipped the cloth in the wash pan and went after Robert again.

The boy squirmed, giggling as Joel reamed his ears with the cloth. "Stop it! It tickles!"

"Hold still an' I'll be done a lot faster." Joel clamped his knees on Robert's hips to hold him in place. Another twist of the cloth, and then he peeked at Robert's ear. He let out a whoosh of breath. "Finally." He released his hold, and Robert scampered several feet away, shaking his head like a dog dislodging a tick.

Joel glanced at the face of his windup timepiece. "Get dressed now. We need to leave in less'n fifteen minutes or you'll be late to your program."

"Yes, sir!" Robert darted for the bedroom.

Johnny, wearing his Sunday clothes, sat on the long wooden bench that served as a sofa. Joel quirked his finger at him. "Come here, Johnny—lemme see your ears."

The boy's eyes flew wide. "They're clean, Uncle Joel, honest. Scrubbed 'em good."

Joel didn't doubt him—Johnny rarely fibbed. But he said, "Lemme check anyway, just to be sure. Hard for a fella to see behind his own ears."

With a sigh, Johnny rose and scuffed across the floor. He patiently allowed Joel's scrutiny. Joel grinned. "Clean as a whistle."

"Told'ja," the boy huffed. An impish grin creased his face. "How 'bout yours? Should I check 'em for you?"

"Mine?"

"You said it's hard for a fella to see his own ears. Might be you got dirt hidin' in there an' don't know it."

Joel aimed a teasing swat at Johnny's backside, and Johnny ducked away, giggling. Shaking his head, Joel carried the wash pan and rag to the dry sink. He dumped the pan and draped the rag over its edge, then turned to spot Robert bounding out of his bedroom. The boy careened to a halt and held out his arms.

"All dressed! Let's go!" He charged for the door.

"Hold up there." Joel strode across the floor and captured Robert. He untucked the boy's shirttails, then retucked them neatly. "That's better. Got to look dapper for your program."

Robert squinted up at him. "Dapper? What's that?"

Johnny ambled to join them. "It means handsome."

"Oooh." Robert stuck out his belly and ran his hands up and down his shirt front. "Am I handsome, Uncle Joel?"

"You'll do. Now grab your coats, scarves, and mittens—it's a cold one."

Joel and the boys rode in companionable silence beneath a clear black sky peppered with stars. For once, the wind had calmed, and even though the air was crisp, it didn't cut. Surely the pleasant evening would bring everyone to the school program.

The wagon rolled into the schoolyard, and Joel's pulse doubled its tempo when he spotted all the wagons already lined up. Johnny called from the back, "Lookit! Lotsa folks here, huh, Uncle Joel?"

"Looks to be half the town. You boys climb down an' go on in so Miss Amsel knows you're here." The boys leaped out and dashed away. He chuckled. Used to be, the only way he could get them to run toward the schoolhouse was threaten to set the wagon on fire. Miss Amsel had worked a miracle.

Perspiration broke out across his back, sending a prickle of awareness up his spine and over his scalp. He wrapped the reins around the brake and hopped down. But then he stood beside the wagon, as if his feet had frozen to the ground. *Miss Amsel . . .* He'd seen her in church every Sunday since Thanksgiving, but like a bashful schoolboy, he hadn't been able to gather up his nerve to talk to her. Tonight he'd have to speak to her—she'd be handing out the pupils' half-year marks at the end of the program. Torn between anticipation and anxiety, he curled his hand over the edge of the wagon bed, seeking the courage to move forward.

The rattle of wagon wheels intruded, and he jerked to life. He waited beside the door for the Jeffers family to alight, then he held the door for them. Patience and Sophie hunched their shoulders and giggled as they passed him, and their parents thanked him. Joel grinned in reply, tipping his hat to Miz Jeffers. But once they'd all cleared the door, he had no excuse to linger. Drawing a breath, he stepped inside.

Coats, scarves, and mittens decorated the small cloakroom. He added his to the mix, wondering at the likelihood of finding them again when it came time to leave. Running his hands over his smooth-tucked shirt front, much the way Robert had, he turned toward the door leading to the classroom. The cloakroom reeked of damp wool, but he picked up the scents of cinnamon and apples drifting from the other room. The pleasant aroma drew him forward.

Townsfolk filled the schoolroom. Their voices created an unmusical hum. All of the seats were taken by women and small children, so the men and older boys lined the walls. Miss Amsel stood at the front corner of the room with the children clustered close to her. He almost waved to her but caught himself in time. Shoving his hands into his pockets, he wriggled into a tiny wedge of space between bulky Andy Bride and Terrill Sterbinz.

He'd no more than settled his shoulder blades against the cold windowpane than Miss Amsel stepped onto the teacher's platform. As if they'd received a signal, everyone hushed. She smiled, but Joel thought he detected a slight tremble in her lips. *Lord, let her relax an' enjoy the evenin'. Give her peace an' assurance.*

"Welcome to our program." Her voice came out strong.

Joel couldn't hide a grin—she'd be fine.

"We appreciate your coming out on this frosty night. The children have worked hard, and I trust you'll enjoy what they've prepared." She briefly described the monthlong study Johnny and Robert had jabbered about for the past weeks, then she turned to the students. "We'll start with Sweden—Martha, Sophie, Ada, Johnny, and Josephine."

Joel swallowed chuckles at childish mishaps and clapped with the other audience members at the close of each group's presentation. He hadn't known Swedish girls wore a crown of candles in honor of St. Lucia as part of their Christmas celebration, or that the first steam engine was built in England. From the pleased nods and murmurs of other attendees, he figured they were also impressed with all the kids had learned.

After the final group shared their project about America, Martha Sterbinz stepped up and explained, in a voice so soft he had to strain to hear her, the history behind the beloved hymn "Silent Night." Then all of the students from oldest to youngest joined Martha on the platform. Some wore makeshift costumes, and they formed a manger scene as Miss Amsel led them in a sweet, if slightly off-key, rendition of "Silent Night."

While the kids sang, Joel glanced around. Folks who'd questioned Miss Amsel's tactics in the past beamed with approval. A few sang along, their heads bobbing slowly with the music. Even Hank Libolt had shed his usual scowl. Joel's chest expanded in pride for what the schoolmarm had accomplished. On this night, at least, everyone seemed to agree she'd done something right.

Chapter
TWENTY

"Thank you for bringing treats to share." Edythe gave Mrs. Sterbinz's hand a warm squeeze. "Everyone enjoyed the Swedish bread braids." Edythe's tongue still tingled pleasantly from the flavor of cinnamon.

"You are very welcome, Miss Amsel." Mrs. Sterbinz smiled shyly, much like her daughter often did. "Martha and I enjoy baking together."

"She's as good at baking as she is at schoolwork." Edythe slipped Martha's grade report into the woman's hands. "Highest marks in all subjects." She sent a warm smile in Martha's direction. The girl flushed bright pink.

Terrill Sterbinz stepped behind Martha and reached past his sister's shoulder to take Edythe's hand. "She's got a fine teacher. Thanks for all your hard work, Miss Amsel." The man winked.

Edythe's cheeks heated. She jerked her hand free of Terrill's and glanced down the straggling line of remaining families. Had anyone witnessed the man's brazen behavior? Her throat tight, she squeaked out, "Merry Christmas." The Sterbinz family moved on, and others took their place.

Edythe greeted each family with a smile and

expressed her appreciation for their attendance. She handed parents grade reports, offering a kind word about every child—even William Sholes, who achieved excellent grades despite his misbehavior. Her heart swelled as she mentioned Louisa's tender spirit, Jane's hardworking attitude, or Andrew's advanced mathematical abilities. Occasionally her voice quavered with emotion. Could her year with them really be half over? It had gone far too quickly.

Edythe forced herself not to cringe when the Libolt family stepped forward. She fully expected criticism from Mr. Libolt. But he gave her hand a quick, impersonal shake, then stepped aside without a word. Stunned by his uncharacteristic silence, Edythe gave a little start when Mrs. Libolt touched her arm.

"Hank and me both enjoyed the program." The woman spoke so softly and hesitantly, Edythe had to tip forward to hear her voice. "Especially the singing. Been a long time since we heard 'Stille Nacht.' Took us back to when we were young'uns." She closed her eyes for a moment, a sweet smile curving her chapped lips, and Edythe's gaze flicked to Mr. Libolt. She tried to imagine the taciturn man as a child singing "Stille Nacht," but the image wouldn't form. Mrs. Libolt shifted her youngest child, Claude, to her other hip and went on, "You did a fine job tonight."

Edythe nodded her appreciation for the kind words, making certain she met Mr. Libolt's gaze directly. Although he didn't smile in return, neither did he frown. She slipped the Libolt children's grade reports into their mother's hand. Little Will and Anna barreled against her for a hug, but nine-year-old Henry opted for a handshake. After wishing her a merry Christmas, the Libolts moved on. Still smiling, Edythe shifted to greet the next family. Her heart somersaulted in her chest when she found her hand captured by Joel Townsend's.

"Good program, Miss Amsel."

She'd heard similar words from many other parents, but coming from this man, they meant more. She couldn't understand why, but his compliment weaseled its way to the center of her soul and lingered. "Th-thank you." She glanced at Johnny and Robert, who stood at their uncle's side, beaming up at her. "The boys did a fine job. I was proud of them."

"It was fun!" Robert rocked in place. "I wanna do a program every month."

Johnny shook his head at his brother. "Don't be silly. Christmas don't come every month."

Robert hunched his shoulders. "Oh, guess that's right . . ."

Edythe laughed and tugged Robert into a hug. "If everyone studies as hard the last half of the year as you did the first half, perhaps we'll have an end-of-the-year program. Would you like that?"

"Yes, ma'am!"

"Go get your coats an' things, boys," Mr. Townsend said, and the boys shot off. He sent a quick glance over his shoulder. "Others're waitin', so I don't want to take too much of your time, but . . . you did fine tonight. Real fine."

Her lips trembled with her smile. "Thank you, Mr. Townsend. The children worked very hard."

"I'm sure they did, but I wasn't speakin' of the children." He risked another quick glance behind him, then lowered his voice. "You brought everybody together tonight . . . gave 'em a reason to be proud of their kids an' proud of the school. You did real good, Miss Amsel."

Edythe's face flooded with fire. She knew she would never forget his words, his expression, or the way he made her feel. Competent, talented, wanted. Her chest ached with the desire to thank him for recognizing the depth of her care for the children. But her voice seemed to have fled. All she could do was offer a nod and hope he read the appreciation in her eyes. His expression softened, and somehow she knew he understood.

He started to move on, and she remembered the boys' grade reports. "Wait!" The word burst out, and he sent her a startled glance. She waved the reports. "The boys' . . ." Her voice cracked.

He grinned and reached for the reports. His

fingers brushed hers as he took the folded pages from her hand, and a delightful tremor traveled from her fingertips all the way to her scalp. She giggled, the sound similar to the one she'd heard leave Missy's lips when the girl flirted with William Sholes. She clamped her hand over her mouth. He gave another dimpled grin and then clumped away.

Ducking her head, Edythe brought herself under control and then managed to turn her attention to the Wolcotts. But even as she hugged Ada and praised the little girl's tremendous progress in reading, her stomach trembled. She'd grown to love these children, yes, but a part of her recognized the stirrings of love for someone else, too. And that feeling had no place in her heart.

"There you are, Joel." Wally Scheebeck pushed a crate across the counter. "Looks to all be there."

Joel peeked in the box, grinning. Wouldn't the boys be surprised to find toys under the tree on Christmas morning? They'd pored over the Montgomery Ward catalog, circling nearly every item on the six pages committed to play items. Not being a wealthy man, he couldn't indulge the boys' every wish, but he thought they'd be satisfied with iron mechanical banks, tin soldiers, and a chariot pulled by a tin horse painted in similar colors to their own dependable Jody.

"Lucky they came today," Wally said, swishing his palm across the wood counter to remove bits of sawdust. "Tomorrow's Sunday an' the day after that's Christmas—if they hadn't come today, you'd have some disappointed young'uns."

"True enough." Joel balanced the crate against his hip. "They'd still have gifts to open—I got 'em each a new shirt an' britches, an' I've got apples, peanuts, and a striped stick candy for their stockings. But that's not the same as toys."

"Nope. Runnin' the store like I do, my young'uns seem to think every toy on the shelf is meant for them rather than for payin' customers." Then he chuckled. " 'Course, at Christmas, it's hard not to indulge 'em."

If Joel had endless cash on hand, he'd indulge Johnny and Robert. Probably spoil them good. Maybe it was best he had to limit his spending.

"Will we see you an' the boys at the church Christmas service?"

" 'Course. Wouldn't miss it." Joel looked forward to this service every year, when the whole town came together to hear the Christmas story read from the Bible, sing carols until their voices were hoarse, and then visit. Although every church service held meaning for Joel, the Christmas one was extra special with its focus on the Gift sent into the world by God so long ago. "Will your family be there?"

"Sure will." Wally's chest puffed. "It'll be the first time to take baby Wallace out, y'know."

"Doc gave the go-ahead, huh?" Joel figured the women in town would flock around Mrs. Scheebeck and that new baby. Women's fascination with babies didn't make much sense to him—newborns were about as pretty as baby birds and didn't do much more than cry and sleep. But women cooed and carried on like babies were the most clever thing around. Would he feel differently if the babe were his own?

"Doc says it's fine 'long as we bundle him up good an' don't let nobody cough on him." Wally's grin stretched across his thin face. "He's really somethin', Joel. Growin' like a weed—still tiny, for a month-old baby, but doin' good." The man heaved a sigh. "Our prayers've been answered for sure. Need to get him to church an' tell God how thankful we are to have him."

For a moment, Joel experienced a pang of jealousy. But he pushed the emotion aside and bounced the crate. "It'll be good to see you all in church again. I best be gettin' back. I left the boys alone, and Robert gets fidgety if I'm gone too long."

Joel swung open the door and nearly plowed headlong into Miss Amsel, who bustled across

211

the boardwalk with her head down. "Whoa!" The word left his lips involuntarily, and she looked up, surprise widening her eyes.

"Excuse me!" She clutched mittened hands to her throat.

Joel chuckled. His breath hung heavy on the crisp air. "No harm done. Here . . ." He held the door for her. "Get on in there out of the cold."

But she remained on the porch and stared at him, standing so still he wondered if her shoes had sent down roots. If he hadn't known better, he would've thought she was looking at a ghost.

"Miss Amsel?"

She gave a little start. "Please forgive me. My mind . . . it wandered for a moment."

He laughed. "Christmas'll do that to a person." He released the door, and it slapped into its frame. "You doin' some last-minute Christmas buyin'?"

She rubbed her lips together and looked off to the side. Her mind sure was wandering. What had her so lost in thought? Finally, her head bobbed, shifting the knitted scarf that covered her hair. "Yes. Well, actually no."

Joel chuckled softly, puzzled by her strange response.

She grinned sheepishly. "I suppose it is last-minute, but I haven't done any shopping at all yet. I-I've been so busy at school."

"Ah." Her dedication to her students continued

to impress him. "Well, last-minute's better than not at all."

She hung her head. "I hope my family echoes your sentiments."

"How's that?"

When she looked at him, he read remorse in her pinched expression. "My first year away, and I didn't mail any packages home. Although our Christmases were never elaborate, I always tried to do . . . something. They'll surely think I've forgotten all about them."

Joel was struck once again by how little he knew about the schoolmarm. The town council had announced she'd come from Omaha, and town gossip had it she'd been jilted by a beau, which was why she wouldn't let any men get close to her. He knew she'd lost her mother when she was younger and he suspected she held a lot of sadness over it. But most of her life remained a secret.

He braved a question. "Got a big family, do you?"

"Pretty big."

"They all back in Omaha?"

Two town ladies he didn't know well bustled up the walk. They smiled and chirped, "Merry Christmas!" Joel returned their greeting, and Miss Amsel shifted aside, allowing them to enter the mercantile. He expected her to follow them in—it was cold out here on the porch, and she had shopping to do—but she stayed outside. However, she kept her face angled away from him, presenting her profile. He didn't mind the view. Gave him a chance to examine her without her knowing it.

She spoke in a distant voice, almost as if she was talking to herself. "My brothers and sister— besides Missy, of course—reside in Omaha. As does my father."

Joel had only one brother, and he was dead. His folks and his aunts and uncles were gone, too, which left just him, Johnny, and Robert. Much as he loved the boys, he'd give most anything to be part of a big family Christmas like the ones they'd had with his relatives when he was small. "Kind of lonely, bein' without family this time of year," he mused.

"And sometimes it can be a blessing."

Joel wanted to ask her what she meant, but the bulky box resting on his hip bone reminded him he'd left the boys alone far too long. He inched toward his wagon. "I need to get home. I reckon the boys an' me will see you in church on Christmas, but just in case we don't get a chance to talk to you, have a merry Christmas."

Her brow crinkled as if she was confused. Then she offered a small nod. "Thank you. Merry Christmas to you. Please greet the boys for me."

"Will do." He plopped the crate in the back of the wagon, then tipped his hat. By the time he'd settled on the high wagon seat, she'd disappeared inside the store. He flicked the reins, setting Jody into motion. Her comment about it sometimes being a blessing to be far from family haunted him. Whatever kind of life she'd had before coming to Walnut Hill, it must not have been pleasant. Sympathy squeezed his chest, coupled with a strong desire to make things better for her.

His heart skipped a beat as an idea settled in. Clearly, Miss Amsel needed a family. And he had a ready-made family in need of a wife and mother to make it complete. He and Miss Amsel were perfect for each other.

She just didn't know it yet.

Chapter
TWENTY~ONE

Edythe moved slowly between the mercantile's aisles, fingering items. The usually well-stocked shelves looked picked over, mute evidence that many shoppers had already made their Christmas selections. The women who'd entered a few minutes ahead of her kept Mr. Scheebeck busy with a lengthy grocery order, giving her time to peruse the shelves and select Christmas gifts for Missy and Luthenia.

Unbidden memories from past Christmases clouded her mind. She'd done her best to make sure each of her siblings had something to open on Christmas morning, but the gifts were always handmade or practical items—never the things the children wished for. Her part-time job as a clerk and Pa's odd jobs when he felt up to working hadn't allowed for extras. She'd always felt guilty at Christmastime, as if she'd let everyone down. Surely there had been happy Christmases when Mama was alive and they all lived out on the farm—the days before Pa's bitterness fell like a thick wool blanket over their lives—but those times were buried under too many years of unpleasantness.

She rounded the corner, her gaze drifting to the window where Mr. Townsend's wagon had stood just a few minutes ago. She'd been thinking of him—thinking of his kindness—when he'd stepped out of the mercantile as if stepping directly out of her thoughts. Unnerving. Yet she'd stood and visited with him. Had opened up a small piece of herself to him.

The dread she'd experienced the night of the school program returned. The man was weaving himself into the fiber of her life. But she couldn't allow it. She could *not* give her heart to a man, no matter how handsome and kind he might be.

Mama had told her love was a wondrous thing, and Edythe admitted a part of her thrilled at the glorious feelings Mr. Townsend conjured within her. Never had her heart felt so light and fluttery as when he praised her. But beneath the warmth of blossoming affection resided an icicle of fear. If he felt the way she suspected, and if he asked to court her, she'd have to say no.

Marrying Joel Townsend meant becoming an instant mother to someone else's children. She'd already given fourteen years of her life to raising five children not her own—and she was still responsible for Missy. In addition, marrying meant she'd have to give up teaching, the dream she'd had for so long, the dream she'd only now achieved. Her heart plummeted as she faced the truth. She wanted freedom. No matter how appealing she found Joel Townsend—no matter how endearing his nephews—she did not want to be a surrogate mother to the orphaned boys and she did not want to give up her career. Somehow she must detach herself emotionally from Mr. Townsend.

"Miss Amsel?" Mr. Scheebeck bustled up beside her, brushing the front of his work apron with both palms. "You doin' all right?"

Although she couldn't honestly say she was all right—her emotions were tied into knots—she flashed a halfhearted smile and set aside her inner reflections. "I'm fine, thank you."

"All right. Holler if you need me." He ambled back to the counter as the door opened and another customer entered on a gust of chilly air.

With Mr. Scheebeck busy again, Edythe forced

herself to complete her selections. She preferred personal gifts, but the lack of merchandise limited her options. For Luthenia she chose two lace-embellished handkerchiefs and an ivory hair comb. The creamy ivory would look lovely against the older woman's brown-and-gray-streaked hair. Missy's recent infatuation with a boy proved she was growing up, so Edythe selected a bottle of lilac-scented toilet water, several lengths of ribbon, and a package of hairpins. Usually Missy wore her long hair down her back in unruly waves, but she was old enough to begin pinning it up. They might even have fun doing each other's hair.

After she paid for her selections, she slid a fat envelope across the counter to the mercantile owner. "I need to post this." She hoped Justus would forgive her mixing Christmas wishes with a request, but she needed him to ship Missy's belongings to Walnut Hill. If her sister was staying, she'd need more clothing and other personal effects.

Mr. Scheebeck squinted at the envelope. "Won't go out now 'til the day after Christmas."

"That's fine." She followed the man to the corner that housed the post office and watched him don his little blue hat. He found a stamp and pasted it into place for her while she checked her mail cubby. No letters waited for her, and for a moment, disappointment tried to take hold. Then she scolded herself for the silly thoughts. Hadn't she left Omaha to find freedom? Then why feel disheartened when her brothers and sister did not send her Christmas greetings?

In the letter to Justus, she'd included messages for her other brothers, Albert and Loren, and her sister Frances. But she didn't enclose a note for Pa. He wouldn't look at it, so there was no sense in wasting precious paper writing to him.

"All stamped an' in the bag, ready to go out on the twenty-sixth." Mr. Scheebeck returned his postman hat to its nail and swished his palms together. "You want me to wrap any of them things you bought? I still have some nice paper left—be glad to fancy them up for you."

"That would be very kind of you, Mr. Scheebeck. Thank you."

The man wrapped her gifts in bright-colored paper and bound each with red or green ribbon. Edythe marveled that her simple gifts could look so elegant. The packages bedecked, he shook out a discarded gunny sack and stacked them inside it. "So nobody can peek 'til you're ready," he said with a chuckle.

Edythe started to thank him, but he bent over behind the counter, disappearing from view. When he emerged, he held an oblong wooden box sporting a huge red ribbon. He pushed it across the counter to her. "This here is for you. Chocolates. Ordered 'em in from Chicago."

Edythe took the box, stunned into silence. She'd sold candy when she'd worked at the store in Omaha, but she rarely got to taste it. "What an extravagant gift!"

"Young'uns insisted on it. They think an awful lot of you, Miss Amsel." His voice turned gravelly, as if he'd embarrassed himself. "Hope you'll like it."

Edythe blinked, fighting the sting of tears. "I'm sure I will. Please thank Lewis and Jenny for me."

"Will do."

His reply mimicked Mr. Townsend's, bringing the man back to the forefront of her thoughts. "G-good day, Mr. Scheebeck. Merry Christmas." Edythe tucked the box of chocolates under her arm, lifted the gunny sack, and hurried outside. She turned her attention to her surroundings, trying to chase away the image of Joel Townsend that plagued her mind.

During her time in the mercantile, clouds had rolled in. They shielded the sun, making the day feel much colder. She shivered and sped her pace. The air smelled crisp and clean, and she walked briskly, her feet crunching on firm-packed snow and her breath hovering around her head in wisps of white that billowed and dissipated. Her gaze drifted across the rows of houses where lanterns glowed behind lace curtains. Tiny, quiet Walnut Hill . . . a lovely town.

A family town.

Her feet slowed. Joel's face once again loomed in her memory. Blue eyes fringed with thick lashes. That boyish dimple that appeared when he smiled. A handsome, clean-shaven, sincere face. A lump formed in Edythe's throat. If things were different—if she were different—she'd be flattered to have a man like Joel Townsend look at her with tenderness in his gaze. But things weren't different, and she couldn't accept his attentions.

She forced herself to resume a swift pace. As she rounded the corner to Luthenia's house, she made a decision that stung more fiercely than the cold air that nipped her nose. It would be impossible to separate herself from Joel and his nephews if she remained in this little community. If she couldn't bring her errant heart under control, she and Missy would have to leave Walnut Hill.

"Why do we have to go to church today?" Missy gave her long brown tresses furious swipes with Edythe's brush. "It's not Sunday."

"The town has a special Christmas service." Edythe pinned the cameo her mother had given her for her thirteenth birthday to the banded collar at her throat. She touched the ivory profile. At times like these, she missed her mother so badly her chest felt empty. "Luthenia said everyone goes—it's a tradition in Walnut Hill."

"But it isn't *our* tradition." Missy smacked the brush onto the dresser and whirled to face Edythe. "So why do *we* have to go?"

Edythe drew in a breath, searching for patience. "It's the town's tradition, and we are part of the town." *For now,* she added silently. "Besides, it won't hurt us to go. Here." She plucked a ribbon from the assortment she'd given Missy earlier that morning. "Let me tie your hair back—it'll show off the pretty embroidered collar Luthenia made for you."

Missy turned around but folded her arms over her chest. "You said everyone goes?"

Edythe's hands paused in brushing her sister's hair into a tail. She met Missy's gaze in the mirror. A conniving glint entered her sister's eyes as she gave a nod.

"I suppose I can go, then."

Edythe's fingers trembled slightly as she tied the ribbon in a neat bow. "Does your sudden interest in attending have anything to do with a certain young man?"

Missy giggled. "It sure isn't because I want to listen to Reverend Coker!" She touched her hair, smiling at her own image, then spun around and made a sour face. "Church is boring, Edie. And it doesn't seem fair to have to go on Christmas."

Sinking onto the edge of the bed, Edythe caught Missy's hand and tugged her down next to her. "Missy, about church . . . I know I didn't take you much when you were young, and I think I made a mistake." Edythe considered Luthenia's peaceful countenance, her giving ways. The older woman reminded Edythe of her mother. "Mama took great stock in attending services, and before she got so sick she always took us. But after she died—"

Missy's lips pinched tight, her gaze narrowing.

Edythe ignored her sister's rebellious look and continued. "It was easier to stay home. But church was important to Mama, so I think it should be important to us."

"Forever? Or just while we're stuck in this town?"

Stifling a sigh, Edythe put her arm around Missy's shoulders. "For at least while we're here. We can decide later if we want to continue going somewhere else."

Missy shrugged, dislodging Edythe's arm. She bounced up and checked her image again, tipping her head one way and then the other. "This collar is babyish. Do I have to wear it?"

Edythe nearly choked. Luthenia must have spent hours meticulously embroidering the tiny forget-me-nots and trailing vines on the crisp white muslin. Couldn't Missy appreciate the older woman's efforts? "You'll hurt Luthenia's feelings if you don't."

Another huff left Missy's lips. Edythe was

growing weary of Missy's dramatic expulsions of breath. "All right. But just for church," her sister said. That devious grin twitched at her cheeks again. "I'll tell her it's too nice to wear while I'm eating—I might soil it." She flounced out of the room before Edythe could form a reprimand.

Rolling her eyes heavenward, Edythe wondered when Missy had become so self-centered. She couldn't remember behaving so inconsiderately at her sister's age. The thought drew her up short. She'd had no opportunity for selfishness—responsibility had been thrust upon her far too early. Her irritation melted away. She would allow Missy a bit of self-indulgence. The time to grow up would come soon enough. And being around Luthenia and the churchgoing members of Walnut Hill would provide good examples for Missy to follow.

She reached for her gift from Luthenia—a Bible bound in black leather with gold gilt letters. She hadn't wanted to accept such an elaborate gift, but the older woman had waved away all her arguments. Then she'd teasingly said, " 'Sides, I wrote in it. Can't send it back!' "

Edythe opened the front cover and read the message again. *The Bible that is falling apart usually belongs to someone who isn't.* She puzzled over the odd transcription. It didn't make sense to her, but Luthenia sometimes possessed a strange sense of humor. She had no time to decipher it now—she needed to head downstairs or she'd make them all late to the Christmas service.

Hugging the Bible to her chest, she bustled down the stairs.

Chapter
TWENTY-TWO

" 'For unto you is born this day in the city of David a Saviour, which is Christ the Lord . . .' "

Edythe followed along in her brand-new Bible as Reverend Coker read with his usual serious, resounding tone. Memories of Christmases from long ago, and Mama's sweet voice reading the nativity story from the Bible, winged through her heart—precious memories of Mama sharing how Jesus Christ came to walk earthly soil, adopt human flesh, and fulfill His destiny as the world's Savior.

" 'Glory to God in the highest, and on earth peace, good will toward men . . .' "

A lump filled Edythe's throat. Something seemed to pull on her heart, bringing the desire to cry.

" 'And the shepherds returned, glorifying and praising God for all the things that they had heard and seen.' " Reverend Coker closed his Bible and smiled at the crowded congregation. "Shall we rise and praise God through song? Let us begin with 'It Came Upon a Midnight Clear.'"

Everyone stood—except the widow Meiner, whose hips gave her trouble, and Missy, who had apparently fallen asleep. Luthenia reached past Edythe and poked the girl. Missy leaped up, her face bright red. As it should be!

The beautiful carol, sung in perfect four-part harmony, echoed from the rafters and chased away Edythe's irritation with Missy. Chills of pleasure traveled up and down her spine. She sang at full voice, some words winging closer to her heart than others. "Look now, for glad and golden hours come swiftly on the wing . . ." If only she could capture glad and golden hours . . .

When they finished the carol, Reverend Coker led them in several more, each sung more robustly than the one before. Edythe's chest felt so full of joy and wonder she could hardly draw a breath, but on she sang, joining her Walnut Hill neighbors in exuberant celebration.

They closed their service with "Silent Night." The boisterous voices that moments ago had sung "Joy to the World" faded into a sweet melody of heartfelt worship. Repeatedly, Edythe dabbed at her eyes. Strange emotions—unfamiliar but not unwelcome—swirled through the center of her heart.

When the hymn ended, men handed out bags of goodies to the children. Their delighted squeals carried over the happy conversations buzzing through the sanctuary. Mr. Jeffers offered a bag to Missy, who took it with a polite thank-you. Then the girl scurried down the aisle to the bench where William Sholes stood with his parents. The two youngsters put their heads together and chatted.

Edythe frowned. What could she do about Missy's fascination with the Sholes boy? She set her worry aside as townsfolk greeted her, offering wishes for a merry Christmas. The two little Townsend boys raced over, and Robert plopped an orange in her hands. "Merry Christmas, Miss Amsel!"

Edythe gave the boy a hug. "Merry Christmas, Robert. And what's this?" She bounced the orange on her palm.

The boy beamed. "An or'nge! It's for you—for Christmas. Didn't have a present for you, so I want you to have my Christmas or'nge."

Johnny held out a fistful of peppermint candies. "An' these're from me."

"Well, my goodness, aren't I the lucky one?" Edythe cupped the goodies in her palms. "I feel so special! Thank you, boys."

Robert swung his sack of Christmas goodies, his grin wide. "You're welcome. I don't much like or'nges anyway."

Johnny socked his brother on the arm and shot him a fierce look. Robert yelped, puzzlement creasing his freckled face. Johnny turned an innocent look on Edythe. "I *like* peppermints. A *lot*."

Edythe swallowed a chortle. What a sweet boy to assure her he wasn't giving her his castoffs. She stuffed the orange and candies into her pockets, then wrapped both boys in a hug, planting a kiss on the tops of their shaggy blond heads. "And I really like being thought of. Merry Christmas, boys."

Robert wriggled loose. "Merry Christmas!" He bounded away.

Edythe slipped one of the peppermints from her pocket and pressed it into Johnny's hand. He flashed a bright smile. "Thank you! Merry Christmas!" He raced after his brother.

Luthenia ambled to Edythe's side, chuckling. "Those two . . . remind me so much of my own Titus and Timothy. My boys were ornery but bighearted scamps." She whisked tears away, and Edythe impulsively slipped her arm around the older woman's narrow waist. Luthenia released another chuckle. "I miss 'em, no denyin' it, but God was good to plant me in a town where I can spend my love on other people's young'uns. Reckon you understand that."

The woman gave a start. "Which reminds me! I want to tell Wally Scheebeck to come by an' get some of my gingerbread men for Lewis and Jenny. Their mama bein' busy with the baby, she doesn't have time for bakin' these days." She bustled away, leaving Edythe alone.

Edythe turned to locate Missy but found herself face-to-face with Joel Townsend. Her heart gave a leap of joy she couldn't squelch.

"Merry Christmas, Miss Amsel."

"M-merry Christmas to you." She wished her pulse would slow. She was as breathless as if she'd run a race. To cover her discomfort, she patted her pockets. "Your boys gave me some Christmas goodies—they're sweet to share."

Joel chuckled. "They're racin' around, getting all their greetings done so we can skedaddle home. I told them they'd have to wait 'til we got back from church to open their presents. They're fidgety—eager to get home, even if it does mean havin' to eat my cookin' on Christmas."

Edythe surprised herself by asking, "I assume one of their gifts is a meal without beans?"

He threw back his head and laughed. It tickled her that she'd amused him.

"No beans. Beef roast, taters, carrots—I put it all in before we left for church, just like Miz Kinsley explained, so we'll have us a fine dinner."

She nodded in approval. "Perfect."

"But I'd best hurry. Not sure how much longer I can keep 'em away from the presents." He took a step toward the open double doors at the front of the church.

Did regret tinge his voice? Even though she shouldn't encourage him, she wanted to chat with him a little longer. "We already opened ours." She trailed along beside him as he made his way through the crowd and held out her new Bible. "This was my gift from Luthenia."

Joel paused just inside the doors and admired it. "A fine gift."

Edythe smiled down at the black leather cover, fondness for its giver washing over her. "I've never had a Bible of my own, but I promised Luthenia I would read it."

Surprise broke across Joel's face. "You . . . you don't read God's Word? But you come to church every Sunday. I thought . . . I thought you were a woman of faith."

She shook her head. "I wouldn't say that." As soon as the words had left her mouth, Mr. Townsend's expression turned gloomy. She hugged the Bible tight against her ribs. "Did . . . did I say something wrong?"

He nodded emphatically. "How can I consider courting a woman who—"

Courting? How dare he blurt out such a thing? And in the church building on Christmas Day. Somehow the word held more meaning on this day in this place. Edythe took a backward step. "I can't be courted, Mr. Townsend. Especially not by . . . by *you*."

His frown deepened. "What's wrong with *me?*"

"N-nothing is fundamentally wrong with you, but . . . but . . ." Edythe reined in her galloping thoughts so she could speak plainly. "You come with a ready-made family. I've already raised one—my brothers and sisters. I have no desire to raise another. Besides, I'm a teacher. My heart belongs to my students." She heard the words and wanted them to be true, yet she knew in the very depth of her being that a part of her heart already belonged to this man who stood staring at her in dismay.

"I see." His voice was flat, devoid of its usual warmth.

Edythe spun to face the wide door opening. Children giggled, racing each other across the snow-blanketed ground. Horses snorted, bobbing their great heads as if eager to get moving. Folks shifted from foot to foot, visiting with neighbors, reluctant to leave the time of fellowship. Happiness filled the yard. She glanced at Mr. Townsend, who stared silently through the open church doors with pain in his eyes. A pain that matched the ache in her heart.

"G-good-bye, Mr. Townsend." She whispered the words and fled.

Chapter
TWENTY~THREE

Joel managed to exclaim over the whistle Johnny had whittled for him out of a twig and even delighted the boys by blasting out a warbling trill. When Robert acted downcast because he didn't have a gift for his uncle, Joel assured him helping with the dinner cleanup would be a fine present, and the boy immediately cheered. Throughout dinner he chatted and behaved as if he overflowed with Christmas cheer. But the enjoyment of a special meal was lost beneath the weight of disappointment.

When dinner was over, he and the boys cleaned up, and he made sure he did lots of teasing to keep the mood light. But when the boys carted off their new toys to play in their room, Joel stopped pretending and allowed his countenance to fall.

She doesn't want to raise a family. . . .

Twice in his lifetime he'd opened his heart to a woman, and twice he'd been disappointed. He slumped onto the rough settee and stared into the fireplace. Flames snapped and danced, seeming to laugh at him. He felt every bit the fool.

After losing Susannah to his brother, he hadn't thought he'd ever find the courage to love again.

232

Then along came Edythe Amsel with her sweet smile and gentle ways, and his heart had stirred to life. How many times had he imagined her in his home? In his mind's eye, he could see it so clearly. Edythe sitting at his table, cooking at his stove, waiting on the porch with a welcoming smile at the end of a day. . . .

He'd never been a man given to fanciful reflections, but somehow it'd been easy to picture her as a part of his life. He shook his head, trying to send the persistent images away. She didn't want him or his boys. Besides, he knew better than to yoke himself with an unbeliever. How could two become one without a solid faith in God at the center of their relationship? It was impossible. He needed to put any thoughts of courting Miss Amsel from his mind.

Giggles erupted from the boys' room. The cheerful sounds contradicted the deep sorrow holding Joel captive. He thumped his feet on the floor and rose to pace the room. He ran his hand through his hair, agitation making his movements jerky. The third time past the fireplace, he stopped and braced his hand on the rough wood mantel. He stared into the fire, which was beginning to die as the logs were consumed. Fires died without fuel. Maybe love would fizzle out, too, if it went unfed. So he'd starve himself of Miss Amsel's company. No visiting at school, no searching her out at church, no stops at Miz Kinsley's. The boys might fuss some, being denied Miz Kinsley's cookies, but he'd be firm.

Heaving a sigh, he mumbled, "It'll be easier to be firm with them than with myself. That woman is near impossible to resist." He drew his hand down his face, releasing a heavy sigh. "Heaven, help me . . ."

"Y'know, Missy's old enough to stay by herself if you change your mind."

Edythe glanced up from reading *The Nebraska Times*. Luthenia stood poised at the front door, her hand on the doorknob. The woman wore her nicest dress—a navy blue worsted with a creamy lace collar. The ivory comb Edythe had given Luthenia glistened in her hair, making her look very elegant. Embarrassed by her own shoddy appearance, Edythe tugged the tattered collar of her mother's old robe closer around her throat and wriggled more fully into the pillows on the parlor settee. "I'm staying in."

"Seems a shame you have to miss the New Year's Eve service." A winsome smile played on the older woman's face. "It's a fine time for the townsfolk. Lots of food, lots of merrymaking . . . sayin' good-bye to the old an' ringin' in the new." She tipped her head, her expression hopeful. "I'll wait if you want to hurry an' get gussied up."

For a moment, Edythe reconsidered. Missy's sniffles, the result of staying out too long on an iced-over pond with some of the other town children yesterday, made her grumpy, but she didn't require constant care. Her sister's illness was a flimsy excuse to miss the service.

After an entire week away from the busyness of school, Edythe longed for a little excitement and noise. But surely Joel Townsend would be at the New Year's Eve celebration. The church building was small. She couldn't possibly avoid him if she went. So she had to stay home.

"I need to be here in case Missy needs something." Edythe forced herself to smile. "Besides, a quiet evening before school starts again on Tuesday will be good for me."

Luthenia huffed, reminding Edythe of Missy. "You've had a slew of quiet evenin's of late. Why, you haven't left the house since Christmas—not even to check the mail. Seems to me what a young woman needs is a little noise an' excitement."

Edythe nearly laughed—once again Luthenia had voiced her thoughts nearly verbatim. Stifling her smile, she answered, "You go on and have a good time. Don't worry a bit about Missy and me." She lifted the newspaper and pretended to read, humming to herself.

Luthenia sighed. "All right, then. I'll be back shortly after midnight. No need to wait up."

"I'll leave the lamp lit for you. Happy New Year, Luthenia."

Her landlady grunted in reply. Cold air whisked into the room when she stepped out the door. Her footsteps on the porch boards *clip-clopped* and then faded away. Silence fell like a club, and melancholy instantly gripped her. Edythe hadn't realized how dismal the house felt without its mistress. Luthenia's cheerful chatter and constant movement filled the little dwelling with life.

Setting the newspaper aside, she padded to the window. Wagons rolled past, all aimed for the center of town, where the church stood. Should she get dressed and go? Missy would likely sleep all evening. She whirled away from the window and flumped back onto the sofa. Hadn't she decided she must stay away from Joel Townsend? That meant no town gatherings, no socializing, and no—

She stopped herself before silently declaring "no church." Luthenia expected her to attend, her own mother had encouraged it, Missy needed it, and Edythe had developed a yearning for it that mystified her. She would go to services each Sunday at the little steepled chapel. "But no other town gatherings," she stated aloud, her voice echoing in the quiet room.

Snatching up the newspaper again, she rattled the pages to make some noise. With determination, she forced herself to focus on reading. She'd purchased a subscription to *The Nebraska Times* so she could use it as a resource at the school. It arrived in her mail cubby a full week after its release, but the information was still valuable.

She'd been amazed at how little understanding her students possessed of the world outside of their town. The newspaper brought bits and pieces of the world to them. Eventually, she intended to require her oldest students to write their own essays on world events. But for now, she simply assigned articles to read. But she couldn't assign something on which she was unaware. So she needed to read it, too.

Flipping the pages from front to back, she scanned the headlines. The words "Married Women's Property Act Adopted" captured her attention. She angled the page to catch the lantern's glow. As she read, her heart began to pound. She finished the article, then crumpled the paper in her lap and stared unseeingly across the quiet parlor. Mixed emotions made her belly churn. What a difference it would have made for her family if this act, adopted in England, was law in America.

Memories tugged Edythe backward in time to her earliest recollections on Grandfather Keiler's farm. How Edythe had loved the farm! Just a simple sod house on a square of treeless plain, miles from town. And so much work to do—feeding the chickens and the baby pigs and helping Mama in the garden . . . Yet joy existed on that plot of ground.

Part of it, surely, was Grandfather's pride of ownership. Even as a very small child, she had recognized the effort required to build a farm on the untamed plains. But Grandfather had worked willingly, pouring his heart and soul into the land. He had bequeathed the property to Mama—his only living child—on his deathbed. But Mama was married to Pa, which gave Pa ownership of the land.

Edythe crunched her eyes, images exploding in her brain. Pa walking behind the plow. She carrying a water bucket so Pa could quench his thirst. Pa backhanding his moist lips, smiling in thanks, and returning to work. Ma greeting Pa at the end of a day with a smile and a kiss. Those days at the farm, despite hard work and battling nature for a harvest, were happy days.

Edythe couldn't recall a single day of bitterness from Pa, no slump to his shoulders—not even when their crop dried up from lack of rain. "We still have land," Pa had declared, his head high. "A man who owns land is never wanting."

And then the railroad men came.

She bent at the waist, across her own lap, crushing the paper beneath her arms. The men had promised Pa money to lay track on the land. Money sounded good—especially since they wouldn't receive a return on their failed harvest. Mama asked to see the contract, but the men said Ma had no standing—their dealings were with Pa, the legal owner of the land.

Had they known Pa couldn't read? Pride prevented him from admitting the inability. He wouldn't dare divulge it to men in fine suits with fancy words on their tongues and glib smiles on their faces. Without reading a word of the contract he made his X. After the men left, Mama read the papers from beginning to end. Tears ran down her face when she pointed out the lines that declared the land now belonged to the railroad, not the family. Pa refused to believe it—said Mama certainly had misunderstood. But he had no choice except to believe when the railroad men came and ran them off the acres Grandfather had crossed an ocean to claim.

In Omaha, Pa took a job cleaning stalls in a livery, but never with his shoulders square or his head raised high. Shame and bitterness became his constant companion. The bitterness broke him down, and when Mama died, he disappeared into melancholy.

Edythe sat up, surprised to find the crumpled newspaper damp with her tears. She wiped her eyes and then flattened the paper as best she could against her knees. She pressed her fingertips to the article. In England, women—even married women—could now legally own property. No longer would their holdings automatically transfer to their husbands.

"America needs such a law." Her voice cracked on the whispered declaration. Had a similar law been in place when the railroad men came, Pa wouldn't have been tricked out of Grandfather's hard-won land. Mama could read—she would never have signed her name to the contract. And Edythe's family might still be living happily on Grandfather Keiler's farm.

Resolve filled Edythe's middle, straightening her spine. When attending normal school, she'd overheard some younger women discuss suffrage—forcing the government to bestow the same voting rights on women that men legally possessed. At the time she'd ignored their talk. Her focus had been on earning her teaching certificate. Now the idea of supporting suffrage returned. She still wanted to teach—none of *her* students would be handicapped by an inability to read—but a new desire burned within her soul.

The town council might disapprove, but Edythe couldn't worry about them. Whatever she could do to bring this English Act to America, she would do it.

Chapter
TWENTY~FOUR

"But that isn't fair!"

Edythe had sent grades one through five to the back half of the classroom and brought the older students to the front for a lesson on government. She'd read the article about English parliament's change in property ownership laws and then explained the laws that existed in America. Her explanation had prompted Jane's uncharacteristic outburst.

Ordinarily, Edythe discouraged the children from speaking out of turn, but she'd never seen Jane so passionate. She sat on the edge of her desk and flipped her palm toward the girl. "Why isn't it fair, Jane?"

Jane's dark eyes flashed. "What's mine should be mine an' what's yours should be yours. If a lady has somethin' that's hers, it isn't fair that she has to hand it over to her husband just 'cause they got married. It should still be hers."

William Sholes, the only boy in the group, snorted.

Jane whirled on him. "I s'pose you think it's fine for a wife to have to hand over her belongings."

He shrugged, examining a hangnail on this thumb. "Yep, I do."

Edythe shook her head. "That isn't a sufficient answer, William. *Why* do you think it's right for a husband to take possession of his wife's property?"

The boy sent Edythe a sardonic look. " 'Cause women don't know how to take care of anything."

The girls erupted with a torrent of protests. Edythe waved her hands. "Class! Quiet now!" Another few seconds of chaos reigned, but then the girls fell silent. They continued to scowl at William, however. Even Missy looked perturbed.

"William, I'd like to hear your reasoning." Edythe ignored the girls' aghast expressions. "A further explanation is needed for us to understand."

William threw his arms wide. "Who works the fields? The men. Who feeds an' waters an' curries the horses? The men. Who builds the barns an' sharpens the plow blades an' harvests the corn?" He sent a triumphant look around the circle of irritated female faces. "The men do the work. So why shouldn't they own the land an' the animals an' the buildings?"

The girls exploded with another round of arguments. The younger children lifted their heads and looked toward the front of the room. Although Edythe wanted the older students to each have their say, she would have to insist upon some semblance of order.

She clapped her hands sharply. "Girls, one at a time." All five waved their hands in the air, each eager face begging to be chosen first. Edythe pointed at Louisa Bride.

Louisa faced William. "Sure the men take care of the plowin' and plantin', but what about the house? What man takes care of the house?"

From the back of the room, a childish voice piped up. "My uncle Joel."

Titters sounded in response.

Edythe gave Robert Townsend a nod. "Thank you, Robert. But you need to finish your arithmetic assignment."

With a sigh, Robert bent back to his work.

Louisa poked William on the shoulder. "What *married* man"—she whisked a frowning glance toward Robert—"takes care of the house?"

William let out another derisive snort. "Wife *oughtta* take care of her husband's house considerin' all the work he does."

Martha's hand shot into the air. "But, William, using your reasoning, if a man should have ownership of the things he takes care of, then it only makes sense that a woman should have ownership of the things she takes care of."

The other girls voiced their agreement. William rolled his eyes and slumped in his seat.

Sophie Jeffers, the youngest of the group, raised her hand, waggling her fingers at Edythe. "Can I ask you somethin'?"

"Certainly."

"How come the law's set up that way?"

"'Cause a bunch of selfish men made the laws," Missy mumbled.

William leaned sideways to sneer into her face. "That's 'cause men know best."

"Says who?" Missy challenged.

"Says me." His chest puffed up. "But not just me. Even God says so."

"God?" Missy yelped. "He does not!"

"Does too." William folded his arms over his chest, looking smug. "Miss Amsel, you got a Bible in your desk. Look it up. There's a verse in Ephesians that says the husband is the head of the wife." He smirked at Missy. "An' if he's the head of the wife, then he's the head of everything she's got."

"Well, you'd never be the head of anything of *mine*." Missy stuck her nose in the air.

William slapped his knee and laughed loudly.

The discussion was moving in a direction Edythe didn't intend to pursue. "That's enough for today. Before class tomorrow, I want each of you to write a three-paragraph essay on property ownership laws. Express your opinion, but also give reasons to support your opinion. We'll share our essays tomorrow, but now it's time for us to take out our readers."

She raised her voice to address all of the students. "Everyone, back to your own seats."

• • •

Edythe carefully turned the pages of her new Bible. Thanks to the table of contents, she'd easily located the book of Ephesians. But the book contained six chapters and many, many verses. How would she locate the verse William had mentioned?

On the opposite side of Luthenia's kitchen table, Missy *scritch-scritched* her pen across a piece of paper. With the tip of her tongue peeking from the corner of her mouth and her eyebrows crunched together, she was a picture of concentration. Edythe wanted to ask Luthenia to leave the dishwashing long enough to help her find the Scripture passage, but she hated to disrupt Missy's focus. Rarely did Missy take schoolwork so seriously.

So she turned pages, her eyes seeking, wondering if she might be pursuing a fruitless chase. William wasn't the most trustworthy source. However, the fact that he attended church regularly made her think he might be speaking the truth. But she wanted to verify it for herself.

Missy slapped her pen onto the table and sat up. "Done!" She lifted the paper and gave Edythe a triumphant grin."You assigned three paragraphs. I wrote *five*. They're long ones, too."

Luthenia hung the damp towel over a rod and turned, wiping her hands on her apron. "Five long paragraphs? Well, I reckon the schoolmarm'll have to give you some extra points for extra work." She winked at Edythe.

Missy waved the page at Luthenia. "It's about why I think property laws in America should be changed." She wrinkled her nose. "William thinks it's just fine and dandy that a woman's property goes to her husband when they get married. You should've heard him in class, sayin' women don't know how to take care of things." She huffed with indignation. "But look at you, Mrs. Kinsley! You have this house an' a little barn an' a horse—you take care of all of it. So I think a woman should get to keep her property."

Luthenia tilted her head, squinting at Missy's essay. "Sounds like you all had a lively discussion."

"Sure did. It'll be more lively tomorrow if Edie lets us girls speak our minds. We had a talk at recess, an' we intend to put William in his place." Missy hopped up, gathering her books. "I'm gonna do the rest of my studying in our room." She pounded up the stairs.

Luthenia retrieved her mending basket and sank into the chair Missy had vacated, her throaty chuckle rumbling. "That's one fired-up young'un."

Edythe nodded absently, her gaze following her sister. "I can't say I'm unhappy to see her siding with the girls in class instead of with

William." She began scanning her Bible again. Where was the verse about men being in charge of women?

Luthenia threaded a needle. "Does my heart good to see you readin' your Bible. Not that I thought you'd break a promise, but—"

Edythe smacked her palm on the table, a frustrated huff exploding from her lips.

"Ouch!" Luthenia stuck her finger in her mouth.

"Did you poke yourself?" Edythe sent the older woman an apologetic look.

"Yes, I did, 'cause you startled me."

"I'm sorry." Edythe slumped against the chair's high back. "I suppose I'm getting impatient. I've been hunting for a particular Scripture for over half an hour." She shared William's statement. "I'm beginning to think the verse doesn't exist."

Luthenia dropped the apron back into the basket and reached for Edythe's Bible. After a few deft flicks with her fingers on the pages, she turned the book around to face Edythe again. "Ephesians five, verse twenty-three."

Edythe bent over the Bible, both grateful to Luthenia for locating the verse and annoyed with herself for being so helpless. When she finished her silent reading of the verse, she released a little sigh. "Well, at least I know William wasn't telling tales—the verse does seem to indicate that men have been placed in a position of authority over their wives."

Luthenia resumed stitching. " 'Course, you can't just read that all by itself. Need to study it along with the whole section from verses twenty-two on to the end of the chapter. Otherwise it sounds like men're supposed to be bossy an' lordin' things over their wives. I don't think that's what the Almighty had in mind."

Edythe looked up. "You don't?"

Luthenia chuckled. "Nope, I don't." Her expression turned serious. "I believe God made man to be the head of his household, but not to stomp all over his family—to protect an' nurture his family, the same way God protects an' nurtures His own. God loves us into obedience. A good husband an' father'll lead his family with lots of love."

Edythe considered her father's style of leadership: manipulative whining and self-centered demands. She pushed aside the memories and pressed her palms to the Bible's smooth, cool pages. "Knowing that our founding fathers built this country's government using the Bible as one of their sources, I'm surprised at how many laws place restrictions on women."

Luthenia's hands paused, but her eyebrows arched. "You one of them suffragists, are you?"

Edythe had never attended a women's temperance convention, and she wasn't a member of the National Woman Suffrage Association, although a few of her classmates at the normal school had invited her to join. Still, she'd been inspired by that article about the new British property act. She wanted to change the laws in America in ways that would benefit women—but did that make her a suffragist? "I'm not sure."

Luthenia set the needle to work again, clicking her tongue against her teeth. Edythe couldn't discern the older woman's reaction—did she disapprove of the suffragist movement, or did she lament Edythe's uncertainty?

"I would like to see the property laws changed." Edythe felt safe in sharing that much with her landlady. A property owner herself, surely Luthenia would be sympathetic toward other women forced to forfeit their holdings. "Being forced to relinquish purchased or inherited property simply because they've married places women in a precarious position." She felt a pang in her chest, recalling what Mama had lost.

Luthenia's fingers busily closed a tear in the apron's skirt. "S'pose it could make a woman wonder if a man was askin' for her hand only 'cause he wanted to take control of the things she owns. Now, when Cyrus asked for my hand, he knew what he was gettin'—nothin' more'n me." A tender smile curved her lips and erased years from her face. "An' that was plenty, he said."

"Did he leave you this home?" Edythe gestured to indicate the walls around them.

"He surely did."

"But the way the law is now, if you were to marry again, your new husband would take possession of it." Edythe's voice rose in fervor as she remembered her pa signing away Grandfather's land. "Even though it originally belonged to Cyrus and you, it would be your new husband's. That isn't right!"

"Right or not, it's the way things is." Luthenia nipped off the thread and set the apron aside. "Sitting here hollering won't change it." She reached into the basket for another article of clothing.

"Someone's hollering needs to change it." Edythe flicked the Bible's pages with her thumb, the subsequent *thwip-thwip* an angry sound.

Luthenia turned the skirt she held inside out and laid it across her knees. "Maybe you oughtta go to that meetin' in North Fork."

Edythe stopped fiddling with the Bible. "What meeting?"

"That one bein' held by Susan Anthony. Didn't you see the article about it in the paper?" Luthenia grinned sheepishly. "Hope you don't mind me readin' your paper before I give it to you—kind of enjoy readin' it while sippin' a cup o' tea midway through the day."

Her heart leaping with excitement, Edythe raced to the parlor and scooped up the newspaper from the sofa's seat. She dashed back to the kitchen and spread the paper flat on the table.

"Second page," Luthenia advised.

Her fingers shook as they flipped the paper to the second page and found the article at the top of the first column. She scanned the opening paragraph while standing, too agitated to sit. Susan B. Anthony, co-founder of the Women's State Temperance Society of New York, was coming to Nebraska! "North Fork," Edythe mused aloud. "Only a stage ride away . . ."

"An' a ferry ride," Luthenia added. "Other side o' the river, y'know. Cold as it's been, they'd probably slide you across. Never cared much for crossin' that river in the winter—always worry the ice'll give way."

"I know it could be treacherous this time of year, but . . ." Edythe slipped into her chair and finished reading the article. Apparently Miss Anthony intended to speak in support of the proposed amendment to the Nebraska constitution concerning women's right to vote. Desire coursed through Edythe's veins. "I want to go."

"Meeting's on a Thursday—that's a school day."

Edythe flicked her hand, dismissing Luthenia's protest the way she'd shoo away a fly. "School could close for a couple of days. Maybe I could take a few of the older students with me." She jumped up and paced the room. "Missy would want to go. And Jane and Martha. It would do William a world of good to hear a different viewpoint than his own."

"Edythe?"

"Of course, it would be best if another parent also accompanied us. I wonder if Mrs. Sterbinz would be interested? We'd need to make arrangements to stay in a hotel. Or perhaps a schoolteacher would offer us a night of shelter."

"Edythe . . ."

"A journey of this magnitude would not be inexpensive, but given its importance, I should hope that—"

"Edythe!"

Edythe came to a halt and spun to face Luthenia. "What?"

Luthenia chuckled. "You surely get caught up in things. Can you stand still for a minute?"

Edythe planted her feet.

"If you're thinkin' of closin' school an' so forth, it'll take approval from the town council. Before you go makin' hotel arrangements an' gettin' the young'uns all wrought up, you best be askin' for a meetin' with Mr. Libolt an' the others."

Mr. Libolt. Edythe's enthusiasm melted like an ice chip on an August day. Mr. Libolt would never approve of her closing the school to attend a suffrage rally. She straightened her spine, deliberately casting aside her despondency. Mr. Libolt was only one of five council members. Just because he disapproved didn't mean the others would. Besides, she'd brought the community together with the successful Christmas program—even Mr. Townsend had said so. Considering the historical significance of this amendment, how could they possibly say no?

Chapter
TWENTY-FIVE

"And so . . ." Edythe stood on the teaching platform, her spine erect and her chin high despite the wild churning in her stomach. The town council members, perched on the recitation benches at the front of the classroom, stared back at her. "I ask approval to close the school the days of January twenty-five and twenty-six, allowing me and a few of my older students to journey to North Fork for this once-in-a-lifetime experience."

She glanced at the wall clock. They'd granted her twenty minutes to present her request; she'd used seventeen. She hoped she'd managed to convince them of the importance of the trip.

During the days she'd waited for this meeting, she'd made tentative plans and was prepared to act. All she needed was their approval.

Mr. Scheebeck sent a quick look down the row of men and then timorously put a hand in the air. Edythe swallowed a chuckle. She hadn't expected the men to behave like her students. Perhaps crunching onto the little benches made them feel like schoolboys again. "Yes?"

"Who'd be payin' for this trip?"

Edythe let her gaze drift across all five faces. She tried not to let their stony expressions intimidate her. "I would pay for my own fares for the stage and the ferry, as well as any necessary lodging accommodations. If any of the students receive permission from their parents to accompany me, I would expect them to fund their own travel expenses."

Mr. Libolt didn't bother to raise his hand. "You really think you can go all the way to North Fork with a passel o' young'uns, put 'em up in a *ho*-tell, an' not have any problems?"

His disparaging tone set Edythe's teeth on edge, but she forced a calm reply. "The students who would likely accompany me are all well-behaved, mature children. I don't anticipate problems."

Mr. Heidrich cleared his throat. "I've heard tell you're still havin' trouble maintainin' order right here in the classroom."

Edythe could well imagine the stories his daughter, Jane, carried home. And about whom. The girl was one of William's favorite targets. Edythe's lips trembled into a weak smile. "Unfortunately, some children are more . . . difficult to control . . . than others. But I feel quite certain the ones who would wish to go along on such a venture would see the opportunity as a privilege and therefore treat it as such."

"How many young'uns you thinkin' on draggin' across the state an' keepin' away from their families for *two days?*"

Mr. Libolt made it sound as though she were planning to kidnap the children so she could involve them in a train robbery. She praised herself for maintaining patience in the face of his blatant scorn. "I would like to make the trip available to the children in my older grades. That would involve Sophie Jeffers, W-William Sholes—" She hadn't intended to stumble over the boy's name, but her inner hope that he would refuse to participate welled up and tripped her tongue. "Jane Heidrich, Louisa Bride, and Martha Sterbinz."

There was no question in her mind that Missy would go, so she didn't bother to include her sister in the list. "These students have actively participated in the study on government and would therefore benefit the most from hearing

Miss Anthony speak on the women's suffrage amendment to the state constitution."

Neither Mr. Bride nor Mr. Jeffers had spoken. During her family visits at the beginning of the year, she'd felt both of the men were less resistant to her unique teaching methods than others in town. She looked at them, hoping one might speak up on her behalf. But they sat silently with widespread knees, their gaze aimed at the floor.

Mr. Libolt lurched to his feet. "Women's suffrage. Bah! Only sufferin' goin' on right now is my own—listenin' to this blather." He paced back and forth briefly, his hands flying around in grand gestures. "Women are called upon to suffer—says so in Genesis of the Bible! 'Sides that, their sufferin' is mostly made up in their heads. Everything they need is given to 'em by their husbands, so they got no cause to be runnin' around, spoutin' about *rights*."

Watching him, Edythe couldn't help but think his commanding presence would be well suited for a politician or a minister. She wanted to interrupt, but she feared facing his anger. So she stood with her teeth clamped on the end of her tongue and allowed him to bluster.

"As for closin' down the school an' shortin' our young'uns two days of learnin', I say no."

"But, Mr. Libolt!" Edythe gathered her courage and held her hands in petition toward the dour man. "Do you realize that if this amendment passes, Nebraska will be the first state in the United States to offer women the right to vote? This is an opportunity for the children to see history in the making!"

He crossed his arms and glowered at her. "They're young'uns an' they belong right here in the classroom 'stead of bein' tugged all over yonder, gettin' their heads filled with wild notions. I say *no*." He turned his scowl on the other men. "There's my vote. What's yours?"

Mr. Scheebeck scratched his chin and rolled his eyes toward the ceiling. "No."

"Bride?" Mr. Libolt barked.

His gaze still downward, the man shook his head in a negative response.

Edythe's shoulders wilted. Even if Mr. Jeffers and Mr. Heidrich said yes, they were outvoted. She'd lost. Her defeat was complete when both men also voted against the trip.

Mr. Libolt swung a sardonic grin in her direction. "Guess there's your answer, Schoolmarm. Put your sights on teachin' the important subjects instead of wastin' time comin' up with crazy schemes." He grabbed his hat from a nearby desktop, plopped it on his head, and marched out the door.

Mr. Bride, Mr. Heidrich, and Mr. Jeffers shuffled out behind him. Mr. Scheebeck slowly rose, the pop of his knees loud in the nearly empty classroom. He offered Edythe a sympathetic look. "Hate to disappoint you, Miss Amsel—know you was set on goin'—but I hafta agree that closin' school just ain't a wise decision." The man shook his head ruefully. "We can't cancel out days for no good reason."

A little bell rang in the back of Edythe's mind. She took a hesitant step toward the man. "What might be considered a good reason?"

"Well . . ." Mr. Scheebeck shifted from foot to foot, his expression thoughtful. "Some years, we've lost days to storms. An' others to illness that came through an' put half the folks in town to their beds . . ." He raised his skinny shoulders in a shrug. "A body never knows what might happen."

A fuzzy plan began to take shape in Edythe's mind. They'd said she couldn't take any of the children on a trip or close the school, but they hadn't forbidden her from going. "What if the teacher falls ill? Must the school close then?"

A snort of laughter burst from the man's throat. "We wouldn't expect the teacher to come in if she was ailin'. But no, it don't close. Past three years or so, if the teacher couldn't come in, the council called upon Miz Sterbinz to step up an' do the duties. She was a teacher afore she married an' had all them young'uns of her own."

Mr. Scheebeck gave Edythe an awkward pat on

the shoulder. "Now, don't be thinkin' we don't appreciate the job you do here. You do things a mite differ'nt, an' there've been times I've wondered . . ." He shook his head. "But my young'uns are happy an' learnin', which makes me happy. Just"—he flicked a glance toward the door, as if afraid someone might be listening—"remember you only signed a one-year contract. If you're wantin' to keep on teachin', you gotta try not to rattle so many folks. You understand me, Miss Amsel?"

Oh yes. Edythe understood perfectly.

Shuffling backward, the man reached for his coat. "Got my wagon an' team outside. Be glad to tote you back to town."

"No, thank you." She gestured toward her desk, where piles of papers waited. "I have work to do. I'll walk back later."

His bushy brows crunched together. "You sure? It's dark. An' cold."

"I'll be fine. Thank you." Stepping behind her desk, she sat and slipped her reading glasses behind her ears. She pretended great interest in sorting the assignments, and Mr. Scheebeck left without another word. As soon as he closed the door behind him, she dropped the papers she'd been holding and put her head in her hands.

How she'd wanted her students—especially Jane, Martha, and Missy, who had expressed such interest in their current study of government—to hear the esteemed suffrage leader's speech. She could still go. She could even take Missy along without having to answer to anyone. But how it hurt to leave the others behind.

Contrary, muleheaded man! If Mr. Libolt had approved the trip, every other council member would have followed his lead, she felt sure. How did one man hold such control? She smacked the papers into a stack and jammed them between the pages of her history book. While she organized the books she needed to carry home for tonight's grading, her mind completed the plan that had begun taking shape earlier that evening.

According to Mr. Scheebeck, a worthy alternate instructor was available to the students if their teacher fell ill. Therefore, an alternate was available if the teacher must be away for other—personal—reasons. If she planned her lessons in advance and shared them with Mrs. Sterbinz, the children could continue as if Edythe were teaching. The town council wouldn't be able to complain the children were being cheated out of days of learning.

She tugged on her coat and scarf, a smile twitching at her cheeks. Mr. Libolt might have control of the town council, but he didn't have control over *her*. Miss Susan Anthony was coming to North Fork, Nebraska, and Edythe Amsel intended to shake the woman's hand and offer her unwavering support to the cause of women's suffrage. And the town council would simply have to accept it.

Chapter
TWENTY-SIX

"I'm tellin' you, Joel, the woman's gonna get herself dismissed before the year is out." Wally shot an anxious look around the store before he turned back to Joel. He lowered his voice, even though they were the only two people in the mercantile. "Town council told her no, she couldn't take those young'uns to North Fork, but she's gone an' bought tickets for the stage—three of 'em!"

Wally pressed his palms to the wooden countertop and leaned toward Joel. "An' she had me send a telegram to the River Walk Inn in North Fork, inquirin' about available rooms. I got a response this mornin'." He waggled his hand in the direction of the post office. "They got a room waitin'." He shook his head. "She's goin', an' she's takin' young'uns with her. That woman's stirrin' up trouble. Mark my words."

Apprehension churned Joel's gut. As much as he'd tried over the past few weeks to set aside his affection for Miss Amsel, he'd failed dismally. He'd even avoided coming to town on Saturdays out of worry he'd run into her. A need for supplies had brought him in this afternoon. He'd figured he was safe, with school in session. But listening to Wally expound on her recent activities—and imagining Hank Libolt's reaction—made his heart ache for the schoolmarm. She was certainly creating a mess. And his reaction proved he still cared.

Joel asked, "Who all have you told about these travel plans?" Wally tended to divulge all he knew to every customer who walked through the door. If the man had followed his usual course of "talk first, think later," Libolt probably already knew Miss Amsel's plans. And the schoolmarm would be sent packing by nightfall.

Wally drew himself up as if insulted. "Haven't told nobody." Then he affected a sheepish grin. "Well, 'cept you, of course."

Joel hoped the man's claim was true. "Why tell me?"

Wally picked up a feather duster and whisked it over the shelves behind the counter. "Ain't no secret how you feel about the schoolmarm."

Heat rushed from the base of Joel's neck to his hairline. "Whaddaya mean by that?"

"Whole town knows you think she's a fine teacher. Anytime somebody says a word of complaint, you defend her." Suddenly Wally whirled and looked directly into Joel's face, his eyes wide. "You ain't *taken* with the schoolmarm, are you?"

Joel looked quickly right and left, seeking listening ears. But they were still alone. "Hush that kind of talk."

Wally laughed. "Oh, now, Joel, nothin' wrong with a man findin' a woman attractive. Even though Miss Amsel's climbin' upward in years, it appears she's still got plenty of life left in her. Other fellas in town seem to think so, though most of 'em have finally give up pursuin' her. She's one finicky woman. But she might like you." He laughed again.

Joel stepped forward, clenching his fists. "Wally, I'm tellin' you—"

Wally raised both hands in surrender, the turkey feathers in the duster quivering beside his face. "I was just joshin' you. Don't get yourself in a dither." He returned to dusting. "I was just thinkin', seein' as how you stood up for her in the past, you might could try an' convince her to give up this wild plan before she causes an uproar that can't be stilled."

Joel leaned his elbow on the counter, worry making his knees tremble. "You really think her taking this trip will create that much trouble?"

Wally paused, looking at Joel as if he'd lost his mind. "Hank Libolt's already got it in for the schoolmarm—always fussin' about what she teaches and the way she teaches it. He's wantin' to be rid of her. Heidrich too. So far me, Jeffers, and Bride've said keep her—at least for the rest of the year, 'cause the young'uns are so fond of her. But if she goes against the council's order not to take young'uns out of school for a trip . . . 'specially to hear some lady spoutin' about women's rights . . ." He snorted. "Jeffers an' Bride'll go to Libolt's side. And the council will dismiss her."

Tossing the feather duster beneath the counter, Wally shook his head. "I know Miss Amsel's got some strange ways of doin' things, but my young'uns like her. They've been learnin' a lot, and they actually seem excited to go to school, not scared like they used to be. I'm afraid if Libolt's good an' het up, he'll be lookin' for somebody as differ'nt from Miss Amsel as he can find. An' that might mean another Shanks."

Joel nodded. Even though he'd meant to avoid Miss Amsel for his own good, he had his nephews to consider. They loved their teacher, they loved school, and he wanted them to continue learning without fear. But would his talking to her do any good?

"I don't know, Wally. She's an independent woman."

Wally chuckled. "Don't I know it." He leaned forward, his expression hopeful. "But you'll try?"

For his nephews' sakes, Joel had to try. "I reckon so." He carted his boxes of goods to his wagon, then checked his timepiece. School would let out in another half hour. He could stick around town, swing by to fetch the boys, and see if Miss Amsel would like a ride to Miz Kinsley's. That'd give him a chance to talk to her.

Joel climbed into his wagon and curled his hands around the traces. But instead of getting Jody moving, he closed his eyes and offered a prayer.

Lord, I believe You brought Miss Amsel to this town. She's a fine teacher, an' my boys would miss her somethin' fierce if she got dismissed. I told Wally I'd talk to her, an' I will, but I'm gonna need Your help. Let me talk to her as a concerned pa, not as a man who harbors feelings for her. Whisper in her heart what she needs to do to keep peace in town.

He closed with the same request he'd made for Miss Amsel since Christmas Day when she'd confessed she wasn't a believer: *Mostly, let her find peace in You.*

Giving the reins a flick, he set Jody into motion. He aimed the horse toward the school. He'd have a cold wait in the schoolyard, but it would give him time to formulate words to convince Miss Amsel to cancel her trip to North Fork. He sure hoped she'd listen to reason.

● ● ●

Nineteen pairs of eyes watched the wall clock. Nineteen bodies poised, elbows braced, feet pointed toward the aisles. Nineteen students anticipated three o'clock—when school let out for the day. Edythe hid a smile. The children's end-of-the-day ritual never ceased to amuse her. The minute hand ticked into position, pointing directly at the twelve, and every pair of eyes shifted to look at Edythe. She bobbed her head. "Class dismissed."

With a whoop, the children thundered toward the cloakroom. Edythe followed at a more sedate pace, pausing to scoop up a discarded slip of paper or push a desk back into alignment. She tucked her coat around her shoulders to block the wind, then stepped onto the porch, where she could oversee the students' departure.

Despite the cold, most of her pupils still walked to school, so she frowned in puzzlement when she spotted a waiting wagon. Then her body gave a jolt—a purely unconscious reaction—when she recognized Joel Townsend on the wagon's seat. He wrapped the reins around the brake handle and hopped down. Edythe took a shuffling step backward when he moved toward the schoolhouse.

His nephews scampered past him and climbed into the back of the wagon. Mr. Townsend

266

reached the porch and stared directly into her eyes. Normally he greeted her with a smile, but today his mouth was set in a grim line. Edythe's pulse sped as an unnamed worry claimed her. She realized she hadn't spoken to him in weeks—by her own choice. But now, looking into his handsome, serious face, she begrudged those lost opportunities.

"G-good afternoon, Mr. Townsend." Though she stuttered a bit, she was surprised how normal her voice sounded.

"I need to speak with you, please."

She'd never seen him so somber. She gulped. "Please come in." She stopped in the cloakroom rather than leading him into the schoolroom. The schoolroom was her domain. The remembrance of the town council members' negative reactions to her recent request had cast a pall over the room in the days following their meeting. Mr. Townsend's solemnity put her defenses on alert. She wouldn't risk a second attack in her place of security.

Shifting to face him, she held tight to her coat lapels. "Is everything all right with Johnny and Robert?"

His nose was red, his eyes watery. He rubbed one gloved finger under his nose before answering. "The boys're fine. But—" He scuffed the toe of his right boot against the floor. "I need to ask you somethin'." He flicked a quick, unsmiling glance at her before staring at the floor again. "Are you really goin' to North Fork after the town council said you couldn't?"

Apprehension faded and was quickly replaced by anger. "Apparently Mr. Scheebeck has been talking."

Mr. Townsend raised one shoulder in a sheepish shrug. "Yep. Is he spoutin' truth?"

Although she should exercise restraint—she was the teacher meeting a parent in the schoolhouse—irritation chased good sense away. "Why do you ask?" she snapped.

He blinked twice. " 'Cause I . . . want to know."

Edythe wadded her coat in her arms in lieu of clenching her fists. "I fail to see why my travels would concern you, but if you must know . . . yes. I intend to go to North Fork and hear Miss Anthony speak."

Mr. Townsend shivered. "Can we step in by the stove?"

"No."

He shot her a startled look.

"The classroom is for school business. We're discussing my personal business, so we can stay right here."

Mr. Townsend's jaw tightened. "All right." He folded his arms over his chest. "Then I have to tell you, you're makin' a mistake. Everyone knows the town council voted against your trip. So far, only Wally Scheebeck an' me know you're plannin' to go, but it won't be long an' word'll spread. You going to North Fork after the council told you to stay here is gonna stir up a heap of trouble. You could very well lose your job, and I'm not looking forward to us losing a perfectly good teacher."

Although he'd started out in a stern voice, by the time he'd finished, his tone had gentled. Edythe sensed his very real desire to protect her, as he'd done numerous times before. It still goaded that he would try to tell her what to do, but she forced aside her aggravation and replied in kind.

"I appreciate your concern, but I'm afraid Mr. Scheebeck has distorted a few of the facts. The town council did, indeed, tell me I couldn't close the school in order to take students to North Fork. What Mr. Scheebeck doesn't seem to realize is that the council did not forbid *me* from going."

Confusion clouded the man's face. "Wally said you got *three* tickets for the stage. Doesn't that mean . . . ?"

Edythe nearly rolled her eyes. Mr. Scheebeck needed to learn to control his wagging tongue. If there were another mercantile in town, she'd take her business elsewhere. "Those tickets are for Luthenia, Missy, and me." She tipped her head and forced the irritation from her tone. "I trust the town council won't oppose me removing my own sister from school. Especially since I have the ability to make sure she keeps up with her studies while we travel. The other students will remain here, with Mrs. Sterbinz stepping in as my replacement for a few days. They'll be well cared for in my absence."

He worked his lips up and down as if seeking words. Finally he blurted, "You sure you know what you're doing?"

His sincere befuddlement made her want to laugh, but the situation wasn't funny. If her family had lost property, surely other families had lost property, too. People—all people, whether male or female—should have the right to maintain what was legally theirs. Unless the laws changed, women would continue to forfeit valuable and dear possessions to men who might not view those belongings as important. She would not sit idly by and do nothing.

"Yes," she answered.

"It's gonna create problems."

"I'm sure it will."

"Town council might even elect to remove you as teacher." Worry laced his tone.

She swallowed. "I know."

"And you're still gonna go?"

She answered with all the fervency she could muster. "I'm going."

Sadness crept across his features. It was a moment before he spoke again. "I'll be prayin'

God's will for you, then. You're a good teacher, an' we need you here. It would be awful hard on . . . my boys . . . to have to say good-bye to you, Edythe."

He turned on his heel and thumped out into the cold January afternoon, leaving her alone in the cloakroom. Not until he'd climbed into his wagon and brought down the reins on the horse's rump did she realize he'd called her Edythe instead of Miss Amsel. Unexpectedly, warmth built in the center of her chest and spread outward, filling her with pleasure. She replayed the sound of his voice speaking her name until tears stung her eyes.

He'd talked to her as a friend. Not as someone wishing to order her about, indifferent to her feelings, but as someone who genuinely cared. She rushed out onto the porch and leaned against the railing, straining toward him as the wagon rolled away. For one brief moment, she considered canceling her plans just to avoid causing Mr. Townsend—*Joel*—undue distress.

But then she spotted Johnny and Robert's blond heads bobbing in the back of the wagon. Reality crashed down around her. Forming a relationship with Joel Townsend would only lead to heartache for both of them. She didn't want the encumbrance his nephews represented, and he needed more than she was able to give.

Cold air whisked around the schoolhouse,

rustling her skirts and sending shivers down her spine. She scurried inside and closed the door against the biting wind. But she couldn't close away the unsettling feeling that she was making a dreadful mistake.

Chapter
TWENTY~SEVEN

Edythe folded her taffeta suit and laid it carefully in her valise. The crisp taffeta in a deep shade of crimson was her favorite dress, and she intended to wear it to the North Fork city hall the evening of Miss Anthony's presentation. Excitement fluttered in her chest. She hoped she'd be able to sleep tonight. Preparing for the trip had taken more effort than she'd imagined. But she was ready.

Detailed lesson plans for Mrs. Sterbinz waited on her desk at school. Her bag contained everything she would need for a two-day journey. She'd tucked the stage tickets and a small roll of paper money in a secret pocket in her reticule. In the morning, she'd add her brush and toiletries to the valise, and then she would be ready.

Snapping the bag closed, she looked across the small room at Missy, who searched through the bureau drawers. "Haven't you decided what you want to wear yet?" she asked her sister. She wanted to choose Missy's clothes for her to speed the process, but Missy hadn't willingly accepted Edythe's suggestions when she was three years old; she'd certainly reject her sister's assistance at fourteen.

"I'm wearing my brown calico for travel and taking the green worsted for the meeting, since it's my most grown-up dress." Missy continued to root through the drawer. "But I want my matching hair ribbon for the green worsted, and I can't find it."

"Perhaps because you didn't put your ribbons in the drawer the last time you used them." Edythe lifted the snarl of ribbons from the corner of the dry sink and held them aloft.

Missy dashed around the end of the bed and snatched the ribbons from Edythe's hands. "There they are!" She tossed the colorful lengths of grosgrain across the bed and began untangling them.

Edythe slid her valise under the bed and then sat on the edge of the mattress and assisted Missy. "You do realize if you'd roll your ribbons and place them in the drawer after using them, they'd always be easily found and ready to wear."

Missy flashed a sour look. "I know."

"Knowing isn't enough, Missy. You also need to *do*."

Missy grabbed the ribbons, pulled the green one from the bundle, and tossed the others into the drawer. She released a huff as she jammed the green ribbon into her bag. "Stop being my teacher or my mother, Edie, all right?"

Edythe, surprised by the vehemence in Missy's voice, stared at her sister in silence.

"You always treat me like I'm still a baby who can't think for herself. I'm not a baby anymore. Can't you stop telling me what to do and just be my sister?"

No, I can't. The words winged through Edythe's mind, but she kept them from escaping her lips. Yet she recognized the truth of her inner thought. She was the only mother Missy had—she'd always taken the role seriously. Now, with Missy sitting in a desk in her classroom, she had no choice but to treat Missy like any of the other students under her care. She couldn't simply remove those titles and close them in a drawer at night—she was, and would continue to be, Missy's mother and teacher.

Missy flopped facedown across the bed, propped her chin in her hand, and frowned at Edythe. "Do you know what I'd really like? For us to be like Patience and Sophie, or like Mary and Josephine. I watch them on the play yard or in the schoolroom during breaks, and they have such fun. Even though there are other kids around, they still like to be together." The frown slipped away, and a pained look crossed Missy's face. "Why can't we have fun, Edythe?"

The question stung. Edythe fiddled with a loose thread on the quilt rather than looking at her sister. "We have fun."

A mirthless laugh burst from Missy as she rolled to her back. "Not like the Ellsworth or Jeffers girls. They have fun without one of them always tellin' the other one what to do."

Edythe could have argued that twelve-year-old Sophie often bossed her younger sister. But she thought she understood what Missy meant. She tried a gentle explanation. "Our relationship isn't the same as the Ellsworth or Jeffers girls, Missy. I'm so much older than you. And since Mama wasn't there to take care of us, I've needed to be a mother to you rather than a friend or . . . or sister."

Missy rolled to her side, resting her head in the bend of her elbow. "But I'm grown up now. I don't *need* a mother."

I still need a mother. Before Edythe could voice her thought, Missy continued.

"And even though you have to be my teacher when we're at school, couldn't you stop trying to teach me when we're here? Couldn't you talk to me like—well, like you talk to Mrs. Kinsley? Or even Mr. Townsend?"

Edythe jerked, yanking the thread from the quilt. "Mr. Townsend?" Simply mentioning the man's name sent a rush of heat through her chest.

"You don't talk to him very often, but when you do, I can tell you're friends. Your voice sounds different, and you seem happier." She sat up, her eyes beseeching. "That's what I want, Edie. For you to be my *friend*. Can't you try?"

Edythe nibbled her lower lip and considered Missy's question. At fourteen, Missy wasn't as grown up as she thought she was. Becoming friends meant releasing her responsibility for her sister. Ceasing to guide and direct. She didn't believe Missy was ready to forge forward without guidance. The fact that she'd fled Omaha and traveled alone across the state proved her lack of common sense. Yet looking into her sister's imploring eyes, she couldn't find the words to deny her request.

"I can try, but it will be hard."

"Why?" The simple query held no resentment, only a desire to understand.

"Because I've been your mother since you were a very small baby. Being a good mother for you as well as for Justus, Albert, Frances, and Loren was important to me. I worked hard at it. I know I didn't always succeed . . ." She paused, hoping Missy might argue, but her sister sat silently, listening with wide eyes. Edythe swallowed her disappointment. "But I did my best. And since being your mother has been so much a part of who I am, it's hard to let it go."

"But you don't tell Justus or . . . or any of the others what to do anymore. Just me!" A hint of petulance crept into Missy's tone.

Edythe laughed softly, hoping to waylay any further rebellion. "Maybe because you're the only one who's still living with me?"

Missy sighed. "I know it isn't your fault you had to be a mother to me. If Mama hadn't died, then we'd just be sisters."

Many other things would be different, too, but Edythe chose not to pursue that topic.

"But I still wish we could be friends. I wish we could have *fun* together."

Edythe pushed off the bed and crossed to the bureau to retrieve her nightclothes. "Maybe this trip will give us a chance to have fun together as sisters. I'll try not to be bossy, and you try not to give me a reason to tell you what to do." She smiled as she finished the statement so Missy would know she wasn't scolding.

Missy crawled under the covers. "I'll do my best."

"That's all any of us can promise." Edythe hoped Missy understood she included herself in the statement.

Missy wriggled onto her side, pulling the covers up to her ear. " 'Night, Edie."

Edythe dressed in her nightgown, brushed out her hair, and then started to blow out the lamp. But her gaze fell on the Bible lying on the table beside the bed. She and Missy had come upstairs after cleaning the kitchen, so she hadn't read the Bible yet this evening. Now it was time for sleep. Yet the Bible seemed to tug at her.

She'd promised Luthenia she would read the book every day. She climbed into bed, careful not to jostle the mattress too much, and leaned against the iron headboard. Shifting the Bible to her lap, she opened it to the book of Acts. Luthenia had recommended starting in the part called the New Testament rather than at the beginning, and Edythe had followed her suggestion. Over the past weeks, she'd read Matthew, Mark, Luke, and John, which had seemed to repeat some pieces of information. She wondered, as she began Acts, if the Bible would tell about someone other than Jesus.

She read while Missy slept, her sister's soft snuffles and the occasional squeak of a bedspring the only intrusions. She came to a block of text, purportedly previously stated by another man named David, and she read slowly, her lips forming the words.

" 'I foresaw the Lord always before me, for he is on my right hand, that I should not be moved. Therefore did my heart rejoice and my tongue was glad; moreover my flesh shall rest in hope: because thou wilt not leave my soul . . . ' " She yawned, tiredness trying to take hold. The words seemed to dance beneath her bleary eyes.

Determinedly, she went back and read the text a second time.

According to the writer of Acts, David was speaking of Jesus. Obviously David and Jesus were very close—so close David believed he would never be abandoned by Him. In all of Edythe's life, she'd never met anyone she'd trusted to always be there. What would it be like, she wondered, to have such a friend?

The Bible slid from her sleepy fingers. She jerked, catching it before it fell off the edge of the bed. Very carefully, she closed the Bible and set it aside. She'd read more tomorrow. She blew out the lamp and then curled on her side. But instead of closing her eyes, she stared at the dark rectangle of the Bible on the side table.

Thou wilt not leave my soul . . . The words repeated themselves in her mind. For so long, she'd felt empty. And alone, even though Missy slept on the other side of the bed. Tears stung behind her nose, and she sniffed hard. What would it take to remove the emptiness that held her captive?

She fell asleep with the unanswered question hovering on her heart.

Chapter
TWENTY~EIGHT

The rattle of the windows startled Joel out of a sound sleep. He opened his eyes to total blackness. So black he wondered if he'd fallen into a hole during the night. He searched the darkness for even a sliver of light. Nothing.

He reached out tentatively and located the table that stood beside his bed. After pawing around, his fingers found a tin of matches. Peering into the dark nothingness made him dizzy, and his hands trembled as he went through the steps of popping the top on the tin, withdrawing a match, and striking it on the underside of the table.

The sudden flare of the match hurt his eyes, and he winced. By squinting, he managed to light the lamp. With the lamp in hand, he padded to the window in his bedroom and pushed aside the curtains to peer out. Once again, he had the sensation of being in a hole. He saw nothing more than a wall of bluish white. Snow. So thick it blocked the moon. Or the sun. He couldn't guess the time.

He set the lamp on the table and scrambled into his clothes. He could already tell the boys wouldn't be going to school today, so he'd let them sleep as late as they wanted to while he saw to the animals. He'd had the good sense to string a rope from the corner of the house to the barn door back in early November just in case a blizzard struck. He sure hoped his neighbors had done the same.

The windup clock on the fireplace mantel showed five ten—still early, which explained some of the dark. Joel combated the shadows by lighting all three oil lamps. He couldn't ever remember being so extravagant in the past, but he found the total blackness unsettling. He tiptoed around, determined not to rouse the boys, and bundled himself against the storm.

When he stepped out the door, the cold hit him as hard as if he'd run into a wall at full tilt. He gasped. The frigid air whisked into his lungs, stinging him from the inside out. His gloved hands turned uncooperative, but with clumsy movements he adjusted his scarf to cover his face up to his eyes. With his nose and mouth protected by the thickly woven scarf, he could breathe more easily.

Keep me safe in this storm, Lord. Pressing his shoulder against the side of the house, he bounced his way to the corner, then felt up and down until his hand bumped into the rope that stretched from the house to the barn. He took a firm grip and stepped off the porch and into several feet of snow. The wind roared, filling his ears with its fury. Snowflakes pelted his face, and he squinted against the onslaught. Tiny pieces of ice clung to his eyelashes, further hindering his vision. Unable to see more than six inches in any direction, he felt completely alone in the world. His heart pounded with fear, and the swirl of the snow made him dizzy.

He planted his feet, trying to gain a sense of direction. Should he forge on to the barn or return to the house? Every bit of him wanted to turn around and seek the safety of his log house, but the animals required care. He had to go on. Whispering another prayer for protection, he curled his left hand more firmly around the rope, stuck his right hand straight out in front of him to keep from walking smack into the barn, and stumbled through the drifts of snow.

The barn was roughly ninety feet from the house—thirty wide strides. He tried counting his steps to get an idea of when he might reach the enclosure, but the snow would not allow him to take long strides. Instead, he shuffled with painstakingly slow steps as he forced a path through the heavy snow, his balance precarious in his blindness. He counted thirty steps, then fifty, and he still hadn't reached the barn.

A sudden worry brought him to a halt. If the boys awakened, Robert would be scared. He'd never liked storms. When the boys couldn't find their uncle in the house, would they search for him? Two steps off the porch, and they'd be lost.

He should go back, wake them, and let them know to stay put. Joel tried to turn around, but the sensation of spinning returned. He froze in place, his heart trying to pound itself right out of his chest.

His hands felt numb from the cold. Would he even know if the rope slipped free of his grasp? A bitter taste filled his mouth—the flavor of fear. *Go . . . get to shelter.* Hand outstretched, Joel propelled himself forward. He hit the side of the barn so hard it jarred his wrist and bounced him backward. He lost his grip on the rope and landed on his backside. A panic unlike anything he'd ever experienced struck. Flailing both arms in the air, he searched for the rope but came up empty. The wind screeched like a wild animal determined to tear him limb from limb. His mouth went dry. His eyeballs burned.

He pawed the space around him, his hands churning up snow, trying to get his bearings. But the roaring wind and blinding snow confused his senses. His shoulders heaved with frantic breaths. Gooseflesh broke out all over his body. *Dear Lord in heaven, where is the barn?*

The storm awakened Edythe before she heard the stove lids clang—Luthenia was up.

She glanced at the top of Missy's head poking out of the covers. Her sister lay very still, the quilts rising and falling with her deep, even breaths. Tenderness welled in Edythe's breast. How Missy could sleep so soundly with the wind howling like a chorus of angry wolves, Edythe couldn't fathom, but at least the storm hadn't disturbed her.

Edythe considered snuggling back under the covers and trying to drift back to sleep. Then a duller clank—the stove door—sounded from the kitchen. Luthenia was getting the fire started. She'd have water on to boil soon. Tea sounded good, so Edythe crept out of bed, shoved her arms into her mother's robe, and padded downstairs.

Luthenia knelt on the kitchen floor, layering wood into the stove's belly. Her gray hair stuck out wildly around her thin face.

"Good morning," Edythe greeted. Her throat sounded croaky, so she cleared it and tried again. "The storm woke me."

"Me too." Luthenia pushed to her feet, her movements slow and jerky. "It's early to be up, but that wind . . . sets my teeth on edge. Who could sleep through it?"

Edythe laughed softly. "Missy could. She didn't even stir when I got out of bed."

"I'm glad. Somebody might as well be restin'." Luthenia tipped her head toward the window. "Can't see a thing out there, snow's blowin' so thick." Her face pinched into a pout of sympathy. "Reckon we'll have to cancel the trip."

Disappointment fell over Edythe. She'd looked so forward to hearing Miss Anthony's speech. Hope flickered in the center of her heart— perhaps the storm would blow through quickly. If so, they might still be able to reach North Fork in time. She scurried to the window and looked out in a world of . . . nothing. An odd feeling struck— as if the house had been picked up during the night and deposited inside a dark bubble.

A chill shook her frame. Such thick, heavy snow and powerful winds. Even if the storm stopped immediately, drifts would block the roads. The flicker of hope died, bringing the sting of frustrated tears. Common sense told her no one should go out in this blizzard.

She spun to face Luthenia, panic rising within her. "Will any of the children try to get to school this morning?"

Luthenia dipped water from the reservoir into a teakettle. " 'Course not. Folks know to keep their young'uns home on a day like this." She placed the filled kettle on one of the round stove lids, then glanced at Edythe's bare feet. "Your toes'll freeze if you don't get 'em covered. Fetch a pair of slippers from my bedroom. Then we can sit here, sip tea, an' stay warm while the storm blows itself out." Looking toward the window, she shook her head. "Hope it's soon. Poor ol' Gertie out there'll need water. I can't get to her 'til things calm down."

Edythe hurried to Luthenia's room and selected a pair of heavy, knitted slippers from a basket on the floor beside the plain wardrobe. Luthenia had knitted enough pairs to accommodate a centipede—the woman's hands never stilled. With her feet considerably warmer, Edythe returned to the kitchen and huddled close to the stove.

Luthenia stood at the window, scowling out at the storm. "I don't mind tellin' you, I find this downright disquietin'. Been through storms before—even ones as fierce as this—but I've never cared much for feelin' all hemmed in." She sighed, her breath steaming the window. "But I'm mighty thankful it hit when it did."

Edythe spun from the warmth of the stove. "Thankful?" When she considered her carefully laid plans to attend the meeting in North Fork, gratitude didn't come to mind. Couldn't the storm have waited?

Luthenia pulled a chair up to the stove and sat. "What if this'd hit when we was halfway to North Fork? Why, chances are good we'd've froze solid right in the stagecoach. The good Lord knew what He was doin', sendin' it in the night so we'd all stay home where it's safe."

Edythe scowled. "If the 'good Lord' had kept the storm from coming at all, we could be on our way to North Fork without any worries."

To Edythe's consternation, Luthenia chuckled.

"Telling God what He should or shouldn't've done is plenty foolish. His ways are beyond what our human minds can understand." She raised her eyebrows and gave Edythe a pointed look. "It's better to trust He knows best an' leave it at that."

The water burbled inside the kettle. Luthenia rose to pour steaming water into two cups.

Edythe sank into a chair and considered the older woman's statement. How did one trust without understanding? Trusting without seeing would be like stepping out into that storm—foolhardy. The empty ache from last night returned, making her feel hollow and needy. She hugged herself, battling the urge to cry.

Luthenia shuffled to the table with the tea, and Edythe curled her hands around her cup, absorbing its warmth. The wind increased in volume, its shriek raising the fine hairs on the back of Edythe's neck. If she found the storm this unsettling while snug inside Luthenia's little home, how would she feel if she were out in it?

Joel collapsed against the ground, his chest heaving painfully. He had two choices—press his face into the snow and freeze to death, or try once more to find the barn. He couldn't give up without a fight. Robert and Johnny depended on him. *God, help me. I can do it with Your help—just get me up.* His muscles screamed in protest, but he pushed to his knees.

The impression of spinning returned, making him sick to his stomach. He fought down the wave of nausea and swung his arms up and down. No rope. Shifting his position slightly, he tried again. Still no rope.

The fierce wind robbed him of breath. A thousand needles repeatedly stabbed his ears. His eyes burned with the effort to see something . . . anything . . . that would give him a sense of location. Despair tried to crumple him once more, but he gritted his teeth, shuffled on his knees to turn his body a few more inches, and forced his arms into one more swing. His fingertips brushed against something.

The rope! He tipped his body forward and waved again, slowly, determinedly. His palm connected with the rope, and he groaned as he grasped the length of twisted hemp in his cold-stiffened fingers. Still on his knees, he clung with both hands and let his head hang low for a few moments, his chest heaving from the exertion.

When he'd gathered enough strength, he began shuffling on his knees, forcing himself through the accumulated snow. He twisted his head this way and that, unable to ascertain his location but trusting the rope would lead him to shelter. His elbow bumped into something hard and immovable—a wall. Holding tight to the rope with his left hand, he uncurled his right hand and extended it toward the wall. With his palm pressed flat against the sturdy surface, he summoned the courage to release the rope completely. The moment the rope slipped free, he experienced a sense of falling, and he had to swallow bile that rose in his throat.

God, You brought me this far. Don't leave me now.

Knowing he'd tied the rope to the right-hand side of the barn's double doors, he inched his way to the left. But instead of finding the crack between the two doors, he found the corner of a building. Confusion struck, making his head spin. Then he realized he'd returned to the house. The animals would have to wait—he couldn't make the trek to the barn. His chest aching, more exhausted than he could ever remember being, he forced his numb knees to once again shuffle, this time to the right.

The wind roared. Snow blinded him. The rough boards beneath his knees cut through his trousers and tore his skin. But his hands found the indention in the wall created by the door. With arms so weary he could barely lift them, he sought the leather string that would raise the crossbar. He found it, but his fingers were too stiff to grasp it. He swiped at the string once, twice, unable to open the door.

Helplessness sagged his spine. He couldn't just die here on the porch, outside the door, where the boys would trip over his body. His jaw too stiff to open, he groaned through clenched teeth, "Help me, God!" He swatted at the string one more time. And missed.

Chapter
TWENTY-NINE

"I gotta get some help."

Joel battled to make sense of what he'd heard. The voice seemed to swoop in from faraway, high-pitched and slurring.

"But it's stormin'! I don't want you to go!"

The second voice held more panic than the first.

"But Uncle Joel's sick—he might be dyin'! I gotta go get help!"

Realization bloomed in Joel's foggy brain. *Johnny and Robert . . . talking about me. An' one of 'em is fixing to go out in that storm.* Fear roused him from his stupor. Groaning, he fought to open his heavy eyelids and squint at two fuzzy, tear-stained faces—the boys, hunkered down beside him. Johnny wore his coat and wool hat over his striped sleep shirt.

"Take off your coat, boy." Joel tried to speak sternly, but the words rasped out on a weak whisper. It pained him to take a deep breath—the frigid air must've burned his lungs. "You aren't goin' anywhere."

"Uncle Joel!" Robert threw himself on Joel.

Joel somehow found the strength to roll to his left hip and hold Robert to his chest. The boy clung, sobbing. "I'm all right. Hush now." He blinked, trying to clear his vision. Sandpaper scraped over his eyes. He scowled at Johnny, who remained on his haunches close to Joel's knees. "Why're you wearin' that coat?"

Tears winked in Johnny's eyes. "I was gonna go to the Sterbinz place an' get help. I heard somethin' bumpin' on the door, so I opened it, an' you fell down. Robert an' me dragged you in so we could close the door again, but you wouldn't answer us when we talked to you." One tear rolled down his cheek, and his chin quivered. "You . . . you scared me, Uncle Joel. I thought you was dyin'."

Some of Joel's anger melted away in the face of Johnny's real fear. Yet he couldn't ease up until he'd made a point with the boy. "You wouldn't have been able to find the Sterbinz place. You wouldn't have been able to find the road, thick as that snow's blowin'." He pointed his finger at Johnny. "Don't you ever, *ever* head out in a storm, Johnny. Not for any reason. All you'd be doing is putting yourself in danger."

"But—"

"Don't argue with me, boy!" At his sharp tone, Robert lifted his head and reared back in surprise. Joel rarely growled at the boys, but they needed to learn this lesson without experiencing the consequences. "Getting yourself lost wouldn't have helped me. You promise me right now you'll never leave this house on your own—especially not in the middle of a storm."

The boys stared at him with wide, uncertain eyes.

"Promise me!" Barking the words made Joel's throat hurt. He gave Robert a little shake, his glare aimed at Johnny.

"I promise," they chorused, fresh tears welling.

Joel snaked out his arm and tugged Johnny to his side. He held both boys and planted kisses in their uncombed hair so they'd know he wasn't mad. Then he set them aside. "Get the broom, Robert, and sweep this snow to the door so it doesn't leave a puddle in the middle of the floor. Johnny, take off that coat an' put a pot of water on the stove for mush. I'm gonna"—he groaned as he forced his legs to hold him upright—"change out of my wet clothes. Then we'll have breakfast."

Robert trotted alongside Joel as he headed for the bedroom. "What about school, Uncle Joel? Ain't we goin'?"

Joel almost laughed. Who would've ever believed the boy would beg to go to school? He tousled Robert's hair. "No school today, boy—we got a blizzard happening out there. Sweep up now, like I told you."

He closed himself in his bedroom and struggled out of his ice-crusted pants. His knees bore several scratches, and it hurt to pull fresh britches over them. Every muscle in his body ached from his time in the cold. But even worse than pain was fear. The idea of Johnny braving the blizzard made him break out in a sweat. What if he hadn't come to and Johnny'd set out for help?

He shook his head, ridding himself of the frightful speculations. Johnny was safe. Robert was safe. They'd promised to never venture out alone. But would they honor the promise? Joel sat on the edge of his bed, staring at the window where the landscape hid behind a wall of blowing snow. Both boys carried insecurities from losing their parents. They clung to him like freshly hatched ducklings trail after their mother. If something happened to him . . .

He bent forward, burying his face in his hands. The boys needed someone else besides him taking care of them. Johnny would never have considered donning his coat and trekking through the blizzard for help if there'd been another grown-up in the house. Joel needed to marry, needed to provide a mother for the boys.

Immediately, a picture of Edythe Amsel flashed through his mind, but he swept it away like his palm cleared a film of steam from a pane of glass. His fists pressed to his aching eyes, he considered each of the unmarried women in Walnut Hill. Four elderly widows, including Luthenia Kinsley; Miz Sterbinz, not elderly but a good fifteen years Joel's senior; and three women in their late teens or early twenties. He searched his memory for a picture of each of the younger women, considering them by turn. One stood out from the others— Maribelle Jenkins.

She'd been out of school for as long as he'd lived in Walnut Hill. He didn't know her well, but he'd caught her watching him at church picnics or from across the mercantile. She always looked away quickly when his gaze met hers, which might mean she was trying to conceal her interest in him. Miz Kinsley had hinted shortly before the boys had come to live with him that Maribelle would make a fine wife. He hadn't found any strong arguments against the older woman's statement. But then the boys had arrived and his attention had turned to them.

Terrill Sterbinz had courted the girl a year ago, but they'd broken things off. Joel didn't know why, and he didn't need to know. Maribelle was unattached, a churchgoing believer, and maybe even a little interested in him.

Come Sunday—assuming this storm blew itself out by then and he could get to church— he'd speak a few words to Maribelle and see what happened.

• • •

"Edie, read to me."

Edythe looked up from her embroidery work. Missy lay stretched out on the parlor settee, her hands behind her head and her ankles crossed. Edythe couldn't help chuckling. She'd never seen a lazier pose. "Don't be silly. You're capable of reading to yourself. Besides, I'm working on this dresser scarf for Luthenia."

She held the hoop at arm's length and smiled at the array of pansies trailing across the expanse of snowy white linen. She hoped to find enough time, between working on lessons and writing letters of support for the women's suffrage committee, to complete the dresser scarf and present it to Luthenia on her birthday in mid-February.

"But I'm too sleepy to read to myself. And I'm bored. Read to me, please? Just for a little while?"

Fortunately, the storm had eased before noon the day before, bringing an unearthly hush after the wind's wild howls. But the residents of Walnut Hill hadn't tried to venture out. Snowdrifts reached all the way to the roof on the north side of most houses. The stage couldn't get through on the roads, so mail service had come to a halt. Everyone stayed in where it was warm. Listening to the storm had been unnerving, but the eerie silence of a town buried beneath snow and ice was almost as discomfiting.

Today the sun shone brightly, and Edythe hoped it would melt away enough snow for folks to make it to church on Sunday and then to school on Monday. Three days of being trapped inside should be enough for everyone.

She dug in the little basket at her feet for more green thread. "If you're bored, why don't you go in and start supper for Luthenia? She's still lying down with a headache. She'd probably appreciate the help."

Missy sat upright and swung her feet to the floor. "What should I fix?"

"There's a ham hock in the cellar and a bag of white beans in the pantry." The mention of beans brought to mind two little towheaded boys . . . and their square-jawed uncle. She pushed the image away. "Ham and beans, with a pan of corn bread, would make a fine supper."

"All right." Missy bounced out of the parlor, humming.

Edythe watched her sister go, astounded by her cheerful response to preparing supper. Either Missy truly was bored enough to view cooking as a pleasant diversion, or she was doing as Edythe had asked and trying to be more grown-up. Edythe couldn't deny she appreciated the change. She disliked battling with Missy and welcomed the opportunity to transition from mother and rebellious child to sisters and friends.

Luthenia toddled from her bedroom shortly

before five o'clock. Edythe jumped up and held the wadded scarf behind her back. "Is your headache better?"

Luthenia grimaced. "Some. It'll plague me 'til this snow clears—I've always had headaches durin' the wintertime." A weak smile curved her lips. "Cyrus used to call 'em snowfall-aches." She moved to the window and squinted out.

Edythe angled her body to hide the scarf behind her and peeked past Luthenia's shoulder. Dusk turned the snow pale blue. Shadows, cast by the house and the band of cottonwood trees, created darker patches. In the fading light of the low-hanging sun, the snow took on the appearance of spun sugar. "The storm was fierce, but the results are beautiful," she said to Luthenia.

"Yep. Even if it gives me headaches, I could never begrudge the snow—always looks so clean and pretty." A wry chuckle rolled from Luthenia's lips. "'Til it starts meltin' or folks traipse through it. Then it looks like a mouse-eaten quilt."

Edythe giggled at Luthenia's picturesque observation.

Luthenia turned from the window. "I better go make sure poor ol' Gertie's water isn't all iced over."

Edythe backed toward the doorway leading to the kitchen. "Let me do that for you."

"Gert's my horse—I'll see to her."

Missy whisked in front of Edythe. "If you're not feeling well, you shouldn't go out in the cold." She pushed Edythe behind the doorjamb and out of sight. Edythe took advantage of the moment to race upstairs and hide the dresser scarf in her underwear drawer. Missy's voice carried from the kitchen. "Don't be silly. Edythe or I can break the ice just as well as you, and Gertie won't care who does it as long as it gets done."

"But—"

"Let me do it, please?"

Edythe raced back down to see Missy using her best pleading face on Luthenia. She hid her smile—Luthenia would have a hard time resisting the sweetly begging Missy.

"Well . . ." Luthenia massaged her temple with her fingertips. Then she jerked upright and sniffed the air. "Do I smell supper cookin'?"

Missy lifted her chin, her grin saucy. "Yep. Ham an' beans with corn bread. That is"—she hunched her shoulders and giggled—"there'll be corn bread soon as I put it in the oven. I was waiting for you to wake up."

"Hmph!" Luthenia folded her arms over her chest and scowled. But her eyes twinkled. "Seems the two o' you have taken over my house an' don't need me at all. Cookin' supper, carin' for my horse . . . Next thing I know, you'll be sayin' the prayers around here, too."

Edythe might read the Bible every day, as she'd promised, but she wasn't ready to talk to God. "We just want to see to Gertie. We'll leave the praying to you, Luthenia."

Chapter
THIRTY

Edythe lifted her face to the sun and drew in a deep breath of the crisp, cold air. She flicked a quick glance at Luthenia and Missy, who walked along beside her. Both of them also appeared to drink in the bright sunshine. Only three days of being cooped up like chickens in a cage, but it had seemed longer. She smiled. "Sure is good to be out and walking under the sun."

"'Specially since we're headed to the Lord's house," Luthenia replied.

"I'm glad the menfolk got the street cleared," Missy contributed. "It'd be awful hard to walk if they hadn't."

"Yep," Luthenia said, "livin' on the main street has its blessings. Menfolk'll clear it, be it blocked by snow, tumbleweeds, or a busted wagon."

They moved at a brisk pace, their breath puffing out in little clouds. They came to an especially mucky patch of melting snow. Luthenia and Missy plowed straight through it, but Edythe lifted her skirts above the high tops of her lace-up shoes before tiptoeing through the mess. Some might consider it scandalous to show so much leg, but she wasn't keen on ruining her dress by dragging it through the puddle on the street. Folks would just have to understand.

Missy's cheeks glowed bright pink and her nose looked red as a ripe cherry, but she wore a smile. "Mrs. Kinsley, do you think the country folks will make it in for service today?"

"Why, sure. I figure everybody's tired of bein' stuck in their homes." Luthenia shook her head. "I'm eager to count noses in church—durin' a fierce storm, seems someone always falls ill or faces some other tragedy. I've been prayin' everyone stayed safe."

Missy said, "Edie, if Martha makes it in, can I sit with her?"

"*May* I," Edythe corrected.

Missy sent Luthenia an impatient look. "Edie's ready for school. She's bein' my teacher again."

Luthenia chuckled. "Don't reckon she can help it, honey."

Missy sighed. "If Martha makes it in, *may* I sit with her?"

"You may."

"Good!" Missy skipped ahead, humming.

Luthenia's eyes twinkled. She whispered, "Glad she didn't ask to sit with William Sholes."

Edythe nodded in agreement. Up ahead, wagons with sleigh rails in place of wheels stood in a haphazard row alongside the churchyard. Edythe looked down the row of horses, identifying who'd come to church by the animal held in the traces. She recognized the Sterbinzes' horse, the Brides' and the Wolcotts', as well as Joel Townsend's Jody. "Looks as though the families who live south of town made it in."

Luthenia shielded her eyes with her hand and examined the wagons. "I don't see any of the northern neighbors' wagons, but they might make it yet. Another fifteen minutes or so before service'll start—there's time." She slung her arm around Edythe's shoulders, grinning. "C'mon. My old heart's ready for a time of fellowship." Her feet sped, kicking up little clumps of brackish snow. Edythe and Luthenia climbed the clean-swept stairs behind Missy and entered the church together.

Folks visited, laughter ringing from every corner. While she hung her coat and scarf on a hook at the back of the sanctuary, Edythe overheard a comment about the Wolcotts losing three milk cows in the storm. Much as she hated to think of the animals' deaths, she hoped tragedies would be limited to four-legged creatures. Storms could claim human lives, too.

"Miss Amsel! Miss Amsel!" The two Townsend boys dashed to Edythe.

"Hello, boys!" Edythe bent forward and embraced the pair. Her heart lifted as their arms circled her neck, hugging hard.

"That was some storm, huh?" Johnny clamped his hands behind his back and rocked on his heels. "Snowed so hard Uncle Joel couldn't even make it to the barn 'til Friday. He was plenty worried 'bout our horse an' cow an' chickens."

"Yep," Robert added, his eyes sparkling. "He tried goin' out durin' the storm, but he fell down, an' me an' Johnny almost hadda go for help."

Johnny scowled at Robert. "Don't fib, Robert."

Robert sent his brother an innocent look. "Not fibbin'. You was gonna go to the Sterbinzes, an' I was gonna take care of Uncle Joel 'til you got back. That's helpin', ain't it?"

"It's not *goin'* for help."

Robert rolled his eyes, then faced Edythe again. "But we didn't have to, 'cause Uncle Joel woke up an' said he was all right. He sure scared us, though!" The boys dashed off.

Edythe pressed her hands to her bodice. Her heart thudded at twice its normal rhythm. If the boys weren't telling tales and Joel had been out in the blizzard, he might have suffered frostbite or picked up a chill. She wouldn't be able to rest until she knew he was all right. With so many folks clustered inside the church, she had a little difficulty locating him. But she finally spotted him in the corner visiting with Maribelle Jenkins.

She started to cross to them, but then came to a halt, taking a good look at Joel. He stood in a casual pose—his weight on one hip, one thumb caught in his trouser pocket. He looked straight into the Jenkins girl's face, a half smile dimpling his cheek. He laughed softly at something she said, his eyes never shifting away.

Edythe turned her attention to the girl, noting how she held Joel's gaze, her lips curved with a sweetly attentive smile. The young woman lifted one hand and grazed Joel's sleeve with her fingertips, then carried her fingers to her mouth to cover a little giggle. They were flirting! Right in church under the whole town's nose. Obviously Joel had lost his interest in courting the schoolmarm. She should be relieved . . . but another emotion captured her.

She whirled to escape and nearly collided with Mary Scheebeck, who cradled her baby son. "Oh! Please excuse me. I didn't see you there," Edythe said.

A knowing look crept across Mrs. Scheebeck's face. She sent a quick glance toward Joel and the Jenkins girl. "Were you watching Mr. Townsend an' Maribelle? Soon as he stepped through the doors, he hightailed it over to talk to her." The woman absently rocked, her voice soft and singsongy. "Never've seen Mr. Townsend move so fast. And I don't mind telling you, I'm glad to see him takin' an interest in Maribelle. High time he took a wife."

Jealousy blocked Edythe's voice box.

The woman went on. "Wally thought for a while he'd taken a shine to you, Miss Amsel, but considerin' you ain't stayin', it's probably best he set his sights elsewhere."

Edythe frowned. "Not staying?" How on earth would the Scheebecks know if she intended to stay or not?

Mrs. Scheebeck's eyes widened. "Did I speak out of turn? Thought for sure the town council'd already talked to you since Wally said . . ." The woman clamped her lips for a moment, but then she shrugged. "Well, you'll be findin' out soon enough. Maybe it's best you hear it from me rather than one of the men. I kinda hate to see you go. Lewis an' Jenny are so fond of you. But, Miss Amsel, you just got too many wild notions for our little town. All your strange ways of teachin', and then wantin' to run off to hear some woman suffragist speak."

She grimaced. "Mr. Libolt wanted to send you packin' right away, but the others talked him into lettin' you finish the year. But they aren't goin' to ask you to stay." The baby let out a weak wail. Mrs. Scheebeck shifted him to her shoulder and patted his little back, giving Edythe a worried look. "You won't let Wally know I told you, will you?"

Edythe lifted her chin. "I'm not a talebearer."

The woman flushed. The baby's wail increased in volume. "I think Wallace is hungry. 'Scuse me." Mrs. Scheebeck hurried off.

Reverend Coker moved to the raised dais at the front of the church, and people shuffled to their seats. Edythe observed Joel sliding in next to Maribelle Jenkins and her folks. She sat beside Luthenia, her mouth pressed into a tight line. She had no right to be jealous. She'd told Joel she wasn't interested in marriage. But seeing him with Maribelle Jenkins somehow hurt more than knowing the town council didn't want to keep her.

The joy of the storm's passage faded in light of these new developments. Her heart ached, thinking about saying good-bye to Luthenia and the schoolchildren. She consoled herself with the notion that it was best for Joel to look elsewhere. Those little boys would benefit from a woman's influence. And Missy would be happy—she wanted to return to Omaha. Edythe would look for a new teaching job there.

She sniffed hard, an unwelcome sting attacking the back of her nose. Even as she opened her mouth and joined in singing the opening hymn, her heart felt heavy. The congregation sang of things well with one's soul. Edythe closed her eyes, but she could find no peace for her own aching soul.

• • •

Weeks blessed with bright sunshine followed the blizzard that had trapped the residents of Walnut Hill in their homes for three days. Cold days, but clear, with only one brief period of snow that came and went so quickly Edythe thought she might have imagined the glittering flakes dancing outside the schoolhouse windows.

She kept the potbellied stove blazing, and the students placed potatoes along the stove's fender. All morning the potatoes baked, filling the room with a wonderful aroma; then at lunchtime, the students had something warm to eat. Edythe considered bringing a soup kettle and fixings to teach cooking to the middle-grade students, but she sensed the town council members would disapprove of spending reading and arithmetic time on something the youngsters could learn at home, so she refrained. She despised herself for yielding to their old-fashioned thinking, yet she'd need a good recommendation from them to secure another position. She dared not upset the council again.

She continued teaching the amendments to the Constitution—those referred to as the Bill of Rights as well as others both proposed and ratified over nearly a century. She dedicated a significant amount of time to the Fifteenth Amendment, since it dealt with suffrage based on race, skin color, or previous condition of servitude. Insightful discussions followed the lessons, and often she only had to ask a question to direct their thoughts and then allow the students to share. Martha and Louisa in particular had very bright, intuitive minds, and more and more she mourned the recognition that these intelligent girls would not have a say in their country's leadership unless a bill concerning women's suffrage was passed.

In the evenings, after grading assignments and preparing the next day's lessons, she pulled out her writing paper and pen. By the glow of Luthenia's oil lamp, she wrote strongly worded letters to congressmen and state leaders concerning the importance of giving equal rights to all citizens regardless of gender. She never received a reply, and she tired of Wally Scheebeck's dismayed headshaking, yet she continued because she believed change needed to come. Not for herself—she couldn't recapture what her family had lost—but for the young women sitting in her classroom.

Trekking nearly daily to the mercantile to mail letters put her in contact with Wally and Mary Scheebeck, both of whom seemed to relish sharing intriguing nuggets of gossip. Although Edythe did her best to close her ears to their tongue wagging, she couldn't prevent herself from listening when they mentioned Joel Townsend's name.

The entire community predicted that when spring arrived, Joel Townsend and Maribelle Jenkins would announce their intention to wed. The rumor ate away at her insides and kept her awake at night. Jealousy plagued her, and the jealousy made her angry at herself. She had no reason to care if he married Maribelle. Yet she cared deeply, and each Sunday when Joel nodded his head in a distant greeting and brushed past her to speak to Maribelle, she felt as though a knife stabbed through her heart. At least Johnny and Robert continued to greet her enthusiastically, whether at school, the mercantile, or the church sanctuary.

She faithfully read her Bible each night before blowing out the lamp. Knowing William Sholes's parents were church attenders, she memorized verses suitable as reprimands when the boy misbehaved. To her pleased surprise, he responded more readily to phrases from God's Word than any she could construct, no matter how sternly spoken. So she sought others, building her bank of Scripture.

One night, reading in Psalm 119, she came upon the verse "Thy word have I hid in mine heart, that I might not sin against thee." With a start, she realized she'd been hiding God's words away in her heart for the purpose of disciplining William. But this verse seemed to indicate memorization was of benefit to the one who held the Scripture. She pondered that idea for many nights, wondering if God might use His words to impact her life.

February rushed toward March, and the sun—still bright—sent down a little more warmth. Planting season waited only weeks away, which meant Edythe's time in Walnut Hill with Luthenia and the students she'd grown to love would soon conclude. She wished she knew where she and Missy would go when the year was over. She considered asking Luthenia to pray for direction, but she knew Luthenia would tell her to ask God herself. But Edythe's ears didn't seem tuned to His voice, so she stumbled on, wondering and worrying on her own.

The first day of March, Edythe awakened early and padded downstairs before Luthenia roused. She sat at the table in the pink glow of a quiet predawn and stared across the neat, humble kitchen—a place of refuge and peace. Sitting there alone, she made a decision. Since it seemed the town council wouldn't invite her back no matter what she did, she would teach the way she wanted to teach during the remaining weeks of school. She would send out letters of interest to schools surrounding Omaha. And she would begin saying good-bye in her heart to Luthenia, Johnny and Robert, Martha, little Jenny, and all the others. When May arrived, and the school closed, she and Missy would pack their valises, board the stage, and not look back.

"A new beginning," she whispered to the empty room, her words bouncing from the ceiling to ring through her ears. Happy words—words of promise. So why did tears follow?

Chapter
THIRTY~ONE

"Joel! Joel Townsend, wait up there!"

Joel paused on his way to the wagon. The boys also stopped, turning to watch Luthenia Kinsley trot across the churchyard toward them.

She came to a breathless halt a couple of feet away and panted, patting her chest. "Mercy! I'm gettin' too old to be runnin' after folks." An airy laugh spilled out, and she smiled down at the boys. "Been a long time since you come by my place for cookies." She sent Joel a pointed look.

Robert took hold of Joel's hand and swung it. "We can come today, I reckon."

Miz Kinsley laughed again. "Today I have oatmeal raisin. They're for dessert, though. Thought maybe you an' your uncle would like to come help me eat a big ol' pork roast."

"Mmm!" Robert licked his lips and tugged at Joel's hand. "Can we, Uncle Joel?"

Johnny tugged on the other hand. "Can we?"

Joel lifted his shoulders in a sheepish shrug. "We can't make it today."

"Awww!" the boys groaned.

He released their hands and gently pushed them toward the wagon. "Go climb in, boys—and mind where you walk." The spring's first rain had left behind squashed brown grass and muddy puddles.

Both boys scuffed to the wagon, their heads low.

Joel removed his hat and ran his hand over his hair. "I know the boys've missed seein' you. But we've been invited to the Jenkinses' place for Sunday lunch. I shouldn't keep Miz Jenkins waitin'."

A smile—half sly, half sad—tipped up the corners of Miz Kinsley's mouth. "I reckon it's Maribelle you're not wantin' to keep waitin'."

Joel released a self-conscious chuckle. "Well, Miz Jenkins does most of the cookin', but Maribelle's the one who invited us."

Miz Kinsley crossed her arms over her chest. "You been eatin' quite a few Sunday dinners at the Jenkinses' place the past couple months. Are the rumors I've been hearin' around town true? You're wooin' Maribelle?"

Heat rushed to Joel's face. The word *wooing* grated. But what else would he call it? He'd been keeping company with Maribelle for more than six weeks. Folks were bound to notice. He nodded.

"S'pose I oughtta say congratulations, then."

Joel couldn't decide from her tone if she was congratulating him or telling herself she needed to. So he just nodded again.

"Maribelle's a fine girl." Miz Kinsley spoke slowly, as if she had a hard time forming words. "Seems I might've even mentioned that a ways back. As I recall, you told me she was too young for you."

Joel tapped his hat on his leg. "I reckon she's aged a bit since then."

"Yep. So've you." Another odd statement.

Joel gestured toward the wagon, inching backward. "The Jenkinses are waiting, Miz Kinsley, so I better—"

She flapped both hands at him. "Go. I'll wrap up them cookies an' send 'em with Edythe to school. She can give 'em to the boys at the end of the day so the other young'uns won't be jealous."

"That sounds fine. Thanks for thinkin' of 'em." He plopped his hat into place and trotted off before she could say anything else to hold him up. He climbed into the wagon, released the brake, and snapped the reins. He'd removed the sleigh rails and reattached the wheels a few days ago, and they squeaked as they carried the wagon over the deeply rutted road that led to the Jenkinses' farm. The boys hunkered in the straw in the back, dozing. With the boys quiet and nobody else around, it gave him time to think. Maybe too much time to think.

Miz Kinsley wasn't the conniving sort, but he suspected her invitation to dinner was her way of finding out what he was doing with Maribelle. She wouldn't come right out and question him because she was too polite. Others in town had no such compunction. He'd managed to dodge the questions so far, but speculation abounded, and it wouldn't be long before he'd have to announce his intentions. Mainly because Maribelle's folks were asking. As often as they'd fed him and the boys lately, he owed them straight answers.

Maribelle deserved straight answers, too. He'd eaten at her folks' dinner table six Sundays in a row, sat with her in church, and he and the boys even had taken her to the restaurant in Lincoln Valley one mild Saturday evening in late February. All of those things added up in a woman's head. Before long, he'd have to, as the fellows said, pop the question. Which was the reason he'd started seeing her in the first place, wasn't it?

Maybe today . . . His mouth went dry at the thought. Giving himself a little shake, he tugged the reins, guiding Jody to turn in at the lane. Moments later, Maribelle welcomed him and the boys into the house. She picked little bits of straw out of Robert's hair, laughing as she did so.

It was a motherly gesture, one that should've given Joel's heart a real lift. But instead he wanted to leap forward and take over the task. He pushed his hands into his trouser pockets.

Maribelle plucked the coats from the boys' shoulders and flashed a smile at him. "Mother just finished putting dinner on the table—she expected you a bit earlier."

Not a hint of displeasure colored her tone, although Joel suspected Minnie Jenkins would fuss about his late arrival. He'd never met a more punctilious woman. Fortunately, Maribelle didn't emulate her mother in that regard.

"We can eat right away," Maribelle went on. "I imagine you're hungry, aren't you, Johnny and Robert?" Her voice took on a lilt—the way folks spoke if they weren't comfortable talking to children. She'd need to get over that quick when she became his wife.

The boys followed Joel and Maribelle and climbed into the same chairs they'd occupied on previous visits. By now they should've been at ease in the Jenkinses' house, but Joel noted they sat with stiff spines, their hands in their laps, as if afraid of making a mistake. Then he realized he was doing the same thing. He deliberately slumped in the chair, only to catch Miz Jenkins's lips pinch into a disapproving line. He straightened.

Tad Jenkins asked the blessing. His deep voice

reverberated with reverence, and Joel felt a bit of his tension drain away. How could a fellow stay uptight during prayer? Listening to Mr. Jenkins pray warmed him toward Maribelle. A woman who'd been reared by a man with strong faith would know how to pass it along to children.

He took the platter of stewed beef and ladled servings into his and the boys' plates. "Thank you, Uncle Joel," they said in turn.

Maribelle beamed. "Such polite boys." She looked at her mother, her eyebrows high. "Aren't they polite boys, Ma?"

Miz Jenkins's lips quirked into something that might pass for a smile. "Very polite."

Joel continued scooping out food for the three of them. By the time all the dishes were passed, their plates were overflowing. One thing Joel could say about Miz Jenkins—she was a fine cook. The boys thought so, too. They cleaned their plates while the grown-ups chatted.

Joel and Mr. Jenkins discussed the coming planting season. After mentioning his favorite place to get seed corn, Jenkins said, "What's this I hear about your diggin' ditches all over your property?"

Joel stabbed his fork into a mound of boiled beets. "My irrigation ditches? They aren't everywhere—just out in the cornfield."

Maribelle laughed softly and swatted at his arm, as if he'd made a joke.

Jenkins cleared his throat. "I reckon that took some time, diggin' ditches."

"It did." Joel picked up Robert's napkin and mopped at gravy on the boy's chin. "But it was well worth the hours spent. If we don't get rain, I channel the water from the Little Platte."

The man frowned. "I trust the Lord to bring rain in due season."

Joel had heard that argument many times before. But he had a successful corn crop every year thanks to his irrigation ditches. Could the other farmers make the same claim? "I trust the Lord, too. He gave me the brains to come up with a way to water my crops an' the muscle to do the work digging those ditches. I thank Him for my harvest."

"Mm-hmm . . ." Jenkins looked across the table at Johnny and Robert. "I see you boys are done." He sounded gruff but not unkind. At least he spoke to them. Minnie either sent them critical glances or pretended they weren't there. "You like puppies?"

Both boys nodded, their eyes round. "Yes, sir."

"We got puppies in the barn. How 'bout I take you out and show you."

In unison, they looked at Joel.

Joel smiled. "That'd be real nice, Mr. Jenkins."

"Tad." The man shot a quick look at his daughter, his cheeks mottling. "Might as well drop all the mister and missus nonsense, given the circumstances."

Joel read the man's meaning. He turned to the boys. "Wear your coats, an' stay with Mr. Jenkins."

"Yes, sir!" The boys bounced up and shot for the corner of the parlor, where Maribelle had laid their jackets across a chair. They jammed their arms into the sleeves then trailed Tad out the door.

Minnie leaned back and placed her palms flat on the table. "Since your father tucked the children out of the way, I'll begin clearing this table so you two have time to . . . *talk*."

Joel didn't miss the subtle emphasis on the last word. He pushed away from the table and held out his elbow. "It's not too cold today. If you wear your coat"—he glanced at her dress, a lightweight flowered frock that didn't look as though it would offer any protection from a chill wind—"we could take a little walk and . . . talk." He used the same inflection her mother had.

"That sounds grand, Joel." She giggled, the sound very young and feminine. She donned her coat, then slipped her fingers into the bend of his elbow. He felt their quiver, a sign of nervousness. Would an independent woman like Edythe Amsel tremble like a leaf in a stout breeze when walking with her beau? They strolled side by side to the fenced corral, where a lone sorrel horse nosed the muddy ground.

Maribelle released his arm and draped her hands over the top rail. Then she rested her cheek on her knuckles and peeked at him, her eyelids fluttering. "What did you want to talk about?"

He leaned against the fence, hooking one heel on the lowest rail. "I . . . um . . ."

She giggled again. "Joel . . ." One hand slid across the rail and grazed his upper arm. "Are you comin' over here just to eat my ma's cookin', or did you have somethin' else in mind?"

He blinked twice, gathering his wits, then cleared his throat. "I reckon it's more'n your ma's cookin'." He grinned, his lips twitching. "Although the cookin' is a powerful draw. I suppose you know all her recipes?"

Her green eyes twinkled. A strand of honey-colored hair slipped free of her ponytail and whisked across her chin, drawing his attention to her smiling mouth. Not once had her lips enticed him to kiss her.

"A few. But not all. I'm the only child, you know. I've been a little spoiled."

Her honesty surprised him. So she might not be a good cook—did that matter? He and the boys had gone more than two years eating mostly beans, and they'd survived. He considered the things he liked about her. She was a Christian—that was important. Open. Honest. And she was pretty. Young, certainly, but she'd mature in time.

Suddenly she popped upright, pinning him with a serious look. "Are you wantin' to marry me, Joel Townsend?"

He swallowed a snort. She was open, all right.

" 'Cause Ma an' Pa would approve. They know you've got a fine farm, with a good crop every year, and that you're a God-fearing man." Her lashes fluttered again, but Joel suspected she was winking back emotion rather than flirting with him. "If you want to marry me, I'd surely like to hear you say so."

He recalled similar words from Susannah so long ago. *"A woman wants to hear how a man feels about her."* But he'd never been good at flowery speech. He still wasn't. But he'd do his best. He opened his mouth to tell her what she waited to hear, but something shouted in his head: *Wait!* He jerked.

She frowned. "Joel?"

He pushed off the fence and faced her. They stood so close he could see his own reflection in her green irises. The green reminded him of the flecks in Miss Amsel's eyes. "Maribelle, I—" *Wait!* That voice again. He slapped the fence. "I'm havin' a hard time finding the right words. . . . Maybe we should—" He intended to say "wait," but Johnny and Robert came charging out of the barn and straight toward him, each cradling a puppy.

319

Maribelle turned to meet them, reaching out to scratch the pups and also tousle the boys' hair. She flicked a smile in Joel's direction. "Don'tcha want to pet the pups? They're real sweet."

Heaving a sigh, Joel stepped forward and placed his big hand over the head of the puppy Robert held. Maribelle cupped her hand over his, smiling shyly at him. He needed someone to help take care of his boys, and she was willing. "Maribelle . . ."

Wait!

He shook his head. Waiting didn't make sense. He needed a wife *now*. He pushed the irritating voice aside. "Let's go ask your pa for his blessing."

Chapter
THIRTY~TWO

By Monday morning, Joel knew he'd made a mistake. A restless night spent under the weight of regret convinced him he'd forged forward when he should've held back. Instead, he'd stated his intentions to Maribelle, received her father's blessing, and by noon today half the town would know he'd asked Maribelle Jenkins to be Mrs. Joel Townsend. How could he turn back now? Especially since she'd already suffered the humiliation of another beau changing his mind.

As he spooned cornmeal mush into bowls for the boys, he told himself things would be all right in the end. After all, Maribelle was a fine girl. Even though he didn't love her, he held a fondness for her. Love would come in time. At long last, he'd have a helpmeet. Someone to nurture his boys, someone to help in his home, someone to sit with beside the fire late in the evening and talk about the day. The Bible said man shouldn't be alone, and now he wouldn't be.

Joel sat down and prayed for their simple breakfast, and when the boys picked up their spoons to dig in to their bowls, he cleared his throat. "Johnny and Robert, I got somethin' important to tell you."

Both popped a spoonful of mush into their mouths, their eyes on him, interested and innocent.

He wiped his hand down his face. "It's been just the three of us ever since you came to live with me, an' we've got along pretty good, but . . ." His mouth felt dry. He gulped a sip of coffee, scalding his tongue. Clapping the cup back on the table, he sucked air to cool his tongue. The boys sent each other a curious glance, then turned in unison to face him again. He swallowed. "Somebody else'll be joinin' us soon."

Robert flipped his spoon upside down in his mouth and let it rest there, his lips pursed around it. Johnny leaned toward his uncle. "Who?"

"Maribelle Jenkins."

Both boys sat straight up in their chairs, their eyebrows shooting high. Robert lowered his hand, but the spoon still dangled from his mouth. Joel removed it before the boy choked.

"What do you say about that?" Joel forced joviality into his tone. "Won't that be nice?"

Johnny scowled. "You're talkin' like *she* does."

Joel sent Johnny a puzzled look. "What?"

"Real high and sweetie-sweet. When she talks to me an' Robert, she changes her voice."

Joel had observed the same thing and had credited it to a small amount of discomfort. He hadn't realized he'd adopted the singsong, sugary tone. Did that mean he was uncomfortable sharing the news? A man should feel joyful, saying his intended's name out loud. The sense of dread that had fallen on him during the night increased in intensity. To combat it, he tweaked Johnny's ear. "I reckon she's just tryin' to be extra nice."

"She won't talk like that forever, will she?" Robert yanked up his spoon again and shoved it deep into the mush.

Joel chuckled. "I figure she'll talk to you just like she'd talk to anybody once she gets to know you better." His gaze darted back and forth between the pair of freckled, fresh-scrubbed faces. "So . . . do you think you'll like it . . . having Maribelle here to cook for us an' help take care of . . . us?"

For long seconds, neither boy spoke. Then Johnny offered a hesitant nod. "Sure, Uncle Joel."

"Sure," Robert echoed. Then he shrugged. "Never once had beans at the Jenkinses' place, so she prob'ly don't know how to fix 'em."

Joel released a genuine laugh. Trust Robert to find the most important reason to bring Maribelle into the house. Then he sobered. "Boys, you know this means she'll be—well, like a ma to the two of you. I want you to be happy. If you don't think you can be happy with Maribelle, I want you to tell me." He held his breath. If either of the boys voiced strong feelings against his marrying Maribelle, he'd call things off immediately, even if it did mean upsetting her parents and putting her in an embarrassing position. His heart pattered—part in apprehension and part, he realized, in hope.

"It'll be all right." Johnny spoke with confidence, his skinny shoulders squared. "When we came here to live with you, we just wanted Ma an' Pa. But we love you now. We'll get to lovin' Maribelle someday, too." He looked at his brother. "Right, Robert?"

Robert nodded silently.

Joel tugged Johnny out of his chair and wrapped him in a tight hug. "You're a fine boy, an' anyone would be proud to have you as a son. Maribelle will be lovin' the two of you in no time." He released the boy with a light pat on the seat of his britches. "Finish up your breakfast now so I can get you off to school. Slow goin', with the roads muddy—you'll need to leave a little early."

"Yes, sir." The boys turned their focus to emptying their bowls.

Joel pushed the mush around in his bowl, unable to eat. He hoped he'd been truthful with the boys. Maribelle hadn't acted disinclined to taking on his boys, but she was so young and she was an only child. What kind of mother would she be? Then Joel realized Miss Amsel had been even younger when she'd stepped into the role of mothering her brothers and sisters. If she could handle it at fourteen, surely Maribelle, who was already twenty-one, would manage.

Sure she would. They'd be just fine . . . wouldn't they?

A few seconds before three o'clock, Edythe stood behind her desk and clapped her palms sharply together to gain the attention of her students. "William, it's your turn to clean the blackboards." She ignored his grimace of displeasure and turned to face Johnny and Robert

324

Townsend. "Boys, I need to speak with you before you leave." She grinned to assure them they weren't in trouble, then glanced at the clock. The minute hand clicked up to the twelve. "Class dismissed."

The children charged toward the cloakroom, and William trudged to the blackboard along the east wall. Edythe stepped off the teaching platform to speak with the Townsend boys. Aware of William's listening ears, she spoke softly. "I have a little something for you from Mrs. Kinsley." She pressed a cloth-wrapped bundle into Johnny's hands.

The boys' faces lit. "Thank you, Miss Amsel!" they said in unison.

"You're very welcome." Her fingers itched to smooth Robert's hair into place—one tuft stuck straight up on the left side of his head. She linked her fingers together before she succumbed to the urge. How she would miss these boys when she left town . . . "Be sure to tell her thank you when you see her next. She's kind to treat you."

Robert blinked up at her, his expression filled with an emotion Edythe couldn't quite define. "She prob'ly won't have to bake us cookies anymore, though. We're gettin' a new mother to bake us cookies."

Edythe's eyebrows shot up. "Oh?"

Johnny scowled at his brother. "Robert, Uncle Joel didn't say we could tell."

"Didn't say we couldn't, either."

"Even so . . ."

Before they could launch a full-fledged argument, Edythe interrupted. "That's fine, boys. You needn't share any personal information with me." Besides, she'd already heard the news. Maribelle Jenkins would receive a real gift in the form of two towheaded, round-cheeked boys with big hearts and tender spirits. Tears stung behind her eyes.

"You two better hurry on home now before your uncle starts to worry about you." Her voice came out unnaturally high, an attempt to hide her writhing emotions. "Johnny, put that packet in your lunch bucket, hmm?"

"Yes, ma'am."

Robert poked Johnny on the arm. "Wanna race?"

"I can beat you hoppin' on one foot," Johnny bragged.

Robert spun and shot toward the cloakroom, and Johnny tore after him.

William wadded up the cleaning rag and placed it in the bucket beside the blackboard. "All done, Miss Amsel."

Smudges clouded the square of black, but Edythe decided to let William go rather than insist he use a wet cloth to thoroughly clean the board. Eagerness to hurry to Luthenia's and ask if she knew about Robert's announcement made her wave a hand of dismissal at the boy. He dashed out the door with a grin.

Edythe quickly performed her end-of-the-day duties, then scurried outside and locked the door behind her. All of the children were gone except Missy and Martha Sterbinz, who stood chatting beside the Sterbinzes' wagon. Terrill sat on the high seat, his elbows on his knees, looking toward the schoolhouse. When Edythe stepped off the porch, he whipped off his hat.

"Afternoon, Miss Amsel. Told Missy here I'd tote you ladies to town. Gotta take Martha anyways—no trouble to give you a ride, too."

Edythe walked slowly toward the wagon. She'd managed to hold herself aloof from Martha's older brother, and she didn't want to give him the impression she'd changed her mind about keeping company with him. But desire to quiz Luthenia about Joel Townsend prevailed over determination to keep Terrill at a distance. "Thank you, Mr. Sterbinz. That's very kind of you."

Missy and Martha clambered into the back, giggling. Edythe moved toward the rear of the wagon, intending to join them, but Terrill leaped down and stepped into her pathway. "Plenty of room on the seat." He clutched her elbow and propelled her along the ground. Then he grabbed her around the waist and lifted her. She let out a little squeak of surprise. Martha and Missy exploded in a fresh round of giggles.

Edythe's face burned with embarrassment as she settled onto the wagon's seat, and she flashed a stern look at her sister. Missy grinned impishly in response, even daring to wink. Edythe whirled around and sat straight-spined, her face aimed ahead, while Terrill jogged to the other side and climbed aboard. He gave her a broad grin and took up the reins. "Giddy-yap!"

The wagon jolted forward, and Edythe smacked her hands over her books to keep them from flying off her lap. Missy and Martha visited in the back, but Edythe and Terrill rode in silence. She sensed him sending her sidelong glances, but she determinedly kept her gaze forward, pretending not to notice.

Terrill drew the horse to a stop outside Luthenia's house. Missy scrambled out of the back. "Bye, Martha! See you tomorrow!"

"Bye, Missy," Martha said.

Edythe shifted to the edge of the seat, hugging her books to her chest with one arm and clutching the seat's raised lip with the other. She placed her foot on the wheel's hub, prepared to hop down. "Good-bye, Martha. Thank you for the ride, Mr. Sterbinz."

Terrill caught her arm, holding her in place.

She sent an unsmiling look over her shoulder, but he didn't let loose.

"I was wonderin' if you'd care to drive over to Lincoln Valley Friday evenin' for supper at the hotel?" His grin stretched wide, his bearing sure.

How many times must the man be told no before he finally accepted the message? Edythe drew in a breath, seeking patience.

"Their dining room serves up a good meal. Be a pleasure to take you. Missy could come, too, an' Martha. Be a real treat for the girls."

Martha beamed, curling her hands over the back of the seat. "It'd be fun, Miss Amsel."

Missy stood on the ground, her hands clasped in supplication beneath her chin. "I've never eaten at a hotel dining room."

Edythe looked from Missy to Martha to Terrill. Two pleading faces and one overconfident one.

Missy crooned, "Please, Edie? Can't we go?"

Martha's blue eyes begged.

Edythe wanted to refuse, but how could she do so without crushing the girls? She blew out the air she'd been holding. "I suppose."

The girls squealed with glee, startling the horse into nervous shifting. Terrill held tight to the traces. When the horse settled down, he caught Edythe's elbow again and helped her over the edge. "I'll pick you ladies up from school on Friday an' we'll head straight to Lincoln Valley. 'Bout a thirty-minute ride. I'll see you then." He flicked the reins, and the wagon rolled away with Martha waving from the back.

Edythe shot Missy a stern look. "A lot of help you are."

Missy feigned innocence. "What did I do?"

Edythe rolled her eyes. "Never mind."

Missy dashed for the house. She banged through the front door, calling, "Mrs. Kinsley! Edie an' me are going to Lincoln Valley for supper on Friday!"

Edythe closed the door behind her and dropped her books on the sofa. Luthenia bustled in from the kitchen as Edythe let out a groan of frustration. The older woman chuckled. "For someone who got a dinner invitation, you don't look too happy."

Edythe scowled. "I'm not." She shifted to look at Missy, who leaned against the kitchen doorway and grinned. "Take my books upstairs, please. Then get started on your homework."

"But—"

"*Now,* Missy."

Missy let out a little huff, but she disappeared around the corner.

Edythe folded her arms over her chest and scowled at Luthenia. "Terrill Sterbinz asked Missy and me to accompany him and Martha to Lincoln Valley Friday evening for supper."

Luthenia didn't even blink an eye.

"If the girls hadn't been so excited, I would have declined. But I suspect he knew I wouldn't be able to disappoint them."

A slight grin twitched at Luthenia's cheek. "I reckon you're right there."

Edythe sank onto the edge of the sofa, looking up at Luthenia in dismay. "I've done my utmost to convince him—and the entire community—that I'm not interested in being courted. Going to Lincoln Valley with Terrill will send the opposite message."

"But it might be a good thing you're goin', 'cause it'll send a message to—" Luthenia clamped her lips shut, her face clouding. "Oh, but it won't matter anymore because . . ."

Edythe frowned. "What is it?"

For a few seconds, Luthenia stood, her lips pressed so tightly they nearly disappeared. Then she sat next to Edythe and took her hand. "I gotta ask you somethin'."

"Of course."

"Have I imagined you an' Joel Townsend lookin' at each other in a special way?"

Edythe's heart leaped into her throat. "W-why do you ask?"

"'Cause there's somethin' I gotta tell you, an' I don't want to hurt you. It'd be a lot easier if I was sure I only imagined sparks flyin' between the two of you."

Forcing a light laugh, Edythe angled her chin high. "I've told you again and again, I have no desire to court anyone, and that includes Joel Townsend." Even to her ears, her statement didn't sound convincing.

Luthenia stared at Edythe, seeming to ponder

something. "I'll just out an' tell you, then. When I went to the mercantile today to fetch the mail an' newspaper, Wally Scheebeck told me Miz Jenkins had been in, an' she said Joel and her Maribelle will be gettin' hitched."

So the rumors were true. A fresh wave of sadness flooded her frame.

Luthenia nodded, her face somber. "Be good for Johnny an' Robert to have a woman in their lives. An' Joel—he won't be alone anymore."

"How . . ." Edythe's voice cracked, and she had to swallow and try again. "How nice for them. Maribelle is . . . is a lovely girl." Her nose stung too much to continue. She jumped up. "I need to get started on grading papers." She dashed around the corner before she broke down and made a complete fool of herself.

Chapter
THIRTY-THREE

With Missy sitting cross-legged in the middle of the bed, books strewn all around her, Edythe couldn't do what she longed to do—throw herself facedown across the rumpled quilt and indulge in a good cry. She couldn't remember the last time she'd allowed herself the unrestrained release of emotion. Being the oldest, the one in charge, the one setting the example, she'd always had to hold herself in check. To be mature and responsible. But just once she wished she could weep and pound her fists on the feather mattress and expend all of the bottled-up feelings that swirled through her middle.

Instead she sniffed hard, squared her shoulders, and sat stiffly on the edge of the bed. "Missy?"

Missy, her focus on the book resting on her crossed ankles, didn't look up. "Hmm?"

"I'm going to start sending letters to schools around Omaha to see if they have need of a teacher next year. Do you have any preferences for where you'd like to live?"

Missy sat up so quickly the braids wrapped around her crown quivered. "What do you mean?"

"I know you wanted to return to Omaha to be near Justus and Eulah when the baby comes, but I was wondering if we should—"

Missy shook her head hard. "Don't you like teaching here?"

The emotions Edythe had pushed down tried to rise again. She cleared her throat in an attempt to keep the tears at bay. "Of course I do, but—"

"Then why do you want to leave?"

Edythe lowered her brows and stared at her sister. "You wanted to leave. You said you didn't like it here."

Air exploded from Missy's lips in a loud huff. She flopped her arms outward. "Since when do you listen to anything I say? I was mad at you for leaving me with Justus, mad because you paid attention to other kids more than you did me, mad at . . . well, just *mad*." She grinned sheepishly. "But I'm not mad anymore. I like it here. I like Mrs. Kinsley, and Martha's the best friend I've ever had. I don't want to leave. Can't we stay?"

Edythe sighed. "No, we can't."

"But why?"

Because I'm in love with Joel Townsend and he's marrying someone else. Edythe swallowed. "The town council doesn't like me."

"Pffft." Missy made a sound similar to one Luthenia made when she wanted to disregard something. "They could change their minds. After all, the kids really like you. They want you to stay—they've told me so."

Pleasure flooded Edythe's frame. "But the students don't make the decision as to who teaches. And the council isn't planning to renew my contract." She discovered stating the truth aloud hurt more than thinking about it. She had to swallow again.

"Well . . ." Missy nibbled her thumbnail for a moment, her brow puckered in thought. "What if you didn't teach? What if we just . . . stayed?"

"We can't *just stay*. I have to have a way to support us."

"So get a job."

Edythe quirked one brow. "In Walnut Hill?" She pictured the business district—a mercantile, a feed and seed store, a small butcher shop that sold mostly wild game, and the requisite barber. The doctor didn't even have an office, but saw patients in a room in his home. "The town isn't exactly bustling with opportunities for employment, Missy. Especially for a woman."

Missy chewed the other thumb. She jerked, her face brightening. "You could get married!"

An image of Joel Townsend flashed in Edythe's mind. She sucked in a breath so sharply it tickled the back of her throat. She coughed into her fist for several seconds. The coughing dislodged the tickle but not the picture of Joel. "W-what?"

"Married. Martha said Terrill thinks you're pretty an' wants to court you." Missy's voice rose in excitement. "If you married him, we could move into Martha's farmhouse with her an' her ma an' Terrill. Then we wouldn't have to leave Walnut Hill at all! Don'tcha see?"

"I see you're quite adept at planning my life." Edythe tried not to sound sarcastic, but she didn't succeed. "I have no desire to marry anybody, including Terrill Sterbinz." Her heart ached anew. She'd worried that Joel Townsend might be falling in love with her, and it had frightened her. But knowing he loved someone else hurt much more than she could have anticipated.

Missy sighed, her head low.

"So we need to be thinking of where we'd like to go. Give it some thought and let me know, all right?"

Missy shifted her head slightly to look at Edythe with narrowed eyes. Her mouth formed a firm upside-down U. "I want to stay here."

Edythe reached for her sister's hand. "I know, but the town council—"

Missy bounced off the bed so fast two books slid onto the floor and landed with a loud smack. She didn't bother to scoop them up but stood glaring at Edythe with her hands on her hips. "You're giving up. And you *never* give up. I'm ashamed of you!" She flounced to the door, her nose in the air. "I'm going downstairs to Luthenia. I'll ask her to pray for the council to change its mind. *She'll* be willing to fight for us to stay. And you better start fighting, too, 'cause I won't leave Walnut Hill!" She slammed the door behind her.

Edythe stared after Missy, her mouth hanging open. She hadn't realized how attached her sister had become to the town and its people. Knowing Missy wanted to stay should have delighted her—she'd love nothing more than to continue teaching the students of Walnut Hill. But now, even if the council changed its mind and renewed her contract, she couldn't stay.

How could she remain here, watching

Maribelle Jenkins with Joel and Johnny and Robert without her heart breaking a little more every day? She flopped sideways onto the bed, hiding her face in the bend of her elbow. When had the thing she thought she wanted the least become the thing she wanted the most? And why had the desire come when it was too late to lay claim to it?

A light tap sounded on the door. Edythe sat up and sighed. "Missy, you can come on in. I'm not upset with you."

The door opened a crack and Luthenia poked her nose in. "It's me. Can I come in?"

Edythe patted the mattress. "I guess Missy told you she wants you to pray for us to be able to stay?"

Luthenia chuckled, shaking her head. She sat beside Edythe, making the bed springs squeak, and curled her work-worn hand over Edythe's knee. "Keepin' up with that sister of yours is like tryin' to catch a sunbeam. Never can quite get a grasp."

Despite her melancholy, Edythe laughed. Luthenia had gotten to know Missy well. And she'd been a wonderful influence for Missy.

"Your sister asked me to pray the council would invite you to stay another year." Luthenia's bony fingers tightened on Edythe's knee. "I told her I'd be prayin' God's will for both you and her. Bein' the selfish old woman I am, I'd like to have you stay. But not if it's against what God wants for you."

Edythe closed her eyes. "Luthenia, you talk about God's will, but I don't understand. Does a God in Heaven really care what happens to us down here?"

" 'Course He does!"

Looking Luthenia in the eyes, Edythe asked quietly, "Then why have I always had to take care of everything myself? I took care of my mother when she was ill. Then I took care of my brothers and sisters. And my father. And now my students." She picked up the Bible resting on the little bedside table and flipped it open. "I've been reading this, like you asked, and again and again I find Scripture that indicates we're loved and that God gives strength, peace, and comfort. But it must not be for me."

Slowly, reverently, Luthenia lifted the Bible from Edythe's hands. She laid it across her knees and turned pages. "Have you read the book of Mark yet, Edythe?"

Edythe nodded. She'd gotten as far as Romans.

"Do you remember the story about the rich man who came to Jesus an' asked what he could do to inherit eternal life?"

Edythe crunched her brow, trying to recall the story. "He claimed he'd been a good person who had obeyed the commandments."

"And what did Jesus tell him he needed to do?"

Glancing at the open book on Luthenia's lap, Edythe replied, "Jesus instructed the man to sell all he had, take up his cross, and follow Him."

"That's right. But the man couldn't do it—he was very wealthy, an' he couldn't bring himself to let go of what he had. Edythe . . ." Tears pooled in the older woman's eyes. "You got the same pride as the rich man in the Bible. You aren't holdin' tight to gold an' such, but you don't want to let go of bein' in charge. You've had control for so long, lettin' somebody else take it from you feels like weakness. But if you'd ever just lean into God's strength instead of relyin' on your own . . . why, you'd discover joy like you've never had before." She flung her arm around Edythe's shoulders and squeezed. "Just let go, Edythe, an' trust Him to guide you."

A tug-of-war more fierce than any she'd moderated on the schoolyard took place in Edythe's soul. Desire to lean into God's strength—to discover complete trust that the Lord would carry her—battled with the long-held practice of seeing to her own needs. She clenched her teeth and spoke between them. "I . . . don't know how . . ."

The arm on her shoulders tightened, and Luthenia lowered her head. Her eyes slipped closed, and her lips moved, although no sound emerged. Edythe sat very still, uncomfortable, yet unwilling to disturb the dear woman while she talked to the God she trusted, followed, and loved. Although Edythe didn't hear a word of the prayer, she knew Luthenia was lifting her and her needs to God. Her muscles ached from sitting so still and stiff, but she remained until Luthenia let out a mighty sigh and slid her arm away.

Luthenia rose. "Reckon I might as well tell you, I been prayin' ever since you came for God to do whatever it takes to bring you around to the knowledge of His love an' care for you. Knowin' the year's endin' soon, an' knowin' you're fixin' on leavin', I just now asked Him to act swift." She shook her finger in Edythe's face. "So you be watchful, Edythe Amsel. God's gonna move, an' when He does, you'll finally understand." A knowing smiled tipped up the corners of her lips. "Yep, you're gonna understand."

Chapter
THIRTY~FOUR

Rain fell steadily Tuesday and Wednesday, creating a gray curtain that dampened more than Edythe's clothing. Walking to school in the rain was even less pleasant than trudging through snow. Although the temperature had risen somewhat with the arrival of March, being soaked left her feeling chilly and out of sorts.

The children were impatient with indoor

activities after enjoying the days of outdoor play, and William Sholes—after a brief respite from prank playing—renewed his orneriness in earnest. Edythe caught herself looking forward to the last day of school when she'd be able to tell the boy farewell for good. Then her heart sank, realizing how many painful good-byes would accompany the one to William.

Luthenia had promised to pray for God's will, and Missy believed that meant she'd be staying in Walnut Hill. She refused to discuss any other possibilities, frustrating Edythe. Without telling her sister, Edythe sent out letters of interest to every school in Douglas County. Surely one of them would have need of a teacher, and she and Missy would be close to Justus and Eulah, Albert and Loren, and Frances and her husband, Clyde, again. Missy would be devastated when they had to leave at the end of May, but Edythe believed she'd accept a new town in time, just as she'd accepted Walnut Hill.

On Thursday, Martha approached Edythe during recess with a reminder from Terrill about their dinner in Lincoln Valley on Friday evening. Her face flushed as she whispered, "He'd like it if you'd wear your red dress. It's his favorite."

Edythe managed to smile and reply, "It's my favorite, too." But as Martha scampered back to her lunch bucket, Edythe decided she would not wear her red dress on Friday. She'd make sure, by the evening's end, Terrill understood she was not interested in being courted. Not by him.

When Edythe came down to breakfast Friday morning, Missy glanced up from the breakfast table and dropped her jaw in shock. "Edythe!"

Edythe smoothed her hands over the skirt of her frock. Once a lovely shade of dove gray with white lace, the dress had faded over the years to a dingy dead-mouse hue with yellowed lace and a tattered hem. But it had been Edythe's favorite dress for several years, so she hadn't been able to discard it, regardless of its worn appearance. Today it provided the perfect means of letting Terrill Sterbinz know she had no desire to dress to please him.

Luthenia turned from the stove, her gaze bouncing from Missy to Edythe, where it traveled from her neckline to the hem of her dress and up again. Her brows rose, and she chuckled low in her throat. "Never seen you wear that dress to school before."

"I've never planned to dig soil and pot seeds with the students at school before." Edythe glided to the breakfront cabinet and removed a coffee cup, her chin high. "I can't wear one of my good dresses for such a messy activity, can I?"

Missy gawked at her, her breakfast neglected. "But, Edie, we're goin' to Lincoln Valley for supper. I wore my best dress." She indicated her blue skirt and shirtwaist. "Martha said she'd be dressin' up fancy, too. You'll just look silly in that old rag."

Edythe poured coffee into her mug. "Perhaps Terrill shouldn't have made plans to leave directly from school without asking me what would be best."

A loud huff exploded from Missy. "You're doin' this on purpose—trying to make him mad, aren't you?" She scooted her chair back so quickly the legs screeched against the wood floor. "I told you I wouldn't expect you to marry him if you didn't love him, but can't you at least give him a chance?" She clattered up the stairs.

Edythe turned and caught Luthenia sending her a frown. She scowled back. "Are you going to lecture me, too?"

"If you don't want to go to dinner with Terrill, you ought to just say so instead of playin' tricks."

Edythe plopped the cup onto the table with force. Coffee sloshed over the edge, creating a dark puddle on the scarred wood. "I'm not playing tricks!"

"Mm-hmm." Luthenia returned to stirring eggs in the pan.

Edythe started to storm upstairs, but then remembered Missy was there. So she charged into the parlor. She stood in the middle of the room, her shoulders slumping. Luthenia was right—wearing an old dress as a means of dissuading Terrill from paying attention to her was no better than William Sholes dipping Jane Heidrich's pigtail in the inkwell to garner her attention.

She returned to the kitchen on leaden feet. Luthenia handed her a rag, and she mopped up the mess she'd made on the table. "I guess I'll go change my dress. The seed potting can wait until Monday."

Luthenia gave Edythe's cheek a gentle pat. "I think that sounds like a fine idea."

Edythe changed into her green bustled skirt and lace-embellished shirtwaist. Missy fussed, "Martha said Terrill likes your *red* dress."

Edythe snapped back, "Well, *I* like the green!"

In retaliation, Missy lagged behind rather than walking beside Edythe all the way to the school. The gloomy sky of days past had cleared, promising a clear sky of robin's-egg blue. The sight of the blazing orange sun breaking through a backdrop of pink and dusky lavender should have given Edythe's heart a lift, but Missy's attitude colored Edythe's. By the time she reached the schoolhouse, irritation boiled under her skin.

She loaded her arms with a few pieces of wood for the stove—she'd get it going to fight away the morning's chill and then let it die out, as it would become unnecessary in the afternoon. It gave her pleasure to thump the wood into the

stove and then close the door with a solid *bang!*
As she turned toward her desk, she heard feet
scuff around the corner from the cloakroom. Was
Missy coming to complain about something
else?

Without turning around, she flung her hand
upward and sniped, "I don't want to hear another
word from you. Stay outside until the other
children arrive."

An "ahem" rumbled—deep and laced with
amusement.

Edythe froze in place. Very slowly she angled
her head to peer over her shoulder. Joel
Townsend stood in the cloakroom doorway, an
impish grin bringing out the single dimple in his
left cheek. Edythe wished she could dissolve into
a puddle.

"M-Mr. Townsend . . ." She turned to face him.
Surely the heat in her face exceeded the roaring
blaze in the stove's belly. "My humble apologies.
I—I thought you were Missy."

His grin climbed higher. "I had my share of
scuffles with my brother. I reckon I understand."

Resuming her teacher poise, she asked, "What
can I do for you?"

He took two forward steps, his boots echoing
on the wood floor. "Wanted to let you know"—
streaks of red brightened his cheeks—"Johnny
and Robert are goin' with Maribelle Jenkins after
school today. She's gonna pick them up an' take

them to her place, let 'em play with the litter of pups in her barn. Thought it best to tell you, so you wouldn't be concerned. They've never gone with Maribelle . . . before."

Edythe hoped the dismay that filled her heart didn't reflect in her face. "I—I think that sounds fine. They . . . they need to become acquainted, since . . ." She couldn't bring herself to voice the words *she'll be marrying you*.

"Yep. Well . . ." He inched backward. "I reckon you've got things you need to be doin', so I'll just . . ."

"Yes. I should be . . ." Couldn't either of them complete a sentence? Edythe stomped her foot lightly against the floor. "Thank you again for alerting me to this change in routine, Mr. Townsend. Have a g-good day." She abhorred the stutter, yet at least she'd managed to speak with a shred of normalcy.

He touched the brim of his hat and clumped out the door. Edythe followed slowly, allowing him time to reach his wagon and leave the yard before stepping onto the porch. Children swarmed the side yard. Even though it was early, she gave the bell's rope a tug. At the resounding ring, the children scooped up their books and charged toward the schoolhouse.

Missy pranced by with her nose in the air, but the others greeted Edythe enthusiastically. The moment the children slid into their desks,

Andrew Bride jammed his pudgy hand in the air.

Edythe acknowledged him while moving up the middle aisle toward her desk.

"I was talkin' to Pa at supper last night about how we been learnin' about seeds an' how they grow." The boy wriggled in his seat, his eyes round and bright. "I told him we was gonna plant beans in a pot so we could watch a plant grow right here in school, an' he said he had a better idea."

Oh, he did, did he? "Yes? What was that?"

Andrew sat up a little straighter, his chest puffing importantly. "He said the schoolyard needs a tree or two. 'Stead of planting itty-bitty beans in a pot, why don't we plant a tree so's we can have some shade?"

William Sholes slapped his knee and exploded with laughter. "Now I know why Andrew's so lame-brained—he takes after his pa!" He pointed at Andrew, who hunched into his seat in shame. "It takes years for trees to get big enough to give off shade, dummy. You'd hafta stay in school ten years or more to see it happen." He snorted. " 'Course, dumb as you are, you might be in school more'n another ten years—"

Every irritation from the morning reared up and launched itself at William Sholes. Edythe screeched his name. "William!"

He threw a lopsided grin in her direction. "What?"

She marched to the boy's desk, took hold of his ear, and yanked him out of his seat. His grin disappeared. The boy yowled, struggling to get loose, but she held tight. "You have spoken out of turn for the last time in this classroom. I have repeatedly cautioned you about treating others kindly, yet you persist in despicable behavior. Well"—she gave his ear a shake, earning another howl of pain—"it will not happen again because you will not be here to mistreat another classmate."

Releasing his ear with a shove, she pointed toward the door. "Go home!"

William stood staring at her, rubbing his ear. "W-whaddid you say?"

Her finger still aimed at the door, she lifted her chin another notch. "I said go home. You are dismissed."

William lowered his hand. His ear glowed bright red. "For the day?"

"For the remainder of the year." Gasps echoed through the schoolroom. Edythe sensed more than a dozen shocked gazes trained on her. "I've had my fill of your disrespectful, unacceptable behavior, and I won't tolerate it one more minute." She spun and charged for her desk. "Go home, William. And do not return."

Ignoring the rows of stunned faces, she looked directly at Andrew. He'd slid so far down in his seat, it was a wonder he hadn't fallen off the edge. "Sit up," she ordered, and he did. "I think your father has a fine idea. Even though this class of students won't have the benefit of shade from trees we might plant today, your children will certainly be grateful we had the foresight to plant them."

A plan quickly formed in her mind. "On Monday, wear your oldest clothes to school. With all the rain we've had lately, the ground should be soft enough for us to dig. Andrew and Lewis, each of you bring a shovel and buckets. I'll make sure I have Mrs. Kinsley's wagon, and we shall make an excursion to the Platte River to dig up two or three seedlings for transplanting in the schoolyard."

William stood rooted to the floor beside his desk, looking as distraught as Edythe had ever seen. Instead of shooing him out the door, she pretended he wasn't there. With a smile, she added, "I think it would be a fine idea to have a class picnic while we're at the river."

A murmur of excitement rippled across the room.

Edythe snatched up a pad of paper and pencil. "Let's see, what will we need for a picnic?" She tapped her lips with the pencil. "Sandwiches, of course. Who would like to bring sandwiches?"

Martha, Ada, and Louisa all raised their hands.

She smiled and wrote their names on the pad. "And maybe . . . apples?"

Henry Libolt nearly came out of his desk in excitement. "I can bring half a bushel, Miss Amsel! They're a little wrinkly from bein' in the cellar all winter, but they got plenty o' taste left in 'em, Ma says."

She nodded at him. "Thank you, Henry. Now, every picnic should end with dessert. Might someone bring cookies?"

"I'll make some!" Sophie Jeffers waved her hand in the air. Her younger sister, Patience, chirped, "I'll help."

Edythe rewarded the girls with a beaming smile. "Excellent. And Missy and I will bring jugs of ginger water. We'll have a grand time at the river on Monday, digging our trees and enjoying a time of relaxation." She slapped the paper pad onto her desk and glared at William. "Why are you still here?"

The boy's face mottled with anger. "You can't dismiss me from school."

Edythe moved toward the boy, her skirts sweeping the floor. "I am the schoolmarm of Walnut Hill. I have the right to decide who attends school and who is dismissed. William, you are dismissed."

With a growl of frustration, William spun and stomped to the back of the classroom. "You'll be sorry! Wait an' see!" He bolted around the corner.

With a smile of triumph, Edythe marched to the

teaching platform. "Grade three, please come to the recitation benches. Everyone else, open your books to the next story and read quietly."

Although the students remained somewhat subdued, the day passed with no other conflicts, and at three o'clock Edythe stood on the porch to observe their leave-taking. Johnny and Robert scurried to the Jenkinses' waiting wagon. They started to climb into the back, but Maribelle patted the seat beside her. The boys used the wheel as a ladder and clambered aboard. Edythe's heart lurched as the wagon rolled away.

The other children scampered in various directions, and only Martha and Missy remained on the porch with Edythe. Martha muttered, "Wonder where Terrill is. Figured he'd be here early." She wandered to the middle of the yard and peered down the road with her hand cupped over her eyes.

Missy nudged Edythe none too gently with her elbow. "You picked a good day to dismiss William."

Edythe frowned at her sister. Missy had witnessed William's misbehavior on days past, and she'd certainly heard him speak so abhorrently to Andrew. He deserved dismissal. She'd had good reason to send the boy home.

Missy folded her arms over her chest. "No way the town council will keep you now—not after you sent William home. An' Martha says Terrill is friends with William's pa . . ." She blew out a breath. "So he's probably mad an' won't come take us to dinner. He won't want to marry you, either." Swinging a furious gaze upward, she snapped, "We might as well say good-bye to Walnut Hill right now."

Missy stormed down the stairs and joined Martha. Missy slipped her arm around Martha's waist and Martha responded in kind. Edythe's chest ached at the sight. Unbidden, Luthenia's warning that God would act ran through Edythe's memory. She nibbled her lower lip, contemplating a possibility. William had misbehaved from the first day of school, but she'd chosen this day to dismiss him. Was her action her own impatience rising to the fore, or had her action been prompted by God as a means of guiding her away from Walnut Hill?

Chapter
THIRTY~FIVE

"Sure am grateful to my folks for keeping Johnny an' Robert this evening so we could have some time alone." Maribelle's smile, lit by the candles in the center of their table, looked sweet and tender. Joel wished the sight would stir something deep inside him. Because it didn't, and because he felt guilty that it didn't, he put his hand over the top of hers.

"Me too." On the drive over, Maribelle had chattered on and on about the changes she wanted to make to his little log house. He'd found himself gritting his teeth—did the house really need lace curtains at the windows or store-bought carpets laid out on the floors? He and the boys had managed just fine without frippery.

"This is the first time we've been truly alone." Her words slipped out on a breathy sigh.

He forced a smile, even as a band seemed to wrap around his chest and squeeze. When they married, he'd have lots of alone time with Maribelle. The thought brought a sense of panic.

Her fingers trembled beneath his. "With Ma an' Pa so close, they can keep the boys lots of times for us." She ducked her head a bit, peeking at him shyly through her eyelashes. "Or maybe you'd think about lettin' them go to a school."

"The boys already go to school." With Miss Amsel.

Maribelle nodded rapidly, the curls on her forehead bouncing. "Oh, I know. But Pa was tellin' me there're these schools where kids go an' live."

Joel jerked his hand free of hers. "What?"

She pursed her lips into a pout. "Now, don't get all ruffled, Joel. You've done real fine, carin' for your brother's kids, but don't you want some time to yourself? We'll be newly married, and we . . ." Her face flooded pink in the lamp's glow. "We'll want our own young'uns. Takin' care of our own *and* Johnny an' Robert . . . ?"

Joel lowered his brows and spoke sternly, the way he would if one of the boys got a fool notion. "I'm not sendin' Johnny an' Robert off to some school with a bunch of strangers. Besides that, the only boarding schools I've heard tell of near here are set up by missionaries for Indian kids. My boys aren't Indians."

She laughed softly and reached for his hand again. "Well, Ma says boys are little heathens." She grinned as if she'd made a fine joke.

Joel removed his hand from her cloying grip and tucked it under the table. "Your mother called *my* boys heathens?" He'd left them with the woman for the evening. He experienced a strong urge to drag Maribelle out of the restaurant and go back to Walnut Hill right now.

"Oh, not yours specifically—just boys in general. She's not used to boys, Joel. She only had me, you know." Maribelle fluttered her eyelashes. "She'll get used to 'em over time the same way I will." A slight grimace creased her face so quickly Joel thought he might have imagined it. Then she brightened, her gaze focused on something behind his shoulder. "Why, look there! It's Terrill Sterbinz with the schoolmarm."

Joel's gut clutched.

Maribelle waved her hand in the air. "Yoohoo! Terrill! Over here."

Joel rose as Miss Amsel, escorted by Terrill, approached their table. Terrill's sister and Missy Amsel trailed behind. Maybe Terrill was treating his sister, and Martha had invited her friend to join them. Maybe Miss Amsel had come along as a chaperone of sorts. Maybe it wasn't what it appeared.

"Hey, Maribelle . . . Joel." Terrill's hand slipped around Miss Amsel's waist. She sucked in a quick breath and stiffened. "Wish I'd known you folks were comin' tonight. We could've rode together—might've saved me some aggravation."

"How so?" Maribelle asked.

Terrill made a sour face. "Just as I headed for the school, my horse threw a shoe. Took me a while to get 'im reshod." He chuckled, winking at Joel. " 'Course, you're prob'ly glad we didn't ride with you. Reckon you'd rather have Maribelle all to yourself, same as me with Edythe here."

So he called her Edythe, did he? The schoolmarm had let Terrill get familiar in a hurry. Joel offered a brusque "no" and slid back into his chair. Maribelle's hand immediately slipped across the table to link with his again. It took all of his self-control not to push it away.

Terrill jabbed his thumb toward Missy and his sister, who stood a few feet away, admiring the dining room. " 'Course, I don't have Edythe to myself, as you can see. Where're your young'uns, Joel?"

Maribelle answered, "They're with my folks, gettin' acquainted. After all"—that little grimace puckered her face again—"they'll be callin' my folks Grandma an' Grandpa before too long."

Joel glanced at Miss Amsel. Her mouth looked white around the edges. Probably from pinching her lips closed so tight. He blurted, "You an' Terrill ever come here before?"

Terrill blasted a laugh. "Nope. But I'm hopin' to come again soon." He glanced at the girls. " 'Course, next time we'll come alone. Right, Edythe?"

Miss Amsel stepped free of Terrill's restraining arm. She gestured the girls forward then flashed a quick, impersonal smile at Maribelle and Joel. "We're keeping you two from enjoying your time together. Mr. Sterbinz, didn't the maître d' indicate we were to take the table near the fireplace?" She grabbed the girls by their elbows and steered them toward the table. Terrill spun and trotted after her.

Joel watched the group until they settled at their table. Miss Amsel chose the chair with its back to him. Disappointed, he turned to face Maribelle, who gave him an uncharacteristic scowl. He started to ask her what was wrong, but the waiter approached their table with plates balanced in his hands. Joel sent up a short prayer of gratitude for the waiter's timing.

Right or wrong, he suddenly had no desire to ask what Maribelle was thinking.

Sitting on the wagon seat beside Terrill, Edythe silently bemoaned the dismal evening. Throughout the meal in the beautifully decorated dining room of the Lincoln Valley hotel, she'd had to fight the urge to peek over her shoulder and see if Joel was holding Maribelle's hand. It wasn't any of her business, but curiosity had nearly driven her mad. Besides, she'd needed to stay alert. Twice before their food arrived Terrill had reached clear across the table in search of her fingers, but she'd eluded him both times. Fortunately, Missy and Martha had kept up a constant chatter or their table would have been cloaked in uncomfortable silence.

Now they rode beneath an endless expanse of star-laden sky. Moonlight bathed the landscape in a gentle glow and shimmered on the horses' sleek rumps. Delightful scents teased Edythe's nose while the steady *clop-clop* of the horses' hooves, the crunch of the wheels, and the cry of a night bird created a unique lullaby. This was the kind of night that should inspire romance. But her heart felt like a lump of lead.

The girls nestled in a pile of hay in the back of the wagon, whispering and occasionally giggling. Terrill glanced at Edythe now and then, opening and closing his mouth as if wishing to talk but uncertain of what to say. Shadows cast by his hat brim hid his expression, yet Edythe sensed his displeasure. She couldn't fault him. As soon as she had an opportunity to speak to him away from Martha's and Missy's listening ears, she would apologize.

Terrill dropped Martha at their home before taking Missy and Edythe into town. He stopped on the street outside Luthenia's house, set the brake, and hopped down. He reached for Missy first, swinging her from the back.

She giggled, skittering away from him. "Thank you for the delightful evening, Mr. Sterbinz. I had a fine time."

"You're welcome." Terrill's words followed convention, but his gruff tone ruined the effect. "Why don'tcha head on in. I need to speak to your sister."

Missy flashed an uncertain look at Edythe but scampered off. Terrill waited until the door closed behind her. Then he aimed his unsmiling gaze on Edythe. "Edythe, I—"

"Please let me speak first."

He folded his arms over his chest.

Edythe wished she'd climbed down. She felt awkward, looking at him from the wagon's high seat. "I apologize. You gave Missy and me a real treat by taking us to Lincoln Valley, and I ruined the evening for you."

He yanked his hat from his head, displaying the deep furrows in his brow. "What did I do to make you so standoffish?"

You're forward and presumptuous. The words flitted through Edythe's brain, but she kept them from spilling from her lips. "It's no fault of yours. I simply was unable to relax." She forced a light chuckle. "To be perfectly frank, Mr. Sterbinz, this was my first dinner with a gentleman."

Terrill's jaw dropped open. "You never been taken out to dinner?"

She shook her head. Responsibility had always presided over pleasure.

"That's a shame. Pretty gal like you, never havin' a beau . . ." Propping his elbow on the edge of the seat, he leaned in. "A fellow has a hard time makin' a lady feel special when he's got two gigglin' girls watchin' his every move. Could we maybe go again . . . next Friday?"

Edythe pulled in her lower lip.

"Folks around here—even Miz Kinsley—will tell you I'm not a bad fellow." He grinned, tipping his head to the side. He looked very boyish and approachable with a light breeze ruffling his blond hair. "Gimme one more chance to show you a nice evenin'. An' if you still don't think you like me after that, I won't ask you again. That sound fair enough?"

Should she prolong this façade, knowing she had no interest in Terrill? A denial trembled on her lips—it seemed unkind to continue seeing him when her departure from Walnut Hill waited around the bend. But looking into his earnest, hopeful face, she discovered she didn't have the strength to utter it.

"It . . . it's very fair to me, Terrill." She swallowed against an urge to cry.

"Good." He returned his hat to his head with a grand sweep. Then his arms snaked out and he caught her around the waist. The moment her feet touched the ground, he released her. "I'll see you in church Sunday, I reckon."

She turned toward the house, but he put out his hand, delaying her. "Miz Kinsley'll probably tell you soon as you go in, but—" He scratched his jaw, twisting his lips into a grimace. "After the service on Sunday, town council's wantin' to have a few words with you."

About William.

"Lloyd Sholes has got up a full head of steam." Even with his face shadowed, Edythe believed she read sympathy in Terrill's earnest gaze. "I know him pretty good—even count him a friend. I've watched his boy grow up, an' I know William's a mischief-maker. Martha fusses about him plenty at home. So I was thinkin' . . ." Terrill lowered his head, scuffing the ground with the toe of his boot. "If you need somebody to speak up for you, I'd be willin'."

If she were honest with herself, Edythe didn't care about Terrill's support. She longed for the support of the only man who had ever set her heart aflutter. But he was promised to another. "Thank you, Terrill. I would appreciate it."

"Count on it, then." He gestured toward the house. "It's late—better let you head in before Miz Kinsley waves a fryin' pan at me for keepin' you so long."

Edythe laughed—unexpectedly, delightedly. How good it felt to laugh. She lifted her hand in a wave and hurried toward the house, but when she reached the door her feet came to a stumbling halt. Worry smote her as forcefully as a star releasing its grip in the heavens and plummeting to earth.

She'd been right to dismiss William. He deserved a severe punishment for his months of misbehavior. But the decision had brought down so much anger—from William, Missy, Mr. and Mrs. Sholes, the town council . . . Her breath caught. What if they chose to dismiss her immediately? The planting season was only weeks away—they might decide the children had received enough schooling for the year. She and Missy had nowhere to go except back to her father's home.

A groan escaped her throat. Why didn't God act, as Luthenia had promised He would, and rescue her? If she had to return to Omaha—and Pa—she'd be trapped. Looking up at the twinkling stars, she whispered, "What are You trying to do to me?"

Chapter
THIRTY~SIX

Edythe's stomach flip-flopped as Reverend Coker closed the service. She'd heard little of the sermon—her focus had been on keeping her breakfast where it belonged. If only she could appear calm and composed when she faced the town council. But the way her stomach churned, she feared she looked exactly as she felt: terrified.

Reverend Coker ended his prayer with a resounding "Amen," and then he held up his hands. "If you have children in school, the town council would like you to stay for a meeting. We'll give the children and the folks who don't have youngsters a few minutes to leave."

Mumbling, people rose and began shuffling toward the aisles.

"We can't leave our young'uns unattended durin' a long meeting," Mrs. Libolt called from a back pew.

Edythe's gut clenched. They were expecting a long meeting? How many complaints would they launch at her? And how would she bear the council's censure with dozens of witnesses looking on? Unconsciously, she reached for support, and she found Luthenia's hand. The older woman curled her work-roughened fingers around Edythe's hand, the grip tight and sure.

"My wife an' I will oversee the children in the churchyard," the reverend said in a calm voice. He strode down the center aisle.

Luthenia leaned close, her breath stirring the fine hairs at Edythe's temple. "I'm goin' to help the reverend an' his missus with the young'uns, but don't you worry. We'll be prayin' for you. Whatever happens here today, you just trust God's got it all under control." Luthenia took hold of Missy's shoulders and guided the girl from the building. Edythe remained on the bench alone. Nausea created a foul taste in her mouth, and she swallowed hard.

Hank Libolt strode to the front of the church. "You all know why we're here." He sounded grim.

Edythe caught herself nodding. She imagined dozens of other heads bobbing up and down in unison. A hysterical giggle tried to worm its way upward, but she forced it down.

"It's my stand that Miss Amsel here"—he flapped a hand in her direction—"acted in foolishness an' spite when she dismissed William Sholes from school."

She dared a quick look over her shoulder. Stoic faces peered forward. She let her gaze bounce across the rows, hoping for a glimpse of understanding or sympathy somewhere, and her eyes locked with Joel Townsend's. Maribelle Jenkins sat close beside him, openly declaring herself as Johnny and Robert's soon-to-be parent. Something tangled around her chest, making it hard to breathe. She zipped her face forward again.

Mr. Libolt's strong voice echoed from the rafters. "We got two things need to be set right today. We need to get William Sholes back in school, and we need to get Miss Amsel straight on what kind of teacher we want for our young'uns."

A rustle at the back of the room indicated someone stood. "I think we oughtta ask E— Miss Amsel why she dismissed William." Terrill Sterbinz spoke up for her, just as he'd promised.

"Only parents get a say in this meetin', Sterbinz," Mr. Libolt growled.

"I'm the closest thing to a pa Martha's got. So I'm stayin'."

Mr. Libolt set his mouth in a disgruntled line.

Terrill went on. "You claimed Miss Amsel sent William home out of foolishness an' spite, but I don't know how we can call it such 'til we know exactly what happened."

A few murmurs sounded, some approving and some carrying a note of protest. Mr. Libolt turned his angry gaze on Edythe. "Teacher, tell us why you sent William home."

His commanding tone made Edythe want to curl her hands around the bench and refuse to move. But this was her opportunity to exonerate herself. On quivering legs, she made her way to the front of the room and stood beside Mr. Libolt's glowering presence.

"I have reprimanded William Sholes on numerous occasions for speaking out of turn or treating the other children unkindly. On Friday morning, without having been given permission to speak, he harshly criticized an idea Andrew Bride shared with the class." Remembering Andrew's embarrassment, indignation filled Edythe's frame. She lifted her chin. "I decided the other children had been subjected to William's bullying long enough. So I sent him home."

A snort carried from the left side of the church, and Mr. Sholes jolted to his feet. He pointed at Edythe, his face red. "You haven't liked our boy since the first week—comin' out to our place to complain about him." He flashed his angry gaze around the room. "She wanted me to take 'im in hand for her. I told her to handle him herself and if she couldn't, then she's got no business teachin'."

Edythe's cheeks filled with heat. How many parents would agree with Mr. Sholes's assessment?

Mr. Bride, nearly as wide as he was tall, struggled upright. "I'll admit I've wondered about some o' the things Miss Amsel's done by way of teachin'. Seemed a mite peculiar to me, them ropes in the schoolyard and using school time to study bugs. But"—he shifted from foot to foot, the floorboards creaking beneath his oversized boots—"the only fussin' Andrew or Louisa have done about school is to complain about William pickin' on 'em. They came home Friday right pleased that they wouldn't have to put up with no more pesterin'."

Mr. Sholes spun on Mr. Bride. "Young'uns tease. They all do it. I'd wager even your young'uns do it."

Mr. Bride nodded his great head. "Sure they tease." He looked down, reminding Edythe of his bashful son. "But few take such pleasure in tormentin' others. Truth be known, I'm glad Miss Amsel sent your William home." He sat amidst a fresh round of murmurs.

Mr. Sholes charged to the front of the room. Edythe reflexively drew back, but the man stopped on the other side of Hank Libolt. With his hands on his hips, Mr. Sholes glared at the gathered folks. "Anybody else glad Miss Amsel dismissed my boy?"

Feet shuffled on the floor, and people whispered to each other. But no one responded. Mr. Bride looked around, his face sad. Edythe's heart went out to the man—he'd taken a stand and ended up standing alone. But then Joel Townsend rose. Edythe's heart leapt into her throat.

"Lloyd, I'd like to understand somethin'. You said you didn't want to be bothered about troubles at school—you wanted Miss Amsel to handle William on her own."

"That's right," Mr. Sholes blustered.

"Seems to me she did what you wanted her to do. She handled William." Mr. Townsend chuckled softly, and a few folks echoed it. "Didn't handle it the way you might've preferred, but you didn't want to be involved." His gaze swept the room, his brow puckered. "In years past we let the teacher discipline however he saw fit. Never had a big meeting to tell the teacher he'd done wrong. So why're we doin' it now?"

Mr. Scheebeck jumped up. "'Cause of her odd ways of doin' things. Like Bride said—she don't teach like other teachers. Half the town's been carryin' a bee in its bonnet over some of her methods. Includin' me." He sent a repentant grimace in Edythe's direction. "But if you're gonna get all het up over keepin' William out of school, then you've gotta get het up at me, too. 'Cause I've told him he can't come into the

367

mercantile no more. He pulled a prank that could've got somebody hurt bad."

Terrill stood again. "My sister's done a heap of complainin' about William. How many others' young'uns have come home, upset over somethin' William did to 'em?"

To Edythe's amazement, almost every parent in the room put a hand in the air, and voices called from every corner.

"Anna's downright scared of him—says he's mean."

"Had to cut two inches off Mable's hair, it was stained so bad from ink. William kept dippin' her braid in the inkwell."

"He tied up the outhouse door with Patience inside. She's been scared of the dark ever since."

Mr. Sholes's face grew redder and redder during the recitation of offenses. His shoulders rose, his chest expanding, and Edythe held her breath, waiting for the explosion. Finally, he waved his fist. "So are you all sayin' you approve of William bein' dismissed? That what you're sayin'?"

Silence fell. Mr. Sholes charged down the center aisle and grabbed his wife by the arm. "We don't gotta listen to none of this." The pair bustled out, the man leading and the woman tripping to keep up.

Everyone looked back at Mr. Libolt. He stared at the door, his jaw slack.

One by one, the town council members left the benches to move to the front of the room. Edythe stood with her shoulders square, her hands clasped in front of her. Mr. Bride, Mr. Jeffers, Mr. Heidrich, and Mr. Scheebeck lined up beside Mr. Libolt in a solemn row.

Mr. Jeffers addressed those seated. "We're gonna take a vote. If you're a parent of one of the school's young'uns, you got a say." His lips twitched. "Miss Amsel oughtta be happy the mothers can vote, too." He cleared his throat, removing the humor from his tone. "Those in favor of lettin' William Sholes come back to school tomorrow, say 'aye.'"

Mr. Libolt thundered, "Aye!" His lone voice hung in the room like the sulfuric odor from William Sholes's rotten eggs. He took a shuffling step backward.

Mr. Jeffers spoke again. "Those in favor of William Sholes bein' kept out of school for the rest of this year, say 'aye.'"

Although few voices rang with enthusiasm, every person remaining offered their agreement. Edythe's heart pounded so hard she felt certain her ribs would break. The greater part of the town had supported her decision. Her knees went weak, and it took all the power she possessed to remain upright. Needing to sit, she moved toward the front bench.

Mr. Libolt leaped forward to seize control of

the meeting again. "There's the second issue." He pinned Edythe in place with a fierce scowl. "Her ways of teachin'. We haven't got that settled yet."

Mr. Heidrich pulled out his timepiece and frowned at its round face. "Hank, it's well past noon. Our young'uns are needin' to be fed. I say we hold off on this for another meetin'."

Several people called out their agreement.

Mr. Libolt hesitated, then gave a nod. "Tomorrow evenin', then. Seven o'clock, right here in the church. All parents are invited." He looked at Edythe with squinted eyes, reminding her of a lizard ready to devour a fly. "We'll see you tomorrow evenin', Miss Amsel."

People filed out while Edythe remained at the front of the church. No one approached to offer a word of encouragement or appreciation, but neither did anyone condemn her. Relief that she could finish the year without William's distracting behavior battled with worry about what tomorrow would bring. Hope that the town might rally in support and choose to keep her hovered on the fringes of her heart, and she longed to grasp it with both hands and hold tight.

A giggle carried to her ears—Maribelle Jenkins, clinging to Joel Townsend's elbow as he escorted her from the church. Hope crumbled, and it was replaced with a stab of pain. If she stayed in Walnut Hill, she'd be forced to witness

Maribelle with Joel, Maribelle with Johnny and Robert. Still pondering that fact, she jumped when someone touched her arm. She turned to find Terrill standing beside her.

He grinned. "Went a little different than you thought, huh?"

Joel and Maribelle disappeared around the corner. Edythe drew in a steadying breath. "Oh yes. I'm quite relieved."

"Me too. Martha'll be happier'n a farmer with a bumper crop when she hears the news. She's never liked William."

Edythe's lips formed a quavering smile. Then she sobered. "But there's still tomorrow's meeting . . ."

Terrill started to say something, but clattering footsteps intruded. Missy barreled down the aisle, her face alight with joy. She flung her arms around Edythe's neck. "I heard! They're not lettin' William come back. You won!"

Terrill met Edythe's gaze over Missy's head. "See you at the meetin' tomorrow, Edythe." He ambled out of the building, his stride long and sure.

Missy pulled back. "What meeting tomorrow?"

Edythe slipped her arm around Missy's shoulders and aimed her for the doors. "Let's talk about it at Luthenia's, hmm? I would imagine by now that pork roast she put in the oven is close to becoming a burnt offering."

Missy giggled at the silly phrase Luthenia always used. She skipped ahead, humming to herself. Edythe envied her sister's lightheartedness. Even if tomorrow's meeting went well—even if the town elected to offer her a contract for next year—Edythe would refuse it. She'd allow Missy these moments of happy abandon, because by tomorrow evening, her sister's joy would crumble to despair.

Chapter
THIRTY~SEVEN

Edythe smiled as she listened to the jabber of children's happy voices in the back of Luthenia's wagon. The river, their trees, and the promised picnic waited ahead, and her excitement matched the children's. She wished she could hurry old Gertie, but she wisely held the horse to a sedate pace down the side of the road where the ruts weren't as deep. She didn't want to bounce anyone out of the back.

The morning air held a bite, but it smelled crisp and clean, and the sunshine beaming overhead assured her the day would be warm. Tender green shoots had appeared across the brown landscape, and tiny dots of white set in little green bowls indicated chickweed was already in bloom. Looking from the rolling countryside to the clear sky lit by a bold yellow sun, Edythe deemed it a perfect picnic day. Not having to worry about William's shenanigans made the day even brighter.

Ahead, water burbled. She smiled over her shoulder. "Children, listen! Do you hear the river's song?"

Their voices fell silent, their heads tilting like a flock of robins listening for worms. Little Will cried, "I hear it! I hear it!" Several others hushed him.

Edythe guided Gertie off the road and across an even expanse of prairie. She drew the wagon within twenty yards of the river and set the brake. Turning on the seat, she sent a stern look into the back. "Now remember what we discussed at school—no one wanders off alone, and stay well away from the water. As much rain as we had last week, the water's high and moving faster than usual. I want everyone to be safe. Do you understand?"

"Yes, Miss Amsel," they chorused.

Edythe smiled her approval. "Andrew and Lewis, grab those shovels. Louisa, Ada, and Sophie, each of you take a bucket. Jane, bring the roll of burlap."

Terrill had advised Edythe on the best way to keep the roots on the little trees from drying out. He'd also volunteered to go to the school this morning while she and the children were away and dig holes to receive the trees. She'd pounded pegs in the places she wanted the trees transplanted. Now, imagining him there in the schoolyard, preparing for their return, a little niggle of apprehension plagued her. She appreciated his help, but she hoped her acceptance of assistance didn't give him the idea she was accepting *him*.

Clapping her hands, she called, "All right, everyone, line up behind the boys. We'll go choose our trees."

With a cheer, the children leaped from the back of the wagon and formed a scraggly line. Edythe delegated Martha and Missy to the rear where they could make certain no one fell behind and got lost. Then she joined Andrew and Lewis at the front. Avoiding the shovel bobbing on Andrew's shoulder, she thrust her fist into the air. "Let's go!"

The children marched along, singing "Yankee Doodle" interspersed with giggles. When they reached the riverbank, Edythe issued another warning about staying away from the water. It rushed past, debris rolling on the surface. She hadn't realized the river would be so angry, and for a moment she wondered if they should return on another day. But looking at the happy, eager faces, she didn't have the heart to disappoint them.

She called out the instructions Terrill had given

her. "Look for well-shaped trees, no taller than Mable's head, with tiny buds on all the branches."

The children scattered, the youngest ones accompanied by the older ones. Within fifteen minutes, amidst a few good-natured arguments, they'd made their selections.

Edythe examined the trees, pretending to frown as she counted branches and measured them against Mable's height. Then she flashed a smile. "Perfect choices!" Exuberant shouts rose, and little Jenny jumped up and down. "Andrew and Lewis, begin digging. Remember to leave a big ball of dirt around the root—we want these little trees to live."

The boys nodded solemnly and pressed the shovel heads into the rich, sandy soil. Edythe ushered the others back toward the wagon and put the older girls to work setting up for their picnic. The younger children linked hands, formed a circle, and began to play one of their favorite games in an open area nearby.

Unbidden, a lump filled Edythe's throat. When these children grew up and left the school and their own children began to attend, perhaps they would point to the trees growing tall and strong in the schoolyard and say, "Miss Amsel helped us plant these. When I look at them, I remember her."

"Miss Amsel?"

Lost in thought, it took Edythe a moment to realize the hushed voice and gentle tug at her skirt wasn't a part of her daydream.

Robert Townsend crinkled his nose, dancing in place. "Miss Amsel, I need the outhouse."

Edythe pointed to a thick stand of brush several yards downriver. "Go there." The boy started to dash off, but she caught one of his suspenders. "Don't go alone."

Robert darted to the circle of children. He tugged Johnny away from the game. Robert whispered in his ear, and the boy trotted off alongside his brother without a fuss.

"Miss Amsel!" Andrew's voice carried from the riverbank.

Edythe addressed Missy and Martha. "Keep an eye on the other children—I'll be right back." The girls nodded in reply, and Edythe lifted her skirts a bit and scurried to Andrew. He'd successfully uprooted one of the trees, so she soaked a length of burlap in the river. The water tugged at the heavy fabric, threatening to carry it away, but she held tight. With Andrew's help, she wrapped the burlap around the broken tangle of roots and then set the tree in a bucket.

"Run up to the wagon and get a drink," she instructed the red-faced, sweaty boy, "before you start digging the last tree."

Just as Andrew trudged over the gentle rise leading to the picnic site, Lewis called for help.

Edythe assisted him, excitement filling her at the sight of the two sturdy little trees standing upright in buckets. Wouldn't they look lovely in the schoolyard? She put her arm around Lewis's scrawny shoulders, which heaved from the morning's work.

"Why don't you go get a drink, Lewis, and rest a bit before you and Andrew dig the last tree?"

"Thank you, ma'am." Wiping his brow, Lewis headed for the wagon.

Edythe caught the handle of the nearest bucket. She curled her other hand around the tree's spindly trunk and lifted. The dirt-crusted root ball was heavier than she expected. Her skirts hindered her progress, and it took several minutes to carry the tree to the wagon. She set the bucket beside a rear wheel, where the tree could rest until it was time to return to the school.

Cupping one hand over her eyes, she observed the children. They now chased each other in a wild game of tag. Instinctively, she began counting noses. The task proved difficult, with the children darting here and there, but it appeared the group was smaller than it should be. Edythe called, "Missy?"

Her sister left the game and trotted to Edythe's side. "Ready to set out the food?"

"Not yet." Edythe continued to scan the group. "Someone's missing." A chill attacked when she realized whom she couldn't find. "Robert and Johnny . . . haven't they returned?" The boys had been gone longer than necessary for Robert to relieve himself.

Missy's lips puckered. "We were so busy playin', I didn't notice they hadn't come back."

Edythe clutched Missy's arm. "Missy, you—" Before she could complete her instruction, wild crying carried from a distance. The children's game abruptly stopped, their voices falling silent. They all turned toward the sound. Johnny stumbled toward them, his pants wet and muddy and his cheeks stained with tears. Edythe ran to meet him. "Where's Robert?"

The boy buried his face against her gray shirtwaist. "He washed away. I couldn't catch him."

Edythe grabbed Johnny's shoulders. "He's in the river?" Fear made her voice shrill and angry.

"Wasn't his fault—William pushed him!" He broke into fresh sobs.

Edythe shook her head, confused. "Johnny, William isn't here."

"He is! Robert had to go, an' when he was goin', we heard a puppy whimperin'. We went to find it, but it wasn't a puppy—it was William in the bushes, makin' the sound." Johnny's voice hiccupped as he told the tale. "Robert said he was gonna tell on him—he wasn't s'posed to be here—an' William said he'd had enough of the little teacher's pet tattlin' on him. He pushed Robert, an' Robert fell in the water. Then William ran away. I . . . I tried to catch Robert, but I couldn't."

The boy fell against Edythe again, wailing brokenheartedly. "He's drowned an' it's all my fault."

Edythe transferred Johnny to Missy, then turned to Martha. "Get everyone in the wagon and drive to the mercantile for help. I'm going to look for Robert."

"What about our picnic?" Josephine Ellsworth whined.

"What about the trees?" Lewis wrung his dirty hands.

"Later!" Edythe snapped out the word—who cared about picnics and trees when Robert's life was endangered? "Hurry now, children!" Edythe lifted her skirts and ran.

Joel stepped out of the feed and seed, fingering the smooth handle of the new axe—a purchase he shouldn't have had to make. He berated himself for breaking the old one. A careless swing while chopping wood for Miz Kinsley had splintered the ash handle. Lucky for him, the axe head had landed harmlessly on the ground, but it could've sliced his leg.

He sent up a silent prayer of gratitude to God for looking out for him when he wasn't looking out for himself. His mind had been on other things—wedding plans. Sweat beaded across his forehead. Maribelle wanted to set a date in early June. She was eager to become his wife. He wished he felt as eager to become her husband.

He placed the axe in the back of his wagon and ambled to the front. As he prepared to heft himself onto the seat, the sound of pounding horses' hooves caught his attention. Runaway team? He squinted against the midmorning sun. Miz Kinsley's Gert thundered toward town. Miz Kinsley had said Miss Amsel borrowed the horse and wagon to take the kids on their picnic, but the schoolmarm should know better than to run a horse like that. Especially with a wagonful of youngsters.

He started to call out a warning, but then he realized Martha Sterbinz held the reins. Fear clutched him. Why wasn't Miss Amsel driving the wagon? The wagon raced past him, and he took off after it. Martha drew Gert to a stop in front of the mercantile and leaped down. Joel captured her before she made it inside the store.

"Where's your teacher?"

The girl wriggled loose. "Lemme go! I gotta get help!"

"Uncle Joel!"

Martha darted into the mercantile as Johnny launched himself from the back of the wagon and into Joel's arms. The boy clung, blubbering out a story about a puppy, William Sholes, and Robert being swept away in the river's current. Although Joel only caught half of it, he understood enough.

Wally and Mary Scheebeck stepped out of the mercantile. Wally waved his hand in the direction of the church. "Gonna go ring the bell, gather up some menfolk. Then we'll head to the river."

Mrs. Scheebeck moved to the edge of the wagon bed. "I'll stay with the young'uns."

Joel handed Johnny to Mrs. Scheebeck and searched the back of the wagon for Miss Amsel's sister. "Missy, come with me—show me where you were picnicking."

The girl scrambled out of the back. He grabbed her hand, and they ran to his wagon. He lifted her aboard before swinging himself up beside her. The girl clutched the wagon seat. Her knuckles glowed white, matching her pale, frightened face. Joel lifted the reins and barked out, "Don't worry—everything'll be fine."

Missy didn't look reassured. He repeated the statement to himself again and again as he drove the team toward the edge of town, planting imploring words in between. *Lord, let Robert be all right. Lord, don't let anything happen to my boy. Lord, keep Robert—and Edythe—safe.*

Chapter
THIRTY~EIGHT

"Robert! Robert!" Edythe screeched the child's name until her throat felt raw. She fought her way through brambled shrubs and close-growing saplings. The hem of her dress dragged in the murky water along the river's edge, weighing her down. But she battled forward, eyes seeking, ears strained for any cry for help, heart pounding, muscles aching. She must find him!

She scanned the turbulent water. As fast as the water moved, it may have carried Robert clear to the Missouri by now. Perhaps it had rolled him to the river's bottom, where she'd never find him. "Robert. Oh, Robert . . ." Tears distorted her vision as she imagined the boy's lifeless body lying cold and abandoned.

Helplessness washed over her, driving her to her knees. Her head hanging low, her shoulders heaving with exertion, Luthenia's voice echoed through her mind—*"If you'd ever just lean into God's strength instead of relyin' on your own . . . why, you'd discover joy like you've never had before."* At that moment, Edythe couldn't imagine feeling joyful. Her throat ached; her heart constricted with fear and worry. A longing swept through her, as powerful as the rush of water rolling past, a longing to unload her worries and apprehensions and allow someone bigger and stronger to carry them.

On her hands and knees, she raised her face to the crystal blue sky above and choked out, "If You're there, God, help me. I can't find Robert, but You—You're all-seeing. You know where he is. Hold him tight, God—keep him safe. Help me find him." Her voice broke, and she squeezed her eyes tight. "Please, God . . ."

For several seconds she remained with her face upward, eyes closed, heart begging. She listened for a rumbling voice from Heaven. None came— only the river's roar and the wind's whisper filled her ears. Yet she didn't crumple in despair. An odd sensation flooded her frame—a comforting warmth that began in the center of her chest and inched its way through her extremities.

With the warmth came a burst of strength and renewed energy. Edythe's eyes popped open in surprise. "God, is that You?" Her heart pounded with a hope more intense than anything she'd experienced before. She pushed to her feet. Raising her face to the sky again, she cried, "Help me find him, God! Please!"

A frightened whimper reached her ears.

Edythe sucked in a startled breath. She stumbled in a circle, her gaze seeking. "Robert? Robert, is that you? Call again!"

A second whimpering cry, weaker than the first, came in response—somewhere ahead. Gasping with ragged breaths, she forged forward. Branches caught her hair and tore at her dress, but she ignored them, her heart beating out a steady prayer: *Help me find him; help me find him.* And there he was, on the opposite side of the river, a tiny figure on the bank.

She came to a stumbling halt, her body straining toward Robert, who lay facedown with his legs dangling in the water. The force of the current tugged at his pants, shifting his body by mere inches. She clutched her hands beneath her chin, fear once more taking her captive. The boy was exhausted. If he were pulled into the raging stream again, he wouldn't be able to fight his way out.

Cupping her hand beside her mouth, she called, "Robert! Robert!"

The boy moaned, his head moving slightly.

"Crawl up the bank! Try, Robert—you have to try!"

He lay still and unresponsive.

Edythe paced on her side of the river, her mind racing. She had to get to him and pull him completely from the water. But how? She couldn't walk across—thanks to last week's rains, it was too deep. And the current would certainly pull her downstream. She groaned, "What can I do? Oh, help me, God! What can I do?"

Use the current.

Although the words formed inside her head, Edythe jumped as if someone had shouted them in her ear. A simple directive, yet complete understanding accompanied it. Her limbs trembled as she scrambled upriver five yards, then ten. She spun and looked at Robert, his body so small and helpless. "Far enough?" She whispered the query aloud, contemplating, then decided it would do.

Gingerly, she stepped into the river. The water pulled hard, tugging at her skirt and nearly sending her onto her face. She cried out, "I'm putting myself in Your hands, God! Guide me safely to Robert!" And then she plunged into the uncontrolled current.

Missy pointed. "There's our tree!"

Joel squinted ahead and spotted a bucket lying on its side with a small, shriveled sapling spilling out of it. He drew back sharply on the reins and called, "Whoa!"

The wagon rattled to a stop, and Joel leaped out of his seat. Instinctively, he reached under the wagon and snatched up the coil of rope that always rested there in case he needed to pull the wagon from a muddy rut. "Stay here," he ordered Missy and then raced for the river's bank.

He pushed his way along the bank, searching for any sign of Robert or Edythe. Muddy footprints, obviously made from a woman's shoe, captured his attention. In the branches of a bush, he found a piece of gray fabric. The schoolmarm had come along here. He stumbled onward, calling, "Robert! Edythe! Robert!" His heart continued to pray even while he called their names.

The coil of rope on his shoulder caught branches, but he trudged on, his feet sinking in the soft mud along the bank and covering the prints left behind by Miss Amsel. Imagining Robert's small body in the roiling water made him sick to his stomach. *Keep him safe, God. Keep 'em both safe.* "Robert! Edythe!"

"We're here!"

He stopped, his body alert. His eyes darted everywhere, seeking, but the water's roar prevented him from determining from which direction the cry came.

"Here! We're over here!"

Several yards downriver, Joel finally spotted Miss Amsel seated on the opposite bank. She waved one hand in the air, cradling Robert's limp body against her chest with the other. Joel broke into a stumbling run, stopping when he was directly across from her. Dropping the rope, he cupped his hands beside his mouth.

"Are you all right?"

"Wet and cold, but otherwise fine." She looked down at Robert, then pulled him more firmly into her embrace. "He's breathing, but his lips are blue. We need to get him to the doctor."

Joel looked around, searching for the place where she had crossed. But he couldn't spot a low area. "How'd you get over there?"

Even from this distance, he could make out an odd smile playing on her lips. "God carried me."

"What?"

"I swam."

Joel gaped in wonder. Against that current? In a skirt? Only a miracle would have kept the water from sweeping her downstream. Perhaps God had carried her. He scooped up his rope. "We'll need a strong enough tree to hold this on both sides. If I toss one end to you, can you tie it off good?"

Gently, lovingly, she transferred Robert from her lap to the moist, mossy bank. She rose and moved several feet away from the boy. "Of course I can."

Her confident spunk made him smile. He knotted one end of the rope around a good-sized tree. Then he dug under the brush for a short length of driftwood and tied the other end of the rope around it. He held the driftwood aloft. "This'll hurt if it hits you, so be careful." He gave the wood a heave. It landed near the water's edge. Edythe darted forward and snatched it up before the water carried it away.

"Pull it as tight as you can," he called. "Soon as

it's secure, I'll come across." He sat and yanked off his boots and socks. He placed his hat on top of the pile and stood on bare feet. The damp ground was cold, and he danced in place, waiting while Edythe tied the end of the rope around three close-growing saplings.

She raised her hand in triumph. "All done!"

The rope stretched a foot above the tumbling surface of the water. Joel gave it a tug—it seemed secure. He took hold of it with both hands and eased into the water. The cold stole his breath and made his teeth chatter. The water pulled at him, and his stomach churned. What fear Robert must have experienced while being swept helplessly downstream. He inched his way along the rope, just as he had the day of the snowstorm, working his way toward safety. How had Edythe done it on her own? He marveled at the risk she'd taken to reach Robert.

Finally, his knees connected with something solid, and he scrambled up the bank. Edythe sat holding Robert again. Joel sank down on one knee beside them and placed his hand on Robert's head. The boy stirred, moaning. His eyes fluttered open and he looked around blearily. "Don't let William push me again." His voice sounded weak and croaky.

"Shh. He's gone. You're safe." Edythe stroked Robert's wet, tangled hair. "God kept you safe, dear one. Just rest."

Looking into the schoolmarm's serene face, Joel's heart caught. Love glowed in her eyes. Love for the boy she held securely in her embrace, but another love—a new love—also lit her from within. Joel believed he knew its source. When had Edythe surrendered to God's love?

She raised her gaze to Joel's. Her normally precise bun sagged, little wisps straggling out in all directions. A lank strand of damp, dark hair hung along her jaw. In her wet, mud-splotched dress, she was a mess—and more beautiful than he'd ever seen her. Emotions welled upward, and to Joel's surprise, the words *I love you* battled for release. "Edythe, I—"

"Joel! Joel!" The noise of many pounding feet accompanied the call.

Joel lurched to his feet and waved both hands over his head. "Over here!"

Men burst out of the brush—half a dozen of them, all looking frantic.

"Everybody's all right. We're comin' across now," he assured the searchers. Then he hunkered beside Miss Amsel. His fingers itched to brush the hair from her face. Instead, he scooped Robert into his arms. "Can you hold to the rope an' get yourself across?" He wanted to help her, but he couldn't leave Robert unattended.

"I can do it." She laughed softly. "I did it

without a rope before, you know." A sigh escaped her lips, and she seemed to slip away somewhere. "God does amazing things when we lean into His strength."

Joel cleared his throat, regaining her attention. "It'll mean another soaking, I'm afraid."

Her smiled turned complacent. "A soaking is nothing. We're fine—that's all that matters."

As Joel followed her to the water's edge, a bitter thought flooded his mind. She and Robert might be fine, but he wasn't. He'd run ahead of God, asking Maribelle Jenkins to be his wife instead of heeding the command to wait. As a result of his rashness, he might never be fine again.

Chapter
THIRTY-NINE

Edythe relaxed as Luthenia's fingertips massaged her soapy hair. Foamy water lapped against her chin, the warmth welcome after the chilly plunge into the Platte River. Not since she was a small girl had anyone assisted her with a bath. She wouldn't have imagined allowing someone to assist her now, but today it felt perfectly natural to succumb to Luthenia's ministrations. Perhaps surrendering herself to God's care had opened her to the idea of releasing a bit of her stubborn independence.

Missy fidgeted on the edge of a kitchen chair, nibbling her nails. Edythe caught her sister's eye. "Stop looking so worried over there. I'm fine, you know."

"But you could've drowned!" Tears flooded Missy's tawny eyes. "What if somethin' happened to you?"

The cooler air of the room attacked her moist flesh, raising goose pimples as Edythe lifted her hand from the water to give Missy's knee a reassuring squeeze. "There's no sense in worrying over 'what if.' Besides, Missy . . ." Her eyes slipped closed as she relived that wondrous moment when God's strength had infused her frame. "I've come to realize there's Someone bigger and stronger who will always be there to take care of you, even if I'm not. Lean on Him, and you'll always have what you need to make it through."

Luthenia's fingers ceased their massage. She tugged Edythe's head backward to peer directly into her face. "Are you tellin' me you've finally decided to let God take control instead of grabbin' it for yourself?"

Edythe laughed. "Well, isn't that what you prayed for?"

"Thank You, good Lord Almighty!" Luthenia threw both hands in the air, sending a shower of filmy soap suds in all directions. She pressed her cheek to the top of Edythe's head. "Oh, dear girl, you've made my heart so happy it just might burst clean in two."

Missy slipped to her knees beside the tub. "What are you talking about?"

Luthenia began pouring cupfuls of water over Edythe's head. "Your sister discovered the joy of leanin' into God's strength. Sure am sorry it took such a scary event to make it happen, but sometimes we gotta face a mighty storm to realize just how much we need a shelter."

Edythe swiped soapy water from her eyes. "You're right, Luthenia. God is a shelter—I literally felt the warmth of His presence on that riverbank before I went in after Robert."

Missy stared at Edythe with wide eyes. "Did William really push him in?"

Edythe recalled Robert reciting the events that led to his frightening downriver ride. "He did." Her heart constricted. She hoped William only intended to give Robert a soaking, underestimating the strength of the river. Or perhaps he hadn't meant for Robert to fall into the water at all. Surely the boy wasn't so malicious he'd try to drown a smaller child. "William said I'd be sorry I dismissed him from school, but I certainly didn't expect him to take out his anger on one of my students. I thought he'd do something to me."

"He *did* do somethin' to you." Luthenia wiped

her hands on her water-spattered apron. "He knows how much you love the kids in your class. By hurtin' one of them, he was sure to hurt you."

Edythe released a heavy sigh. "I'm just so grateful Robert is all right."

"I don't imagine William's doin' so well right now, though." Luthenia's lips formed a grim line. "Menfolk out lookin' for you an' Robert found William skulkin' in the bushes alongside the road, blubberin' how he'd killed Robert for sure. They hauled him home to his pa an' made the boy 'fess up before they left. Last they saw, Lloyd was draggin' William into the woodshed. I reckon it'll be a while before William pulls another of his pranks."

Edythe took little pleasure in William's chastisement. Perhaps if Lloyd Sholes had shared in the discipline of his son earlier, Robert could have been spared today's fright. Then she gave a little start. If Robert hadn't fallen into the river, she might never have called upon God for help.

Her gaze fell on the wall clock, and she let out a gasp. "The meeting at the church starts in less than twenty minutes! I need to get dressed." She reached for the towel draped across the nearest chair.

Luthenia clicked her tongue against her teeth while Edythe frantically wrapped herself in the length of rough cloth. "You ain't goin' to any meetin' tonight."

"But—"

"You got yourself good an' soaked in an icy river rescuin' one of Walnut Hill's young'uns." Luthenia plunked her hands on her hips. "Nobody's gonna expect you to be at that meetin'. Only place you're goin' is up to bed with a cup o' hot tea, an' that's that."

Edythe bit her lower lip, uncertain. "Bed does sound heavenly."

Luthenia picked up Edythe's discarded clothes and gave them a toss through the pantry door. "I'll mosey on over to the church an' sit in on the meetin' for you so I can tell you all about it." She shrugged. "You bein' there won't change the outcome no how."

Missy followed Edythe to the staircase. "Edie, do you think they'll keep you, since you saved Robert today?"

Edythe held the towel with one hand and brushed Missy's cheek with the other. "What I did today doesn't have anything to do with my teaching methods. I don't think today's events will change anyone's mind about me as the schoolmarm."

"So we still have to leave?"

Pain stabbed Edythe's chest. How she hated to see her sister disappointed again. "Let's pray for God's will. What He wants for us is better than what we want for ourselves." *God, You gave me the strength to face that raging river today. Can*

You give me the strength to accept whatever You have in mind for Missy and me?

"I'll join you in that prayer." Luthenia bustled across the kitchen and slung her arms around Edythe's and Missy's shoulders. The three bowed their heads, and Edythe placed her concerns into God's capable hands.

Joel hated to leave the boys alone after their harrowing day, but Robert fell asleep right after supper. The doctor had said sleep was the best medicine for the boy, so Joel didn't want to rouse him for a ride to town. But he couldn't stay away from the meeting that would determine Miss Amsel's fate.

He closed the bedroom door and moved to the dry sink, where Johnny scrubbed the supper dishes. "Will you be all right here if I go on into town?"

Johnny flicked a glance at the closed bedroom door. "Robert sleepin'?"

"Yep."

"We'll be all right. I'll keep an eye on him."

His solemn tone and serious face, too old for his not-quite-nine years, tugged at Joel's heart. He pulled the boy into a hug. "Thank you, son. Soon as the meetin's over, I'll be right home. You close the damper on the stove an' go to bed when you're finished with the dishes. You had a big day, too."

Johnny sighed. "Sure am sorry Robert got so scared. Sorry we didn't get those trees brought to the school, too. We didn't even get to have our picnic."

Joel tousled Johnny's hair. "If I know your schoolmarm, she'll make sure you get that picnic. As for the trees . . ." An idea started ticking in the back of his mind. "Don't worry. Your schoolyard'll get some trees, too."

He plopped his hat onto his head and trotted to the barn. Rather than hitching the wagon, he saddled Jody and rode the horse to town. The pale sky, all rosy in the west as the sun slinked downward, made for a pleasant backdrop. But Joel's thoughts were troubled. Maribelle had indicated she'd be at the meeting. After coming close to blurting out his love for the schoolmarm on the riverbank today, he didn't know how he'd be able to look Maribelle in the face without her seeing guilt in his eyes.

Lord, help me. I made a commitment, an' I'm duty-bound to honor it. Maribelle hasn't changed. Isn't fair to make her suffer because I acted foolishly. Help me do what's right for all of us.

He slipped into the meeting late, but Maribelle had held a spot for him. He listened to Hank Libolt share his concerns about Miss Amsel's unconventional ways. It seemed the man lacked some of his usual bluster, however. Maybe the schoolmarm's unselfish actions today had softened the bullheaded man just a bit.

With Maribelle beside him, Joel held his tongue in speaking words of support for Miss Amsel. He felt as though he failed Miss Amsel by staying silent, but speaking up would somehow be traitorous to the woman he'd pledged to marry. So he let others do the talking, and silently cheered when the Scheebecks, Jefferses, Sterbinzes, and Ellsworths all indicated approval of the schoolmarm.

At the end of the meeting, Hank Libolt asked for a vote. It split evenly with eleven votes to retain Miss Amsel and eleven votes to close school early and discharge the teacher. Libolt cleared his throat. "Lloyd an' Betsy Sholes aren't here tonight to give their vote. They can give it come Sunday, when we're all gathered here again. Then we'll have a final count."

Joel's heart sank. Neither of the Sholeses would vote in favor of Miss Amsel—not after she'd dismissed their son. Edythe was as good as gone. People shuffled out the door, talking quietly. Maribelle curled her hands around Joel's elbow as they moved into the churchyard. He escorted her to her wagon, but she didn't climb up. Instead, she placed both palms against his chest, peering up at him with wide, probing eyes.

"Joel, we need to talk."

He rubbed his finger under his nose, hoping the

double-thud of his heartbeat didn't come clear through to her hands. "I left the boys alone. I oughtta get back."

Her fingers curled, catching the fabric of his shirt. "It's important."

He gently removed her hands from his shirt. "All right, then. But hurry."

She pursed her lips into a disgruntled scowl, but she didn't step away from him. "You know Terrill Sterbinz and me kept company . . . an' then parted ways. The partin' ways was my idea." She ducked her head, toying with a button at the throat of her dress. "I liked Terrill—I really did—but there was one thing I couldn't set aside. He wanted us to get married an' then live with his ma an' brothers an' sister. He said I could be a big help in takin' care of the house an' the farm an' so forth. I admired him for wantin' to look after his family. But . . ." Her chin lifted, her gaze seeking his. "I couldn't help thinkin' he didn't want a wife as much as somebody to ease his ma's load."

Joel's stomach flipped.

"Maybe I'm wrong—an' if I am, I apologize—but I worry that's why you asked to marry up with me. Not because you have such fondness for me, but because you need somebody to come in an' help ease the load of carin' for your house an' your nephews."

Joel stifled a groan. "Maribelle, I—"

"I like you. I have for a long time, an' havin' you callin' on me was like a dream comin' to life. But . . ." Tears winked in her eyes. "Now I'm not sure. Spendin' time with Johnny an' Robert in little snatches is fine, but I don't know about takin' 'em on full time. It's scary to me." She blinked rapidly.

Joel curled his hands around her upper arms. "The boys aren't goin' anywhere, Maribelle. Not to some school or anyplace else. Even if they weren't born to me, I love 'em. An' if you marry me, you'll have to love 'em, too." His heart clenched at the worry reflected in her eyes, yet he didn't have the means to set her fears to rest.

"You want me to love your boys, but . . ." She gulped, her fingers twitching beneath her chin. "You still haven't said whether you love me." She seemed to hold her breath, looking into Joel's face with expectation.

He couldn't speak.

She waited for long seconds, her body so still it appeared she'd turned to stone. And then her breath whooshed out in a rush. She turned her face away. "I think my bein' with you is too much dream an' not enough truth to carry me for the rest of my life."

He swallowed. "I'm sorry." And he was. Sorry for tangling her in his selfish needs. Sorry for running ahead of God's plan for him. Sorry . . .

She started to climb into her wagon, but her

skirts hindered her. Joel caught her around the waist and lifted her onto the seat. She glanced at him, her lips quivering and her face white. "Thank you." Softly. Politely. Then she flicked the reins and the horse jolted forward.

Joel watched the wagon roll away in the dusk. Although neither of them had said so, he knew their betrothal was broken. He'd willingly take the blame and let Maribelle criticize him all over town if she wanted to. Because even though he was sorry he'd hurt her, he'd never been so relieved in all his life.

Chapter
FORTY

"We vote to let her stay."

Edythe shook her head, unsure she'd heard correctly. Missy let out a delighted gasp and clutched Edythe's hand.

Lloyd Sholes stood at the front of the church with his hands shoved deep into his trouser pockets, his face set in a resigned frown. "The missus an' me, we decided we owed her after the trouble William caused." He shuffled back to his bench and plopped down beside his wife.

Hank Libolt stared after him, looking as stunned as Edythe felt. Libolt said, "I reckon since that's thirteen for an' eleven against, the town council will be keepin' Miss Amsel on 'til the end of this term."

"What about next year?" The question came from Mrs. Jeffers.

Mr. Libolt scowled. "Town council already decided to—"

"An' I think you oughtta reconsider," the woman said in a tart tone. Murmurs followed.

Edythe shook loose of Missy's grasp and rose. "I thank those of you who have given your support, allowing me to complete this term with the children. I realize some of my ideas are unusual. However, I can assure you I've never had anything but the students' best interests at heart. Everything I've done has been out of genuine affection for the children of Walnut Hill."

A few people nodded in response. Others looked away, apparently embarrassed.

Over the previous week, she'd prepared a little speech to be given regardless of how the town voted. Although peace had flooded her when she'd prayed about it, now that the time had arrived to form the words, her tongue turned clumsy. She offered a silent request for God's strength, and then continued.

"As much as I love the children, I must inform you of my decision to leave at the end of this term. In order to be an effective teacher, I must feel at ease, and I cannot feel at ease knowing there are several people who oppose my methods. Additionally, God has placed a calling on my heart unrelated to teaching." Excitement stirred through Edythe's middle as she considered using her abilities not in a classroom, but in ways that could still impact generations. As much as she would miss her students, she knew she'd made the right choice.

Her gaze bounced past Luthenia's teary-eyed face to the dismayed children and somber parents. She spotted Joel Townsend sitting between Johnny and Robert, and her heart fluttered in response to the steady, unwavering gaze he aimed in her direction. For a few seconds she froze, unable to turn away from his tender blue eyes. The desire to dash across the church sanctuary and leap into Joel's strong arms washed over her.

Quickly, she faced Mr. Libolt before the longing overcame good sense. "I thank you for allowing me to spend these past months with your children. I . . . I will treasure the memories of my time in Walnut Hill." She sat so the townspeople—especially Joel—wouldn't witness her tears.

An uncomfortable silence fell, lasting for several seconds. Then Mr. Libolt cleared his throat. "That ends our meetin'. The council members'll start searchin' for a new teacher soon."

His impassive tone juxtaposed sharply the myriad emotions tumbling through Edythe's heart. Benches creaked as people stood. Feet shuffled against scarred floorboards, mumbled voices diminishing as folks left the building. Edythe remained on her bench until everyone had gone, unwilling to face them. When all was quiet, she finally rose and turned to leave. Her gaze fell upon the bench where she'd seen Joel and his boys. The empty bench became representative of the aching place in the center of her chest. How she would miss those towheaded boys and their bighearted uncle.

"What I'm wantin' to know," Luthenia groused as she scooped a second helping of lima beans and stewed tomatoes onto her plate, "is why you didn't tell me you'd decided not to teach no more. Shock nearly made my ol' heart forget to keep beatin'. It's not good for a woman my age to get a scare like that."

Edythe covered her mouth with her napkin to hide her smile. She'd miss Luthenia's crusty ways when she and Missy left. "I'm sorry. I should have talked to you and Missy."

Missy looked up from her full plate. She hadn't eaten a bite. "You really mean to go, then?" She sounded more sad than resentful.

"I don't intend to *teach* next year, Missy. As for where we'll live . . ." Edythe sighed. "I'm still praying about that. I'll need a job of some sort—but something not as time-consuming as teaching. I intend to dedicate considerable time to the women's suffrage movement."

Luthenia gawked at Edythe.

Edythe sent a serious look across the table. "The more I think about the inequities—and the effects the current laws will have on Missy and other girls like her—the more I realize change must come. As you told me, God doesn't intend husbands to run roughshod over their wives. If men and women should share responsibilities in the home, shouldn't they also share responsibilities in government?"

Luthenia's brow puckered. "Guess I haven't given it much thought."

"I've thought of little else since the children and I began our study on government. I've become convinced, listening to Missy, Martha, and the other girls, that women have much to offer—their voices should be heard." Edythe linked her hands and rested them on the table's edge. "I don't want to oppress men or demand to be given rights beyond what's held by them, but neither do I want men to oppress women. As God's creations, we should be held in equal esteem."

Luthenia shook her head, her eyes wide with wonder. "You *have* been thinkin'."

Edythe's thoughts slipped backward in time to

the joyful days on her family's farm. "It's a battle that must be won, and it will take time and dedication. I have the desire—now I simply need the means to see it through." She looked at her sister, who pushed a lima bean back and forth on her plate with her finger. "Are you angry with me?"

Missy sighed. "No. Me an' the other girls, we want to be able to vote an' own property an' all those things men can do when we grow up." She met Edythe's gaze. Although sadness lingered in her eyes, she smiled. "I'm proud of you, Edie, for lookin' out for other people. It's what you do best."

Luthenia clanked her fork onto the table. "Why, Edythe, it *is* what you do best! An' doesn't it just seem as though God's been preparin' you for this with the responsibility He gave you way back when?" She reached across the table and took Edythe's hand. "You got a givin' heart, an able spirit, a smart mind . . . an' you can string words together in a way that inspires people." Missy nodded emphatically, and Luthenia smiled. "He picked the perfect person to do battle when He picked you."

Edythe laughed, her joy spilling over at the open support offered by her sister and her dear friend. "I'm so glad you understand." She grimaced, raising one shoulder in a sheepish shrug. "I don't imagine the good men of Walnut

405

Hill will approve, but I must follow my heart."

When word spread of her intention to become a suffragist, she'd surely face another round of censure from the community. And she would bear it. Only one man's opinion really mattered, and she'd trust God to give her the strength to face his criticism, should it come.

"There." Joel stepped back and admired the sturdy little walnut tree with its branches pointing toward the sky. His gaze roved the schoolyard, taking in the other two trees. Small and spindly now, but in time their branches would provide shade for the students at play.

He and the boys had spent all of Sunday afternoon digging up new trees and then planting them in the ready holes on the school grounds. Joel had worried Robert would balk at returning to the river, but the boy had gone willingly, eager to fetch the trees. He'd stood well back from the water's edge and occasionally looked over his shoulder, searching for William, but he hadn't cowered in fear. Joel hoped having survived such a scary event might help Robert face his other fears—such as storms.

Now Robert scampered from tree to tree, touching the trunks or ducking low to peer at the sky through the scrawny branches, happy and carefree. Joel curled his hand around Johnny's neck and pulled the boy snug against his side. "So what'cha think? Will Miss Amsel be pleased?"

Johnny grinned, slinging his arm around Joel's waist. "Uh-huh!"

"Now remember—let's keep it secret that we put those trees in." Joel couldn't be certain why he didn't want the schoolmarm to know he planted the trees, but he sensed it needed to remain a secret.

"I won't tell. But Robert might. He can't keep a secret." Johnny spoke matter-of-factly, not at all critical of his brother. "The very day you told us Miz Jenkins was gonna be our new ma, he came right to school an' told Miss Amsel."

Joel needed to let the boys know they wouldn't be getting a new ma, after all. He hoped they wouldn't be too confused.

Johnny's brow puckered. "Is she really leavin', Uncle Joel?"

For a moment, Joel thought the boy referred to Maribelle. Then he realized Johnny meant Miss Amsel. His heart twinged. "So she said."

"I don't want her to go. I like her."

"I know, boy." On the riverbank last week, looking into Edythe's face—peaceful despite the frightening time she'd spent searching for Robert—he'd wanted to gather her into his arms and never let go. But she'd made it clear she didn't want a ready-made family.

At least he'd had a chance to gift her in a small

way before she left. With his arm around Johnny, he held his free hand to Robert. "C'mon. It's suppertime, an' then you two need a bath— you're as dirty as if we'd planted you in the ground."

"Awww, Uncle Joel!"

Joel laughed and swung them into the back of the wagon. As he drove out of the schoolyard, he looked once more at the trees. He wished he could be at the school tomorrow morning to see the look on Miss Amsel's face. But then again, maybe it was best he couldn't.

Edythe spotted the little trees when she was still a quarter-mile down the road Monday morning. Missy must have noticed them at the same time, because she pointed. Edythe nodded. "Come on—let's hurry."

Together the sisters jogged the remaining distance and stopped, panting, beside the tree closest to the road. Edythe touched the wilting leaves while Missy circled the tree, examining it from top to bottom.

"This isn't one we picked out." Missy held her hand over her head, measuring the tree's height. "The ones the boys dug were barely to my shoulder, but these are as tall as you."

Who could have planted the trees? An entire week had passed since the interrupted picnic at the river. She'd cautioned the children to stay away from the holes Terrill Sterbinz had dug, and last Friday when Terrill had taken her to Lincoln Valley for dinner, she'd asked him to stop by and fill them in. After the ordeal with Robert, she had no desire to take the children back to the river for more trees. Terrill had agreed, but he'd asked if she could wait a few more days, since he'd planned a Saturday trip to Aurora to look at a horse, and of course Sunday was a day of rest. Edythe had consented to wait.

But the holes were filled . . . with trees! They had to have been planted on Sunday—she'd worked at the school on Saturday and hadn't seen anyone. Could Terrill have decided to forego his day of rest and plant these trees for her?

"Who do you suppose did it?" Missy wondered aloud.

"I don't know. But the poor little things look like they could use a drink. Why don't you get the bucket and water each of them while I unlock the school?"

Children began arriving, and all exclaimed over the trees. Only Johnny and Robert held back. Edythe assumed seeing the trees brought back unpleasant memories, so she didn't encourage the boys to examine the tiny, unfurling leaves of palest green or rub their palms on the sandpapery bark. When Martha arrived, Edythe took her aside.

"Did Terrill come here yesterday and plant the

trees?" She held her breath as she awaited the answer. She feared Terrill may have done it as a way to manipulate her into another dinner in Lincoln Valley. He'd been none too pleased at the end of their evening when she'd told him she didn't intend to let him court her.

Martha shook her head, her face innocent. "Couldn't've been Terrill, Miss Amsel. He came home straight after church an' spent the day restin', like he always does on Sunday. Even heard him snorin' while Ma an' I were doin' the dishes." She tilted her head, her face crinkled in thought. "Maybe Mr. Sholes did it—he sure seemed sorry in church yesterday. Might be his way of makin' things right."

Edythe hadn't considered the trees might be an apology from Lloyd Sholes. She thanked the girl, then pulled the rope to bring everyone in from the yard. She discovered that when she sat at her desk and looked out the northeast window, one of the trees stood directly in her line of vision. She glanced out repeatedly, wondering who had gifted the children with the trees.

Near the end of the day, Edythe perched on the front edge of her desk and clapped her hands. The students set aside their work without delay and gave her their attention. "As you know, our school year is rapidly coming to a close."

The children's expressions shifted from attentive to apprehensive.

"I know all of you enjoyed treating your parents with the Christmas program, and—"

Robert Townsend burst out of his seat. "Are we gonna do another program?" He flashed a grin around the room, showing the gap from his newly missing front teeth. "She tol' me at Christmastime we might have one if we all worked hard."

Edythe laughed. "Do you think you've worked hard enough?" Excited mutterings filled the room, interspersed with statements of affirmation. "Very well, then. We'll begin preparing."

Louisa Bride raised her hand. "But, Miss Amsel, end of the term's not a holiday. What'll our program be about?"

"We'll show your folks the things we've learned this year." The children had learned, but so had the teacher—valuable lessons she'd cherish for the rest of her life. "We can have a spelling bee and multiplication races"—she named the children's two favorite learning games—"and you can recite one of the poems we memorized from our readers. We could also make a book, a big one on butcher paper, telling the story of our school year. What do you think?"

The students cheered.

"I think we should call the book *Our Year With Miss Amsel*," Andrew Bride blurted. Then he slunk low in his seat, his face red. Children tittered.

Edythe smiled at Andrew. "I appreciate being given such recognition, Andrew, but perhaps *Memories of Our Year Together* might be more appropriate."

Martha waved her hand. "Will there be a commencement for Missy an' me?"

"Of course we'll have a commencement, complete with diplomas." Edythe had already ordered sheepskin diplomas and several ribbons from the Nebraska Department of Education. "There will be other awards, too. We'll make it a grand close to the school term."

While the children chattered excitedly, offering their ideas for pages in the memory book, Edythe battled sadness that threatened to emerge as tears. *God, I have complete peace about taking on the challenge of winning rights for women, but it's so hard to think of leaving these children. Give me strength, God, to say good-bye.*

Chapter
FORTY-ONE

Joel couldn't recall a more perfect spring for preparing the fields for planting. Gentle rains had fallen during sleeping hours in mid-March, moistening the soil. Then the sun had chased the clouds away and dried things enough for Joel to turn the ground. He never tired of watching the mineral-specked clumps of earth roll away from the plow blade. Often he stopped the oxen to lean down, squeeze a fistful of the moist dirt, and inhale the rich aroma.

He began pressing his seeds into the ground on the twenty-third of the month—two weeks earlier than his neighbors, who waited for April's full moon. But his pa had always planted on the day of March's new moon, so it felt right to him. Besides, the rains ensured the seeds would have enough moisture to sprout, even if the other farmers in town thought he was rushing things.

The sixth of April—the day before the full moon—Joel discovered the first tiny shoots of green peeking through the sod like little arms reaching for the sun. After school, Joel took Johnny and Robert to the field and let them run their fingertips over the tiny, fragile sprouts. They insisted on visiting the field each day thereafter, engaging in good-natured arguments about how many stalks filled the acreage and how much each had grown overnight.

Joel delighted in the boys' excitement, which matched his own at the signs of new life burgeoning across the once-barren expanse of ground. The cornstalks grew in strength and height daily, promising a successful harvest. And within Joel's soul—despite how hard he worked to set the feelings aside—his love for Edythe Amsel continued to grow, too.

He saw her in church each Sunday, dressed in her schoolmarm frocks, with her dark hair smoothed into a sleek bun that rested precisely at the base of her skull, and he reminded himself she didn't fit the picture of a farmer's wife. When the boys jabbered about something she'd taught them that day in school and his heart pattered in response to the sound of her name, he told himself she'd be leaving soon—it was pointless to pine for her. But pine he did. In his prayers, he asked God to erase the feelings he held for her. But God stubbornly refused to respond to his request. So Joel went on, confused and heartsore, battling his own emotions.

By the second week of May—the final week of school for the boys—the corn stood more than a foot tall, with stalks as thick as Joel's thumb supporting long, slender leaves of green that caught the sunlight and rustled in the wind. Joel went out every day with his hoe to chop at the dirt around the base of each stalk. His father had taught him to soften the soil around the growing stalks, making it easier for rain to reach the roots, and to hack away any weeds that dared to rob his corn of nutrients.

On this sunny afternoon, while he carefully tapped the hoe's blade against the ground, something his ma had told him winged through his mind. He paused, remembering her sweet voice as she'd told Joel a life was better lived when the person let God do what was needed to soften his heart and to carve away the influences that could rob his soul of joy. Even now, twenty years after she'd been laid to rest, he remembered and treasured her influence on his life. *But my boys'll never again benefit from a mother's touch, unless . . .*

He blew out a mighty breath, his hands stilling on the warm hoe handle. In a few more days, the boys would be home all day for the summer months. He'd be working the fields and trying to keep two active boys occupied. The longing for a helpmeet rose again, and he squinted toward the ball of fire suspended high in the clear sky. "God, those boys need a ma to look after them an' teach them. I need a wife. Your word says man isn't meant to be alone. So what am I supposed to do?"

Wind gently rustled the leaves, creating a familiar lullaby. A bird called—its cry lonesome—and a second one answered. *Won't You answer an' tell me how to fill up this lonesome side of me?*

Edythe Amsel's face flashed in his mind's eye.

With a groan, he set the hoe to work again, his thoughts tumbling like the little clods of dirt that hopped away from the blade's *chop-chop*. He hadn't been able to drown his feelings in hard work, and the Lord hadn't seen fit to simply take them away. If he spoke them out loud and heard them rejected, would he finally be able to let go?

He paused for a moment, his gaze drifting in the direction of the schoolhouse even though it was too far away to see. This coming Friday evening the schoolchildren would host their end-of-the-year program. He'd put on his finest suit, splash his cheeks with bay rum, and present his best face. And when the program was over, and everybody else had gone home, he'd tell Miss Edythe Amsel flat-out how he felt about her.

He jabbed the hoe into the dirt. He'd listen to her final rejection, and then he'd move on.

Edythe caught Missy's wrist. "Stop chewing your nails. You've got them nibbled down to nubbins already."

"Can't help it," Missy whispered. "I'm scared. What if I forget what I'm supposed to say? Everybody in town's out there . . . and they'll all laugh at me!" She began gnawing at her thumb.

On the other side of the muslin curtains, which Luthenia had dyed a rich, royal crimson before helping Edythe string them the length of the classroom on a sturdy wire, muffled voices confirmed Missy's speculation. Edythe hadn't peeked yet, but she felt certain the entire town of Walnut Hill—even those who didn't have students—had come out for the school's closing program.

Edythe pried Missy's hand away from her face.

416

"You'll do fine." She shifted her gaze to include the entire class of children who huddled in a group beside the teacher's platform. "You all will. You've worked hard, and I'm so proud of you." Her voice caught. The past weeks had moved too quickly. Eagerness to see what the next year would bring couldn't quite remove the sting of this farewell. She'd loved teaching, and she knew a part of her heart would always belong in this little schoolhouse.

Jane Heidrich pointed at the wall clock. "It's seven. Time to start."

Edythe turned a wobbly smile on Missy. "That's your cue." She found the slit between the two curtains and pulled, creating an opening. "Go welcome our guests."

From Missy's welcoming statement to the whole-class recitation of William Wordsworth's "I Wandered Lonely as a Cloud," the program proceeded without blemish. After the applause died away, Edythe presented awards to deserving students—Mathematics Excellence to Andrew Bride, who blushed crimson and then hugged Edythe so hard she gasped; Quality Penmanship to Jane Heidrich; and Most Improved Reader to Patience Jeffers. She stifled her laughter when Little Will Libolt scratched his head and announced quite loudly upon receiving a red Perfect Attendance ribbon, "I'd ruther have green, but thank you, Miss Amsel."

She blinked back tears as she handed beautifully calligraphed diplomas to Martha and Missy. She hugged them in turn, and in the midst of the embrace Martha whispered in her ear, "Ma says I can go to high school next year. Someday I want to be a teacher just like you." Edythe clung extra hard to the girl, her heart swelling with pride and love.

All too soon she stood on the platform with the children and thanked the audience for coming. The year hadn't been easy in many ways—she'd faced criticism and suspicion—but looking across the faces, she realized nearly every person in attendance had helped her grow into a stronger, more resilient, more loving person. A tear escaped, but she swept it away and managed to smile as she turned to the students. For the final time, she pronounced, "And now . . . class dismissed."

The students came at her in a rush, arms reaching for hugs, some children laughing and others crying. Edythe laughed through her tears. One by one, the parents approached to retrieve their children and offer words of gratitude. Edythe accepted their thanks, whether stated firmly or muttered reluctantly, responding to each with equal warmth.

At last the room cleared. Edythe pushed the curtains to the walls, then stood in the middle of the floor. Muffled voices of folks milling in the yard drifted through the open windows, carried on the sweet scent of a spring evening. The voices seemed to fade into the background as her gaze roved freely from the blackboard behind her desk to the row of letters printed on white cards along the ceiling line. The walls were bare, the children having taken home their papers the day before, but in her memory she saw arithmetic pages, child-drawn maps, and thoughtfully scripted essays.

Edythe moved to the south window and pulled loose the little sign she'd tacked beneath it on her very first day. Little Jenny Scheebeck's high-pitched squeal echoed in her mind: *"Window, Miss Amsel! That says window!"* She closed her eyes, smiling, remembering. For long seconds she stood, lost in thought, and then a floorboard creaked.

She spun toward the sound. Her hand flew, almost without her realization, to her throat where her pulse suddenly doubled its tempo. "M-Mr. Townsend."

He held his hat in both hands with the brim flat against the front of his black suit jacket. A sheepish grin creased his cheek, showcasing the single dimple that so intrigued her. "I wondered if I m-might have a word with you?"

His timidity, so unlike him, stirred Edythe's sympathy. She pointed to the nearest student desk. He shuffled forward and wriggled into the seat, his knees poking out in the aisle. Edythe crossed to the desk in front of his and perched sideways as well, resting her elbow on the edge of his desk so she could face him. A delicious scent—citrusy yet earthy—reached her nose, stirring her senses to life. His Adam's apple bobbed, drawing her attention to the ribbon tie beneath his clean-shaven chin. He looked nothing like a farmer on this evening.

A longing to reach out and take his hand swirled through her. Her fingers twitched. She clasped them together and blurted, "Thank you for the trees."

His brows rose, his lips parting in surprise. "H-how'd you know?"

Edythe smiled, recalling how Robert excitedly whispered the truth in her ear, followed by a sheepish request to keep his telling her a secret. "A little birdie told me."

A short huff of laughter left his throat. "I should've known."

She tipped her head. "Why didn't you tell me?"

He shrugged. "Didn't want you to think . . ." His voice trailed away, and he swallowed twice, his gaze dropping to the desktop. He laid aside the hat and then rested his elbows on the desk. The position brought his shoulders forward, and he tucked his chin low, his eyes avoiding hers. "Miss Amsel, there's something I've been feelin' for a long time, an' now that . . . that you're leavin' town, I figured I better tell you."

Edythe wanted to say calmly, "Oh? What's that?" But her tongue felt stuck to the roof of her mouth. So she sat silently, her heart pounding in her chest as fiercely as the school bell's clapper the day Little Will decided to take the rope for a ride. Being near the man, so close his fingertips would brush her arm if she shifted a mere two inches, was nearly intoxicating.

"My boys . . . they've loved you since the first day of school. An' you've been real good for them. I know you're their schoolmarm, but in ways you've been . . ." He gulped, color climbing from the crisp white collar of his shirt toward his ears. "Motherly."

Affection rolled through Edythe's chest, images of the boys—little bookends, she thought of them, with their matching freckles and straw-colored cowlicks—flooding her mind. Tears stung the back of her nose.

Joel continued in a low, almost growly voice. "I remember once you told me you'd already raised a family, but watchin' you, it sure appears you've grown to love the young'uns in this school. Includin' Johnny and Robert. So . . ." His head shot up, his blue eyes connecting with hers. "I wondered if you might consider marrying up with me and becomin' a real ma to my boys."

Edythe drew in a sharp breath. Several thoughts struck at once. *He proposed! Luthenia said he was a fine man—one of the best. Missy and I can stay here in Walnut Hill!* But then some of her own words returned, and her elation dimmed. As much as it pained her, she had to be honest with him. And herself.

"I won't deny that I love Johnny and Robert." *Almost as much as I love you.* "They're wonderful boys, and being their ma would"— tears threatened, and she blinked rapidly—"give me much joy. B-but I can't accept."

Abruptly, he rose. "I understand." He reached for his hat, and her hand snaked out to catch his wrist. He seemed to freeze in place, his gaze aimed at her fingers holding the sleeve of his jacket. She jerked her hand back as if stung. His gaze lifted slowly, meeting hers. No anger resided in his blue eyes, just a sad acceptance that was somehow more piercing than fury would be.

She clasped her hands at her waist. "May I explain?"

He nodded.

"Marrying you would give my sister and me a place of security. It would allow me to remain here in Walnut Hill and watch the children I love grow into adulthood." Her nose stung fiercely, and she sniffed. "Terrill Sterbinz also proposed marriage, but I refused him, as well, because I cannot marry for security or selfishness. Only for . . . love." The last word escaped on a breathy whisper.

Joel nodded. "'Course you'd want to love the man you marry. Only one person lovin' the other would make for a lopsided relationship." He turned and began scuffing slowly toward the doors. "Even as much as I love you, I couldn't expect—"

She raced after him. "What did you say?"

He looked at her, his face sad. "I said, even as much as I love you, I couldn't expect it to be enough. You'd want to love me, too."

She grasped her throat, holding back a burble of laughter. "B-but I do love you!"

His eyes flew wide. "What did you say?"

Laughter escaped, light and joyous. "I said I love you."

"You *do?*"

She laughed even harder at his shocked expression. "Yes." She reached out, and his hat fell to the floor as his hands reached toward her in response. Their fingers intertwined, their palms meeting. Their elbows bent, drawing them together like two halves of a hinge. "I planned to leave Walnut Hill because I couldn't bear living here while being apart from you."

Wonder lit his face. "So you don't want to leave?"

She shook her head wildly, tendrils loosening from her bun to slap against her cheeks. "I love the town—the people. You." She laughed again, unable to hold back her delight.

"But you said you weren't going to teach anymore."

"No, because—" Would he denounce her desire to work for women's suffrage? She had to be honest with him. She quickly explained her plans, watching his face for signs of disapproval. But he merely nodded, his eyes never wavering from hers. "So that's why I won't be teaching. I won't have time."

"All that battlin'—can you do it from Walnut Hill?"

"I can write letters and articles from anywhere."

Without warning, his arms encircled her. He scooped her off her feet in a hug that robbed her of breath. Then he made sure she wouldn't draw another breath for half a minute by capturing her lips in a kiss that made her world spin.

When he set her back on her feet, she clung to his shoulders, her legs wobbly. He grinned, and she found the courage to press her fingertip to his endearing dimple. With a light chuckle, he turned his face and kissed the exploring finger. Then he sobered.

"I need to do this right." Very slowly, his gaze still pinned to hers, he slipped to one knee. A band of moonlight flowed through the window, lighting the golden strands in his walnut-husk hair. Her fingers trailed away from his shoulders, and he caught them, carrying them briefly to his lips. Then his handsome face tipped upward. "Miss Edythe Amsel, I love you. Would you honor me by consentin' to become my wife?"

Epilogue

Edythe would never have guessed Hank Libolt possessed such talent at playing the fiddle, but the man stood on the church steps, his elbows high, his bow flying across the strings to create a cheerful tune.

The early-September sun beamed down brightly, warming her hair, while a gentle breeze teased her skin. The perfect day had brought out the entire town to witness Joel and Edythe pledging their lives to one another, and she'd never seen a more merry celebration than the one taking place now in the church's grassy yard. She could scarcely believe the festivities were in her honor. Well, hers and Joel's.

Her eyes automatically sought her husband, and like a bit of iron drawn to a magnet, she found him in the center of the dancers . . . with another woman in his arms. She smiled. Missy looked so pretty in her pink dotted-Swiss dress, and so happy.

Edythe's heart swelled, a prayer rising effortlessly. *Thank You, Father, for bringing Joel into our lives.* He'd be a wonderful, loving husband to her, but she also trusted him to be a loving father to Missy.

Someone jostled her elbow, and she turned to find Luthenia beside her. In her new two-piece suit of apricot with white lace ruffling beneath her chin, Luthenia's appearance rivaled Edythe's in her wedding suit. Knowing she and Joel would board the stage at the end of the day, Edythe had chosen a soft gray travel suit and gaily flowered bonnet in lieu of the traditional wedding gown and veil. Joel had pronounced her too lovely for words. How had she managed to find a man who appreciated her uniquenesses? Only God could have arranged such a union.

Luthenia curled her hands around Edythe's elbow and sighed. "It's been a splendid day. An' what a pleasure to meet your brothers an' other sister." She chuckled softly. "I'd've known they was yours even if I hadn't been with you to meet the stage—never seen such a strong family likeness between kin."

"We all resemble our mother—everyone's always said so." Edythe's heart panged briefly. She wished Mama were here to witness her happiness. Or even Pa. But having Justus and Eulah, who nestled their month-old son in her arms, and her other brothers and sister here to celebrate was a blessing beyond description. Besides, she and Joel would see Pa on their wedding trip. She prayed Pa would be pleased to know she was happily wed, but if he wasn't, she wouldn't allow his melancholy to destroy her joy.

"Met the new teacher, too." Luthenia bobbed her chin in the direction of the older man standing on the fringes of the circle with hands locked behind his back, observing the dancers with an interested air. "Not as comely as you, that's for certain." Luthenia's brow pinched. "You sure you aren't gonna miss bein' the schoolmarm?"

Edythe answered honestly. "I suppose there will always be a hint of chalk dust trapped in my fingertips, but I'm doing what God called me to do. I don't regret the decision."

"Well, the young'uns'll miss you, that's for sure. But if you're happy, I'm happy." She proved it by beaming at Edythe. Then she pointed at Edythe's brother Albert, who began dancing with Maribelle Jenkins. "Lookee there—grabbin' himself some fun before the stage comes." She sent Edythe a crooked grin. "Tonight's stage'll be a mite crowded with all those Amsels plus you an' Joel on board."

"We'll make do." Edythe giggled. "If I have to, I'll sit on Joel's lap."

Luthenia's eyes crinkled merrily. "An' I'll have me a fine time with Missy, Johnny, an' Robert while you an' Joel are on your trip. Gonna spoil 'em rotten for you."

427

Edythe groaned, and Luthenia laughed.

"Miss Am—I mean, Ma!" Johnny and Robert, wearing identical black suits, white shirts, and black ribbon ties, dashed across the grass and huffed to a halt before Edythe. She straightened Johnny's tie and smoothed Robert's unruly hair into place, her pulse skipping a beat at the glorious title *Ma* reverberating in her ears. "We wanna dance!"

She touched her chest with her fingertips, feigning surprise. "With me?"

"Yep!" They each caught one of her hands and dragged her into the midst of the dancers. The three formed a circle, their giggles running the scale and their feet kicking up dust in a frolicking jig.

The music transitioned to a sweeping, wistful tune that created an ache of pleasure in the center of Edythe's chest. The boys' wild stomping ceased and Edythe's feet slowed, then Joel stepped behind the boys. His hands gently separated the pair. With knowing grins, they crept away. Joel held his arms open to Edythe.

In Joel's eyes she read everything her heart could hope to receive. She drew a deep breath, drinking in the scent of this man—her husband. And then, without hesitation, she stepped into Joel's arms, the place she was meant to be.

Acknowledgments

Mom and Daddy, my first teachers—thank you for the Christian example you've always set for me. It was easy for me to know Jesus because I saw Him in you.

Don—thank you for marrying a teacher and then learning to live with a writer. You didn't sign up for make-believe people sharing your house and the craziness of deadlines . . . but you love me anyway. What a gift.

Kristian, Kaitlyn, and Kamryn, my daughters and now also my friends—thank you for giving me a reason to pen these tales of God's grace. I hope you're as proud of me as I am of each of you.

Connor, Ethan, Rylin, Jacob, Cole, and Adri, my precious grandbabies—thank you for making Gramma smile and filling my life with joy.

Connie, Eileen, Margie, Ramona, and Donna, my crit partners—thank you for being there!

Craig Harms and Lorna Seilstad—thank you for sharing your knowledge of Nebraska with me.

Charlene and the staff at Bethany House—thank you for your encouragement and support. I couldn't ask for a better publishing home.

Finally, and most importantly, *God*—thank You for planting dreams and abilities in Your children and then paving the pathway so dreams can come true. May any praise or glory be reflected directly back to You.

About the Author

KIM VOGEL SAWYER is the author of eighteen novels, including many CBA and ECPA bestsellers. Her books have won the ACFW Book of the Year Award, the Gayle Wilson Award of Excellence, and the Inspirational Reader's Choice Award. Kim is active in her church, where she leads women's fellowship and participates in both voice and bell choirs. In her spare time, she enjoys drama, quilting, and calligraphy. Kim and her husband, Don, reside in Central Kansas and have three daughters and six grandchildren. She invites you to visit her Web site at *www.kimvogelsawyer.com* for more information.

Center Point Publishing
600 Brooks Road ● PO Box 1
Thorndike ME 04986-0001 USA

(207) 568-3717

US & Canada:
1 800 929-9108
www.centerpointlargeprint.com